Some Good Memory

Jo Hershberger

Outskirts Press, Inc.
Denver, Colorado

This a work of fiction. Although references are made to well-known people, places and events, the story and characters themselves are products of the author's imagination. The opinions expressed in this manuscript are solely the opinions of the author and do not represent the opinions or thoughts of the publisher.

Outskirts Press, Inc.
http://www.outskirtspress.com

ISBN: 978-1-4327-2513-6

Outskirts Press and the "OP" logo are trademarks belonging to Outskirts Press, Inc.

PRINTED IN THE UNITED STATES OF AMERICA

"You must know that there is nothing higher, or stronger, or sounder, or more useful afterwards in life, than some good memory, especially a memory from childhood, from the parental home . . . If a man stores up many such memories to take into life, then he is saved for his whole life. And even if only one good memory remains with us in our hearts, that alone may serve some day for our salvation."

Fyodor Dostoevsky—*The Brothers Karamazov*

Prologue

May 2002

Kate Kirkpatrick was so immersed in drafting the framework for her latest children's book that she dropped her yellow tablet when the phone rang. She decided to let her machine pick up, but her pen paused in midair when she heard the voice from long ago.

"Kate? It's me—Doris. Doris Lochschmidt. I was hopin' you was home. Uh, well, guess you're not. Give me a call at—"

"Doris?" As she grabbed the phone, Kate mentally flipped through the files in her mind back to 1947, when they had been seventh-grade friends at Sweet Briar School in Rockwell. The image of Doris' shabby house was so strong that she could almost smell the odor of cabbage simmering. "Where *are* you?"

"Here. At home. In Rockwell." Doris' penchant for abrupt answers never had changed. "Honey, I need you. Need you to come down here real bad."

Before Kate could stammer a single question, Doris gave a brisk explanation. Rosie Mulgrew, the rowdy and revered leader of their grade-school pack of four, was so consumed with grief over the death of her husband that she literally was wasting away.

"She's just skin 'n bones." Kate could hear the tears in Doris' voice. "I'm scared if we don't do somethin', she's gonna wither up and die."

"But I thought she was in Arizona." Kate was confused.

i

She had heard that Rosie had married later in life and had settled near Phoenix with her husband.

"Well, she was. But her 'n Bud moved back to Illinois a couple of years ago. Me 'n her—we pretty much picked up where we left off."

Kate sighed as she stared out the window at the tip of Notre Dame's gold dome and the square that marked the top of the university library. Flipping through her calendar, she realized she was already two weeks behind schedule with this new book, and three local schools were hounding her to come and speak to their junior-high students before classes adjourned for the summer. Still, hearing Doris' voice transported her back to the time of her own seventh grade, when she would have walked on hot coals for Rosie Mulgrew.

"I—I haven't even seen her since high school," she mumbled, almost to herself.

"I know all that, honey. But we was friends back then. The three of us 'n Cheryl." Doris sniffled. "And Rosie needs us. Needs all of us right now."

Kate never gave her schedule a second thought. "Next Tuesday, at 11:30, at The Boulder in Rockwell—your restaurant, right?" Already she was erasing the phone conference she had scheduled with her agent and penciling in the trip to her hometown.

"I was sure you'd come." Doris' pace quickened. "Now, if I only knew how to get in touch with Cheryl. That'd be the icing on the cake. I don't even—"

"Cheryl? I've got her phone number here somewhere. We ran into each other a few years ago in Chicago. Want me to call her?" She waited as Doris weighed her offer.

"That'd be so great. But know what? I think I'll call her myself. Just give me the number and I'll do the rest."

Rummaging through her desk, Kate found the scrap of

paper with Cheryl's information. Doris promised to confirm the date after she had talked with Cheryl and Rosie, adding, "You won't be sorry, honey."

* * *

Cheryl McTavish had one foot out the door when the phone rang. She'd be late for the benefit luncheon in Lake Forest if she stopped now. Oh well, what the—

"Hello? This is Cheryl." No matter how rushed she was, she always used her cordial phone voice—an old habit she'd developed from her years as a singer.

"You don't sound a day over twenty," cracked the voice on the other end. "Hey, it's me. Doris. Doris used-to-be Panczyk. Your old friend from Sweet Briar. Remember me?"

Slowly Cheryl lowered herself onto a chair by the phone table and took a deep breath.

"Doris? Doris Panczyk? How could I forget?"

Cutting right to the heart of the issue, Doris told her the reason for her call and explained that she had just talked with Kate.

Stunned, Cheryl murmured, "I've only been back to Rockwell once—well, since—"

"Yeah, Kate's folks said you stopped to see 'em one day several ago. Honey, it's been way too long."

Cheryl gripped the side of the phone table to steady herself. The sound of Doris' voice brought back such a flood of memories . . . of her frightening ordeal at the train trestle, of the pact the four of them had shared, of her family's abrupt departure from Rockwell. She wasn't sure she wanted to unearth that painful time of her life.

Reading Cheryl's thoughts, Doris pressed on. "This isn't about us, Cheryl. It's about Rosie. And she needs you here next Tuesday."

In an instant Cheryl was certain of two things. She *would* be late for the charity luncheon today. And she'd definitely drive the ninety miles to Rockwell the next week.

"Count me in." She wondered why she felt like a seventh-grader again agreeing to a trip to the movies with her old pals. "I'll be there."

* * *

"Damn." Rosie Laughlin's first reaction to the sound of the phone was to let the thing ring. Grumbling, she made her way back into her house and waded through the stacks of unread newspapers, old magazines and forgotten mending on her living room floor. She debated as she stared at the phone. "Damn," she muttered again as she picked up.

"Hey, it's me. Are you all right? I had to let the thing ring twelve times."

Rosie was relieved. At least the call was from Doris and not from the lawyer or the bank with some nuisance detail about Bud's estate.

"So?" she asked. "I wasn't sure I wanted to answer it."

She grimaced as Doris told her she needed her to get herself to Rockwell for lunch on Tuesday.

"I might be busy," she hedged. Doris persisted.

"Naw, I'm not into lunches right now." She stood her ground. Doris was always trying to get her to do something. "I don't feel like it."

Doris' mood changed.

"Now, listen here, Rosie, and listen to me good." Doris took a deep breath. "I've lost track of the number of times I've been up to your place in the last couple of years. But this time I need *you*. Plan to be at The Boulder at 11:30, on Tuesday, you hear?" Pausing, she anticipated the next question. "And no, I can't tell you why. Not on the phone. Just be there." Her words were strong, but her voice quavered.

"Okay, okay!" Doris could be so stubborn sometimes. "I'll be there. Damn!" she muttered as she slammed down the phone.

* * *

Doris Lochschmidt's hands were damp as she took a deep breath at her desk in the tiny office off the kitchen at The Boulder. She, the shyest of their group of four, had just assumed Rosie's old role and organized their first get-together in over fifty years!

"Just a minute—give him a cup of coffee," she replied when a waitress informed her that a wholesale food rep was waiting to see her. She needed a moment to absorb the fact that her restaurant would be the site of their reunion.

A wave of anxiety brought a tremor to her fingers as she wrote the entry on her calendar. What would they talk about? Cheryl had been a longtime singer in the Chicago area, Kate was a successful author of children's books, and Rosie—well, she was no longer the take-no-prisoners leader they'd loved in junior high. Depleted by grief and depression, Rosie would do well to show up at all.

It was amazing, Doris reflected, that they had jelled as a group so quickly in seventh grade. After the episode on that October afternoon when they had made their solemn pledge, they had become a unit so strong, so loyal to each other that they'd assumed nothing would ever separate them.

Patting her hair into place, she took her time as she ambled toward the counter by the cash register. "I'm comin'. I'm comin'." She winked at the sales rep, knowing in advance every item she would order from him.

* * *

Rosie scolded herself after she'd practically hung up on Doris. After all, Doris was her best friend, but she was always pushing her. Pushing her. And pushing her some more. She'd have to talk with her about that.

Weaving around the piles on the floor, she wondered what was eating Doris. She lowered the blinds so the spring sunshine wouldn't glare off the TV, then shoved aside a tangle of blankets as she plopped on the couch. Cruising with the remote, she settled into the familiar grooves, pulled a piece of flannel up under her chin and opted for an old episode of *Bewitched* to get her through the morning.

* * *

Usually Cheryl would have admired Chicago's spectacular tulips along Michigan Avenue as she made her way north. But she found herself so preoccupied with the call from Doris that she almost rear-ended the cab that stopped suddenly in front of her. She decided she'd better give more attention to her driving.

Moments later, as she threaded her silver Jaguar through the late-morning traffic on Lake Shore Drive, she allowed herself to recall those days at Sweet Briar School. The fun, the fellowship with her three friends had filled the void at home—that empty space that yearned for more than the dollar bills her dad peeled off to her on his way out the door on Friday nights.

"Gotta get down to Rigoni's Tap," he'd always explain. "Gonna talk with a guy about selling him a new car."

Her mom had always been too absorbed in reading movie magazines and touching up her nails to pay much attention to her, so she'd found solace in two places—her music and her group of friends. She wondered how much Rosie, Doris and Kate really knew about her family's sudden move from Rockwell and hoped they wouldn't talk about it next Tuesday.

As she always did when she was stressed, Cheryl began to hum the one song that soothed her, "Gonna Take a Sentimental Journey . . ." When she pulled into the country club in Lake Forest, she barely remembered driving through Winnetka.

* * *

From her window, Kate watched a cluster of Notre Dame students shuffling toward their 11 a.m. classes. She was too distracted now to give any thought to her next book. Her mind spilled over with memories as she anticipated the following Tuesday. She smiled, wondering if they would wolf down bologna sandwiches with mayonnaise on white bread as they had so often done in Rosie's kitchen years ago.

Sipping her mid-morning cup of coffee, she was amazed at the wave of emotion that Doris' call had created. She remembered how uncertain she had felt when her family had moved to Rockwell during the spring of her sixth grade. Her uncles had offered her father a job in their grain and coal business with the caveat that he and her family live with her elderly grandmother. She'd had to go to Sweet Briar School on the wrong side of the tracks, but her parents insisted that she also make friends with girls who attended Longworth School on the more affluent side of town.

Right from the day they unpacked, she had felt like a person with one foot on the dock and the other in a rowboat starting to drift away from land. Split between loyalties, split between obligations, split between identities, she had longed to be accepted. So when Rosie Mulgrew had invited her to go with her and two other girls on a bicycle ride to the cemetery on a smoky afternoon the following October, she had jumped at the chance. After all, Rosie practically ran seventh grade, although none of the teachers would admit it. Kate had never once stopped to consider that one little outing with Rosie and her pals might alter the direction of her entire life.

Pondering the following Tuesday, Kate put down her cup to straighten a pile of papers on her desk. Her little gang had known her well back in seventh grade, and they might have read the updated bio info on one of her book jackets. Those were the bookends of her life. She wondered how her old friends would react if they knew what had transpired during the years in between. There were some chapters of her life that she wished she could rewrite.

* * *

Part One: Kate

1947 - 1949

Chapter One

I t was the hobos who had drawn them together, Kate realized later. If the four of them had not stumbled onto the two tramps camped under the railroad trestle that dusky autumn afternoon in 1947, they would not have been sucked into action to protect their friend. There would have been no need to make their solemn pledge never to tell another soul about the episode. And without that secret, they would never have forged the foundation for their friendship—a bond so strong that it would carry them through the trials of seventh and eighth grade and surface again years later to salvage life itself for one of them.

The chain of events had begun so innocently. Kate Freeman was thrilled to be included when the bold and brazen Rosie Mulgrew suggested a bicycle ride to the cemetery after school. Still feeling the pangs of being "that new girl from Texas" after arriving at Sweet Briar School the previous April, she longed to find a circle of friends. To receive an invitation from the most feared and respected girl in seventh grade was the equivalent of finding a top prize in a box of Cracker Jack.

"C'mon." Rosie raised her chin in Kate's direction. "The three of us are riding our bikes out to the cemetery." Her blue eyes were somber as she explained her purpose. "My sister, Colleen, said her and some of her friends thought they saw a ghost around that grave with the statue of the little girl." Tossing her shoulder-length auburn hair, she pulled her bike from the rack by the school. "I want to

1

see for myself, and Doris 'n Cheryl are coming with me."

"I'll tell my mom and catch up with you down the block. It'll only take me a minute." Feeling a rush of excitement, Kate bounded across the street, raced up to her front door and called to her mother. She promised to be home by 5:30, then hopped back on her bike and bumped over the brick pavement until she pulled alongside Doris Panczyk at the end of the line.

Smoke from burning piles of leaves curled into the air as they rode by the tarpaper shacks at the edge of town and pedaled past stubbled cornfields one mile north to the cemetery. Rosie took the lead on the bike that had been her sister's. Following closely behind was Cheryl Allison, the shortest and prettiest girl in Sweet Briar's seventh grade. Her brown pageboy bounced as she skimmed along on the red Sears bike her parents had given her for her birthday in June. Kate labored a little harder on the dark maroon bike that had belonged to her cousin. Still, she felt that her two-wheeler seemed almost new compared to the rusty boy's bike that Doris shared with her younger brother, Tommy.

She was grateful to have a bike at all, she thought as they outraced a mangy dog that chased them. Otherwise, she would have been home at this very moment, playing Chinese checkers with her grandmother or entertaining her eight-year-old sister, M.J., while her mother fixed supper. Life just hadn't quite settled out since they had moved from Texas to help take care of Gran, she thought. She knew her father was glad to have the job keeping books at the grain elevator his two brothers owned, but coming to live in Rockwell had sure turned her life upside down.

Dodging a large stone in the gravel road, she thought of how different things were here. In Texas they had rented a house in an area where everyone worked at the military base or munitions plant. Her friends—and their homes and their families— were pretty much alike. But here they lived with Gran in her aging two-story home on the Sweet Briar side of town. The kids at school eyed her with suspicion, thinking her family had money like her dad's brothers, Uncle Art and Uncle Henry who lived on the Longworth side of town. Boy, were they wrong! She slowed, waiting for Doris.

She'd had to go to a few parties given by Longworth kids because her parents and their parents were friends. But she hadn't felt comfortable—especially when that snooty Nancy Dawes had snickered under her breath about "those dirty kids from Sweet Briar." Already she had come to hate the silver tracks of the Nickel Plate Railroad that split Rockwell into two halves—Sweet Briar to the north and Longworth to the south. With a foot in each camp, she was never quite sure where she stood. She braked as they entered the cemetery, happy that she could be part of a group again, at least for the rest of the afternoon.

"Let's stop here for a minute," Doris called as they passed through the stone gates and came upon the grassy circle covered with white crosses honoring those from Rockwell who had died in the war. "I wanta see my brother's grave."

Kate felt a wave of dread wash through her. She knew Doris' brother, Chet Jr., had been killed on the beach at Normandy during D-Day over three years ago—the second tragedy for the Panczyks. When Doris was six and living with her family near Chicago, she had lost her father when a tree he was sawing fell on him and killed him instantly. Months later, her mother had packed her brood of seven children into her old Ford, said good-bye to the home where they had known such grief, and moved eighty miles south to Rockwell, where she could start over with a decent job on the assembly line at Midwest Manufacturing.

Methodically Doris stepped off four rows across, five places down, counting as she went.

"Here it is." Her uncertain smile brightened her pale face.

The three circled around her. Standing next to Cheryl, Kate felt like a giraffe—all legs and half a foot taller. "Chester Joseph Panczyk Jr.: May 3, 1924—June 6, 1944," stated the brass plate on the cross. A tear trailed slowly down Doris' cheek.

"Mom says the good die young," she murmured philosophically. "But it's just not fair that all we have left of him is the Silver Star. Well, that and a few other medals."

"Medals sure don't make up for nothin'," Rosie agreed bitterly. "Geez, we'd sure give back Brian's Purple Heart and everything else if we could have our brother the way he used to be." Her wide mouth hardened into a thin line. "He'll probably spend the rest of his life listening to the radio in our living room and playing those sad songs on his harmonica."

Feeling inadequate because she'd had no brother to sacrifice, Kate exchanged a quick look with Cheryl. Neither had been scarred by the war, as most of their classmates had been. Kate's father, although too old to serve on active duty, had worked as a bookkeeper in a munitions plant in Texas. Cheryl's had been rejected because of a mild heart condition. Kate shifted her feet uneasily until the war talk passed.

"C'mon, sweetie." Rosie gave Doris a little hug. "Let's go find that statue and see what's there."

Doris pushed a strand of light brown hair away from her face. Then, placing her left foot on the pedal, she began to run with the bike and threw her right leg over the boy's bar. Once again, Rosie assumed the lead as they followed the maze of lanes through the cemetery. Finally, at the far

Sr5

northeast corner, just beyond the goldfish pond, she spotted
the little girl in granite. One of the most ornate markers in
the cemetery, it showed a child with a bird in her outstretched palm. "Mary Margaret Morris: 1871—1879," the
carving read. The same age as M.J., Kate thought.

"She was younger 'n us," Doris observed. "Wonder
what she died from."

"My grandpa knew some of her family," Cheryl volunteered. "They said one day she woke up and was fine. Then
later that morning she came down with scarlet fever and
was dead by five o'clock."

"I always heard she was playing outside. Then a big
cloud—you know, like a evil spirit—came roaring through
her yard, and when it was gone she was dead. Just like
that." Rosie snapped her fingers dramatically. "The hired
girl saw it and claimed it was 'cause the ladies who'd been
to see Mrs. Morris the day before left their umbrellas open
in the house." She nodded her head and tightened her lips,
affirming the truth of her version.

"You're kidding." Kate spoke before she could stop
herself. Anxiously she glanced at Rosie, hoping she had not
aroused her quick temper.

"It's the God's truth," Rosie declared. "And whether
you believe it or not, I'm warning you—don't *ever* leave an
umbrella open in the house." She narrowed her eyes. "Especially not in *my* house!"

Kate nodded, making a mental note to herself never to
bring an umbrella anywhere near the Mulgrew home.

The four wandered in different directions, pausing to
study the names engraved on the ancient tombstones. As
Kate ran her fingers over a rose carved into a granite stone,
she realized the ridges felt almost as sharp as real thorns.

"Oh, my god, here's a family that lost five little babies,
one by one," Doris knelt beside a small square of granite.

"This place is too sad. Let's just go home."

"Is your dad buried here?" Cheryl asked.

"No, he's up near Chicago, in a big Polish cemetery with his brother. But when we go, our whole family goes there all together—the whole bunch of us. In the middle of the day, not late afternoon like this." She pushed up her little round glasses and gazed at them mournfully. "Can't we just leave?"

Rosie studied the sky. "See those pink streaks? It'll be dark in an hour. We'll just wait behind that tool shed and watch for a few more minutes."

Doris berated herself under her breath for allowing Rosie to talk her into making this trip. Once again, Kate exchanged glances with Cheryl as they reluctantly pushed their bikes behind the gray wooden building, but neither was ready to question Rosie's mission. Dry leaves crunched under their feet as they settled themselves for their vigil.

"Do we have to be so quiet?" Cheryl was brave enough to ask the question that gnawed at Kate.

"If you were a spirit, would *you* come out if you heard a lot of noise?" Rosie snorted in disgust.

"Well, excuse me!" Cheryl rolled her eyes.

Kate and Doris began to snicker.

"Shh!" Rosie ordered. "I just heard something."

Instantly all four were on guard.

"Me too." Doris stood, rooted to her spot.

"There!" Rosie said triumphantly. "I heard it again."

"Do you think it could've been a walnut fallin' into the fish pond?" Doris never failed to have a common-sense solution for everything.

Rosie put her finger up to her lips, signaling for silence. Hardly daring to breathe, they waited. Then, without warning, the leaves crackled as a blur sped past. Panicky, they

6

squealed and grabbed each other.

"Oh, my god!" Doris made the sign of the cross.

"Lordy, it's—" Cheryl began to laugh "It's a squirrel! He's got a nut in his mouth."

"I thought whatever it was would get us!" Under her jacket Kate felt her heart flopping like a freshly caught fish.

"Well, I guess we're not going to see a ghost around here today." Rosie tried to sound disgusted; however, she was pale and a little shaky as she mounted her bike. "Let's go home."

"I need to pee," Cheryl said as they made their way back to the main gate.

"Well, not here. It's disrespectful," Rosie scolded.

Cotton-candy streaks in the sky widened into deep pink as the sun began to sink. Kate shivered as an early evening chill pierced her thin windbreaker.

"I can't make it home." Cheryl was almost in tears. "I really—"

"Okay. Do this." Rosie was planning as she spoke. "Turn at the great big tree down there and take that little trail along the field until you come to the train trestle. There's lots of trees there and no one's ever around."

"That place gives me the creeps," Doris rubbed her arms as if she were freezing.

"Yeah, I know." Rosie shook her head. "My pa's told us he'd take a belt to us if he ever heard of any of us playing around on top of the trestle. But we won't go up there."

"Lordy, just stop talking about it and hurry!" Cheryl's new red bike zipped out in front. "I'm going on ahead."

"Weak kidneys," Rosie grumbled. "You can hardly take her anywhere."

The three giggled as they followed Cheryl to the sprawling oak. When they turned toward the trestle, Kate studied the huge cement blocks that stair-stepped like a pyramid to support the floor of the bridge that carried the Chicago & Eastern Illinois Railroad over a branch of the Iroquois River. Although her grandmother had told her about two boys who had suffered broken legs when they jumped from the top to escape an oncoming train a few years ago, she could see nothing foreboding about the viaduct itself. In fact, she and her father had ridden across it on a passenger train just last summer on their way to Dearborn Station in Chicago. Her thoughts were pierced by a scream.

"Cheryl!" The three shouted in unison.

Pounding their pedals, they bounded over the rocky path until they found the red bike lying beside the remnants of a campfire. Kate scanned the site, spying a wad of blankets, a crumpled green Lucky Strike cigarette package, a wrapper from a PayDay candy bar and a tin cup filled with coffee.

"Leave your bikes," Rosie commanded. "We gotta get her!"

Although Kate wanted to turn and run, she realized Doris had already picked up the tin cup and was heading in the direction of the screams. She followed and was shocked to see Cheryl struggling with two hobos, her pants down around her ankles. Instinctively she grabbed a dead limb off the ground and smacked one of the tramps soundly across the back of the head. She felt solid contact as the branch met his skull. Doris dumped the coffee into his eyes and left him writhing on the ground.

The second man groaned and swore as Rosie landed a swift kick to his groin and grabbed Cheryl by the hand. Together, the four of them climbed onto their bikes and scrambled toward the main road.

"You ain't seen the last of us yet," one of the men called after them.

"Yeah, we had sumpin' real purty to show the rest of

you too!" The other cackled as he zipped up his pants and
threw a stone, narrowly missing Doris.

Kate's hands were so clammy that they slipped off the
handlebars. Her wheels seemed anchored in mud as she
tried to force the pedals harder than she had ever pushed
before. When they reached the oak tree and turned onto the
main road, she felt her knees wobble from relief. As the
men's shouts faded in the distance, she imagined she could
still smell their sour breath on her neck.

"Oh, my god," Doris wailed.

"Shut up!" Rosie forged ahead. "We gotta get to my
house—fast!"

Panting, they churned their way through the smoky air
until they reached the safety of Rosie's front yard. They
dropped their bikes and ran inside, letting the screen door
slam behind them. Immediately Kate sniffed the comforting
aroma of hamburger and onions browning in a skillet. From
the living room came the soft moan of Brian's harmonica.

"Rosalie? Rosalie Annette?" Mrs. Mulgrew called.

"Yeah, Ma, I've got some of the girls with me." Rosie
gasped as she tried to catch her breath. "We're going up to
my room to look at movie magazines."

"Well, just for a few minutes. I need you to set the table
and watch the potatoes that I just started."

"Sure, Ma."

They followed Rosie up the dark flight of stairs that led
to three bedrooms. Once inside the room that Rosie shared
with Colleen, they fell onto their double bed that was
tucked under the steep slope of the unfinished ceiling.

"Oh, my god," Doris repeated.

"They grabbed me!" Cheryl sputtered as if the others
had not been there to witness the incident themselves.
"They could've—they would've—" Her shoulders shook as
she began to cry.

"But they didn't!" Rosie's tone was triumphant, but her left eye was twitching wildly as it did whenever she was upset. "We took care of 'em, all right. Kate, I didn't know you could swing a piece of wood like that."

Kate felt her face grow warm. "I played a lot of ball with the neighbors in Texas," she explained. "It was Doris throwing the coffee in his face that really got him."

Doris smiled wanly as she comforted Cheryl.

"Yeah, and I don't think the one I kicked will be bothering anyone for a day or two neither." Rosie's wide grin spread across her face. "I got him pretty good."

As Cheryl's sobs subsided, the four sat in silence, contemplating the adventure that had almost turned tragic and had left them all shaken. Kate watched Doris' trembling finger trace the rows of dark green chenille on the bedspread.

"Do you think we should turn 'em in?" she wondered.

Kate considered the possibility, knowing she would savor the sight of them being hauled off to the Rockwell jail.

"I don't know . . ." Cheryl wiped her face with her sleeve. "My mom would kill me, just for being there."

Slowly each one nodded in agreement. Cheryl had spoken the truth.

"My folks sure wouldn't let me go anywhere on my bike for a long time," Kate said. "We've heard Gran tell about the men like that used to beg at our house for something to eat before the war. She always gave them a sandwich until she saw one of them throw it into the neighbor's bushes one day. Boy, did that make her mad! If she heard about this—"

"Well, then, that's it. Kate, you've just settled it." Although Rosie sounded strong, her eyelid continued to quiver. "Today will be *our* secret—and ours alone. Chances are those old hobos'll move on in a day or so anyway.

They're just a couple of tramps." The color was gradually filling in under her freckles.

"We have to promise not to tell," Cheryl urged. "*Really* promise. I mean—nothing like this ever happened to me before."

"Me neither." Rosie was serious for a moment. "It's gotta be official. Hey—I know—" Hurrying over to Colleen's dresser, she picked up her sister's Bible and laid it on their night stand. There she thumbed through the pages until she found the Twenty-Third Psalm.

"I know this part," she said, putting her right hand on the scripture.

"Me too." Kate felt the solidness of the trusted book as she placed her unsteady hand on top of Rosie's.

"I don't—but then I don't go to church. Does that matter?" Cheryl seemed to question her own worthiness.

Rosie gave her a tolerant look. "Right there, Cheryl." She pointed to the back of Kate's hand and watched with approval as Cheryl and Doris stacked their palms on top of it.

"Wait—wait a minute." With her free hand, Rosie reached up and pulled the string that hung from the ceiling so that the light bulb over the bed cast a yellow orb on the open book.

"Now," she directed. "Repeat after me: We promise—" Rosie began.

"We promise," the rest echoed.

"Never to say anything about what happened on the cemetery road."

They parroted the phrase after her and watched as she ceremoniously closed the Bible. Their lips were sealed. Forever.

"Hey, Rosie!" Her brother, Mike, two years younger, burst into the room. "I'll trade you three—look, three—

Wonder Womans for your new *Captain Marvel*." He held up a fistful of wilted comic books, his blue eyes trained hopefully on her.

The four jumped as if the hobos themselves had pounced on them. Although Mike had broken the solemnity of their spell, Kate was glad to see him. His blond crew cut, crooked smile and chipper ways made her wish that she had a younger brother just like him.

"Get outta here!" Rosie nudged him toward the door. "I read those old things months ago." Stopping suddenly, she scrutinized him. "Have you been hanging around outside the door listening?"

"Naw!" he protested vehemently, tugging on his prized St. Louis Cardinals cap. Kate studied his face and, realizing he had failed to blush, believed him. Disappointed, he turned and left the room muttering, "Darn. Guess I'll have to try Teddy Moody."

He started to shut the door, then poked his head back in. "Hey, Kate, your Cubs'll never come close to the Cardinals next year. Musial's better'n your whole team put together!" He grinned at her wickedly.

"I told you—" Rosie threw a shoe at her brother, who stuck his tongue out at her and scampered down the stairs.

"Gosh!" Kate jumped up, jolted back to reality. The jab at her beloved Cubs had brought her to her senses. "I've gotta get going. It's almost 5:20."

"Kate." The tone in Rosie's voice stopped her short. "Don't even think about telling your mom about this."

"You know I wouldn't. After all, I promised. On the Bible." Kate returned Rosie's steady gaze, knowing that her loyalty was being weighed. Finally Rosie glanced away.

"Good." she nodded her head, satisfied at last.

"Rosie," Doris asked as they descended the stairs. "What was it you yelled—you know, when we were—"

She motioned in the general direction of the cemetery.

"Yell? I didn't yell anything."

"Yeah. Yeah, you did." Cheryl agreed with Doris. "When we were riding home—something about critters or—"

"Oh, that!" Rosie chuckled. "Must have said, 'Fried fritters!' It's what Ma always taught us to say when we thought we needed to cuss."

Outside the pungent smell of burning leaves engulfed the group. As Kate turned in the direction of her home, she saw the eerie old Naughton mansion, its red bricks blackening in the remaining light. Wisps of smoke cast shadows across its long windows and wove images over its turrets.

"I'm heading home," Cheryl announced as she took off in the opposite direction toward her house.

"C'mon, Doris. Ride with me—just up to the corner of my block," Kate urged. "We'd better hurry."

Scrambling once more onto their bikes, Kate and Doris rode like the wind. Thankful for Doris' presence for at least part of the way, Kate never let her gaze wander in the direction of the Naughton place as they sped by.

She nodded her head in gratitude when Doris left her at the corner. Then, teeth chattering, she began to mumble a phrase of reassurance.

"Fried fritters! Fried fritters!"

Rosie was right, Kate thought. The words did help. Faster and faster she chanted as she pedaled all the way home.

* * *

Chapter Two

"You look flushed." Kate's mother barely glanced up from the potatoes she was stirring. "I rode fast to get home by 5:30."

Hesitating just long enough to take a deep breath and savor the safety of home, Kate tried to make her voice sound confident, like Rosie's. She went straight to the bathroom just off the kitchen, washed her hands in the little sink and studied her face in the mirror. Her usual fair complexion *was* ruddy, and her hazel eyes stared back at her as if startled at her own reflection. She splashed cold water on her cheeks, then grabbed five sets of silverware from the cupboard drawer and began to place them on the red floral piece of oilcloth that covered the square wooden table.

As if on cue, M.J. appeared at the precise moment that the meal was ready. Their father followed closely behind, his hand tucked carefully under Gran's arm as she inched toward the table with her cane. Although her pace had been slowed by a stroke the previous year, her mind was as keen as ever.

Kate tried to act nonchalant, but the secret weighed so heavily on her that she felt like a changed person. Although she tried to focus on passing the meat loaf and green beans, she knew her mother suspected something.

"What did you girls do at Rosie's house?" There it was—her mother's sixth sense suggesting that Kate might have done something out of the ordinary.

"Just looked at movie magazines and stuff." Kate made

ridges with her fork in the mashed potatoes.

"You missed *Jack Armstrong.*" M.J.'s thick brown braids fell over her shoulders as she extended her reach for the meat loaf platter. "And it was extra good."

For once Kate was grateful to have M.J. join the conversation. Still, her mother persisted.

"Do the Mulgrews have many books—or mostly just magazines?" Mother's eyebrows arched the way they did whenever she asked a question and already knew the answer. Handing the salad to Kate, she studied her carefully.

"Guess I never really noticed." Kate shrugged. Then, feeling the need to defend the entire Mulgrew family, she countered, "But they like to tease each other—especially that Mike. He's such a card. At least *they* have fun at *their* house!"

She did not regret her sharp retort. Her mother had no reason to undermine Rosie's parents, just because they ignored classic books and the opera! It was her subtle way of voicing a hint of disapproval without stating it openly.

Her father and grandmother came to her rescue.

"Henry wants to put up another large storage bin, but Art's not so keen on it." Changing the subject was her dad's way of getting her off the hook and salvaging a peaceful mealtime. M.J. sighed, indicating that she would rather have listened to Kate and her mother trade barbs than to endure another conversation about Dad's two brothers and the challenges they faced in their grain and coal business.

"Art says too many farmers are building silos for their grain and we might get stuck with a white elephant." He scooped a second portion of potatoes onto his plate.

"You're gettin' a elephant?" M.J. let her fork clatter to her plate.

Her father laughed so hard that he almost choked.

15

"John!" Gran chided. "No, Mildred Jean, that's just an expression. A 'white elephant' is something that is of no use to anyone. Like my left arm and leg sometimes."

M.J. was pensive, then the light dawned on her round face. "Oh—and kinda like that ugly vase that Aunt Iris gave you for your birthday?" She licked the mustache of milk from her upper lip.

When everyone chuckled, M.J. looked both puzzled and pleased with herself. Then she switched gears abruptly. "Can I stay up for *Fibber McGee* at 8:30?"

Relieved, Kate finished her meal as the talk switched to evening radio shows and the action that day on *Stella Dallas*, Gran's favorite soap opera. But that night, long after she and M.J. had gone to bed, she tossed and turned. The strident strains from a symphony on WGN's Philharmonic program unsettled her as they drifted up to the room she shared with M.J., then she counted the deliberate thumps of Gran's cane as she made her way up the steps to get ready for bed. She wondered if the hobos were still camped out by the trestle or if they had moved on. Or, worse yet, if they had come into town. Trying to convince herself that she was safe in her own room, she scrunched deeper under the covers.

The following day at school she learned that she was not the only one who had experienced trouble fighting off the memories of the after-school encounter.

"It took me forever to go to sleep last night." Doris' gray eyes drooped behind her glasses as the four made their way down the hall to the social studies room.

"Me too. I musta used the chamber pot three times till Colleen got after me for being so fidgety." Rosie shook her head. "But I had a idea during the night. Here's what we need to do. Let's start a club—you know, a secret group so the four of us can talk about stuff we won't tell anyone else."

Kate sucked in her breath. A club? An exclusive group with Rosie, Cheryl and Doris that would include *her*? Cheryl responded before Kate could find the words.

"When we go home for lunch I'll ask Lila if you can come over and stay all night tomorrow." Cheryl chewed on her bottom lip. "You're right, Rosie. We really need to talk this over some more. It still gives me the creeps."

Cheryl was all smiles after lunch.

"Lila says it's okay for you to come. Besides, I want to show you the new hi-fi that Bertie brought home last Saturday. We can make some popcorn and listen to records without anybody bothering us."

"Why do you always call your parents by their first names?" Rosie wrinkled her nose.

"They don't care. It's what they call each other." Cheryl's answer seemed perfectly logical. "Think you all can come?"

Secretly crossing her fingers, Kate assured Cheryl that she would be there. Sometimes her mother seemed to have an invisible list of homes where Kate could not stay because of "bad situations." That evening Kate was greatly relieved to learn that Cheryl's house was not one of them.

The next afternoon, clutching a grocery bag filled with her pajamas, her toothbrush and a pillow, Kate approached Doris' house. The two of them then planned to stop and get Rosie so that all of them could arrive at Cheryl's place at the same time. It was the first occasion, Kate recalled later, that they felt compelled to travel together as a cluster.

She stepped aside to avoid the rusty truck resting at a cockeyed angle on the sidewalk by the Panczyks' front steps. Shifting the paper sack to her other arm, she watched with interest while Doris' older brothers, Vic and Charley, gently transferred a piano from the truck bed onto a long-handled cart.

"You're lookin' good!" Stumpy dark-haired Violet, Doris' oldest sister, heartily encouraged her brothers. Violet had graduated from high school three or four years ago and worked as a live-in maid for Nancy Dawes and her family across town.

"Okay, okay now." Vic's muscles bulged under his T-shirt as he eased the load over the porch and through the front door. Charley was equally intense as he guided the piano from the front. Now in their junior and senior years of high school, they had been the two top scorers on the varsity basketball team the previous season. Their success had guaranteed that Doris, who had failed to inherit their dark handsomeness, would enjoy at least some degree of popularity and acceptance.

"Crap!" Vic muttered as he banged into the screen door and knocked it loose.

"You can fix that later," Violet said. "Just be more careful."

The heavy odor of coal oil mingled with cooked cabbage greeted Kate as she stepped inside the dark hall and followed as the boys slid the piano into the living room.

"Right over there, so it's not too close to the stove," Violet directed. Against the faded yellow wallpaper stood Doris' youngest brother, Tommy. His thin face and pale blue eyes wore the same expression of wonder that M.J. usually showed on Christmas morning.

"It's a present for our whole family—but mostly for Tommy," Doris explained, her eyes never leaving the piano. "Violet bought it off Dr. and Mrs. Dawes. They let her have it real cheap because no one in their family really plays and, besides, they're redoin' their house and don't have nowhere to put it."

"I've heard Tommy in the music room at school." Kate watched Tommy run his fingers reverently over the keys without sounding a note. "He's really good—I mean, for a fifth-grader. Almost as good as my dad—and *he* plays the organ at church."

"Mom's so proud of him." Doris' grin was full of admiration for her younger brother. "Me 'n Vic 'n Charley— we've promised to do Tommy's chores and ours too if he'll play for us while we work. Mom says it's a poor family that can't afford one piano player."

Before Vic even carried in the dark wooden bench. Tommy was bent over the keys. His left hand picked out the bass beginning of "Bumble Boogie."

"It has a great sound," he murmured.

"Ought to," Violet straightened her shoulders. "They just had a tuner down from Chicago two months ago."

Stuffing her pillow case with a change of underwear and tooth brush, Doris said, "Violet, tell Mom when she gets off work that I'll be home by 8:30 tomorrow morning to help her baby-sit."

"Baby-sit?" Violet's heavy brows met in a fierce scowl.

"Yeah, Lorene's bringin' the kids over tomorrow morning so her and Cletus can go look at a different apartment."

"Well, keep them kids away from the piano," Violet warned.

"Don't worry—I'll find somethin' for 'em to do."

Once they were outside, Doris explained that Violet had little use for their sister, Lorene, and her husband. "She thinks Cletus and Lorene are always dumpin' on Mom," Doris said. "But if we didn't watch little Vickie and them twins, I don't know what would happen to 'em."

Kate inhaled deeply, welcoming the rush of cool air into her lungs. Although her family had very few luxuries, she felt guilty when she saw how the Panczyks managed to slide by with the barest of necessities. Their strongest asset was the love and support that they showed for each other.

Rosie was waiting for them at the corner. Even if she had been blindfolded, Kate would have recognized her from the smell of hamburger and onions that lingered in all of her clothes.

"Boy, am I glad to get out of there." She pulled at her left eyelid, obviously annoyed that it was twitching.

"What's the matter?" Kate adjusted her pace so that her feet moved in perfect sync with Rosie's.

"Oh, it's just Brian. Again." Kicking a stone, she grumbled, "He's in one of his moods and thinks he has to make everyone else miserable."

"C'mon," Doris challenged her. "Race ya!"

Cheryl greeted them with a smile at the front door.

"Drop your bags by the couch," she instructed. "We'll put down blankets and just sleep in here tonight. That way, we can listen to records as late as we want to."

"You got new curtains." Doris nodded toward the shiny gray folds splashed with maroon leaves that hung limply at both windows.

"Yeah, Lila decided to try those plastic ones from Schultz Brothers. You know how she's always coming up with different ways to decorate."

It seemed to Kate, however, that in spite of Mrs. Allison's frequent changes, the living room still felt harsh and brittle. Maybe it was the sharp corners of the blond coffee table or the boxy new couch. Feeling her sinuses clear as she sniffed the strong fragrance of nail polish that came from the kitchen, she suddenly was concerned about what Cheryl's mom might be fixing for supper.

"Geez, you got new curtains and this hi-fi too?" Rosie pulled open the bottom drawer of the Philco table model and looked inside.

Cheryl nodded. "The radio's in the top half, and the record goes in here." She slid a black 78 record into the slot and closed the door.

"Or would you like to swing on a star, carry moon-beams home in a jar?" As the voice of Bing Crosby filled the room, Cheryl began to dance.

"I know—it's an old song, but I still like it." Her brown eyes sparkled as she added, "Bertie let me buy two new ones too."

Kate wondered what her parents would think of the Allisons' vast collection of pop music and jazz that filled the built-in shelves beside their hi-fi. There were endless albums of the Dorsey brothers, Glenn Miller and Les Brown—plus many of the top singles from recent years lined up in their paper jackets. Her own family had collected a few heavy albums of classical music, their sound now thick and fuzzy from constant use.

"Supper's ready, girls!" Cheryl's mom called from the kitchen. Shoving aside a stack of romance magazines on the table, she motioned toward a platter of bologna sandwiches, a large bag of chips and bottles of cream soda. The syrupy scent of "Evening in Paris" that trailed after her failed to camouflage the bittersweet smell that floated out of her glass and seemed to seep from her pores. Kate assumed that it came from the half-empty bottle of Jack Daniel's sitting on the counter.

As tiny as Cheryl, Mrs. Allison always dressed in skirts and sweaters like the ones Colleen Mulgrew and her high-school friends wore. Still, she appeared more wrinkled and worn than Doris' mom, who toiled five days a week on the assembly line at Midwest Manufacturing. Just a few days earlier Kate had heard her parents commenting on Mrs. Allison when they thought she wasn't listening. Mother had been convinced that her aging skin was the result of too many cigarettes, while her dad had speculated that it was caused from wondering why Bertie spent so much time at

Rigoni's Uptown Tap.

"You girls jush make yourselves a'home. There's 'um butter cookies in the drawer." She waved airily toward the cupboard. Cheryl cast a concerned look in her mother's direction and assured her they could find everything they needed. Telling them twice that she would "jush be in the bedroom," she filled her glass, picked up her magazine and stumbled upstairs.

After supper the girls donned their pajamas and spread blankets over the living room carpet. Although the brassy harmony of the Andrews Sisters filled the room, Kate thought the place seemed oddly void of activity. At Rosie's or Doris' house there would have been people tripping over them, teasing and tormenting them just for occupying some of their space. But since Cheryl was an only child ("Lila said she'd *never* go through that again"), there was an absence of life that oozed from every corner.

Even in Gran's home. Kate knew they would have had to deal with keeping M.J. out of their hair and her dad coaxing the girls to sing with him while he ran through the score from *Oklahoma!* on the old upright piano. And Rosie would have tried to get him to plunk out the bass of "Heart and Soul" while her fingers expertly stated the melody. In the few months Kate had known Rosie, she had watched her play that song on every piano she came across—in stores, at school and in other people's homes— because she said it made her feel like she could win the "Morris B. Sachs Amateur Hour" hands down.

Later that evening, Cheryl's mom emerged again and managed to fix them a large bowl of popcorn, slightly scorched. They had just stationed themselves around the popcorn when they heard Cheryl's dad come in, closing the back door quietly behind him. Mrs. Allison greeted him with a kiss that seemed to last much longer than necessary.

"Hi, Bertie!" Cheryl ran to give her father a hug.

"Hey, Punkin'." His eyes twinkled as he surveyed the group. "And ain't they sweet . . ." Serenading them with a few bars, he did a few nimble steps as he brushed their heads with his hand. He reminded Kate of Fred Astaire, only with restless eyes that seemed to dart constantly from one person to another.

Wolfing down the sandwich that would serve as his late supper, he spoke with pride about their new hi-fi.

"Lila Baby, I've got time for one quick dance. Then I'm off to Rigoni's—gotta meet a guy who wants to talk about a '48 Mercury."

He shuffled through the records as Cheryl scooped up the popcorn bowl and waved the group to the sofa. Then, as the Pied Pipers filled the room with their mellow rendition of "Dream," he wrapped his arms around Cheryl's mom and swept her around the living room. Although Rosie and Cheryl grinned with admiration, Doris fixed her gaze on the draperies and Kate tried to scrape a spot of ketchup from her jeans, secretly thankful that her parents never acted mushy like that.

"You girls might be asleep when I get home. But enjoy the hi-fi in the meantime." Bertie flashed his best sales-man's smile, then murmured, "You, Lila Baby, better stay awake."

In a moment he was gone. Clutching a stack of *Modern Romance* and *Movie Star Parade* magazines, Mrs. Allison waved him another kiss and tottered up the stairs.

Alone at last, the girls unloaded their latest complaints about their parents and siblings before they tackled the list of people they really hated. Between mouthfuls of popcorn, Rosie complained about her lack of equal rights in the room that she shared with Colleen. Kate disclosed that their mealtimes took forever because her grandmother was such a slow eater and her parents talked too much. Eventually they launched into the topic of Panczyks' piano.

"It's not new." Doris described how her sister had bought the piano for Tommy from Dr. Dawes, who "has so much money he doesn't know what to do with it." Her words poured out as she spilled other Dawes family secrets that she had gleaned from Violet—about Mrs. Dawes ordering most of Nancy's clothes by catalog from an exclusive shop in Chicago and Nancy's dressing table with the fluffy little skirt made to go with her fairy-tale white bedroom furniture.

"Well, lah-di-dah. And I bet they got indoor plumbing too." Rosie glanced at Cheryl and Kate. "'Course, so do both of you. But Doris 'n me—we gotta go out back."

"Lordy, I sure can't imagine Nancy Dawes doing that." Cheryl chuckled at the thought of Nancy traipsing to the outhouse.

Like an actress playing her audience, Doris revealed more inner secrets about the Dawes family, describing the expensive vacations they took to Florida and the desolation Nancy suffered because her parents were always at the country club.

"Every Saturday night Violet has to sit and listen to the Hit Parade with her 'cause she can't stand to be by herself." Her voice was filled with pity.

"Oh." A small sigh escaped from Cheryl. She covered her mouth as her eyes filled with tears. "What about Brucie?" she wondered.

"That's another thing. Brucie—her brother? He's nine years old and still wets the bed," Doris confided. "Violet says she has to change his sheets three or four times a week."

Rosie pounded her pillow and laughed out loud.

"That's the thing about the kids who go to Longworth."

Cheryl chewed on her thumbnail. "They're aren't any better than us, but some of them are so stuck up. Just last Saturday Bertie and I saw Nancy with Adele Atwater and Ellen Gilchrist when we were buying records. They pretended like we weren't even there."

Cheryl went to the hi-fi and slid in another record. Over the strains of Vaughn Monroe's, "Dance, Ballerina, Dance," they agreed on two facts about the Longworth kids: They were a bunch of snobs and they didn't have as many cute boys as Sweet Briar had.

"I mean, they've got Skip Stone and Walt Hamilton," Cheryl began an impromptu inventory. "But look at our class—Stan Piechocki, Larry Collins, Kenny Kroll—"

"And Jimmy McPherson." Rosie was adamant. "He's definitely the cutest with his blond crew cut and his red slipover sweater."

"Yeah—like your little brother," Doris snorted. "And just about as tall too."

"Yeah? So who's your heartthrob?"

Doris reddened and rubbed the mole near her chin as she often did when she was weighing an answer. "I don't have any—you know that. The boys in our class are too young for me." Assuming a false air of superiority, she said haughtily, "I'm holding out for an older man!"

They laughed but didn't push her. Doris, they all knew, was sensitive about the fact that she had repeated second grade after a near-fatal bout with the "hard" measles just before her family had moved to Rockwell. While the others were still waiting for their thirteenth birthdays, she would turn fourteen just before Christmas. She also was self-conscious about having to wear a bra and dealing with "the curse" each month.

"I think Russell Logan's kinda cute," Kate volunteered.

"But he wears glasses." Cheryl definitely gave him

poor marks for that defect.

"But he looks good in them," Kate responded defensively. "Plus he never has warts or dirty fingernails."

They all burst out laughing as Cheryl slid another record into the Philco and turned on the floor lamp. Kate marveled at it because it had a little switch at the base that controlled a soft circle of light that cast a glow over the entire room.

"But I'll go there again 'cause I want to believe the gypsy," crooned The Ink Spots. Doris sighed contentedly as she listened to the song.

"I'd sure like to go *somewhere*, but it wouldn't be to see some gypsy. And it wouldn't be to Florida like Nancy Dawes neither," Rosie scoffed as she picked out the last good kernels of popcorn. "I'd go to Hollywood. And sit in a drugstore, like Lana Turner, and just wait to be discovered. Geez," she mused, as she surveyed the unpopped kernels, "that'd have to be the best day of my life. Ever."

"My best day was just last Saturday." Cheryl smiled as she remembered. "When Bertie got us the hi-fi."

Kate thought for a moment, knowing full well that hers was the day during the previous summer when she had gone with her father to Chicago on the train. They had lunched at the Palmer House and viewed the city from the top of the Chicago Board of Trade building.

"Look at the world spread out before you," he had told her. "There's more to life than Rockwell or even Texas."

But she knew in her heart that she couldn't tell her friends about that. It had been such a grand experience that she was afraid it might devalue one of their treasured memories. Instead, she groped for another special time.

"My best day was when my cousin gave me her bike." She rubbed a nubby flaw on her pajama pants.

"That old thing?" Rosie was always ready to challenge.

"Well, I guess mine's not much better, come to think of it."

Doris spoke so softly that they had to strain to hear her as she recalled the reunion her father's family had held just before his death.

"It was at a Polish campground—somewhere west of Chicago, I think." She paused, remembering. "Some of my dad's cousins dressed in clothes they had brought from Poland and did a dance. And we ate kielbasa and sauerkraut and drank buttermilk."

"Buttermilk? Ugh!" Cheryl made a face.

"Yeah. But it was real cold and creamy. And later there were big plates of kieffles with powdered sugar on them." She closed her eyes as if she could picture it all in her mind. "Mom and Dad even danced a polka and got out of breath. We all laughed so hard. Yeah. Oh, my god, that was a good day." She paused, her concern evident even in the darkening room. "Do you think I had the best day of my whole life when I was only six?"

"I dunno, but mine was kinda like that too." Rosie hugged her knees. "It was right before Brian went overseas. He was home in the summer, and all of us went to the Old Settlers Fair over at Smithville. We ate fish sandwiches, then Mike puked on the Tilt-A-Whirl." She chuckled at the memory of it. "Colleen was fussin' 'cause she was afraid she wouldn't get home in time to go to the show with Danny Rigoni, but Brian made her wait while he threw darts at balloons. He won two little baby ducks and gave 'em to me 'n Mike."

The others sat stone still as they realized Rosie hadn't quite finished.

"Pa let Brian drive the car home. Then Brian made Colleen *really* mad by taking the time to go past Sandra Bishop's house—even though she was going steady with his best friend. But, mostly, we all had fun together. And

Brian was—well, just how he used to be."

A larger-than-life picture of the Mulgrews filled the room as each imagined the rowdy family on that fine day— laughing, kidding, bossing each other around. At last Doris broke the silence.

"The war sure changed everything. We lost Chet Jr. and—"

"And we lost Brian. At least the Brian we knew." Rosie stood abruptly and re-played "The Gypsy." "Now Colleen says we're walkin' on eggshells all the time."

"It's weird because—" Cheryl started, then stopped.

"Because why?" Rosie's tone challenged Cheryl to state her reasons.

"Well, you know." She looked helplessly at each of the others. "I mean, now that the burns on his arms and face have pretty much healed, he looks so—well, so normal."

"Yeah, well—" Rosie sighed.

"I guess I don't really know what happened." Kate decided that she should confess her ignorance.

Rosie wiped her salty hands on her pajamas and looked her straight in the eye.

"His balls got blown off is what happened." She colored slightly. "He's still got his thing, Ma said, but not the rest. And he could still—well, you know—*do it*, if there was anyone he cared about. He just can't have kids."

"Oh," the rest chorused, reeling from the weight of so much information. Later, Kate thought, she would ask Doris to explain exactly what Rosie had meant. She just didn't quite get it.

"Ma says that Brian 'can but he can't,'" Rosie continued as if she had read Kate's mind. "And until something comes along that makes him want to get out of the house, he's goin' to sit there and play his harmonica and tell himself he's not a man. Geez, I hate it—especially when I remember how great he used to be!" She pounded her fist on the rug so hard that she made the floor lamp jiggle. "I think that's the worst thing that's ever happened. Yeah. Somehow, my best *and* worst times are all because of Brian." She put her head on her knees so the others could not see her eyes fill with tears.

"I guess I have two worst days. Does that make me the winner?" Doris' small, sad smile broke Kate's heart. "You know—the day my dad got killed and the day we got the telegram about Chet Jr. What else can I say?" Her smoky eyes were somber behind her glasses. "Mom would prob'ly add even a third day—when Lorene came home from school her junior year and said her'n Cletus were getting married 'cause she was pregnant. Mom looked like she'd been slapped, then Lorene had to go and make it even worse by sayin' something smarty about the church not believin' in birth control anyway."

"Oh, boy—that better not happen to Colleen and Danny," Rosie whispered to herself.

Cheryl and Kate sucked in their breath simultaneously. Again, they felt they had nothing to contribute. Searching her memory, Kate knew she was lucky to have both parents, her sister and her grandmother. Her insides churned, just anticipating the grief she would feel if she ever lost one of them.

"My worst day was last year when we heard Gran had had a stroke and my dad said we'd have to leave Texas and move back here to take care of her," she heard herself contributing. "Later my dad was crying in the night. He thought I was asleep, but I heard him, just the same."

"Your dad cried?" Rosie made a face.

"Yeah." Immediately Kate felt guilty that she had stolen one of her father's worst moments and claimed it as her own. Still, it seemed to have made an impact on Rosie and, for that, she was grateful.

"Boy, I've never seen Pa cry—not even when Brian came home so bad."

Their eyes switched to Cheryl as they anticipated hearing about her worst day.

"We need more music. And more light." She jumped up to turn on a table lamp and to change records.

"Come on, you have to tell us your worst," Rosie urged.

"I just don't—" Cheryl protested.

"You don't really have to." Doris was quick to sympathize.

"Oh, no—it's just too weird. I don't know how to say—"

"Maybe it's too bad a day to tell," Rosie said. "Or maybe it was last Tuesday when those old hobos—"

"Oh my god." Doris shook her head, then began to snicker. In a moment all four were rolling on the floor with laughter. "Nobody told no one. Did you?"

Still convulsed with giggles, they shook their heads, reassuring her that their precious secret was well guarded.

"Till the end of time . . ." came the words from the Philco. The group grew solemn as the lyrics filled the room. Quietly they listened to Perry Como.

"My worst is just never knowing," Cheryl whispered at last.

The words hung in the air, unfinished, like a sentence without a period.

Everyone stared, but no one uttered a sound.

Finally, brushing the smooth hair away from her face, Cheryl began to elaborate. "Just not knowing when Bertie is coming home. He works down at Adler's—all hours, you know," she added hastily. "He likes to be the first one there in the morning, and then he spends a lot of evenings down at Rigoni's 'cause he says you just never can tell when somebody's ready to talk about a new car. So he's not home much. But he's always buying us such nice stuff. And he's so proud of Lila—she was homecoming queen in high school, you know, and he wants the best for me and—"

Her words spilled out, faster and faster, like a bike running downhill out of control. They let her ramble, listening with compassion to each excuse she dredged up in defense of her father. Finally, she sighed.

"But, as good as he tries to be, it's just hard—you know—every day, not knowing."

For an instant Kate recalled an evening three or four years before, when a spring storm had cut off the electricity and the only light in their house in Texas came from scary jagged streaks that shot across the sky. She and M.J. had huddled between their parents under a blanket on the sofa, believing in their hearts that the storm could not harm them. Their family unit was too strong, too solid.

After several moments of silence the four girls spread their arms and, over the empty popcorn bowl, formed a circle as they sat cross-legged on the floor. In the stillness they gazed from one to another, realizing in some way that they, too, were becoming a family. By sharing their brightest joys and darkest fears, they were forming a bond that nothing could penetrate.

Rosie was the first to speak. "If we're gonna have a club, we should be thinking about a name. But we don't have to have regular meetings or officers or stuff like that."

Pausing, she seemed to try to envision their new organization. Deep down, during the cushion of silence, Kate knew in her heart that this group would never be a democracy. One person would call most of the shots—and that, of course, would be Rosie. Inwardly she smiled as she realized that she, the new girl from Texas, would be one of that charmed circle.

At last Rosie announced her decision.

"We'll be the Fearless Four. And we'll have one rule. Just one, you understand?" She searched the faces of the three who surrounded her "And this is it: Nothin' we've said here tonight leaves this room."

Kate looked at Doris and Cheryl. All three nodded in agreement as Rosie proclaimed one more time, "Never!"

* * *

Chapter Three

K ate felt she was home free. Now a recognized member of Rosie's clan, she was regarded with respect at Sweet Briar. No longer did the sticky ball of dread rise from her stomach to her throat each morning as she dressed for school. No longer did she want to shrink from every eye when she was called upon to recite in class. No longer did she have to amuse M.J. each afternoon before supper. She had places to go and friends who went with her.

Being one of Rosie's inner circle, she decided, was even better than getting to meet Peter Lawford. After all, Rosie had the kind of clout revered by other seventh-graders. She had showed it when she'd sassed Mrs. Beckwith for assigning extra homework in social studies and, once again, when she'd stood up against Shirley Ann Melowicz and the other cocky eighth-grade girls who'd tried to bully her. Sensing that they dare not push Rosie too far, teachers shared the unwritten understanding that to be on Rosie Mulgrew's targeted list of enemies was to make life unnecessarily difficult for themselves.

During the weeks that followed their slumber party, Kate felt that the four of them were thicker than peanuts in a Baby Ruth candy bar. Then came The Invitation. Later she wondered how one little white envelope could create so much grief and misery.

She was on her way to an after-school session at Rosie's house where they were going to make plans to see *Blondie's Lucky Day* at the Pinnacle Theater a week from that Saturday. Stopping at home first, she sniffed the rich sweetness of freshly baked cookies the moment she turned the knob on the front door. She waved to Gran, who was huddled against the living-room radio listening to *Backstage Wife* and scowled as M.J. swiped a cookie and rearranged the remaining ones on the cooling rack as if she thought Mother might be dumb enough not to notice that there were only eleven left.

"They're peanut butter." Her mother looked up with a smile that softened the harshness of her thin face. Sometimes Kate wished that she would wear her hair in a fluffy style, like Cheryl's mom, instead of pulling it back in the severe bun she preferred, but she never could actually picture her like that. "And, yes, you may take some down to Rosie's. Oh, you also have some mail." Without ever turning her head, she caught M.J. right in the act. "Mildred Jean," she warned, "you've had two extra cookies—and that's quite enough for now."

Abashed and pouting, M.J. slunk out of the kitchen. As Kate tested the chewy warmth, she glanced down at the November issue of *The American Girl* and the little white envelope on the kitchen table.

"Great, Mom. The best ever." Kate gave her mother an appreciative hug. "Guess what: Doris said today that she thinks her mom can drive us to the basketball game this Friday night at the high school. Everybody's real excited to see what Vic and Charley can do this season."

"That's really nice." Her mother shook her head. "With all that Cora Panczyk has to do, she seems to make time to be a good mother to her children. I really admire her for that."

"Yeah," Kate agreed. "Doris is so sweet. Oh—and you know what else? We're going to see *Blondie* together next week. On Saturday night. The four of us."

"Mildred Jean will want to see that one too." She slid her apron over her head and hung it on a hook by the refrigerator. Seeing Kate's look of consternation, she added, "Maybe your sister and I will go to the matinee together."

Flashing a grin of appreciation, Kate thought how comforting it was to have a mother who understood the importance of spending time with good friends. She cast aside her new magazine and ripped open the envelope that bore her name. Inside she found a card with a picture of a birthday cake and an invitation:

A Supper Party for My 13th Birthday!
Where: My House When: November 1, 1947
Time: 5—8
Nancy Dawes
Please RSVP, Phone Number: 859

"What's in your envelope?" Her mother stopped flattening the last lumps of dough with a fork and gave her an expectant look.

Kate threw the invitation on top of the magazine, relieved that she already had plans that night and could not possibly go to Nancy Dawes' party.

"Nothing really." Spreading out an old bread wrapper, Kate selected eight of the best cookies to take to Rosie's. "Somebody's having a birthday."

Kate felt her heart quicken as her mother picked up the card. It seemed to take her two hours to read it, then she sighed. "That was the evening you were planning to see the movie with the other girls, wasn't it?"

Kate felt her defenses rise when she heard her mother use the past tense. "That's the night when we *are* going."

"I know you had talked about it, but this is a formal written invitation that was mailed before you had your conversation about the movie." Mother was easing into that calm, brick-wall tone that she had used so much since they had returned to Rockwell to live at Gran's house. "You should call Nancy this evening and let her know you'll be there."

"I don't want to go." Crossing her arms defiantly, Kate added, "She's not my real friend. Her parents are *your* friends, not mine."

"Nancy's father has taken care of all the Freemans. For years." Her mother's voice was glacial.

"That's different!" Frantically, she tried another approach. "Mom! Do you realize what Rosie and the rest of the group would think? If they know that I've been hanging around Nancy and her rich friends again, I'll be an outcast at Sweet Briar for the rest of the year!"

Her mother merely arched an eyebrow, always a bad sign.

"Besides, I don't have a thing to say to the kids from Longworth. Especially for three whole hours." Again she waited for a reply. Hearing none, she charged ahead. "I mean, they're just a bunch of stuck-up snobs. Everybody knows that!"

Methodically, Mother began filling her big speckled blue cookie jar. When she still said nothing Kate knew she was in trouble. Desperately she wished that her mother wouldn't dump her own frustrations over having to share a house with her mother-in-law on *her*. It just wasn't fair!

"I'm *not* going!" she repeated angrily as she headed toward the front door. "I already made plans to go to the show that night with the girls."

"You're forgetting your cookies, Kate," her mother said evenly.

"I'm not takin' 'em," she called over her shoulder, trying to sound as much like Rosie as she could. She would

36

show her mother *where* she would go and *who* her friends would be. After all, she was almost thirteen years old—and she knew how she wanted to live her life!

She grimaced at her grandmother as she strode through the house, then grumbled to herself all the way to Rosie's house. There she banged on the front door until Mike, chomping on an apple, let her in.

"Rosie's fryin' up somethin' out there." He motioned with his head toward the kitchen. "Just go on in."

As Kate entered the kitchen, she saw Rosie jump back to avoid being splattered with grease. Across the room Cheryl and Doris slumped in the dark wooden chairs, looking unusually glum.

"What're you cooking?" She plopped down on an empty seat next to Doris.

"Pork steak." Expertly Rosie turned the sizzling slabs with a long-handled fork.

"What recipe are you using?" Kate wondered.

"Recipe? For pork steak? You crazy?" Rosie hooted. "You just fry it till it's done. Simplest thing in the world."

Trying to hide her embarrassment, Kate picked at a circle of dried milk on the faded piece of oilcloth. Now, she decided, was not the best time to mention her invitation from Nancy Dawes.

"Lorene 'n Cletus are movin' in with us." Doris' ominous news hung more heavily in the kitchen than the cloud from Rosie's skillet. Cheryl telegraphed a quick look of dismay to Kate.

"Violet's jus' gonna shit a brick." Doris' brow formed a network of wrinkles. Kate studied her shoes as she often did when a "crude expression," as her mother called it, tumbled so innocently from Doris' mouth. "But Mom says they don't have no choice. Cletus wrecked his pick-up over the weekend while he was drunk, and they hafta use their rent money to get a new one, else he won't be able to work."

"Lordy, where will you put everyone?" Cheryl's words echoed Kate's concern.

"Mom says she'll just sleep on the couch so Cletus and Lorene can have her room," Doris explained. "Vickie can use Violet's old bed in my room and we can squeeze in one of the twins' cribs with us if we set the bureau out in the hall. Vic and Charley can make space for the other crib in their room."

"What about Tommy?" Rosie wondered.

"Oh, he'll just stay on that little cot under the window space at the end of the hall. He'd rather do that than move in with Vic and Charley." She circled her mole with her finger. "Mom says she's gonna need me more 'n ever."

"But you'll still be able to—well, to do stuff with us, won't you, Doris?" Kate was afraid their newly formed group was about to crumble.

"Well, yeah. But lots of times I'll have to go home right after school to help with the kids or start supper."

"Then we'll come too. We can peel potatoes and help watch the kids." Rosie poured a little water into the skillet and slammed down the lid. "We're not givin' up that easy!"

Next to the trauma in Doris' home, Kate felt that her disagreement with her mother was a family picnic. She never mentioned her dilemma to her friends and that evening, when her mother warned her that she would be missing every basketball game in November if she didn't change her attitude, she obediently went to the phone and accepted Nancy's invitation. Later, when she sulked around the house and her grandmother asked her to play a game of Chinese checkers, she felt her shoulders sag. Her social life, as she knew it, was over.

"A bit of rough going tonight?" Gran never looked up

as her withered fingers carefully placed each of her yellow
marbles into their holes.

"I just don't get her sometimes." Kate spat out the
words under her breath.

They played in silence, then her grandmother smiled as
she skipped over several of Kate's cherry-red marbles with
one move.

"I never had any girls—just the five boys, you know."
Gran wiped her eyes with her handkerchief as she always
did when she thought of the sons she had lost. Robert, the
oldest, had died of a ruptured appendix when he was nineteen, and fun-loving Earl had stumbled in front of a Chicago streetcar after an all-night session in a bar. "We didn't
have disagreements over parties—just fistfights sometimes." She stuffed her handkerchief inside the sleeve of
her lavender sweater where she could find it when she
needed it.

"Pretty lucky, if you ask me." Scanning the board, Kate
made one small jump.

"But Katie Sweet, I'll tell you one thing." Gran's hand
trembled as she lifted her yellow marble to make another
leap. "I've always been glad that we built this house in the
Sweet Briar section where we did. We've had friends on
both sides of town."

"You must've been a miracle worker or something."
Kate watched as Gran made another move, totally absorbed
in her game.

"No, not that." Gran triumphantly dropped her last
marble in its place, smiling but never mentioning that she
had beaten Kate once more. "What I am saying is to go to
the party and try to work things out with your friends at
Sweet Briar. Someday you'll be glad you did."

"I dunno, Gran." Kate felt as if she were hugging a frail
bird as she wound her arms around her grandmother's tiny

body. "Right now I wouldn't bet on it."

She avoided her mother as she grabbed a jacket from the coat rack and picked up the supper garbage to take to the alley. Outside, under the light of a full moon, she dropped the paper sack into the dented metal can and decided to take a stroll to the corner just to cool off. Her life at that moment seemed as bleak as the bare branches that were silhouetted against the gray sky. And it was all her mother's fault, first preaching to Kate about the value of relationships and then forcing her to do something that would make her friends angry. The only good thing about the evening had been her conversation with Gran. When Kate and her family had made their annual visit to Rockwell from Texas, she and Gran had baked cookies and gone to the library together, but Gran had never before talked to her as if she were an equal.

Jamming her fists into her pockets, she turned around and kicked a pebble all the way back to her house. The sharp wind stung her eyes, a stern warning that winter was just around the corner.

For the rest of the week she was careful not to jeopardize her chance of going to the first basketball game. On Friday evening she joined the other girls at Doris' house, where her mom greeted them heartily and instructed Doris to scoop the trash out of the back seat of her pre-war Chevy so everyone could fit in.

"Gotta get Lorene to pick up after herself and her kids," Mrs. Panczyk reminded herself as she stood on the accelerator. The car coughed, lurched and finally cooperated. "I'll meet you girls at the main door after the game. And, Doris Bernadette, don't act silly and embarrass your brothers—you hear me?" She patted her gray hair into place and smiled so they all would know she was only kidding.

"I wish she wouldn't use my middle name," Doris muttered as they entered the gym. Inside the band was playing a college fight song as the Rockwell players warmed up in their new white jerseys with royal blue trim. Vic was swishing free throws without missing, and Charley was practicing his signature shot from the left corner. As the girls made their way up the bleachers they passed Nancy Dawes, who acknowledged Kate with a bored little wave.

"See you at the party."

Kate stopped, one foot on the next bleacher, and looked down to see Peggy Birdsong smiling up at her. Chunky, with sparkling brown eyes and freckles, she was one of Nancy's good friends.

"Yeah," Kate replied quietly, not wanting the others to notice. She managed a weak grin.

"Who's that?" Doris asked as the girls settled themselves on the next-to-the-top row.

"Peggy Birdsong. I see her at the Methodist Church sometimes." Kate glanced around, hoping Rosie hadn't heard.

"My dad hates her dad's guts." Rosie made a face. "Ralph Birdsong's the manager down at Midwest, you know. My dad doesn't have much use for anyone in management." She snickered. "Him and the other guys on the line call him 'Tweetie' behind his back."

Kate took a deep breath, relieved to hear the shrill horn signaling that tip-off was just minutes away. They stood as the band started the national anthem, feeling the bleachers swaying ever so gently beneath them. Then the roar began, "Go, Boulders, Go!"

Basketball in Texas, Kate thought, had been nothing like this. For the next two hours she joined the cheers as Vic muscled his way through the knot of green-and-gold Buffalo Creek uniforms for seventeen points. But it was

Charley, with his sweet smile, who won the hearts of every-one when he stopped to make sure a little boy in the front row was all right after the ball hit him in the leg. He also contributed five baskets from his "hot corner" and made five free throws for fifteen points.

It was going to be a great season for the Boulders, jubi-lant fans predicted as they streamed out of the gym.

"Somehow, I'll get to every game if I have to hitch-hike." Doris' mom sat straight and tall behind the wheel as she drove the girls home. "Their dad and Chet Jr. would be so proud of them boys."

On the following Thursday, as they helped Doris peel potatoes in her kitchen, Kate mumbled under her breath that she would not be able to join the others for the movie on Saturday night, then abruptly changed the subject. "What's that song that Tommy's playing?"

"Oh, somethin' called 'New York, New York, a helluva town.'" Doris handed little Donnie a saltine cracker as she bounced him on her hip. "I'm sick of it."

"Oh, yeah, my dad was playing that a while back. That's where I heard it." Kate continued to steer their con-versation away from the movie.

"Your dad dropped off some sheet music for Tommy the other day." Doris wiped Donnie's mouth with the back of her hand. "Didn't he tell you?"

"No." Kate felt her face redden. That was so typical of her dad to share his music without mentioning it to anyone else.

"What did you say about not goin'?" Rosie set down her paring knife. "You know, a few minutes ago."

Kate felt her palms began to sweat as she realized that Rosie had heard her after all. "I can't. Mom says I have to go somewhere else." Her voice sounded small and far away.

"Doesn't she approve of the movie?" Cheryl dropped her last potato in the pan and stared at her incredulously. "It's only *Blondie*."

"It's not that. She's making me go somewhere." Kate's shrug signaled how defeated she felt.

A scream split the air, as Vickie charged into Doris.

"Ronnie hit me, 'Oris!" Her white-blond hair was matted, and her face was blotchy from crying. She looked like a doll whose owner had neglected it for months.

"Just a minute." Doris planted Donnie on the floor and went into the living room to scoop up the other. "Ronnie, no," she said emphatically. "Do not hit!"

"How can you tell them apart?" Cheryl looked from one twin to the other.

"See, it's easy." Doris held one boy up close so the others could see him. "Ronnie Dean here—he's got one eye that's almost brown. The other one is blue. Both of Donnie Gene's are blue as can be. A shame," she added under her breath, "that they both look like their hillbilly dad."

The girls giggled, causing both of the twins to laugh. Seeing she was getting no sympathy, Vickie stomped off to the living room.

"Well, it's your loss. You're gonna miss a good show." Rosie tied her headscarf around her head. "We'll tell you all about it. Geez, it's gettin' dark early. We'd better go."

As Kate started out the door, Doris pulled her back. "Violet said you're goin' to Nancy's party Saturday." Her eyes were wide behind her glasses.

"My mom said I hafta." Kate hung her head.

"I won't tell." She squeezed Kate's arm to let her know she understood.

"Thanks, Doris," she grinned. "I owe you one." Her burden felt lighter as she skimmed down the steps. "Wait up, you guys!"

By Saturday afternoon, however, Kate complained that she felt hot and her stomach ached.

"Wonder if I'm coming down with something," she suggested hopefully.

Expertly, her mother placed the back of her hand against Kate's forehead.

"Cool as a cucumber," she pronounced. "You'll feel better, once you get to the party. Oh, your father picked up a record for you to give Nancy. Melba Dawes told me that they were getting her a new hi-fi for her birthday."

"What is it? Something by Perry Como, I hope." Kate brightened at the thought of taking a gift that Nancy might appreciate.

"No, actually it's a red-label RCA Victor recording of 'Ave Maria.' It's excellent quality."

"Geez," she muttered as she walked away. Who in their right mind would ever listen to something like that? She could feel her mother's stare boring a hole in her back as she weighed the value of doling out discipline for being disrespectful.

Because her mother had ignored her remark, Kate bristled but remained silent when her mother insisted that she wear the good red-and-green plaid wool skirt and bright red cardigan that her Uncle Art and Aunt Janet had sent the previous Christmas. Sensing Kate's disapproval, her mother stated calmly, "Nancy will be wearing something nice that her mother bought in Chicago. You should dress accordingly."

But her mother, who usually had excellent instincts for social events, was dead wrong. When Kate arrived, bearing her "Ave Maria" record, Nancy Dawes met her at the front door wearing rolled-up jeans, a new striped tailored shirt and saddle shoes.

"Oh, hi, Kate." Flashing her phony smile, Nancy accepted the tell-tale flat package. "Perry Como or Frank Sinatra?"

Kate stared at the floor in response, then followed her into her living room to join the group. She felt as if she had stepped right into a *Better Homes & Gardens* magazine picture as she surveyed the smooth white wood furniture with floral cushions so plump that they appeared to have swallowed everyone who was sitting on them. The entire floor space was blanketed with pale blue carpet so that not a single inch of bare wood was left to attract dust balls. Matching draperies made her realize that Mrs. Dawes must have bought everything all at the same time, rather collecting odds and ends of furniture from relatives, the way Sweet Briar families did.

The rest of the girls, all sporting jeans and cotton shirts, glanced up when she entered then resumed their conversations. Only Peggy Birdsong acknowledged Kate's presence by motioning for her to come over and sit by her.

"I love your skirt." At least her warm smile was genuine. "I wish I could wear plaid, but my mother says it's not flattering." Peggy sighed.

"My mom said everyone would be dressed up." Studying her watch, Kate realized she still had two hours and fifty-six minutes to go! She longed to be walking to the Pinnacle with Doris, Cheryl and Rosie rather than suffocating in Nancy Dawes' beautiful living room, listening to her beautiful friends discuss beautiful topics!

"My mother is putting in a new powder room downstairs," Adele Atwater purred. "It's going to have a pink sink and toilet and wallpaper with pink poodles on it." Kate thought of Doris and Rosie trudging to the outhouse on the coldest day of the winter.

"Neat. My mom and dad have started to build a new

house at the edge of town," Ellen Gilchrist added. "It'll be a ranch style made of gray stone."

"You'll still be in the Longworth area, won't you?" Nancy expressed concern.

"What do you think?" Ellen scoffed. "Do you s'pose my parents would allow *me* to go to Sweet Briar?"

Kate felt a deep burning bubble up in her throat and ascend all the way to her scalp, but no one seemed to notice.

"You know who's cute from Sweet Briar though?" Judy Fuller's nasal tone drilled the air like a buzz saw. "Those Panczyk boys on the basketball team. Vic is hubba-hubba, and that Charley just has the dearest smile."

"Oh, yeah?" Nancy asked with a smug grin. "Well, their sister is working right here in our kitchen, right this minute. Only *she* missed out on all the looks!" Her shrill cackle made Kate want to cover her ears.

"So did the one who's our age." Judy brushed the cashmere on her sweater sleeve back and forth, admiring it as she spoke. "She's about as mousy as they come. But I hear that people put up with her 'cause she's Vic and Charley's sister."

"Hey, Nancy, when are you going to open your gifts?" Peggy sensed that the conversation was making Kate squirm.

"Not till we play this nifty game." She ripped open a box and lifted out a set of movie-star pictures. "It's called 'War of the Studios,' and we have to choose partners and guess which movie star works for MGM and which one is at 20th Century Fox. Mom ordered it from Field's for the party."

Kate suffered through the choosing of teams and tried to be nonchalant when she was the only one left without a partner.

"Gee, sorry." Nancy batted her eyes in Kate's direction.

46

"Betty Pinckley was coming but got sick at the last minute."

"That's okay." Kate felt as if her skin had shrunk a size and was suddenly too tight for the rest of her. "I'll see if I can help in the kitchen." Relieved for a respite from their artificial chatter, she pushed open the door of the kitchen. "Hey, Violet—need anything?"

Violet jumped, then grinned. "Pretty miserable out there?"

"Pretty different." Scooting out a chrome stool with a turquoise Naugahyde seat, she said, "Tommy's sure doing great on the piano." She began to spoon dip into a bowl for Violet. "He gets all of us jitterbugging so hard sometimes that we forget to help Doris with her work."

Violet snorted as she spread a variety of pretzels and chips around on a platter. "If Lorene would get off her butt, Doris wouldn't have to do so much." She placed the bowl of dip in the middle of the plate. "I don't know how Mom puts up with it. And that lazy Cletus and them poor little twins always hangin' around with runny noses and poopy diapers." She shuddered.

"But you're right about Tommy." She studied Kate for a moment. "Did you know your dad is payin' for him to take lessons with Gertrude Smoot? She's got him workin' on everything from classics to jazz."

Kate swallowed as she recalled that her dad didn't even have enough money to buy her a different bike! This was definitely not a good day.

"Miss Smoot said he struck a deal with her—that he'd substitute for her at the early Presbyterian service for nothin' next summer if she'd give Tommy lessons at half price so he could afford 'em." Again she scrutinized Kate long and hard. "Your dad's okay—you know that, don't you, kid?"

"I've always kinda thought so." Kate grinned. "Know what? Those girls out there think your other brothers are pretty cute."

"Yeah?" Violet's bushy eyebrows raised at least two inches. "And I'll tell you a secret. Vic and Charley wouldn't have nothin' to do with the likes of them. They're spoiled rotten. Can you imagine any one of those girls havin' supper at *my* house?" she whispered. A derisive chuckle escaped from her lips, and she covered her mouth to keep from laughing out loud.

"Not much." Kate lifted a chip from the bowl she had prepared. "But know what, else, Violet? I wish *I* was there. Right this minute." Sighing, Kate had purposely lapsed into the grammar that she knew sounded familiar to Violet.

"I bet you do, kid. I bet you do."

Kate's visit with Violet was the highlight of Nancy Dawes' party, although she did commiserate with Peggy about the fact that both of them would be heading to the orthodontist in Danville in a few months. Kate had never thought that her teeth looked that bad, but when her mother had insisted that her social life could be impaired if she didn't have them fixed, Kate had gone straight to the bathroom mirror. Examining her "large but healthy Freeman teeth," she found them straight and not crooked, like Doris'. They just had a hard time finding enough room in her mouth.

"Maybe we can suffer through it together." Peggy inspected the contents of her cucumber sandwich before biting into it. "I'm going to feel like a real ugly duckling for awhile. They say I may still be wearing braces even when I'm a freshman."

Kate appreciated Peggy's kindness that evening, especially when Nancy rolled her baby-blue eyes when she opened the recording of "Ave Maria." Thanking her only after her mother nudged her, Nancy went wild over Art Lund's recording of "Mam'selle" and Vaughn Monroe's "Let It Snow! Let It Snow! Let It Snow!" "Ave Maria" was laid aside and never made it to the turntable. Still, Peggy continued to chat with Kate so she wouldn't feel so isolated.

When her mother came to pick her up and exchanged pleasantries with Mrs. Dawes, Kate could not get to the car fast enough.

"Melba said that your gift was so thoughtful." Her mother guided the Pontiac away from Nancy's curb. "I hope you had a better time than you anticipated."

"It was okay." Kate felt there was no reason to cause more trouble.

"I knew you'd be glad you went," her mother assured her as their car bumped over the railroad tracks that separated the Longworth from the Sweet Briar side of town. "The more friends you have in different places, the more you'll enjoy life."

"I suppose." Kate stared out the window as they passed the Naughton mansion, not one bit convinced. She only hoped that Rosie wouldn't find out about the party.

* * *

Chapter Four

B ut, of course, she did. Kate knew the minute Rosie gave her the cold shoulder in the cloakroom the following Monday morning that she had learned about Nancy's party. Rockwell sure wasn't like Texas, she thought. Here, it seemed that the harder you tried to hide something, the sooner it would come back to haunt you.

"I didn't tell," Doris whispered as they hung up their coats just before music class. Already the air in the tiny closet reeked with the winter odors of kerosene and scorched navy beans that were entrapped in the shabby wool jackets of their classmates. "She sat in front of the Atwaters at mass yesterday and overheard Adele talkin' with her mom about the record you gave Nancy."

Kate's stomach flipped as she thought of Adele Atwater discussing that stupid record for everyone at St. Peter's to hear. She nodded her appreciation to Doris.

"S'pose you're better'n us now." It was more of a cutting statement rather than a question that Rosie hissed as they took their seats next to each other with the sopranos. Across the room Doris and Cheryl eyed them uneasily from the alto section.

"What do *you* think?" As frightened as she was of Rosie's wrath, Kate was surprised to find herself challenging their leader. This whole episode was beginning to get under her skin.

"I think you lied about not bein' able to go to the show with us Saturday night. That's what I think." Rosie folded her arms across her chest as if to signify that their conversation was over. Her eye quivered ever so slightly.

"I had to go. My mom *made* me." Kate was shocked that her voice sounded cold and calm, like her mother's when she was making a point. "I didn't have a choice."

Their conversation stopped abruptly at the sound of Miss Brennan's baton tapping lightly on her metal music stand. Sending a radiant smile as a warning in Rosie and Kate's direction, she announced in her lilting voice that auditions for the annual operetta would be held in two weeks.

Kate sat up straighter and wondered who *wouldn't* want to try out—except, maybe, Otto Rutledge, who was fifteen and mumbled obscenities under his breath to all the girls, and Earlene Compton, who fell asleep at her desk every day! Everyone else adored the tiny, golden-haired teacher who, Cheryl had said, looked like a combination of Jane Powell and June Allyson.

But the group had more pressing issues than auditioning for the operetta.

"We've gotta talk, the four of us," Cheryl suggested after school. "We can go to my house." Rosie shrugged and refused to look at Kate, agreeing that she guessed she could be there.

Kate felt her stomach churn with the same nervousness that she had every time she had to recite a memorized poem in front of the class at school. Although she welcomed the chance to explain why she'd gone to Nancy's party, she thought the whole thing seemed like a big deal over nothing. And there she was—caught in the middle.

When they arrived, Cheryl had already lined up four little purple bottles of Grapette and a box of soda crackers on the Formica kitchen table.

"We'll go up to my room." She picked up the crackers

and one of the bottles. "Nobody will bother us there." As they passed through the living room, they waved to Lila, who was engrossed in a game of solitaire and the daily radio episode of *Lorenzo Jones*.

"I hate it when we're mad." Sorrowfully Doris fell onto Cheryl's chintz bedspread and extracted a few crackers from the box. "It makes me feel like Lorene when Cletus comes in and yells at her."

"We're not yelling at nobody. But if we have our own club, we shouldn't be lying to each other neither." Rosie took a long swig of her pop and set her mouth in that straight line that indicated she wasn't about to give an inch.

"Okay, look, you guys." Taking a deep breath, Kate set her bottle on the floor and stated her case. "Nancy Dawes sent me an invitation to her party. I told my mom I didn't want to go. I begged her—actually begged her—but she made me. That's all there is to it."

"How could she make you?" Cheryl's eyes were somber.

"She said if I didn't go—and if I wasn't nice about it—I wouldn't get to go to any basketball games in November."

Doris whistled softly. "The whole month?"

"The whole month." Kate fought back the tears that stung the corners of her eyes. "Do *you* think I had fun there? Do *you* think I liked being the only one from Sweet Briar at Nancy Dawes' perfect house . . . with about forty kids from Longworth?" She knew she was exaggerating, but she had to make her point.

"Violet said you came out in the kitchen and talked with her. She felt sorry for you." Doris tried to make her feel better.

Kate bit her lip and nodded.

"But you could've told us," Rosie insisted. "Geez, I heard about it at mass." Angrily, she plunged her hand into the cracker box.

"I knew you'd get mad. Besides, I didn't lie. I just said I had to go somewhere else."

"I—I think it took guts to go." Cheryl spoke deliberately, like a judge issuing a verdict in a movie. "I can't even imagine having to do that."

"Me neither." Doris' quiet support was firm. "That's just what Violet said."

"So, lemme ask you one thing, Miss Party Girl." Rosie's tone was spiteful. "Do you think you're better 'n us 'cause you went to Nancy's?"

"Geez," Kate scoffed, trying to do her best Rosie imitation. "I'm not better 'n anyone."

"Oh. Okay." In one word and with a smile that emerged like a rainbow after a storm, Rosie welcomed Kate back to her inner circle. Then she frowned thoughtfully. "If we're gonna be the Fearless Four though, we need to know we can trust each other—forever and always." Her gaze settled directly on Kate.

She hoped that Rosie couldn't see her heart thumping under her scratchy blue cardigan. "Yeah?" Kate asked tentatively.

Rosie let her thoughts wander aloud. "Still no officers and rules but we oughtta have to do stuff, like—"

"Requirements?" The moment the word dropped from her mouth Kate was filled with regret. She always tried to scale back her vocabulary when she was with her Sweet Briar friends. She knew they thought her mother was weird because she actually read books for pleasure instead of indulging in romance magazines and radio soap operas like the other moms.

Rosie gave her a withering look.

"Like I said—there should be stuff we gotta do to be a full member." Rosie's eyes began to sparkle as she threw out suggestions—"walk a whole block on Kate's stilts or swipe a pack of gum at Lil's grocery when her back is turned or—"

"Hey, wait a minute," Cheryl interrupted, "not so fast. Each of us should get to make a rule—you know, like come up with one thing that everyone else has to do." She sipped her Grapette. "I think we should each have to sing one popular song—with all the words—in front of the others."

"That's easy for you. You love to sing," Doris protested. "I'm worse than Judy Canova. But, yeah," she reflected, "I guess I could do that once."

"Everybody agree?" Rosie questioned. "Okay, that's Test Number One."

Kate sighed inwardly, knowing she would die many deaths before she could squeak out the words of a popular song in front of her friends. Somehow, though, she knew she would summon the courage.

"Okay, I got one." Rosie squared her shoulders as she dared to be denied. "Everybody has to write and ask three movie stars for their pictures. And none of us can choose the same one; I'll take Guy Madison," she added all in one breath.

Kate began to feel a sense of calm wash over her as they all nodded in agreement. That would be fun. Filled with new courage, she suggested that the third rule would be that each would have to sit on the steps of the Freeman attic for five minutes. "Alone."

"Naw. Naw, naw, naw." Rosie spoke out with vehemence. "That's not fair. Because it's your attic and you're already used to those steps."

"She's right," Cheryl brushed back her hair and shot Kate an apologetic look.

"I'd die of fright." Doris' brow looked like a road map. "You'd have to call Dr. Dawes to come and try to bring me back to life."

Kate understood. As the group quietly considered other requirements, she thought about Gran's large Queen Anne house that her family had called home for the last months. She, too, had felt its imposing quality when she first moved in. She just wished that her Sweet Briar classmates didn't think her family was wealthy because their house was so big. What they didn't know was that it had no heat upstairs and was badly in need of major repairs. Still, everyone at Sweet Briar assumed that, because her last name was Freeman, her parents had a lot of money like her Uncle Art and Uncle Henry. Suddenly she had an idea.

"I've got it. Each one of us will walk the three blocks from my house to Rosie's by ourselves. After dark." She took a swig of her Grapette while her friends considered the possibility.

Doris' eyes grew large. "But that's past the Naughton mansion. It's spooked."

"Yep. That's what they say." Kate was enjoying playing the tough one for a change.

"I think I could do that," Cheryl agreed hesitantly, "but I'll probably run."

"Me too! They'll just have to catch me if they want me!" Doris seemed energized by the prospect.

"I dunno." Rosie had paled beneath her freckles. "I guess so." Not appearing to debate Kate's suggestion, she raised her eyebrows. "Doris?"

"Oh, my god, I just don't know—"

"Well, you've gotta think of somethin'." Rosie was growing impatient.

Doris stood and walked over to the window. "We could climb a tree—or read the same book—or . . ." She turned, her eyes brightening. "I know! Each one of us will have to change one of Donnie or Ronnie's poopy diapers," she stated triumphantly.

"Oooo!" Cheryl wrinkled her nose.

"You're not serious." Rosie made a face.

"Yeah. Yeah, I am." She lifted her chin to show her determination.

Kate chuckled out loud. Doris was fun to watch when she stood her ground.

"What's so funny?" Cheryl wondered.

"I was just thinking," Kate said. "Poor Donnie and Ronnie. I've never changed a diaper in my life!"

Cheryl and Rosie looked at each other and began to snicker. "Me neither," they chimed in unison.

Laughing, they stacked their hands on top of each other and pledged they would complete the requirements before the end of December. Rosie was quick to add that she would also write to Perry Como and Lon McCallister. Kate knew her three in an instant—Peter Lawford, June Allyson and Van Johnson; they were all her favorites. Plus, of all the studios, MGM sent out the best pictures. Cheryl put her claim on Judy Garland, Jane Powell and a new star, Doris Day.

"No guys?" Rosie wondered.

"Nope. I'm collecting girl singers because maybe someday I can be one," she added almost shyly.

"I'll take Ingrid Bergman . . . because she is so beautiful." Doris paused and considered her options. "And Penny Singleton . . . 'cause I just love *Blondie*."

"You don't have to tell us why, just who." Rosie drummed her fingers on the bureau.

"And . . . and Ronald Reagan." Doris completed her list proudly. "Because he has such a cute smile," she said to herself.

They didn't need addresses; they already had them. Collecting movie star pictures was a hobby they had just discovered. It didn't cost much—just a three-cent stamp—and the thrill of coming home from school and finding an envelope with the return address of MGM, 20th Century Fox, Paramount or RKO was exhilarating. Sometimes Rosie even wrote to the cowboys at the Republic studio because Mike liked those pictures, but Kate considered them a waste of good postage.

The four became so preoccupied with thinking about their obligations to the club and waiting for the results of their auditions for Miss Brennan's operetta that they scarcely noticed that the last remaining leaves in their neighborhood had been raked into mountainous piles and burned. Rosie, Cheryl and Kate auditioned for roles in *New York, Here We Come!* which would be centered around two girls and two boys who visit the city. Doris said a spot in the chorus would be all she could handle.

"Hey," Rosie expounded, "it's not Hollywood, but I'd give anything to star in a show about New York." Kate, whose ears had been punished by Rosie's energetic but off-key tryout, was not surprised when the casting list was posted on the music room bulletin board a few days later.

"Fried fritters! I don't want a place in no chorus!" Although she spat out the words, Rosie's shoulders sagged as she turned to Doris. "Guess you 'n me will be together though."

Because of Rosie's disappointment, Cheryl tried to contain her excitement when she discovered that she and Russell Logan had won two of the four coveted lead parts. Kate's stomach took a dive when she realized that she had been cast as the Statue of Liberty and would have to sing a solo with her hand held high in the air the entire time. First practices would be held during individual music classes, then the full cast combining students from Sweet Briar and Longworth would begin rehearsals in January. Kate hoped that she would be down with pneumonia by the actual performance dates in mid-February.

"Geez!" Rosie kicked a stone after school. "You're no better'n me at singing, Cheryl. I can't figure why Miss Brennan didn't give me a big part. I know she likes me."

"Aw, hon, she probably just needed somebody real short, that's all." As Cheryl tried to take the sting out of the news, she shot Kate a quick glance indicating that she hoped Rosie would believe her. "Besides, Miss Brennan has to have people in the chorus she can count on."

"I guess." Rosie booted the stone into the gutter. "But when I get to Hollywood, she'll be sorry!"

Rosie's bravado failed her, however, when the other three asked her to sing the solo required of her for club membership as they met together after school at Doris' house. The living room was already lined with boxes of faded Christmas decorations awaiting the tree that Dr. Dawes always bought for Violet.

"I'm not in the mood today," Rosie grumbled, still smarting from Miss Brennan's lack of confidence.

"Then I'll do it!" Cheryl popped up and spontaneously danced around on Panczyks' threadbare living room rug as she belted out the lyrics to "Winter Wonderland." Little Vickie ran in to join her, and the twins, toddling around in diapers and stained shirts, tried to mimic her. Everyone cheered when she finished.

"Cheryl, you've got that great catch in your voice," Kate told her. "Like June Allyson when she talks—or Kay Starr when she sings."

"Thanks." Cheryl beamed. "Trouble is, I never know when it's going to break."

"But that's what makes you so—oh, my god, Ronnie Dean!" Abruptly Doris sniffed the air. "Whew! Somebody better be changin' your pants."

When Rosie looked away, Kate decided she might as well volunteer.

"But you'll have to show me how," she reminded Doris.

Fumbling with the wet cloth and a clean diaper, Kate attempted to distract Ronnie. "Zip-a-dee-do-dah, zip-a-dee-ay . . ." she crooned. He stopped wiggling and held still as he listened for the word, "Zip!" Vickie joined him, laughing at the lyrics, as she tried to imitate Kate. When she had finished, she saw that poor Ronnie was wearing a diaper that pinched him on one side and hung loose on the other. Still, Doris deemed that she had fulfilled her requirement.

"Looks like you can check off your song too," Rosie said generously.

"Aw, c'mon and do it one more time." Perched on the arm of the sofa where she had joined them to watch the fun, Lorene snubbed out her cigarette in a chipped ashtray. "Vickie just loved that, didn't you, cutie?"

Blushing, Kate hurried through one more chorus. But when it was Doris' turn to sing, she declared, "Not here— maybe at your house, Kate."

"Me too," Rosie added. "I want your dad to play the piano for me cause he'll make me sound so good. I just love to hear him—"

"Crap!" Vic exclaimed as he and Charley burst through the door. "If Coach Armstrong makes me shoot fifty free throws at practice again, I'm gonna tell him where to go!"

"Yeah?" Charley never noticed the people who had gathered in his living room. "That's 'cause you missed half of the ones you shot against Watseka. We can't be missin' free throws. You know that."

Vic muttered something under his breath and headed toward the kitchen.

"Don't eat none of them ham 'n beans!" Lorene yelled.

"Mom cooked 'em last night for supper. And we gotta save some for Cletus when he gets home." Lighting another cigarette, she picked up her ashtray and ambled out to the kitchen to see that the boys obeyed.

The next night, however, Vic's diligence paid off as he made nine out of ten free throws against Onarga Military to keep the Boulders' undefeated string intact.

In the days that followed, the girls established a pattern that was as disciplined as Vic and Charley's practice. First they would race home after school to check their mail for movie star pictures. Then they would proceed on to Doris' house to see if Rosie and Cheryl were ready to meet the diaper challenge. Finally, one afternoon, both of them were able to corner a messy toddler and hold their breath while Doris and Kate held their sides and laughed.

At last, just before Christmas, Rosie announced that she was ready to do her solo. She had two requests, however: She still wanted Kate's father to accompany her, and the rest of the group could not look at her while she sang.

Kate was proud that her dad really got into the spirit of his performance.

"Rosie," he said, "we're gonna knock 'em dead." Then he pounded out such a lively rendition of "I'm Just a Girl Who C'aint Say No!" that Rosie begged to do a second chorus. Although the pained smile on Kate's mother's face betrayed her true emotions, she joined Gran and M.J. in clapping heartily when the song was over.

"You're a born entertainer, Rosie," Mother said diplomatically.

"I never heard anything like it in my life." Gran spoke the truth in such a way that Rosie never recognized it.

Rosie just beamed and, for once, had nothing to say.

"I can play for you too, Doris," Kate's father volunteered. "What's your favorite song?"

Hunching up her shoulders, she squirmed and thought for a moment. "Do you have anything country—you know, like they sing on Grand Ol' Opry?"

He gave her question thoughtful consideration before he finally replied. "I'm sorry. You know, I don't think I do. I really need to get some new sheet music."

Screwing up her mouth and eyes, she considered other possibilities. "Do you have 'Danny Boy'?" she asked at last.

He lifted the lid on the piano bench and pawed through his sheet music. "I think it's in here somewhere." Ruffling through all the Christmas carols, he lifted one up and smiled. "Here it is!"

"But is that really popular?" Cheryl challenged. "I mean—it's not on the *Hit Parade* or anything."

"It'll be good enough," Rosie declared, ready to enjoy someone else's talent. "Take it away, Doris."

As Doris began, haltingly at first, Kate's father slowed the tempo a bit and caressed the keys with his tender touch. Her mother had just plugged in the Christmas tree so that the soft light from the late afternoon dusk created an angelic effect on Doris' pale face. As she whispered the phrase, "And I will bend and tell you that I love you," each one recalled her father and Chet Jr; and the tale of a loved one lost brought tears to the small group clustered around her. When Doris had finished, Gran reached into her sweater sleeve for her handkerchief, and Mother left the room quickly and returned with a box of tissues.

"Here. Pass it around." She took the first one herself before handing it to Rosie. "Then come out to the kitchen and have some Christmas cookies. I baked them this morning. Just one won't spoil your suppers."

Reinforced by their snack, the girls glanced out the kitchen window at the last strand of sunset that stretched across the sky. Each knew what the other was thinking.

"Let's do it!" Rosie exclaimed. "I'll go first." She slipped into the worn pea jacket that Colleen had handed down to her. The others were so filled with anticipation that they failed to notice Rosie's quick phone call.

"I'm ready," she stated resolutely. "The rest of you wait, then follow a couple of minutes apart."

She was out the door in a flash. A few moments later Cheryl was gone.

"Why is everybody running away?" M.J. asked.

Mother was just as curious. "What in the world are you girls doing?"

"Something for our club," Doris answered seriously. "We have to pass the Naughton mansion at dark—all by ourselves."

"Oh." Mother nodded with understanding. "Well, I'm certainly glad that John and I don't have to do that."

M.J. just stared at Kate with new respect.

In the few moments Kate had alone with her family, she asked, "Do you really think the Naughton mansion is spooked?"

"Only during the month of December," her father said cheerfully from behind his newspaper.

"John!" her mother reprimanded him. "Kate, you know yourself that I've played bridge there with Pansy Naughton. Of course, right now she and Ezra are away for the winter."

"Your grandpa and I were there before they even put on their first addition," Gran's eyes were bright behind her glasses. "Back before their first child, Maude, was born. I won't tell you what we saw then," she added secretively.

Chills ran up Kate's back as she recalled that the house supposedly had thirty-one rooms. Old Ezra Naughton had built on a new wing each time one of his five children had been born. Now that his offspring had left Rockwell and his first wife, Madeline, had died, it was rumored that Madeline's ghost had returned to punish Ezra for bringing his new spouse to live there.

"But have *you* ever walked by there at night? By yourself?" Kate wondered.

"No, Ezra and Madeline never asked me to." Gran's smile bordered on mischievous.

"I wouldn't do it—not in a zillion years!" M.J. announced.

"But it's your turn now, Katherine Emily," her dad said, putting down the paper. "Get going. And if you're not back by bedtime, we'll start to worry and call the police."

Behind her, Kate could feel their amusement, although they never uttered a sound. As she closed the front door she felt the slap of cold air against her face. Her breath hung in little white clouds in the blackness. At the corner ahead loomed the red-brick structure on her left, its turrets made visible by a half moon that was making a slow ascent. Unlike the other houses in the neighborhood, it offered no holiday trimmings. Its dark windows stared blankly at anyone who dared to look their way.

When she reached the corner Kate caught a glimpse of the house. From the front bedroom, the one that had been Madeline's, came a soft glow that fogged the long, narrow window. The rest of the mansion was shrouded in darkness. Taking a deep breath, she sprinted all the way down the next two blocks until she toppled into the arms of her three friends who were waiting on Rosie's porch.

"Did *you* see that weird light in the window?" she gasped.

Vehemently they shook their heads back and forth, admitting they had been too scared to peek.

After they had warmed themselves at the kerosene stove in the middle of the living room, Mrs. Mulgrew signaled that it was time for supper.

"Rosalie, I need you to help serve up," she called. The heat from the ribs and sauerkraut simmering in a kettle had steamed up their kitchen windows.

"Geez, you guys look like you seen a ghost or somethin'." Mike elbowed past them on his way to the table. "Hey, Ma! Can I have the label off the new can of Ovaltine? I'm gonna send it in to *Captain Midnight*."

When their hearts had stopped pounding at last, they congratulated themselves on having completed the most traumatic requirement for their club. It was only then that Kate realized that she would have to pass the Naughton house again to get home! Cheryl lived in the other direction, and Rosie, of course, was already on safe ground.

"Doris, walk me back part way," she pleaded.

"Okay." Doris almost seemed to be anticipating her request.

As they approached the mansion, Kate suggested that they turn left and go down two blocks. "That way, we'll already be on your street," she explained.

"Plus, we won't have to pass by that awful place again," Doris replied knowingly.

"That's funny." Kate stared at the old house over her shoulder. "I don't see any light up there at all now."

"Ghosts come and ghosts go, just when you least expect 'em." Doris' answer was philosophical. "I told you it was spooked."

Although their detour took Kate five blocks out of her way, she felt it was well worth it. As she opened her front door she felt embraced by the familiar walls. Suddenly starved, she was happy to smell the aroma of chicken and noodles.

"So . . . you survived your big test." Her father folded his paper and placed it on the end table. "Now you've proved yourself to the Fearless Four and you'll never doubt each other again."

"Yep." Kate nonchalantly tossed her coat over a prong of the hall tree.

"And," he pushed up his glasses on his nose and gave her a wry smile, "that's what it's all about—right?"

She grinned back at her dad. He *was* right. She had paid her dues, and no one—not even Rosie herself—could doubt her loyalty again.

* * *

Chapter Five

"**K**ate, would you do me a favor?"
As soon as she heard her father's voice she quickly slid the package she was wrapping under her bed. Although her door was shoved shut as far as it would go, she didn't want him to catch her in the act of wrapping the recording of Tchaikovsky's "Symphony Pathetique" that she'd bought for him for Christmas.

"What?" Straightening the bedspread so he couldn't see the gift, she hoped he didn't want her to take M.J. for a walk. With only two days left before Christmas, her parents might want to get M.J. out of the house so they could do some wrapping themselves. The gifts from other relatives were already under the tree, but Kate knew that her parents always waited until the last minute to add their presents to the pile.

"I have some sheet music that I think Tommy might enjoy. Would you mind taking it over to Panczyks'?" He nudged the door and handed her a packet.

"Sure!" She welcomed the opportunity to do a favor for her dad and to go see Doris all at the same time. Only yesterday Rosie had passed her last club requirement by changing Donnie's diaper—a squishy mess that made Kate glad she had fulfilled her obligation before the winter colds and diarrhea set in with all their symptoms. Donnie had been feverish and restless, and only Doris' supreme coaching job had steered Rosie through to the end.

When she arrived at Doris' house, Cletus had his truck

up on blocks and was working on it in the front yard.

"Hi, Cletus. Are Doris and Tommy around?" She never was quite sure what to say to him.

"Ye-ahh," he drawled. "In 'er somewheres. Gol-lee. We're sure gettin' the company today!" Wiping his nose across the sleeve of his jacket, he stuck his head back under the hood. Kate shuddered and wondered how Doris could sleep at nights, just knowing he was in the same house.

The screen door was still hanging crooked from its top hinge. Cletus had promised to fix it for Mrs. Panczyk but always seemed too busy doing nothing. Startled, Kate jumped out of the way as Vic and Charley nearly bumped into her as they dashed out of the house, their basketball shoes slung over their shoulders.

"Tommy's in the living room. Doris is in the kitchen," Charley called over his shoulder. "Just go on in."

The combined odors of burned toast and wet diapers hung in the hall. Stepping over three piles of dirty clothes just inside the front door, she found Tommy hammering out piano exercises in the living room. One of the many loops of worn tinsel that Cletus and Lorene had taped over the shabby wallpaper had come loose and dangled over the piano.

"Hey, Tommy. I brought some stuff that my dad thought you'd like to borrow. There's some old Jerome Kern sheet music and a book of classics." Handing him the stack, she added, "Oh—and a little collection of Christmas carols too."

"For me?" He turned and smiled at her. He could have been Doris' twin, Kate thought, but somehow the features and coloring that appeared plain and ordinary on her seemed winsome on him. "Tell your dad I'll cut his grass for him sometime next summer. For nothing."

"I'm afraid that's my job. But you could do it for me!"

She grinned, heading for the kitchen. There she found Doris pulling canned goods from several large sacks. A large turkey occupied the rest of the table.

"Tommy! Get out here right now and take this turkey out to the back porch. We've gotta keep it cold till tomorrow, and there's no room in the fridge!" Doris' voice was unusually shrill with a harsh edge to it. Kate could tell by the puffiness around her eyes that she had been crying. "Oh hi, Kate," she mumbled, keeping her head down.

"Wow—you must have gone to the store early!" Kate surveyed the collection of groceries that covered the counters. "Need some help?"

Doris gave her a look filled with misery. Behind her glasses her eyes were blurred with tears.

"We didn't *buy* this. Perfect Nancy Dawes and her perfect mother brought it to us."

"All of this?" It must have been twenty dollars' worth, Kate thought. Picking up one of the cans, she tried a lighthearted approach. "Yum—ripe olives."

"Yeah, just what we need. What we really could use is soup beans and hamburger—not this fancy stuff!" Bitterly Doris shoved the olives into the cupboard.

"Can I help?" Kate had never seen Doris quite so discouraged.

"No." Hanging her head, Doris looked at her then glanced away quickly. "Oh, Kate, promise me you won't tell Rosie and Cheryl about this. I—I'm just so ashamed." She began to cry.

Unsure of what the problem was and how to help, Kate put her arms around her.

"Oh, Dor, I won't. You know that." She hugged her fiercely, then asked, "What happened?"

"Oh, Mom was in the basement startin' the wash, so I went to the door. There stood Nancy and her mom, all dressed up, holdin' bagfuls of groceries." Her shoulders heaved as she wiped her eyes with her arm and tried to continue. "Mrs. Dawes—well, she looked around our house and rolled her eyes at Nancy. I could tell what they were thinkin'."

Unsure of what she should say, Kate merely remained silent until Doris could choke out the rest of her story.

"Tommy got Vic and Charley—Lorene already had took the kids to her friend's down the street—and the three boys brought in the rest. Nancy just stood there and watched Vic and Charley like—well, like they was movie stars or somethin'." Doris' shot Kate a pained expression. "Her mother kept lookin' at our kitchen, like she'd suddenly been dropped into a hell hole and said, 'So this is where Violet learned to cook.'

"I tried to thank them, but I felt so dumb. Then Mrs. Dawes said that her ladies' club is helping needy people this Christmas and she and Nancy thought it would be nice to do somethin' for Violet's family. She—she was just so goddamn proud of herself." Her whole body convulsed with sobs.

"What'd your mom say?" Kate's own eyes were filling with tears as she listened.

"She came up from the basement, hands all red from bein' in the washtubs, and thanked them. She didn't act ashamed, but she didn't lick their shoes neither." Doris brushed back her tears. "In fact, she even asked if they would like somethin' to drink. I was proud of her for that."

"What'd Nancy and Mrs. Dawes do?" Kate couldn't picture the two of them in Gran's kitchen and tried to realize how terrible it must have been for Doris and her mom.

"They seemed kinda nervous and said they'd better get goin'. They had lots of presents to wrap. On the way out," Doris uttered a little chuckle, "Mrs. Dawes got one of her skinny heels tangled up in a pile of laundry and said in that fakey little high voice of hers, 'Oh, my, oh my!'"

"Too bad she didn't fall flat on her fanny." Kate handed her a can of cranberry jelly to squeeze into the cupboard.

Doris actually laughed, then looked horrified. "You didn't come over with food too!" She clapped her hand to her mouth.

"Heck, no. My dad sent some music over for Tommy to borrow. But if you'll open that can of olives you just put away, I'd sure be glad to test 'em for you."

* * *

The following morning, on Christmas Eve, her dad asked Kate to ride with him to Bakers Corners to deliver a box of Russell Stover creams to a lady who had given him a stack of old *Etude* magazines. She liked going places with him because the two of them always had a good talk without her mother, M.J. or Gran to distract them.

On the way home, as snowflakes began to dance on the windshield of their aging Pontiac, he discussed the songs he would be playing for the Christmas Eve service at church and how proud he and her mother were that Kate would be singing a solo in the operetta. They rode together in companionable silence for a few moments. Then she asked the question that had been gnawing at her since the day before: "Why on earth would anyone ever think that Doris' family is needy?"

"What makes you think they are?" he responded, never taking his eyes from the road. The wipers were working double-time, trying to keep the snow from building up on the windshield.

Kate explained about the groceries that Mrs. Dawes and Nancy had brought. She told him that she thought they had been kind to remember the Panczyks but that their superior attitude had humiliated Doris.

"But don't you dare tell," she warned him. "I promised Doris I wouldn't, but then here I go spilling everything to you."

"You've got my word." He wiped some steam from the inside of the window, then reached out and covered Kate's fingers with his gloved hand. After a few moments he asked, "Got a little extra time? I want to show you something. But you have to promise me, as I just did, never to tell what we see today."

"I promise." Kate wondered what he could he possibly show her in Rockwell that was new. She'd covered every block on both sides of town in the eight months she'd lived there. "Mother's Christmas gift?" she asked at last.

"Nope." He chuckled as he steered the car through the snow that covered Oak Street. "See that house on your side? The brick one with the white columns?"

"Yeah, that's one of the prettiest houses in town. Everybody knows that's where Adele Atwater lives." Kate thought that Adele's home looked like a Christmas card as the snow powdered the pine trees that lined her front sidewalk.

"You're right. Adele's dad, Vince Atwater, even built that place himself. It's beautiful inside. Your mom and I have been to a party there." He slowed so she could get a good look at the house she'd admired so many times.

"But Vince Atwater has—well, as they say— overextended himself. He's put up so many houses since the war, trying to get rich quick. The bad thing is, he hasn't been able to sell all of them." Her dad inched on down the street. "Now he's behind in his bills and owes everybody in town—including us. About eight hundred dollars for coal, if I remember right."

"Whew!" Kate whistled softly. Being in debt, according to Gran, was a sin right up there with lying and stealing. "But Adele has the prettiest clothes. Almost as nice as Nancy Dawes." She cringed again just thinking the pain Nancy had caused Doris the day before.

"That she does. But their bills just keep piling up." He turned the corner and started down Ash Street. "Poor Vince is under a lot of pressure these days, but nothing, I understand, to what Sonny Gilchrist is facing."

"Ellen's dad? That's their new house, isn't it?" She pointed to a the shell of a modern ranch with three separate wings. "Wow—it's going to be huge!"

"Yep," Dad said. "You know, they own the lumber yard, but so many people, like Vince Atwater, aren't paying *their* bills that Sonny is really struggling to keep his business. But that didn't make any difference to Sonny." He snorted. "Sonny and his wife threw a big Christmas party at the country club just last week." Kate could tell that Dad was almost choking on his words. "They owe us close to a thousand dollars, but they think it's more important to look good than to pay their bills."

"Ellen always has new clothes too." She knew she was only adding fuel to the fire.

Dad shook his head and muttered something under his breath.

"Those people, Kate, are known as 'four-flushers'. They spend big to look big, even when they don't have the money. So," he added as they jostled over the Nickel Plate tracks, "don't ever let anyone fool you with appearances."

"Hey—aren't we going home?" she asked as they passed their house.

"In a minute. I want to show you a couple more things. Wipe the steam off your window."

Now she was really curious. As she rubbed the sleeve

of her coat across her window, she realized they were passing an unsteady shack, its thin tarpaper shielding it from the heavy snow.

"That's where Emery Ogle lives," Dad said.

"Cletus' brother?" Kate wondered if Emery was as mean and shiftless as Cletus.

"That's right, but he's cut from a different cloth than Cletus. Emery is a hard worker. But he has five little children, and one was born crippled. It's all he can do to put food on his table."

"I think I know who they are," she said, recalling three girls and their little brother who always came to school in the same clothes. "They wear the same thing, every single day. But they're never dirty." She thought for a moment. "Like Cletus," she added.

"And Emery—" her dad paused. "He comes over to the coal yard and does odd jobs, just to trade work for lump coal that he can put in his stove. He's dog-tired from working a full shift at the foundry all week, but he still asks us if he can shovel coal on the trucks on Saturday runs, just to heat his own house."

"Aw, they probably won't get much for Christmas." Kate's eyes stung as she pictured the children enduring the holiday with no gifts and a skimpy meal. Suddenly she felt guilty about the packages under their own tree.

"Don't worry," Dad reassured her. "I've heard from the best authority that Santa plans to stop there tonight."

She grinned, knowing her dad would give his last penny to help someone else. "Hey—there's Doris' house. I bet she's probably helping her mom with that turkey right now." Even Doris' house looked softer, prettier and almost expectant in the late afternoon dusk of Christmas Eve. Kate noticed that someone had fixed the screen door.

"Doris' mom is a good woman," her father stated with

conviction. "Cora Panczyk is as steady as they come. Every other Friday afternoon, as soon as she gets paid down at Midwest Manufacturing, she comes in with two dollars toward her coal bill. Summer, winter, fall—it doesn't matter. Cora does not get behind."

"Gosh." Suddenly she thought of Doris' mother in a completely different light. Why, she was doing a better job than Mr. Atwater and Mr. Gilchrist!

"Plus she always has a pretty good joke for us too." Dad chuckled to himself.

"I hope she doesn't feel bad about getting all that stuff from Nancy and her mom." Kate wished that Mrs. Dawes had just kept her generosity to herself.

"I don't think she will," Dad assured her. "Cora Panczyk is smart enough to know that Melba Dawes did a nice thing for Melba Dawes' sake—and not really to help Cora. Melba's one of those do-gooders who likes to brag about what she's done for others."

"Gosh," Kate repeated, attempting to digest all the information her dad was dumping on her.

"Okay, Kate—" Dad said as the car crunched into their driveway. Mounding up on the row of spirea bushes in front of the porch, the snow looked like whipped icing on one of Mother's spice cakes. "We made a deal. I won't tell about how upset Doris was—and you won't repeat anything I told you now. About any of those folks. Ever!"

"I won't, I won't. I promise." Kate felt older to think that her dad had trusted her with such confidential information.

"I just want you to know that, if I had to choose, I would have all our customers be as faithful as Cora Panczyk and as hard-working as Emery Ogle. The fancy folks could go somewhere else, for all I care." He peered at her over the top of his glasses. "So don't ever think, Kate, that

74

people are better, just because they might happen to live in a nicer house and wear newer clothes. Sometimes the real stuff—you know, the stuff that matters—just doesn't show."

"I got it, Dad." As she climbed out of the car, she realized that she needed to ask another question before they went inside. "One more thing . . . Cheryl's dad. Does he pay his bills?"

Her father didn't answer immediately. Instead, he removed his glasses and stuck them in the pocket of his corduroy jacket so they wouldn't get spotted from the snow.

"I mean, they always have new things, and I guess I just wondered," she rambled.

As he studied her thoughtfully she wondered if his brown eyes had lost a little of their sparkle. Maybe, she thought, it was because she was so used to seeing them behind his lenses.

"Bertie always seems to have money for his bills," he said evenly. "Yes, Cheryl's dad pays us."

"Good." She wasn't sure why she felt so relieved. "Thanks, Dad."

The huge snowflakes that landed on her face made her cheeks tingle.

"Look, Dad." She watched as the flakes dissolved in her outstretched mitten. "We never had anything like this in Texas."

"You're right," he agreed. "There's a lot that we have here that we didn't have in Texas."

That night, as M.J. dreamed of Santa and sugarplums, Kate stayed awake and once again tried to sort out all that her father had shared. She thought of the Panczyks, who would sing with gusto the next day while Tommy played carols on the piano. And she remembered Adele Atwater's family in all their finery and wondered just how merry their

Christmas would be as they tried to hide their shaky financial situation.

She was glad her dad had showed her the difference. The Longworth kids, for all of their fancy stuff, really weren't superior after all. She would remember that next time she was forced into going to one of their parties. But, in the meantime, she was proud that she lived on the Sweet Briar side of town, where real people laughed and loved amid the smells of cooked cabbage and kerosene.

Sometimes, she concluded drowsily, it's hard to figure out who's needy—and who's not.

* * *

Chapter Six

Armed with the knowledge her father had given her, Kate strode into 1948 with new confidence. He had shown her both a chink in the Longworth armor and a strength in the Sweet Briar fabric that she hadn't realized existed. She made no secret of the fact that she was a Sweet Briar student and proud of it.

On New Year's Day, as Dad's brothers and their families returned to have dinner with Gran, Kate heard herself entering the conversation. She'd always enjoyed the company of Aunt Janet and Uncle Art. Childless, they were generally cheery and had money to spend on concerts, theater and travel. As soon as they took off their coats, pudgy Uncle Art whisked M.J. and her off to a corner where he slipped each one a five-dollar bill to wish them Happy New Year.

But the air crackled with tension when the other relatives arrived. Uncle Henry, who was lean and lanky like her dad, and Aunt Iris, a skinny, dried-up lady who looked as if a smile would split the tight skin on her face, liked to snoop. Kate knew their nosiness made her mother "nervous as hell," as Doris would say. Their son, Marvin, felt that, as a Purdue sophomore, he deserved the last word on every topic discussed, while his emaciated sister Mavis spent the afternoon in a corner reading a book of British poetry. Mavis' only redeeming quality, as far as Kate was concerned, was that she'd outgrown her maroon bike in time for Kate to use it. They were not the people she would have chosen as her companions for the first day of the new year.

As her dad placed the steaming brown goose on the dining room table, Kate could see her mother, normally calm and collected, wiping her brow with her apron in the kitchen. It was not the heat from the oven that was making her perspire. Kate wondered if Brian's melancholy would ruin the day for the Mulgrews and if Cletus and Lorene were allowing Vickie and the twins to run wild through Doris' house. She speculated that Cheryl was eating a cold sandwich and watching her parents dance.

"The goose is perfect, as always," Aunt Iris purred. "But is it quite as large as the one Gran served last year?"

Her father's request that they bow their heads left Aunt Iris' question unanswered. Gran gave the blessing, wiping her eyes as she included the names of her departed husband and sons. After they had stuffed themselves on goose and sauerkraut and finished with her mother's plum pudding Kate was relieved to adjourn to the kitchen so she and M.J. could do the dishes. Although they tried to dawdle so they wouldn't have to endure more adult conversation, their mother came to the kitchen innumerable times to make sure they finished in time to join the others in the living room. They sighed as they sat down on each side of their grandmother, realizing they had not missed the business discussion.

"That Allen coal from West Virginia has been our best seller so far this year." Uncle Henry lifted a Lucky Strike to his thin lips, while his yellowed fingers cradled the heavy Iron Fireman ashtray in his other hand. "If it keeps outselling Brazil nut, I think we should raise the price per ton."

"Maybe on the egg coal but not on the lump." Kate watched as her dad rearranged the logs in the fireplace with the poker as he spoke. "We've got too many folks using lump in their stoves who can't afford to pay more."

"John's right." Gran's left hand fluttered as it always did when she tried to make her point. "Remember, your father said to sell coal at a price that people can bear to pay. Otherwise, everybody suffers."

"We'll wait and see." Always the diplomat, Uncle Art tried to avoid taking a stand as he thumbed through the pages of *The Chicago Tribune.*

Kate was glad to hear her mother artfully steer the conversation in another direction by asking the aunts their opinions of the "new look" with its lowered hemlines and open-toed shoes. Grimacing, Uncle Henry turned to his brothers and challenged them to place bets on how badly Bump Elliott and the Big Nine's Michigan Wolverines would wallop Southern Cal in the Rose Bowl later that day. She daydreamed as they speculated on who the Republicans would run against Truman in November. But when the topic turned to the Boulders and how long they could go undefeated, she spoke up.

"If Vic and Charley are on their game, they'll probably go to state," she blurted out.

Marvin made a condescending comment about the two older Panczyk girls and added that neither of the boys would stand a chance of making the team if they went to Purdue.

"How do you know?" Kate landed a verbal punch that she knew would make even Rosie proud. "How many games have you been to?"

Uncle Art came to her rescue.

"I'll tell you one Sweet Briar kid who could really play ball a few years ago." Tossing aside his newspaper, he leaned forward earnestly. "That was Brian Mulgrew. He was one tough guard. Then he goes to war and gets himself burned all to hell."

"Arthur!" Gran scolded him for dropping a bit of profanity in her living room.

"He sure is a sad one now," Kate said. "Just sits around the house and plays his harmonica."

"Well, Kate," chirped Aunt Iris, her smile overly bright, "You certainly are up on the latest news from Sweet Briar. But, honestly, we don't need to sit here and talk about those people all afternoon. Marvin, Mavis—get your things together. We'll be running along."

"You'll all have to come to the operetta this year," Dad urged as he helped Aunt Iris into her black wool coat with the silver fox trim. "Kate's the Statue of Liberty."

"Well, that's just great, honey." Aunt Janet's smile was genuinely enthusiastic as she chimed in from across the hall. "Maybe someday we'll be seeing you on stage at the Shubert in Chicago."

"Don't puff her up too much now, Janet," Mother said as she put her arm around Kate. "But we *are* proud of her."

"She has to hold a torch for a long, long time. But it's not real!" M.J. tossed her braids. "They're making it out of wet newspapers and paint and stuff."

"Gee, I'm sorry I'll have to miss it." Marvin smirked. "I'll be in the middle of finals. Or something."

After they had closed the front door on the family's New Year's Day, Mother announced that she was going upstairs to lie down. Dad turned on the Rose Bowl game while M.J. took out her new box of modeling clay. Kate accepted Gran's invitation for "just one game" of Chinese checkers.

"Well, Katie Sweet, you're getting to know your friends at school pretty well since you all started that club." Gran's tone was matter-of-fact as she jumped one of Kate's marbles.

"I like going to their houses," Kate admitted. "Each place is so different." She scanned the board for her next play. "I don't know—it's hard to explain. But I think they like me too."

"Then you keep going," Gran said as she jumped three of Kate's marbles in one move. "I like to hear you talk about them." Her eyes twinkled. "Especially when Iris is here. It makes her leave sooner."

The following Monday, when they reconvened at school, Rosie was ready to pop. "I got news!" Her smile spread from ear to ear as she emerged from the cloakroom. Her three friends clustered around as she announced that Brian had agreed to fill in at the basketball games while the official timer recuperated from surgery.

"Coach Armstrong stopped by our house yesterday and talked to Brian about it." She paused for dramatic effect.

"Yea!" they chimed as they headed for their desks.

Kate realized Doris was beckoning to her. "Vic and Charley told the coach to ask him," she whispered. "He's always been their idol and they said he's just gotta start gettin' out."

Kate just shook her head and smiled, thinking of how much happier all the Mulgrews would be just to see Brian taking an interest in something.

As they resumed their schedules that January, Kate began to feel as if everything around her were piling up. She was amazed at the amount of energy she used to wade through the waist-high snowdrifts that had accumulated. The mound of homework assignments coupled with an intense rehearsal schedule for the operetta left her feeling equally drained.

Still, she knew her busy life was a breeze compared to the demands Doris faced each day. Because Lorene had gotten a job as a waitress at the truck stop, Doris now had to fix supper and take care of Vickie and the twins after school. Some days she fell asleep in class, and twice she quietly asked Kate to slide her math paper over to the edge of her desk during a test so she could copy the answers. Finally, she told Miss Brennan that she could no longer be in the operetta chorus because she couldn't attend the rehearsals.

Kate knew that she, Rosie and Cheryl had no choice but to carry on without her. Frequently, as she waited in the wings for the cue for her dreaded solo, Kate could detect Rosie's exuberant voice from the rest of the on-stage chorus: "Liberty, Miss Liberty—finest sight you'll ever see!" The refrain haunted Kate's dreams at night.

"Are you scared at all?" she asked Cheryl one afternoon as the two left the school after rehearsal. Already the deep dark of late January had descended, and it wasn't even four-thirty.

"Not really." Cheryl hugged her homework close to her chest. "If I had to make a speech I'd be terrified, but this is just memorizing lines that someone else wrote for us."

"Well, at least you have two good songs," Kate reminded her. "I've gotta do that stupid 'Miss Liberty' number!"

Cheryl's dark hair flipped as she turned. Kate thought that under the street light she glowed like a model on the cover of *The American Girl.*

"Good songs or not, when I'm out there singing, I feel like I'm doing what I was born to do." Her breath formed tiny clouds in the frigid air. "I just wish I really *were* going to New York!"

In addition to their rehearsals, Kate and her friends made sure they had time to attend the basketball games each week. So did almost everyone else in Rockwell. Her dad even took M.J., while her mother volunteered to stay home with Gran. Kate knew that Mother didn't give a hoot for basketball, so the arrangement worked out well for everyone. The crowds were growing larger with each game, and Doris pointed out confidentially that the out-of-town men in broad-brimmed hats were college scouts in checking on Vic and Charley.

As the team continued to roll through the season undefeated, the excitement seemed to unify the town. It was great, Kate thought: Longworth people were cheering for Sweet Briar boys, and the Sweet Briar parents didn't mind a bit when "that rich little snot Alan Atwater" came in as a substitute in the final thirty seconds and calmly sank two free throws to win the county championship.

Rosie always kept one eye on the game and one eye on Brian.

"Look at him!" She nodded toward the bench during half-time of the New Richmond game. "He's joking with some of his old teammates. And I even saw Sandra Bishop flirting with him earlier."

"Sandra Bishop?" Cheryl asked, munching on one of the licorice sticks that she had bought at the concessions stand.

"Yeah, he always kinda liked her in high school, but she was a year ahead of him and was engaged to Freddy Osgood." She sighed. "Freddy was one of Brian's basketball buddies."

"I remember when he got killed at Iwo Jima." Doris' doleful expression seemed out of place in the midst of a game. "His mom hung a gold star flag in her window."

"Yeah." Rosie was engrossed in her Seven-Up candy bar. Every one of the seven bites had a different filling, and she was always afraid that if she mixed two of them, something dreadful would happen to her. Nibbling into the caramel bite, she told them, "It just about killed Sandra too. She's a secretary down at Midwest, and Dad said she looked like a ghost for more'n a year."

"Is she the one in the pink sweater and pearls—with the

blond hair?" Kate nodded toward the bench.

"Yeah," Rosie wadded up her wrapper and tossed it under the bleachers.

"Oooh," Cheryl giggled. "She thinks your brother is hubba-hubba, all right."

Kate noticed that the buoyant mood generated by the basketball team spilled over into their operetta rehearsals. The longer that her Sweet Briar friends mingled with Longworth students, the more they all seemed to realize that they were dedicated to a common purpose on two fronts. First, they would do anything to back their beloved Boulders and, second, they were bent on presenting the best operetta that Rockwell residents had seen yet.

When performance day arrived, however, Kate felt as if a porcupine had taken up residence in her stomach. She wondered if Vic and Charley felt the same way when they had to shoot a free throw during a tied game. After she had picked at the bowl of Cream of Wheat that her mother had fixed for her supper, Gran pulled her aside and told her, "I never had any girls, you know, but every one of my boys liked to perform. They always said that once you get past your opening lines, the rest is the most fun you'll ever have."

But they never had to wear a scratchy costume, Kate thought glumly. And they never had to open a show while holding a papier mache torch that weighed a ton.

After her father dropped her off at the school and told her cheerily to "break a leg," she entered the back door and sniffed the clean smell of freshly painted flats. Beyond the curtain she could hear the first few members of the audience moving about in the metal folding chairs that had been set up on a canvas covering the gym floor. On stage Miss Brennan flitted around like a hummingbird, making certain that their costumes were hanging perfectly and that they were all in their proper places.

Holding her torch high, she felt the blood drain from her face as the curtain opened.

"Liberty, Miss Liberty—" She heard her own voice, small and frail, sending the words out in wisps. As the silent audience strained to hear, her mind became a blank page. Hot and miserable under the stage lights, she desperately combed the trenches of her memory for the right words. In her damp palm she could feel the handle of her torch turning to goo.

"Liberty, Miss Liberty," she repeated uneasily. Her accompanist struggled to match the music to Kate's lyrics.

"Finest sight you'll ever see," Peggy whispered urgently.

"Finest sight you'll ever see!" she sang out. With her memory on automatic pilot, she poured out the rest of the song. No longer afraid and shaky, she knew that Peggy, swathed in her lace-and-ribboned costume, was right behind her to prompt her if she faltered again.

After the show M.J. threaded her way through the crowd to greet her. "You sure were nervous!"

"We were so proud." Her mother was glowing as she hugged her. She and her father were kind enough not to mention her bad case of stage fright. Humiliated, Kate scolded herself for needing Peggy's help. Rosie or Cheryl would never have blanked their opening lines the way she had.

"And we're already looking forward to coming again tomorrow night," Dad added. "By the way, I want to congratulate Cheryl. That girl sounds just like Betty Hutton!"

The next night, her dad made sure that Gran came along and had a front-row seat. Kate breezed through her song and, after the show, glowed with the rest of the cast members as Miss Brennan assured them they were the best group she had ever directed. Longworth and Sweet Briar students alike basked as one unit under her praise.

Kate felt that same unified anticipation as Rockwell residents from both sides of town packed the gym for the first game of the regional tournament the following week. With their undefeated season a reality, the Boulders had begun to attract statewide attention as newspapers speculated on how far the "Cinderella Team of 1948" might go.

A few fans even cheered when Mrs. Panczyk entered with the rest of the family—Violet, Tommy, Lorene and even Cletus slinking along behind them. Doris said that her mom had persuaded an elderly neighbor to watch Vickie and the twins so Lorene and Cletus could see Vic and Charley play.

The Boulders responded with three games that local supporters would talk about for years. In the first contest Danny Rigoni was brilliant on defense and led all scorers with nineteen points. The second match was such a lopsided victory that every sub scored at least two points. Vic and Charley took over in the championship game, with Vic making ten consecutive free throws and Charley swishing long shots from all over the court. Only the two games of the sectional tournament, to be played in the Danville gym, stood between the Boulders and the Sweet Sixteen.

"I'm telling you—it's my lucky mittens," Rosie shouted after the regional trophy had been awarded. "I've worn these blue-and-white mittens to every game this year and we haven't lost yet! Haven't washed 'em neither!"

"My mom says it's because Vic and Charley're eatin' four hot dogs apiece before they play." Doris nodded, confident her mother was right.

"Well, whatever—we'd better keep doing it." Rosie buried her mittens securely into the pockets of her jacket.

The following week Kate sucked in her breath as she

86

and her friends entered the Danville gym. A huge barn of a building, it was filling with hundreds of fans who had come to see the Rockwell Boulders annihilate the Champaign Maroons. It shouldn't be much of a contest, she thought. After all, Champaign had already lost twelve games! Doris' family was assigned to a special section, and Brian, who appeared with Sandra Bishop's arm linked in his, had prime seats right behind the team.

"Look at Brian," Rosie marveled. "He's smiling! Geez, I just pray that he's finally coming out of it. And cross my fingers too!"

Mike, who had temporarily swapped his Cardinals cap for a Boulders beanie, bounded up the bleachers.

"Hey, Rosie—let me squeeze in there with you guys."

"Dope!" Rosie retorted. "Sit in your own seat."

"Naw!" He nudged her. "It's way up near the top. I can't see nothin'. You can't hardly tell Vic from Charley up there."

"Well, fried fritters! Go find Colleen then."

His face clouded. "Oh, she's so nervous for Danny she won't even listen to me. C'mon, Rosie, pul—eeze?"

"Hey, Mike, I'm pretty skinny. Sit by me." Kate motioned to him as she scooted closer to Doris.

"Ya mean it?" His face brightened. "I'll be good—and you can have some of my popcorn." He offered her his bag with a few burned remnants and a bunch of unpopped kernels.

"If we get in trouble, you're outta here. You got that?" Rosie was emphatic. "I didn't come to Danville to baby-sit with *you*, you little creep."

Mike just grinned and settled in next to Kate.

As the Boulders took the floor, they glanced nervously at the top of the bleachers, taking in the size of the crowd. The tremendous number of Rockwell fans didn't seem to

phase the Champaign team; after all, they were city boys
who were used to playing in large gyms. At the opening
tip-off, the ball ricocheted off the hands of Rockwell's own
Wayne Stevens and into the hands of a Champaign guard—
a bad omen, to say the least. By the end of the first half
their jitters had put the Boulders in a deep hole, 30-18.

"We'll be okay. I still got my lucky mittens, remember?" Rosie fished in the pockets of her coat and came up
with nothing. As play began, her face was a roadmap of
wrinkles. "I know I had them." She was so distracted that
she didn't see Charley make three quick baskets.

"Wahoo, Charley!" Mike was out of his seat. "C'mon,
you guys," he screamed.

With one minute to go, Vic sank two free throws that
finally gave Rockwell the lead by one point. Kate felt the
bleachers trembling beneath her as the rabid crowd roared,
"Sweet Sixteen! Sweet Sixteen!"

Just thirty seconds were left when Wayne Stevens
fouled out, and Alan Atwater came in as a sub. After a
Champaign player made his first free throw, the score was
tied. Boulder fans cheered as Alan captured the rebound of
the second attempt, then watched in disbelief as one of the
Champaign boys stripped the ball from him. In a panic-
driven attempt to retrieve the ball, Alan fouled his oppo-
nent, who calmly sank both shots. When the final buzzer
sounded, the stunned crowd could not believe the score:
"Champaign, 47, Rockwell, 45."

"Damn it! Damn it to hell," Mike whispered as he
brushed his sleeve across his eyes before making a hasty
exit down the bleachers.

"Oh, my god." Doris was too numb to move.

The Champaign boys ran to shake hands with the Boulders, then hopped around the court like a bunch of jumping
beans. Vic, Charley, Danny—the whole bunch—just stood

there, white as hospital sheets. Alan Atwater doubled over as the game ended, and poor Wayne Stevens, his head buried in a towel, was still glued to the bench.

Jaws clenched and too proud to cry, the Rockwell fans filed grimly from the gym. Outside, many tore up their tickets to the championship game, while others uttered oaths Kate had never heard before. The wind had turned raw during the game. Now a driving sleet stung their cheeks and mingled with their tears as they made their way through the parking lot. Once on board the bus, Rosie knelt to pick up something on the muddy floor.

"Look," she said, her face crumpling, "I must have dropped 'em on my way out. It's my mittens—my lucky mittens."

* * *

Chapter Seven

K ate was shocked that the numbing effect from the defeat was powerful enough to filter into every corner of town. In Texas she had witnessed tempers flaring over a football game, but this loss was different. The space in their lives that had once been filled with dreams of a state championship was now a gaping void. On every damp, dismal morning during the last two weeks of March, Rockwell residents, young and old alike, faced their daily routines dull-eyed and listless. The boys from Champaign had succeeded in crushing the spirit of an entire community.

People handled their disappointment in different ways. When Rigoni's Uptown Tap offered a free round of consolation drinks the night after the Champaign game, they had so many takers that they finally had to give rainchecks. Kate's father reported that he'd heard that even Pudgy Pete's, a grimy shack of a bar down by the railroad tracks, had to turn customers away.

Kate, like every other student, ignored homework assignments, and teachers said nothing. Housewives, including her own mother, spent so much of their day in marathon phone conversations that they failed to have supper ready at the usual time. Even Gran grumbled around the house that it was the worst thing that had happened since the Cubs lost the World Series to the Tigers.

On Wednesday following the game, Kate and her friends went home with Doris to help her with her after-school chores.

"I haven't heard so much bawling since we got the news about Chet Jr." Expertly turning a piece of fatty meat with a long fork, Doris stepped back to avoid being splattered. "When we got home from the game Mom cried, and Lorene cried, and Cletus went to the tavern and came home drunk. When Vic and Charley finally came in, they just went straight to their rooms. But I could hear them crying too."

She poured a little water over the meat and slammed a lid on the skillet. "Mom told them they could mope all they wanted to at home, but when they go out, they're to hold their heads up high. She said they've given everyone a lot of thrills and don't have nothin' to be ashamed of."

"How are they doing?" Cheryl studied a shoebox filled with broken crayons and picked out a purple one for Vickie.

"Just ask 'em." Doris turned off the burner under the sizzling pan. "They've been fixin' the back steps with Cletus and are comin' in right now."

"Hey, girlies!" Cletus flashed them the rotten-toothed grin that always made Kate squirm. Heading straight for the refrigerator, he took out a bottle of milk and tipped it to his lips. Kate made a mental note not to drink any milk at Doris' house as long as Cletus was living there.

"Smells good," Charley peeked under the lid. "When's it gonna be ready?"

"Later rather than sooner, if you keep lookin' in the pan," Vic answered testily.

"You guys doin' okay?" Doris wondered. Kate was glad that Doris had posed the question. The rest, even Rosie, were too timid to ask.

"Yeah," Vic replied. "The coach from Southern Illinois called today. He thinks I can start for 'em down there at

Carbondale next year."

"But that's so far—" Doris protested.

"Then *I'd* better keep practicin'," Charley spread peanut butter evenly over two slices of white bread. "'Cause next year, if we have to play Champaign again and you're at Carbondale, I'm personally gonna see to it that we whip their butts!"

"Not if you've still got that good-fer-nuthin' Atwater kid on the team." Cletus smeared his mouth on his filthy sleeve. "There was guys down at Pete's after the game that woulda beat him up good, if'n they'd had the chance. Rich little bastard."

"Hey, Cletus, it wasn't his fault." Charley spoke through a mouthful of peanut butter. "Coach Armstrong told us after the game that we'd all been lookin' ahead—even him. We just didn't come to play."

He folded the second slice of bread and stuffed the entire thing into his mouth. "I mean—shoot, Champaign had all those losses—and we didn't think they were any good."

"They weren't. You guys just stunk." Cletus began to pour milk down his throat.

"I'd a liked to've seen you do any better!" Vic jumped up from his seat, snatching the milk bottle. "You lazy son-of-a—"

"Forget it!" Charley growled as he grabbed Vic by the arm. "There's nothin' any of us can do about that game now. Just leave it alone." He turned to Rosie, abruptly changing the subject. "Hey, it's been great havin' Brian runnin' the clock at our home games. Us guys sure do like havin' him around."

"Yeah." Rosie jiggled Ronnie on her lap. "He's been more like his old self since he started comin' to the games."

"God, he was my idol when I was in sixth grade." Pausing as he screwed the lid back on the peanut butter jars, Vic silently reflected on the athletic ability of Brian Mulgrew.

"Mine too," Charley agreed. "He showed me how to make shots from the corner when we were down at the school playground on Saturdays. You know, he really oughtta go to school and be a coach."

"That's what he always planned on doin'. But then him and bunch of other guys enlisted before their senior year was even over." Rosie blew a bubble with her gum that covered most of her face. When Ronnie stuck his finger in it and laughed, she continued, "Then when he got hurt 'n all, he just came home and fiddled around with his harmonica." She stopped and cocked her head as if she had just been struck with a thought.

"What's the matter?" Cheryl asked.

"Come to think of it, I haven't heard him playin' that thing for awhile. I knew somethin' was different at home but couldn't put my finger on it."

"Maybe he kin work with some of 'em younger kids—you know, like Mike and even Tommy. Somebody's got to start bringin' 'em little 'uns along." Cletus capped the almost-empty milk bottle and put it back in the refrigerator.

"Aw, Cletus, you know as well as I do that Tommy ain't got no interest in playin' ball," Vic lamented. "After Charley graduates, that'll be the end of the Panczyks for the Boulders."

"Well, 'en, that there's another problem yer goin' have if'n you don't get him out there to play." Cletus sniffed and once again ran his sleeve across his nose. "I mean, somebody'd better start makin' a man outta him."

"Just let it go, Cletus," Charley warned.

"Well, it's the god's truth." Cletus squinted a mean look across the kitchen at Vic and Charley. Kate froze in her spot and wished that, somehow, she and the other girls could make themselves invisible. "Yer goin' to end up with a queer on yer hands if'n you don't get him away from that py-annie."

Leaping across the kitchen, Vic grabbed Cletus by the front of his shirt.

"You keep your mouth shut and go do somethin' useful for a change—you hear?" Charley's face was redder than Kate had ever seen it. "Tommy's got a different gift from me 'n Vic, that's all. And I don't ever—you hear me— *ever*—want you to say nothin' like that again!" His fist was right under Cletus' runny nose.

"And that goes double from me," Vic added, surprised at the vehemence of his younger brother. "We'd like to see what *your* gift is, smart ass—other than makin' babies!"

When everyone burst out laughing, Cletus slunk out the back door. Then Charley yelled into the living room, "Hey, Tommy—play us some of that Scott Joplin stuff. We could use somethin' peppy around here!"

"Thanks, Charley." Doris' smile was weak. "You guys are the greatest."

Relieved that the tension had burst, the other girls sighed and murmured their agreement.

"I gotta be gettin' home." Rosie shoved her chair up close to the wooden table. "Colleen's working down at the dime store every night this week and Ma's got stuff I gotta do." Kate and Cheryl were quick to follow.

Once outside, they breathed deeply. The sweet smell in the air and the distant cooing of a turtledove signaled that perhaps spring would come along after all and heal their wounded spirits. A small bunch of crocuses splashed patches of yellow and lavender along the broken chunks of cement that served as Panczyks' sidewalk.

"That Cletus gives me the creeps." Rosie shuddered. "I think he's scary."

"My folks told me I couldn't stay all night at Doris' if

Cletus is around." Cheryl stooped to pick a crocus. "Bertie's heard some stories about him around town."

"Like what?" Kate wondered.

"I don't know. Bertie wouldn't say." Cheryl shook her head. "I sure feel sorry for Vic and Charley though. Do you think they'll be okay?"

"Yeah, I think *they* will," Kate assured her as her mind raced to Alan Atwater. She wasn't so sure about him. It must be a terrible thing to have to carry the blame for disappointing the whole town, she thought.

On the following Monday morning, however, they saw their basketball grief evaporate like mist in a morning wind when Rosie scurried up to meet them in the classroom cloak closet.

"You'll never guess what happened Saturday!" Breathless with anticipation, she withheld her news for a few more moments.

"Tell us!" Cheryl jumped up and down impatiently.

"Yeah, c'mon." Kate and Doris chimed together.

Having piqued their curiosity, she spilled out her bulletin at last: "Brian and Sandra got married!"

"Married!" Kate thought the three of them couldn't have been more in unison if they were the Andrews Sisters.

Smirking, Rosie said no more. Again, she paused, savoring the fact that she held all the cards in this conversation. "Yup. Married. Tell you more about it when we change classes."

Frustrated, they took their seats. Kate tried in vain to focus on the social studies lesson covering the rise of urban life in Illinois during the early twentieth century. Sifting through Rosie's brief announcement, she realized that, because of Brian's injury, he and Sandra didn't have to get married.

The three bombarded Rosie with questions the moment they changed classes.

"Hey—one at a time!" Kate hadn't seen Rosie smile so much since Guy Madison's picture arrived in the mail. Brian and Sandra, she said, had been married in Danville on Saturday morning. The next day they had joined the Mulgrews for supper and had told them their plans: Brian was going to University of Illinois to become a high-school coach. And someday they hoped to adopt a family.

"Ma cried. She said it's a miracle, plain and simple." Rosie's reverent gaze traveled to each of them. "But you know what *I* think?"

Speechless, they waited for her to continue.

"Well, last week I found a penny—heads up—and put it in my pocket. The very next day," she lowered her voice as if she were about to impart a matter involving national security, "I found a four-leaf clover in our back yard. Right under Brian's window!" She clamped her lips together and nodded as if she were agreeing with herself.

"Oooh," they all sighed as they took their seats in Miss Brennan's music class. Love—and good luck—seemed to have blessed the Mulgrews all at the same time.

* * *

Kate could not believe how quickly Rosie's joy translated into success in every project she tackled that spring. Rosie had been able to talk her mom into paying her three dollars a week for doing the family's cooking so Mrs. Mulgrew could take a summer job at the canning factory and had wiggled out of mowing the lawn—a non-paying task—by bribing Mike to do it. But, best of all—at least for Rosie—she'd tried out for eighth-grade cheerleader and made it.

Happy that Cheryl also won one of the three coveted spots, Kate tried not to show her own devastation. She'd worked on her cartwheel for three weeks in an effort to develop her agility, but Nola Nesbitt, a short blond who'd already started wearing lipstick, was elected instead. Kate told herself that it was only because Nola had just moved to Rockwell three weeks earlier and hadn't been there long enough for anyone to hate her. Secretly, however, she fretted that Rosie might start to prefer Nola's company over their group.

She shouldn't have worried, she realized. As they headed into the final week of school, Rosie actually displayed more compassion than Kate had ever seen. When Doris lowered her eyes and confessed that she had to cut dandelion greens for supper instead of admiring their movie-star pictures, Rosie came to the rescue.

"I got it!" She snapped her fingers."We'll take our pictures over to Doris' instead of going to my house. That way, we can help her pick greens and still look at our pictures when we're done."

"Everybody better bring some scissors and a sack then," Doris advised.

Kate thought that the vacant lot across from Panczyks' house looked like a bright yellow slab of butter as they approached it. Kneeling to snip the jagged green leaves from the base of the plants, the four talked about the long summer that lay ahead.

Rosie and Doris warned that they would have plenty of household chores and their mothers wouldn't allow friends in the house while they were at work. Assuring them that she would miss them, Cheryl tried to hide her excitement that she had been accepted to study at the national music camp at Interlochen, Michigan. Kate didn't envy her having to spend eight weeks away from home, but she wasn't thrilled with the plans that had been laid out for her either.

"Gran's going over to stay at my Uncle Art's while our family goes to the Smoky Mountains." She grumbled as she flattened her pile of greens so her sack could hold more. "That means I have to spend eight days with M.J."

Later, as Doris soaked the greens in a sinkful of water, they admired their picture collections and agreed to trade a few of their prized autographed photos. Rosie grinned in triumph as she only had to sacrifice Jane Powell for Cheryl's Dane Clark and Robert Walker.

"But that gives me another girl singer." Cheryl casually shrugged off the loss of two leading men. Changing subjects, she said, "That reminds me. Bertie heard down at Rigoni's that Miss Brennan's not coming back."

"Well, how would anyone down at the tavern know that?" Rosie challenged.

"I dunno. Some guy has a friend in Lafayette who told him that his buddy's going to marry the music teacher from Rockwell this summer."

Quietly they digested Cheryl's information.

"But she's so old!" Rosie wrinkled her nose. "People her age don't get married."

"She's gotta be almost forty. She's in a club with my mom and dad." Kate was glad to have something to contribute.

"That's older than my parents!" Cheryl shook her head. "But Bertie said the guy's wife died and left him with two kids. He teaches music at Purdue or something."

"Maybe they'll break up." Doris' eyes brightened as she offered her solution.

"We can only hope." Rosie tucked her new photos into her brown envelope, then glanced up at the clock on the wall. "I gotta go. Sure hope there's plenty of greens for everyone, Doris."

That evening Kate overheard her parents discussing their plans for the trip to the Smokies as they sipped lemonade together on the front-porch glider. Then Dad made a curious comment.

"I can't imagine where Bertie Allison gets all his money. That camp where Cheryl's going to go for the summer costs a bundle. I've seen ads for it in *Etude* magazine." Kate knew he had no idea that she could hear him through the open window.

"Maybe Lila has something put away that we don't know about." Her mother's voice was low.

"Her family didn't have a pot to pee in." Dad snorted at the thought.

"John!"

"Well, it's true." Kate could hear the rusty creak of the metal glider as he puzzled about the Allisons' financial situation. "Maybe Bertie took out a loan of some sort. Well—at any rate, he always keeps his coal bill paid up."

"Who?" Kate questioned innocently as she closed the screen door behind her.

"Katherine! Have you been eavesdropping?" Mother immediately was on her guard.

"Not really. But *if* you were talking about Cheryl's dad, I know he works hard. Really hard." She studied the fireflies that darted away from M.J. as she chased them.

"Maybe Bertie sells more cars than I give him credit for," Dad said dryly and jiggled the ice in his glass.

"That's what Cheryl says." She jumped at the chance to defend Mr. Allison. "She says that Lila calls them 'extra opportunities'—you know, like when her dad has a beer with a guy at Rigoni's and the guy ends up buying a car from him."

Her parents stared at her for a few moments, considering her wealth of information.

"Hmm." Dad was noncommittal.

"Really, Kate. I wish you wouldn't call Mrs. Allison by her first name." Mother set her glass on the metal table in front of the glider. "And I doubt that you have first-hand knowledge of what goes on at Rigoni's."

"Well, I doubt that you do either!" Indignantly, Kate left the porch and returned to the stuffy living room, making sure that the screen door slammed behind her. Honestly, she thought, her parents were trapped in such dull lives!

* * *

Chapter Eight

The summer days stretched out long and dusty after Kate and her family returned from the Smokies. Grudgingly she admitted to Gran that the trip hadn't been too bad— they'd all enjoyed hiking the mountain trails and had marveled when the head caller at the square dance in Gatlinburg insisted that staid-and-proper Mother join him for one set that had left her giggling and gasping for breath.

But the joy of early June faded as July days baked away one by one. She grew weary of playing Chinese checkers with Gran and tired of picking tomatoes and nasturtiums from the garden every day. The restlessness that nibbled away at her caused her to snap at M.J. and to resent each request her mother made of her.

When Cheryl called late in August to announce that she was home from Interlochen, Kate jumped at the chance to be reunited with her friends. She joined Doris and Rosie, who were free of their commitments for the evening, on Rosie's front steps. Licking popsicles they had found in her freezer, the four commiserated on the confinement that each felt in her own life.

"I never thought I'd say this 'cause school's not my favorite place, but I'll be glad to go back just to get away from them kids." Expertly Doris turned her stick to keep the ice from falling.

"Can't be any worse than what I've been doing!" Rosie examined the chipped red polish on her nails. "I feel like Cinderella. It's 'Rosie-do-this and Rosie-do-that' every single day!"

"Maybe so. But you try chasin' them twins around all day." Doris batted at a mosquito. "The only time they sit still is when they're on the piano bench with Tommy. Then we can't stand 'em bangin' on the keys."

"Lila says she's going to keep me inside until school starts." Cheryl rolled her eyes. "She's scared to death of polio. I'm going to feel like a hothouse plant."

"My mom's the same way." Kate felt the last of her grape-flavored ice slide down her throat. "She wouldn't let me go to the county fair because of the crowds. At least when school starts, polio season will pretty much be over."

"And we'll be king of the hill!" Rosie collected their wooden sticks and set them on the porch rail to dry for a project Mike was working on. "Everybody will have to answer to *us*!"

* * *

It didn't take long for Rosie to make good on her prediction. By the second day of school she had settled into her favorite classroom location—middle-row desk, fifth from the front. From that vantage point, she had always been able to initiate ripples of misbehavior without getting caught.

Unlike the previous September, Kate entered each new class with a sense of ease and confidence. She knew what to expect—that is, until the third day, when she entered the music room and was stricken by the chill in the atmosphere. Gone were the colorful pictures of Lena Horne, Jo Stafford and Perry Como. In their place were a few black-and-white drawings of Mozart, Beethoven and Brahms. The windowsills had been stripped of Miss Brennan's ever-blooming African violets, and the desk was stark and empty except for a metronome and a lesson book.

"Geez!" Rosie's eyes circled the room. "Is he a monk or a priest or somethin'?"

The brisk tapping of a baton against the metal music stand cut short their conversation. As the man's fingers lovingly caressed his director's wand, he flashed a cheerless smile.

"Good morning, class. My name is Mr. Hartley."

A shadow fell across his desk as if a cloud had passed over the sun, temporarily sapping the room of its warmth. Kate's first thought was that their new instructor had made the mistake of buying a gray suit that was at least one size too large for him. A sparse fringe of black hair lined the back of his long, narrow head, which was separated from the rest of him by a charcoal bow tie. His mirthless eyes flitted from one student to another as he continued to rub his little baton.

"Our first order of business will be to have each of you write your name on my seating chart. Then I will ask you to come, individually, to the piano and sing the scales for me so I can evaluate your talent."

"Boy, is he in for a treat when he gets to me." Stan Piechocki's irreverent comment under his breath started an epidemic of laughter.

"Class!" Mr. Hartley sounded like a snake as he spat out the word.

"This is sure gonna be fun." Rosie squirmed in her seat.

It took a full week of music classes—three sessions, in all—for them to complete the auditions. It took only one day for the eighth-grade boys to christen him "Old Fartley".

"He looks just like a worm dressed up for a wedding," Stan observed under his breath.

"He ain't got no neck—that's for sure." Jimmy McPherson agreed. "Yep—Piechocki, you're right. He looks just like a worm!"

No one could squeak out a decent note. Even Cheryl's audition, which should have been as smooth as nylon stockings, was one of the worst.

"They tell me you have been to Interlochen." Mr. Hartley's voice was tinged with sarcasm. "I should have thought that they would have trained that hoarseness out of your voice."

"It's—well, it's kind of a catch. I mean, it's the way I sing." Cheryl became flustered. "At Interlochen—"

"We will work on it during the year." He dismissed her coolly.

Kate felt sorry for her. After all, Cheryl could belt out a song better than anyone at the high school! She squirmed as he announced her name. With the full set of braces that Dr. Frank had cemented onto her teeth just the day before, she felt like a horse with a bit in her mouth.

As she began to sing, the rays from the sun danced on her mouthful of metal, sending reflections onto the bare green walls.

"Sparkle Plenty!" Jimmy snickered. The rest of her classmates—even Rosie, Doris and Cheryl—guffawed at the reference to the character in *Dick Tracy*. Withering, Kate felt the scales dying in her throat.

"I thought you were from a musical family, Kathy. In fact, I understand that your father may be the only parent at Sweet Briar who can actually play the classics." Mr. Hartley flashed his thin smile in her direction.

"It's Kate," She corrected him quietly. What did *he* know about her dad and his musical ability? And who gave him permission to embarrass her in front of her friends?

Glancing at her name in his grade book, he smiled. There was no warmth in his eyes. "This says 'Katherine'. You prefer Kate to Kathy?"

104

"Yes." Kate watched circles of color rise in his hollow cheeks.

"We will try the scales again. But first—" He rapped his baton sharply against his music stand. "Class! Class! There will be no laughter. None! Music is a serious subject. Now, try it again, Kath—Kate." He bore down on her name with obvious disdain.

Leaning away from the ray of sun that washed over the piano, Kate tried to force the strength of her anger into her voice as she took a deep breath and began again. At that moment she hated Jimmy for making her the object of cheap laughter, and she hated Mr. Hartley for his haughty approach. So far, she thought, the first few days of her eighth-grade year—the one she had so eagerly antici-pated—were off to a shaky start.

Her mood darkened even more the next week when she received a formal invitation announcing that Miss Adele Atwater requested the pleasure of her company at a tea to be given the following Saturday afternoon in her home.

"A tea? Gosh, what kind of party will those people think of next?" She could only imagine what Rosie and her friends at Sweet Briar would have to say about that! "Can't I just RSVP that my company will not be all that pleasant and that I have no interest in going?"

Her mother peered over the top of her sewing glasses, then continued to darn the hole in one of Dad's socks. Her silence suggested how she felt about Kate's sarcasm.

"What do they do at a tea?" M.J. stopped practicing her piano lesson. "Just sit around and drink it? How boring! I wouldn't want to go either, Kate."

"Actually it's a British custom—enjoying conversation and light refreshments with a group of genteel friends." Mother stopped to inspect the quality of her work. "I imag-ine there will be some lovely pastries."

M.J. rolled her eyes. "You could just go to the bakery and bring home a bagful of rolls." She returned to butchering the Gilbert & Sullivan medley she had been assigned. Kate couldn't resist smiling at her mother. M.J.'s practical interpretation had cut the tension over the invitation, but it had not changed the fact that Kate would have to attend. She knew it, her mother knew it, and both knew that it was not worth arguing over.

This time, however, Kate weighed the odds and decided to take her chances. She would tell Rosie ahead of time when the moment seemed right.

Her opportunity came as the girls gathered at Doris' house the following Monday. "You guys will never guess what my mother's makin' me do now." Kate injected great disgust into her voice as she stirred a panful of ham hocks and soup beans in the Panczyk kitchen. Doris stopped her iron over the board in midair, and Rosie and Cheryl stopped stacking blocks with Donnie and Ronnie on the linoleum floor. She definitely had their attention.

"That's awful, hon." Cheryl was sympathetic when she heard about the tea. "I just know Lila wouldn't make me do something like that. And if she tried, Bertie wouldn't let her."

"Fried fritters!" Rosie slammed two blocks together so hard that the entire tower toppled. "When's your mom ever goin' to realize that you're old enough to say where you're goin' and where you're not?" She handed Donnie a wooden block so he could start over. "Will you be done in time to go see *Abbott and Costello Meet Frankenstein* with us that night?"

"Don't worry. I'll be the first one outta there," Kate assured her.

"I sure wouldn't trade places with you." Doris finished pressing the front of one of Charley's shirts and buttoned it onto a hanger.

"I do have to wonder what it'd be like to go to one of their parties just once though." Cheryl was wistful, almost talking to herself. When she intercepted the scathing look from Rosie, she quickly added, "Not that I'd really want to."

Relieved, Kate returned to the Panczyks' ham and beans. At least she had learned how to sidestep Rosie's wrath. Now she hoped that Peggy Birdsong would help her survive Adele's big social event.

Kate's mouth was dry the following Saturday as her mother inched the Pontiac along Oak Street. When they reached the large brick home with white columns, her mother gave her final instructions.

"Remember to keep your gloves on until you are served." Her mother's eyes misted over as she studied her. "You look so grown up today, Kate. I know you don't want to go, but I do hope you'll have a good time."

"Don't forget to be here right at four." Kate sighed, indicating that she would rather be anywhere but standing on Adele Atwater's sidewalk at that moment. "I'm going to the show with the girls tonight."

As she crunched through the dry leaves on her way to the massive front door she recalled her father's confidential comments last Christmas Eve about the Atwaters' financial condition: "Don't ever let anyone fool you with appearances," he had counseled. Somehow his words gave her strength as Adele opened the door and greeted her with an artificial smile.

"Hello, Kate," she said as if she had rehearsed her line all morning. "I am delighted that you could come."

"Me too." Tugging nervously at her white gloves, she glanced around the foyer with its large burgundy leaves stenciled onto dove-gray walls. Her mother had mentioned earlier in the week that all the walls in the Atwater home had been hand-painted by an artist from Chicago. Still, Kate thought that even Cheryl's modern house with its sharp edges seemed warm and cozy compared to the museum atmosphere created by the Atwaters.

The shrill laughter of Nancy Dawes cut through the harpist's soft strains like a sharp knife through a Sunday roast. Glancing around the living room, Kate was relieved to notice that her mother had been right this time in suggesting that she wear her navy dress with the white Peter Pan collar. However, her heart sank when she failed to find Peggy Birdsong. Without Peggy's welcoming smile, Kate knew she might as well be one of the large pink roses on the draperies. So far, no one had greeted her or had even noticed that she was there. Perhaps, she thought, it was better that way. She took a seat on a straight-back chair and listened as the conversation flitted from name-brand clothing to winter vacation locations to eighth-grade boys.

"I hope some of the Sweet Briar boys come to the sock hop," Nancy said, pushing back her perfect blond pageboy. "Especially that Jimmy McPherson. I think he looks like one of Bing Crosby's sons."

"You'd better hope that Rosie Mulgrew isn't there then," Judy Fuller snorted. "She'll scratch your eyes out if you horn in on Jimmy and her."

"Oh, she's just a little alley cat from Sweet Briar." Full of contempt, Nancy's words landed with a thud. No one made a sound as Kate realized that each Longworth girl was, suddenly, very much aware of her presence.

"Well, Kate, even you must have tangled with Rosie once or twice." Coyly, Nancy tried to cover her gaffe by shifting the attention away from herself. "Everyone knows that the Mulgrews have terrible tempers."

"I couldn't say." Although Kate felt searing heat rising

in her face, she heard her words drop clearly like single pebbles into a calm pond. "But Rosie Mulgrew happens to be one of my very best friends."

"Ooh, touche!" As Nancy's scornful snicker filled the room, the other girls stared silently at the floor. Adele quickly saved the moment.

"Please come to the dining room." She swirled her skirt as she turned and motioned dramatically toward the doorway. "Tea is now served."

As they filled their china plates with tiny fruit wedges and crustless sandwiches with goopy spreads, it seemed to Kate that perhaps Judy Fuller was trying to cover for Nancy's rudeness.

"Too bad Peggy couldn't be here today." She spoke quietly as she and Kate studied a platter of little cakes that Adele had called 'petit fours'. "She had to go to Wisconsin with her parents this weekend."

"I miss her," Kate admitted.

"Yeah, well Peggy's going to have to shed a few pounds if she ever expects to wear anything shown in *Seventeen*." Nancy was back on her throne of superiority. "She'll have to go to those cheap shops in Danville where they sell fat clothes if she isn't careful."

"Never turn your back on Nancy," Judy whispered pleasantly as she leaned across her to scoop up a few cashews. "Or you may find a knife in it."

Other than the fact that she dribbled a glob of white icing down the front of her navy dress, Kate was able to endure the rest of the tea without calling attention to herself. Instead, she concentrated on the number of times—eleven, to be exact—that Nancy referred to *Seventeen* magazine. Kate made a mental note to get a copy of it at the library so she could see what all the fuss was about. She also promised herself to urge Rosie to wear her blue sweater—the one that brought out the color of her eyes—to the sock hop, just in case Nancy had any plans for flirting with Jimmy McPherson.

At the movie that night, however, she learned that the sock hop was not Rosie's top social priority at the moment. It was the wiener roast that her parents had said she could have the next Friday evening at Sweet Briar Park. A patchy piece of land with a few rusty swings and a couple of broken picnic tables, the area had been established during the New Deal years for the benefit of residents on that side of town. Proudly Rosie announced that she was inviting everyone in their class.

"Ma and Pa'll stop by to help roast the hot dogs." She stopped at the candy counter in the lobby to get a box of Milk Duds. "And Colleen and Danny'll be there to chaperone from 6:30 to 9:00—in case your parents want to know. Oh," she added, popping a piece of chocolate into her mouth, "and if any of you want to bring a bag of chips or somethin', feel free."

Now, that was her kind of invitation, Kate thought. None of this small white envelope stuff requesting the pleasure of her company and asking for a response.

Even her parents liked the idea.

"It's good that she invited everyone," Gran commented as Kate pulled on her warm jacket and prepared to leave for the wiener roast. "I never had any girls, you know, but I always felt sorry for the children in my boys' classes who weren't asked to go to the parties."

"Don't forget to take the chocolate chip cookies." Her mother handed her a heavy shoe box tied with twine.

"Thanks, Mother. The other kids are gonna love these."

Kate was so proud that her mother had gone to the trouble to bake something special for Rosie's party. But when she gave Rosie the cookies at the park, she learned that Mother had called Mrs. Mulgrew earlier that day to make sure that there would be adequate supervision.

"Thanks," Rosie said shortly as she took the box from Kate and set it on the picnic table. "But, geez, Kate, how do ya think Ma felt when your mom phoned her to ask if there'd be adults around all evening?"

"But I didn't know—"

"Is she gonna follow you around your whole life to make sure nothin' happens to you?" She shook her head in disgust and strolled over to join Jimmy, who was shooting baskets at a crooked hoop.

"Don't worry, hon." Cheryl was right at her elbow. "She's just touchy because she wants her party to go okay."

"Well, she's not making me feel very welcome." Disgustedly Kate kicked a walnut against a tree trunk.

"Let's just go over and help Danny and Colleen unload the hot dogs and buns from their car," Doris suggested. "The sooner the food gets unpacked, the sooner we can eat. And I can only stay until 7:30."

With great enthusiasm, they piled the picnic tables high with bags of chips, jars of pickles, mustard and catsup and packages of hot dogs and buns. Danny's biceps bulged as he set cases of Coke, Grapette and root beer on the ground. Then he turned his attention to the bonfire, where Russell Logan was showing Stan, Kenny Kroll, and Larry Collins how to build a log-cabin campfire. When they finally lighted the tiny pieces of kindling, the flames licked through the twigs until they ignited the larger logs.

"Hey—we're good!" Stan never was one for modesty. "Only took one match."

As the sky reddened and smoke from the bonfire drifted into the tall oaks and maples, the landscape around the park softened. Across the street the tarpaper shacks, which housed the Gatlin and Purvis families and their broods of ten and eleven children, looked like cozy cottages. Twilight erased the harsh lines of reality, turning the park into a magical place.

"Hey, Rosie!" Kate turned to see Mike heading her way.

"Geez, creep, who invited you?" Realizing he was carrying something, Rosie asked, "Whattya got?"

"I'm helpin' Ma." Proudly he placed a chocolate cake in the middle of the table. "Ma just finished it and let me lick the bowl. Her 'n Pa are comin' right now."

"Rosalie Annette, move some of those chips over so your pa can set down this tubful of baked beans." Always heavy on her feet when she had to walk much of a distance, Mrs. Mulgrew stopped to catch her breath. "Put it right there, Jack."

All the classmates swarmed on the food like ants on a piece of taffy. Waiting near the end of the line, Kate watched Wanda Gatlin and Fayetta Purvis cast furtive glances as they ladled man-size helpings onto their paper plates. It saddened her to know that many of her peers lived in situations where they faced meager portions at mealtime on a daily basis. She couldn't help but think of Adele Atwater's party with its freshly pressed linens and cascading harp music just one week earlier and, once again, pushed away the nagging question of who is really needy and who is getting along just fine.

This party was way better than Adele's silly tea, she thought, as she heard Rosie's mom encourage Wanda to take another helping. Mrs. Mulgrew was making it her personal mission to stuff every undernourished eighth-grader from Sweet Briar. Slicing a monstrous wedge of cake, she plopped it onto Fayetta's outstretched plate. Shyly Fayetta dropped her eyes and whispered, "Thanks, m'am."

As the fire mellowed and the toasty embers begged for

112

marshmallows, Rosie's parents gathered up the remnants of the meal and announced that they had to leave.

"We're sure glad all of you could come," Mrs. Mulgrew shouted, reminding them that Danny and Colleen would be in charge until the party was over. Mike, who had hoped his parents would forget him, scowled when his mother gave him notice.

"Michael," Kate could tell she meant business. "It's time for you to go too."

"Aw, gee—"

"You'll get your turn when you're in eighth grade." His father playfully cuffed him on the jaw. "This wiener roast is getting to be a Mulgrew tradition. You oughtta know that!"

"This is the bestest time of my whole life." Wanda licked the goo from her fingers and poked two more marshmallows onto the end of a sharpened stick.

"Same goes for me." Tugging her thin sweater around her shoulders, Fayetta stared somberly at the fire.

"Me too," Kate agreed. She'd never felt connected to Wanda and Fayetta in any way, and yet, as they roasted marshmallows together, she realized that they shared the same emotion. In the shadows of the glowing coals each of them grew quiet as they basked in their fleeting camaraderie.

Five minutes later the mood switched abruptly as Jimmy yelled, "Ghost in the graveyard!"

Uncertain which way she should run, Kate stood frozen at the picnic table as her squealing friends scattered to the farthest corners of the park. Her heart turned over when she heard Stan call, "Hey, Cheryl—it's kiss-and-tackle time!"

"Oh, no, it's not!" Cheryl began to run, but Stan quickly caught her, pulled her to the ground and kissed her.

"I got me one, Kenny!" he crowed. "Hey, Rosie—

you're next!"

"Oh, no, ya' don't—that one's mine!" Jimmy shouted defiantly and bolted toward Rosie.

Desperately Kate searched the crowd for someone to take charge. Doris had already left, and, according to their reactions, Cheryl and Rosie didn't object to getting caught.

"Where are Danny and Colleen?" she asked Fayetta.

"Over in Danny's car," she snickered. "We prob'ly won't be seein' 'em agin." Then she gasped and began to run when she saw Henry Simpkins charging toward her. "You'll never catch the likes of me, ya big hillbilly!" Fayetta cackled.

Standing alone at the picnic table, Kate was suddenly aware that she felt more isolated than she ever had at a Longworth party. When Jimmy and Rosie bounded up for a few gulps of root beer, she pretended to be busy covering the desserts.

"Whatsa matter, Kate? You stuck in cement or sumpin'?" he asked.

"Maybe she's thinkin' her ma wouldn't approve." Rosie smirked.

For one brief moment she hated Rosie for using that snide tone that always made her feel different and, somehow, set her apart from her Sweet Briar friends. Wondering how Rosie could have been so callous, she turned away so no one could see the shame that spread across her face.

"Her ma prob'ly wouldn't—and that's why I'm chasin' her!" From out of the woods sprang Russell Logan. Startled, Kate sprinted off until he caught her and pushed her to the ground.

"Ouch!" she yelped as her head hit two large walnuts.

"Don't scream." As she listened to his words, low and even, she realized that Russell knew exactly what he was doing. "If you hate this idiotic game as much as I do, you'll go along with me."

"Huh?" she sat up, rubbing the back of her head.

"There's one for me!" he shouted. Then he whispered, "Just pretend that I'm chasing you and catching you. It's the only way the two of us will ever survive this night without being called sissies for the rest of our lives!"

Thus, for the rest of the evening—until Danny Rigoni blasted the horn of his car and shouted that it was time for everyone to go home—Russell Logan hounded Kate and tackled her. She was never quite sure whether she should feel chagrined over his compassionate gesture or just plain thankful that he had rescued her from the most humiliating social event of her life.

As she struggled to fall asleep that night, she desperately wished that the kids from Longworth would not flaunt their superiority and that her Sweet Briar friends would show a little more restraint. Tears dampened her pillow as she realized that she was destined to be somewhat of a misfit in either group. And there wasn't a soul she could tell.

* * *

Chapter Nine

After Rosie's party, Kate began to notice faint cracks in the solidarity of her group—subtle changes that reminded her of the spidery tracings that wound their way across Gran's antique teapot. Although the four girls still traveled as a solitary unit every chance they had, Kate knew that beneath the surface lay a fine network of lines—minuscule threads that could come between them. And those, of course, were caused by boys.

"Stop moping around!" Rosie scolded her several days later as the four of them scuffled through orange maple leaves that had collected by the Sweet Briar entrance.

Kate sighed and said nothing, still smarting from Jimmy McPherson's request to change seats at the movie the previous Saturday night so he could sit next to Rosie. Since Doris had been unable to go and Cheryl was already sitting with Stan, Kate had felt like M.J. tagging along.

"You want a boy to sit next to you? Then tell Russell Logan." Rosie snickered. "He sure to seemed to have the hots for you at the wiener roast!"

"Lordy, you guys," Cheryl cut in. "Just let it go. Come on over to my house and listen to the new records that Bertie brought home."

"I can't." Doris' tone was flat. "I gotta go home and watch the kids."

"Yeah, me too. I promised to help Gran with something." Kate glanced at Rosie. "Hey—I didn't mean anything. I'm just touchy today."

Rosie punched Kate's arm affectionately—and yet hard enough for the ache to linger.

"Aw—you're prob'ly on the rag," she chortled. "Or a little jealous."

"Or maybe both," she conceded. "Cheryl—maybe we can come over tomorrow to talk about what we're going to wear to the sock hop."

"I won't be goin' to that either," Doris said. "Gotta baby-sit. But you all know I got no interest in the boys in our class. I'm too old for 'em."

"Lordy, Doris, are you sure?" Cheryl expressed a concern that Kate shared. Making light of the situation so as not to embarrass Doris, Kate commented,

"Well, you're missing a chance to mingle with those classy kids from Longworth. You know this is the first big get-acquainted party before our freshman year."

"Just one more reason for me to stay home." Crossing her arms, she gazed down the street where two of Charley's friends were inspecting the engine of Mrs. Panczyk's car. "You'd better watch it, Rosie. Violet says Nancy Dawes has got her heart set on dancin' with Jimmy McPherson that night. Her mom's even bought her a new sweater set. Cashmere."

"Not a chance." Rosie tightened her lips. "She knows better 'n to even try."

Later Kate wished that Rosie had paid more attention to Doris' warning. She was also disappointed when she met Rosie and Cheryl at the front door of the school just before the sock hop to see that Rosie was not wearing the blue sweater as Kate had suggested. Instead she was flaunting a beige angora cardigan, buttoned down the back.

"New sweater?" Kate ran her fingers over Rosie's silky sleeve.

"Naw." Crossing her fingers, Rosie warned. "Pray that

nothing happens to it. I took it out of Colleen's drawer."

"Without asking?" Cheryl was impressed with Rosie's courage.

"She wasn't home." Rosie's eyes flashed with innocent mischief. "And I was tired of that old blue thing I wear all the time."

Kate didn't have the heart to tell her that the beige seemed to sap Rosie of her usually healthy glow, that she looked as if she might be recovering from the flu.

As they entered the doorway of the gym, they stopped in their tracks.

"Geez!" Rosie murmured in admiration. "It don't even look like the same place!"

Kate was impressed with the way that the high-school student council members had transformed the barren gym into a colorful autumn scene. Glittery cardboard letters spelling out "F-A-L-L F-L-I-N-G" were clamped to a rope which sagged between the two volleyball poles on the stage at one end of the room. To soften the vastness of the gym, the decorating committee had placed clusters of gourds and pumpkins around corn shocks in several spots. In front of the stage the refreshment table was laden with jugs of apple cider and mounds of doughnuts.

"Neat!" Cheryl was already a few steps ahead. "I feel like I'm at Rockwell High already."

Jimmy sauntered by as the girls removed their shoes. "Get those things off, girls," he grinned. "Gotta keep the gym floor in shape for our games." Looping his thumbs into the pockets of his jeans, he gave Rosie's sweater a look of approval. "You save a bunch of dances for me. Okay?"

Rosie merely bestowed a broad smile on Jimmy and nodded as an uncharacteristic wave of magenta crept from her neck to her forehead.

118

Kate was relieved when the first dance, a mixer that required Sweet Briar and Longworth students to mingle, came to an end. She had suffered enough as she'd slid through "Skip to My Lou" with a wet-palmed Timmy Timmons. Seeking out Cheryl, the two watched with amusement as Nancy Dawes dashed up beside Jimmy and Rosie and brazenly announced that she was claiming him for the Sadie Hawkins number where girls asked the boys to dance. Kate couldn't help but admire the fact that Nancy's pink-and-blue argyles matched her outfit perfectly.

"Well, gee—" Jimmy stammered.

"Good. See you then." Brushing his shoulder, she purred, "Don't forget now."

His red sweater seemed to swell for an instant as he watched Nancy walk away.

"Geez! What was that?" Rosie bumped him slightly.

"Darned if I know." He shrugged and grinned. "But I guess I'd better do what the lady says—right?"

"Wrong!" Rosie's lips were clenched in a tight line. "You're dancing that dance with me. You just didn't know it yet!"

"I'd better get to Stan before one of those Longworth dolls asks him." Cheryl scurried off, leaving Kate to wonder if it was time to seek out Russell Logan again.

Confused and discouraged, she went in search of him and found him standing alone, waiting for her.

As they two-stepped jerkily to Jo Stafford's recording of "The Things We Did Last Summer," she and Russell were distracted by the commotion in the middle of the gym. They grinned as Rosie planted an elbow across Nancy's nose when she tried to cut in on Jimmy and her.

"Damn it—that hurt!" Nancy stomped her foot on the hardwood floor.

"Oh, sorry." Rosie answered demurely. "I didn't realize

you were so—so close."

Freezing Rosie with an icy stare that would have withered anyone else, Nancy turned and waved across the gym to Timmy Timmons.

"Yoo hoo—oh, Timmy." Even the artificial lilt in her voice couldn't hide her anger. "I hope you're saving this dance for me."

"Score one for Rosie," Kate commented to Russell.

"Does she ever lose?" he wondered as he gave her an adventurous twirl.

"Not that I've ever noticed," she said, humming along with the music.

At the end of the number they attempted an awkward dip. "Somebody's waving to you." He nodded toward the corner. "I think it's Peggy Birdsong."

She turned and saw Peggy motioning for her to join her.

"Guess what!" She drained her cup of cider, then gave Kate her full attention. "I just found out that both of us have appointments with Dr. Frank tomorrow. Right?"

She nodded, grimacing at the thought of spending time in the orthodontist's chair.

"I thought maybe we could take the bus together—you know, have some lunch at Woolworth's. That is, if we can still open our mouths after he's done with us."

"Okay, yeah. That really sounds good." The prospect of riding to Danville without one of her parents seemed like the best thing that had happened to Kate that week. "I'll check with my mom and call you first thing in the morning."

"Oh—and you might want to warn your pal Rosie." Peggy's tone was low and confidential. "Nancy's really steamed. And when Nancy's steamed—" She didn't bother finishing the sentence but raised her eyebrows instead.

As the record player began to pour forth the lively

120

"Mississippi Mud," the boys cleared the floor and let the girls take over. Again, Kate was hit with that old familiar feeling of isolation because she had not learned to jitterbug. Colleen had taught Rosie, and Cheryl had such a natural sense of rhythm that she picked it up right away. As the two of them bopped around in perfect sync, Kate made a prolonged trip to the rest room until the song was over.

When she returned, a breathless Cheryl waved to her. "Hey, Kate—let's get a snack."

As the two of them selected their doughnuts at the refreshment table, Kate felt a wave of wistfulness wash over her. She watched Rosie and Jimmy approach, wishing that she had someone who adored her as much as Jimmy liked Rosie. Then, from the corner of her eye, she was aware of a white blur that shot out onto the floor, scattering an assortment of gourds in front of Rosie. Absorbed in Jimmy's attention, Rosie tripped on one, stepped awkwardly on another and sprawled into the rows of cider-filled cups on the table.

Cups flew and amber liquid splattered in a wide circle. Worse yet, Colleen's sweater was drenched with cider. Quickly Jimmy grabbed a handful of napkins.

"Fried fritters!" As Rosie slid off the table, she surveyed the sticky, matted mess that covered her. "Oh, god," she asked weakly. "Will this come out of angora?"

As she took the napkins from Jimmy, she spotted Nancy watching her from behind the closest corn shock. Paper fluttered to the floor as Rosie charged at her.

"You made me fall me on purpose, you little bit—" Even those in the farthest corners of the gym heard the resounding smack that Rosie landed on Nancy's cheek.

"Did not!" Nancy cowered like a frightened animal as Rosie yanked out a handful of her blond pageboy. "Ow!" she wailed. "Somebody help me!"

Jumping to Nancy's defense, Jimmy turned on Rosie.

"Hey, girl, leave her alone!" Heroically he drew Nancy close to him and yelled, "For God's sake, you're hurtin' her!"

His reaction only made Rosie angrier. Punching Jimmy in the stomach, she snarled, "Well, you just take her then— ya little Longworth lover!" She turned and bumped right into two high-school teachers who grabbed her by the arms, reprimanded her for her behavior and told her she would have to leave immediately.

"See if I care!" As she spat out the words, she rubbed her left eye to try to keep it from jumping. "I was just leavin' anyway."

Although she admired Rosie's spunk, Kate feared for her. She knew Rosie would find a way to handle the punishment she was sure to receive from her parents at home. It was the loss of Jimmy's affection that would eat her up inside.

Across the gym, Jimmy and Nancy sat side by side on folding chairs. As Jimmy dabbed Nancy's cheek with a cloth, her tiny white argyled foot swung triumphantly, and there was just a trace of a smirk at the corners of her mouth.

"Cheryl," Kate vowed, "we're gonna find a way to wipe that snotty little smile off Nancy Dawes' face. We owe Rosie that much!"

She nodded determinedly. "She'd do the same for us. We'll think of something."

* * *

When Kate awoke the following morning, she was not so sure she wanted to spend half the day with someone from Longworth School after the fiasco the night before. Still, if she had to go with anyone, she guessed she would choose Peggy. After all, she would always be grateful to Peggy for rescuing her from her terrible case of stage fright during the operetta.

"Some party last night." Peggy chuckled as they took their seats on the twelve-passenger bus that ran the Rockwell-to-Danville route several times a day. "And know what I heard?"

She then confided to Kate how Nancy had plotted to get Rosie in trouble. Training her big brown eyes on Kate, Peggy continued, "I think it all went just the way Nancy Dawes wanted it to go."

"What—"

"Well, remember I told you that Rosie oughtta look out, 'cause Nancy wanted to be with Jimmy McPherson. I mean—well, Rosie's pretty smart and all and she's not one to pussyfoot around. So, if Nancy figured she could get Rosie in trouble . . ."

"Which is just what she did. You know," she heard herself confessing to Peggy, "I saw something white scatter those gourds in front of Rosie."

"A white sock with pink-and-blue argyles. One that came from Chicago, no doubt." Peggy's droll observations were already making Kate sit up and take notice. Here was a Longworth girl who might be, way deep down, a lot like her!

The next thirty minutes flew as Peggy tapped into her supply of Nancy Dawes stories. Kate barely saw other passengers climb onto the bus at Bakers Corners and Morgantown as she heard Peggy recount the times when Nancy had humiliated most of her peers at Longworth in one way or another. As they neared the Danville bus station, Peggy explained how manipulative Nancy could be with her parents.

"Whenever Brucie gets anything, she demands that her folks give her something just as nice. Today Dr. Dawes is taking Brucie to a U of I football game in Champaign. So good old Nancy told her mom she wants to see *Brigadoon* and go shopping in Chicago."

"I wish that would work at my house." Kate checked to make sure she had her little purse snapped securely. "But it wouldn't. My parents would see right through that and laugh me out of the room."

"Mine too." She went on to say that Nancy and her mother were planning to take the train the following Friday evening and how Nancy had bragged about the fact that the two of them would be staying at The Drake.

"After they get there on Friday night, they're going to 'settle into their suite,' as she put it." Peggy glanced out the window as the bus pulled into the station. "They'll go shopping at Field's on Saturday morning and see the play in the afternoon. Can you imagine how much all of that will cost?"

Kate shook her head. "My mom and dad would love to see *Brigadoon*." She ran her tongue over her mouthful of rough metal. "Instead, they're paying for my braces."

She didn't mind the time she spent in Dr. Frank's torture chamber, as she and Peggy called the dental office. After their appointments they dined at Woolworth's on chili and grilled cheese sandwiches and had time to check out the latest Nancy Drew book at Woodbury's stationery store. Lacking the necessary sixty-five cents to buy the book, Kate reluctantly placed it back on the shelf.

On the way home she thought how much fun she would have if the Fearsome Four could make a trip to Danville together. Nowadays it seemed they were just lucky to get to go to the show once in awhile.

"I had a great time." Back in Rockwell, Peggy gave her a quick little hug before she opened the door of her mother's Hudson. "Maybe having braces won't be such a pain after all if we can go through this together. We'll do it again in six weeks—right?"

Grinning, Kate nodded.

"Know what?" she asked her father as she climbed into the Pontiac. Without giving him a chance to reply, she answered her own question. "Peggy's the first person from Longworth I've met who's okay. Really okay."

* * *

Kate didn't see much of Rosie for the next two weeks. When she called after she returned from the orthodontist, Mrs. Mulgrew said that "Rosalie Annette cannot come to the phone right now." Her tone of voice indicated that Kate should not bother to stop at their house either.

On Monday Rosie appeared to be contrite. She had met with school officials and had agreed to write a note of apology to Nancy Dawes, which they would review. She also had to promise that, every day for two weeks, she would turn in five pages with her handwritten pledge stating, "I will try harder to control my temper."

"The funny thing is that Mom and Dad were a lot madder about Colleen's ruined sweater. I have to buy her another one with my own money." Rosie paused at the drinking fountain. "They didn't seem to care much that I smacked Nancy Dawes."

"But the whole thing was *her* fault—Nancy's, that is." There. Kate stated aloud what everyone had suspected. "I saw her little white foot hit those gourds just before you and Jimmy came along."

"I knew it! I knew it!" Rosie's eyes blazed triumphantly.

"Do you want me to go to the office with you and report her?" Kate could feel a fierce protectiveness welling up inside.

"You'd do that?" Rosie studied her with new respect.

"Sure. I'd back you up. You know that."

Rosie pursed her lips as she weighed the possibilities.

"Naw. That's okay. But thanks." A sly smile formed on her lips. "Someday, when she least expects it, she's gonna be sorry."

* * *

That same evening Kate called Cheryl after supper.

"I think I might know how we can help Rosie get even," she whispered. "Meet me halfway on your street so we won't have to walk past the Naughton place. I'll tell my mom you're coming over to study.

In the gray dusk, under a flickering street light, she could see Cheryl's silhouette gliding toward her like a canoe on a calm lake. Kate wished that she had that same gracefulness.

"What's up?" Cheryl called.

"I've got an idea, but I thought I'd better tell you in person," Kate murmured. "It's too dangerous to say it on the phone. You know how Effie May down at switchboard likes to listen in." Slowly they headed toward Kate's house.

"Right now we can't even tell Rosie and Doris," Kate cautioned. Seeing Cheryl's eyes widen, she added, "Believe me. It's for their own good."

The only sounds in the autumn air were the dry leaves crackling under their shoes and the howling of a neighborhood dog. At the end of the street an orange half moon hovered over the pavement. Taking a deep breath, she began to tell Cheryl about her plan.

"Remember at the sock hop how we promised that we'd make Nancy Dawes eat that nasty smile?"

126

Cheryl nodded. "Yeah."

"Well, here's what I think we should do." Briefly she told her that Nancy and her mother were going to stay at The Drake in Chicago that Friday evening. "Wouldn't it just be a shame if their reservation got canceled—and they didn't know about it till they got there?"

Cheryl stopped so suddenly that Kate ran into her. "How?"

Kate outlined the idea that had kept her awake for the last two nights. She would call the information operator from a pay phone to get the number of The Drake in Chicago. But Cheryl, who could lower her voice to imitate any adult, would have to cancel the reservation at the hotel.

"It could be your best acting role so far." Kate thought that part of the plot would appeal to her.

Cheryl, however, needed no persuading. "Let's do it. We can use my phone. I'll just tell Lila I have to make a quick long-distance call—I've done that a couple of times since I went to Interlochen—and she won't pay any attention to us if she's listening to her programs."

Again Kate stressed the need for secrecy. "If Rosie doesn't know, she can't possibly be responsible for this." She stared up at the first stars that had begun to pop through the dark clouds above them. "Same thing for Doris. I wouldn't want Violet or her to get blamed, 'cause Violet's sure to know all about this trip to Chicago."

"Yeah, we gotta protect them," Cheryl nodded "Just one thing though—could you kinda write out what I'm supposed to say? That way, if I get nervous, I won't forget my part."

"Sure," Kate agreed as they opened her front door and switched their conversation to a homework project.

By the following afternoon, Kate had scribbled out a few lines for Cheryl and had called for the number from the

phone booth in front of Claxton's Meat Market. At
Cheryl's house, however, their plan hit a snag when they
found Lila on the phone, gossiping endlessly about a choice
piece of news involving one of the local beauticians. Impatiently they paced as they waited . . . and waited. Finally, at
5:10 they gave up.

"I've gotta be home in five minutes," she told Cheryl.
"We'll just have to try tomorrow." Pedaling home in frustration, she wondered if her grand plan was about to collapse.

The next afternoon they held their breath as they entered Cheryl's house. Lila gave them a mechanical wave
and merely turned up the volume knob on her little white
kitchen radio when Cheryl mentioned that she had to make
a call.

Kate felt her hands grow damp as she heard Cheryl give
the operator the hotel number and, moments later, launch
into her sad tale as Melba Dawes: There was sudden illness
in her family and she and her daughter would have to cancel their reservation for that Friday night. In a masterful bit
of improvisation, she added that she hoped that the hotel
would not have any trouble renting the room that night.
Placing the receiver back on the hook, she grinned and
gave Kate a thumbs-up sign.

"Done!" Her dark eyes sparkled. "And—guess what?"

"What?" Kate croaked, still reeling from the shock of
their accomplishment.

"They said they won't have a bit of trouble renting the
room. There are two big conventions this weekend, and the
Bears are playing at home. How's that for good luck?"

Triumphantly they hugged each other. "This will just
serve Nancy right," Cheryl proclaimed.

"And remember—we can't tell Rosie and Doris a thing
until after this all blows over," Kate reminded her.

"I know. But in the meantime—" Cheryl pounded the sofa pillow with her fist. "I'm only sorry that the two of us won't be there when Nancy and her mother try to check in." Laughter erupted through her words with such force that she could hardly speak.

Collapsing on the sectional, they succumbed to their giggles until their shoulders heaved from exhaustion. Fortunately the ominous strains from the soap-opera organ on Lila's kitchen radio had swelled to a level loud enough to muffle their hysteria.

* * *

Kate was so jumpy all weekend that she actually welcomed the diversion of taking M.J. to see *Meet Me in St. Louis* at the Pinnacle. However, even Judy Garland's performance couldn't keep her thoughts from drifting to The Drake and Nancy Dawes. Once Monday morning arrived, she didn't have to wait long to hear about the mischief she and Cheryl had caused.

"Oh, my god, you'll never guess what happened." Doris pounced on the three girls at the school door.

"Ronnie and Donnie both got potty-trained over the weekend." Rosie guessed without enthusiasm. "Finally."

"Nope. This news came direct from Violet." Doris nodded her head with authority. "It's about Nancy and her mom." Pausing, she allowed the magnitude of her announcement to sink in. "And, Rosie, you're gonna love it."

"So c'mon, c'mon" Cheryl motioned for Doris to speed up. "Just tell us."

"Well, here's what happened." In dramatic effect, she recounted the fact that Nancy and Mrs. Dawes had arrived with all their luggage early Friday evening at The Drake, only to find that they had no room. The hotel people were very apologetic and even showed them the notation that the reservation had been canceled the day before.

"Well—" she continued, "Nancy and her mom were just plain out of luck 'cause there wasn't a single room in all of downtown Chicago. Mrs. Dawes told Violet that Nancy threw a cryin' fit right there in the lobby." She lowered her voice. "They finally got a room at a little old hotel up on the north side and had a cab take 'em there."

"I hope it stunk." Rosie's eye was starting to jerk. "I hope it was filthy dirty too."

"Actually, there were cockroaches—and Mrs. Dawes didn't close her eyes all night." Doris' smile said it all.

At this news the girls exploded, laughing so hard that they almost fell to the sidewalk.

"I wish I could have seen all that." Wiping her eyes with the sleeve of her jacket, Cheryl avoided looking at Kate.

"Did they still go to the play?" The words tumbled from Kate's mouth before she could stop herself.

"Yeah, but they had to store their luggage at the train station 'cause they didn't want to leave it at the hotel all day. Violet said that Nancy told her the mix-up ruined everything—" Doris stopped and stared at Kate. "How did *you* know they were going to a play?"

Kate's voice died in her throat "I—I guess I heard my mom telling my dad—or something," she stammered, feeling her cheeks grow warm. She hoped that no one but Cheryl noticed her discomfort.

"Serves her right, by golly!" Rosie's face was one big smile. "That little twerp had this one comin'!"

"Yeah," Doris agreed as they stepped from the crisp October morning into the thick heat of the schoolhouse. "Violet said Nancy pouted around all day Sunday 'cause she can't take it when things don't go her way."

130

"Poor baby." Rosie's sympathy dripped with sarcasm.

Kate sidled up by Cheryl as they walked to their language arts classroom.

"It worked! It all worked!" she whispered.

"I thought you were going to spill the beans for a minute. But did you see the look on Rosie's face?" Cheryl's eyes sparkled. "That made it all worthwhile!"

"Sure did," Kate agreed, savoring the moment. She smiled at the thought that her scheme had made life better for Rosie. And, somehow, it made no difference that Rosie didn't know.

* * *

Chapter Ten

The next weeks flew by for Kate as she and her friends shifted their focus to the new basketball season. After losing their first two games, the Boulders finally adjusted to the loss of Vic Panczyk and began to win again. When the team brought home the holiday tourney trophy, fans began to hope once more that Rockwell might have a shot at the Sweet Sixteen in March.

Always the pessimist, Uncle Henry grumbled about the Boulders' chances at the New Year's dinner that Kate's mother had prepared once more.

"They don't have a chance in hell." He stubbed out his cigarette in the ashtray

"Henry—" Gran cautioned as she nodded her appreciation to Kate for dicing her helping of goose into manageable bites for her.

"Actually, I think they're more solid than they were last year." Uncle Art ladled more gravy onto his potatoes. "You know that poor Atwater kid was so down on himself after messing up in the Champaign game last year that he wasn't even going to play this year? If it hadn't been for Charley Panczyk, he'd probably be tooting his trumpet in the pep band."

"How's that?" Dad started the bowl of stuffing around for a second time.

"Well, Vince Atwater himself told me that Alan was so depressed that he wasn't going out for the team. Then the Panczyk kid—Charley, I guess it is—got Alan off by himself and said he wouldn't play if Alan didn't. It must have worked, 'cause they're running like clockwork together."

Charley sure was a good friend to save Alan like that, Kate thought. Then she stopped and realized that the Fearless Four would do the same thing for each other. In fact, she recalled with satisfaction, she and Cheryl had already scored one for Rosie—and it would be a long time before their friend would realize it!

In mid-January a brutal blizzard paralyzed all of eastern Illinois late one Saturday night. The girls barely made it home on the bus from the ball game at Paxton and were still snowbound three days later. Kate relished the first day off from school, working a jigsaw puzzle with her mother. By the second day she was weary of playing Chinese checkers with Gran and "Flinch" with M.J. On Wednesday she was grateful to hear that narrow lanes had been carved through the drifts so that schools could open again.

"Where's Doris?" she asked as she and Cheryl lingered in the cloak closet. The smell of wet wool from their classmates' coats hung like a vapor in the small cubicle.

"Prob'ly got a cold or somethin'." Rosie shrugged. "I'll call her after school."

The next morning, however, Rosie seemed concerned.

"Lorene answered and didn't want to talk. She just said that Doris prob'ly wouldn't be in school all this week and hung up. And another funny thing—Danny told Colleen that Charley hasn't been at practice since the blizzard." Thoughtfuly, she said, "I'm going over there after school and see what's happening. You two wanta come?"

Kate could hardly concentrate on her classes for the rest of the day as she speculated about what was wrong with Doris. She hoped she hadn't worn herself down and gotten pneumonia. Sometimes Doris sacrificed her glass of milk so the twins could split it, and there were nights when she got up with the children so they wouldn't waken her mother. She was stunned, however, when she learned the real reason for Doris' absence.

Shivering in the damp chill as they waited on Doris' front porch, the three grew quiet as Rosie pounded on the door for the fourth time. Finally, Charley shoved open the screen. A purple bruise circled one eye, and his right hand was swathed in gauze.

"C'mon in." He motioned his head toward the living room. "Doris'll be glad to see you guys." As they moved through the hall, Kate noticed that the upstairs railing had been broken—most likely another victim of the twins' boundless energy.

In the dreary twilight that filtered into the living room, Doris glanced up from a picture she was coloring on the floor with Vickie. Squealing with delight, Donnie and Ronnie sprang from the overstuffed chair to the couch as they tried to see who could stir up the biggest cloud of dust.

"Hi." Doris' voice sounded small and far away.

"Everyone else is gone but the two of us right now," Charley explained quietly. "Hey, Dor—take these girls out to the kitchen and give them some pop or somethin'. I'll ride herd on these savages for awhile."

Without a word, they followed Doris to the kitchen, where she mechanically pulled the cord from the ceiling light and took four mismatched glasses from the cupboard. In the glare from the bare bulb they glanced around the table awkwardly. For the first time that Kate could remember, they were all at a loss for words. Finally Cheryl broke the silence.

"So," she said, "you haven't missed much at school this week. Oh, well, except that Otto Rutledge got sent to the office for passing gas in class. And when he left the room, he popped a good one and grinned, just for spite."

"Sure sorry I missed that." Doris managed a wan smile.

Again they sat in strained silence and sipped orange pop.

"Do you want us to get your homework?" Kate knew that would be the first thing her parents would worry about if she missed two days of school.

"Mom picked it up. She told the teacher I won't be back till next Monday." Listlessly, Doris scraped at a crusty lump of dried food on the table.

Rosie could stand it no longer. Setting down her glass, she planted both elbows in front of her and rested her chin in her hands. "What's up?" she asked directly. "Are you sick or what?"

Doris shook her head. "Mom says I don't have to talk about it. To nobody."

"Then don't do it, hon." Cheryl was the first to respond. "Some things are just better kept to yourself."

Doris nodded gratefully. From the living room they could hear Charley's muffled voice trying to direct Vickie and the boys into a worthwhile activity. The plastic clock over the stove clicked off another minute. At last Doris took a deep breath.

"Guess if I can't talk about it with my best friends, I'll never be able to tell nobody." She seemed to be addressing herself.

"It's okay," Rosie said softly. "You just do what you gotta do. Maybe we oughtta just run along home for now."

"No—no, don't go." Doris glanced away from them. For several moments she seemed to be studying the yellowed wallpaper. Then she began.

"It was the night of the blizzard—Saturday night, I guess. We'd all gone to bed after the game. All except Cletus. And he was still out drinkin'." She took a long sip of her pop and picked at a gooey spill that had crystallized on the table.

"I was sleepin' hard and thought I felt Vickie crawl in bed with me. She does that, you know, sometimes when she has a bad dream." Quickly she glanced at each of them for reassurance, then lowered her gaze once more. "Then I smelt the beer—or whatever—and felt his hands all over me. For a minute I thought I was havin' a nightmare an' then I knew it was Cletus and I just started screamin'. As loud as I could."

Kate felt a collective shudder pass over the three as they listened and saw Rosie's eye begin to twitch. They held their breath as Doris continued.

"In a minute Tommy was in there, kickin' and scratchin' at Cletus. Vickie and Donnie had started bawlin'. And then Mom came in and wondered what the hell was goin' on. Cletus just kept sayin' that he got turned around when he came home from the tavern and thought he was in bed with Lorene." Her eyes were expressionless as she recalled the nightmare that had been real.

"Charley was mad. Oh, my god, I've never seen him like that. He punched Cletus good, but then Cletus gave him a fist in the eye. Charley yelled and clobbered Cletus while Mom pounded him on the back.

"The kids was all cryin' by that time, and Lorene came out of her room in time to see Charley kick Cletus down the stairs. He went right through the railing and landed in a heap on the hall floor. Lorene was screamin' language worse'n I've ever heard, and Mom told Cletus to get the hell out of her house and never come back. Then her 'n Tommy put their arms around me to try to stop me from shakin'.

"Charley—he was hurtin' real bad and holdin' his hand. But he picked up Cletus and took him out in all that snow and threw him in Mom's car—like a bag of garbage. He hauled him over to his brother Emery's house and left him there. Just yesterday we heard that Emery gave Cletus five dollars and took him out to the highway so he could hitch a ride to Kentucky. A few trucks was gettin' through, and Emery said one of 'em would prob'ly give Cletus a lift."

Cheryl was the first to go to Doris.

"Oh, hon, we would've been here sooner! You must've been so scared." She hugged her as Rosie and Kate joined in.

Doris' shoulders began to shake.

"But nothin' really happened. You know what I mean."

They held her tight for several moments as she sobbed. After Rosie dug deep in her pocket for a tissue they returned to their chairs and listened while Doris filled them in on the rest of the events:

Charley had seen a doctor, who had set his broken hand, and would be out of basketball for at least three weeks. They groaned.

Lorene had already expanded her shift at the truck stop and would see a lawyer about a divorce as soon as possible. They nodded.

But Doris was still so shaken by the incident that she had no appetite and was nauseated every time she tried to eat. Her mother had given her permission to stay home from school all week until Lorene could take the children to a sitter's house the following Monday. But, in the meantime, Doris was running on empty.

"I hate Cletus for what he tried to do to me. Scared me shitless!" She shook her head dejectedly. "And I just don't know how much longer I can keep runnin' this house, with the kids and meals and all."

Kate felt tears spilling down her cheeks as she listened to Doris. She had allowed herself to be annoyed by her mother, M.J. and even Gran herself while her dear friend had been suffering, really suffering in a way she could never imagine.

"Fried fritters!" Rosie sputtered as she rubbed her watering eyes with her sleeve. "I guess the one good thing is that creep Cletus is gone. And you'll never have to see him again—right?"

Doris gave a faint smile and nodded.

"Somehow—I don't know how—we're going to help you, Doris," Kate vowed.

"But you guys have to promise not to tell what happened." Suddenly Doris was worried that their assistance might only create more grief for her family. "As far as anyone knows, Cletus got mad and left Lorene. And Charley broke his hand when the bathroom sink he was tryin' to fix fell off the wall and hit him. We don't want people talkin'—"

"You know we can keep a secret," Kate assured her.

"And you know we love you. So much." Cheryl was the only one able to put into words what Kate and Rosie wanted to say.

"You guys're the greatest." Doris' eyes brightened." "Just knowin' you're there—" Her voice broke again.

Again they engulfed her quickly, then left her alone in the bleak kitchen. As they tramped through the knee-deep snow, they weighed the possibilities for offering help. There was such a fine line, Kate now realized, between being patronizing in the way Nancy Dawes and her mother had been when they had delivered the Christmas groceries and giving Doris the kind of support she really needed.

"I can't even imagine." Cheryl's words hung in little puffs in the air. "She carries such a load—cooking, taking care of those kids—and then to have that awful Cletus—" She shivered.

An idea began to form in Kate's mind. This time last

year, she thought, she wouldn't have dared to offer a solution, but after creating the scenario that had ruined Nancy Dawes' weekend in Chicago, she felt more entrenched as a vital part of the group.

"You know," she let her thoughts tumble out as she gazed at the Naughton mansion silhouetted against the winter sky, "my mom says everyone needs time alone. Every single day. Doris never has that."

Rosie and Cheryl looked at her, puzzled.

"What does that have to do with anything?" Rosie scoffed. "We don't have *any* of that at our place—unless we're in the outhouse!"

"But I sorta see what you mean," Cheryl said slowly. "I have nothing but time alone at my house. Bertie's always gone, and when Lila's listening to her programs I sometimes feel lonesome. But at least it's quiet. At Doris' house it's never—" Her voice trailed off.

"We've gotta think of somethin'." Rosie rubbed the sleeves of her pea jacket. "But right now I'm freezin' out here. Let's sleep on it."

That evening, at supper, Kate casually mentioned that Doris seemed pretty overwhelmed with her responsibilities. Without ever telling her family about the horrific scene at Panczyks' house, she reeled off a list of Doris' after-school chores—cooking, cleaning, baby-sitting.

"Sounds like she's in jail!" M.J. blew on her soup to cool it, waiting for their mother's scolding.

"Sounds as if she needs some time to herself." Mother shook her head sadly.

"Come to think of it, Cora told us that they'd had a string of bad days when she came in to pay her coal bill this week." Her father stirred his soup. "She said that Cletus had left, which might be no great loss, and that Charley had broken his hand." He rubbed his chin thoughtfully. "She

139

didn't even have a joke for us."

"Yeah." Kate crumbled a cracker into her bowl. "And Doris carries more than her share."

"Well, why don't you bring little Vickie over after school for an hour or so one day a week?" Her mother put down her spoon. "Then on a different day, see if the twins want to come. M.J. could help entertain them and it would give Doris a bit of quiet time."

Kate's spoon paused in mid-air as she wondered if she had heard right. Bring Lorene's children to *their* house? That plan was even better than the one she herself had been devising. Gazing at her with wonder, she admitted that there were times when Mother could be an absolute genius.

"That just might help," Kate replied slowly. "And if Rosie and Cheryl—"

"Don't push them," her mother cautioned. "Everyone's home is different. But, yes, I think we could handle an extra one for an hour or so now and then, don't you, Gran?"

"I suppose Vickie's too young for Chinese checkers, but we could teach her 'Old Maid'," Gran smiled.

"And I could be a big sister for a change." M.J. spoke through a mouthful of crackers.

The next day at school, when Kate shared her mother's idea with Rosie and Cheryl, they thought that they could do the same.

"Lila might only want me to bring one twin at a time, but we'll see," Cheryl said. "She doesn't like to have her house messed up."

"Maybe Tuesdays and Thursdays would be good, 'cause we've got cheerleading practice on Mondays," Rosie reminded her.

"We might not get to spend as much time together," Kate cautioned.

"But we'll be helping Doris," Rosie and Cheryl chimed

in together as if they had rehearsed the line.

Relieved, they all smiled. That, of course, was the most important thing.

* * *

For the first time in her life, Kate felt as if she were doing something really worthwhile. Each day after school she, Rosie and Cheryl bundled up Lorene's children and trudged through the snow with them to their own homes. She smiled one day when Doris actually volunteered to answer a question in class and felt a wave of pride wash over her as Doris turned in every homework assignment. And when Kate gave her a stack of Gran's old copies of *Good Housekeeping,* Doris' eyes shone with a sparkle that she had not seen for months.

"Tell your grandma thanks." Doris thumbed through the pages, stopping to admire a tall coconut cake topped with real flowers. "I just love to see what people have done to make their food look prettier. I seen some hamburger recipes I'm gonna try so I'm not always stirrin' up the same old thing in a skillet. I know Tommy'd like somethin' different, and Charley'll eat anything."

Kate felt satisfied. Just watching Doris unwind and relax was making everyone happy. They all agreed that if a little solitude was helping Doris, the added attention was working miracles on each of the children. Cheryl said that Vickie loved having Lila paint her toenails and fingernails every week. And Rosie reported that Mike had brought out some of his old toy trucks and blocks for the boys.

"He's like a five-year-old kid again himself. But, you know," she confided, "he kinda likes it—even when Ma yells at him to pick everything up after Donnie or Ronnie leaves."

Kate noticed it was the same at her house. Her mother had patiently showed Vickie how to set the table and fold napkins—but only after she had learned to wash her hands thoroughly. One day, after her mother had given Vickie three cents to sort the spools of thread in her sewing box, she promised to help her make a quilt for her doll from scraps.

"I'm goin' to sew with real 'terial." Vickie's pinched face was aglow. "Your mama said I could." Kate was amazed at her mother's ability to teach and have fun with Vickie all at the same time. At Doris' house, it seemed, someone was always yelling at her.

While Gran was excited to have a little girl in the house, she was completely taken with Donnie and Ronnie.

"They remind me so much of Robert and Earl when they were little boys." She sniffled and pulled her handkerchief from her sweater sleeve as the family gathered for supper one evening. "Donnie wants to learn, and Ronnie just wants to have fun.

"I like Ronnie better." M.J.'s words were clouded by a mouthful of peas and carrots. "He's not as rough as Donnie, and he sits right up there on the piano bench with Dad and me and plays with one finger at a time."

"Probably because he's used to hearing Tommy," their father mused.

"Then why don't Donnie—"

"Why doesn't Donnie." Mother was quick to correct M.J.'s grammar.

"Anyway, why doesn't Donnie do the same? They're twins, after all!" M.J. scowled.

"Twins may look alike on the outside but be completely different on the inside." Dad buttered a slice of bread. "Donnie would rather play with your old peg table. Maybe someday he'll grow up to be a carpenter."

"Well, he'll sure be a noisy one," M.J. muttered. "He's the loudest kid I ever heard!"

"But have you noticed how all three love to be read to?" Gran stopped as she struggled to guide some peas onto her spoon. "Each one begs for different stories, but they all snuggle up to me the minute I sit down with a storybook. They like to help me turn the pages."

"One other thing." Dad ladled more vegetables onto his plate. "Maybe Cora's eyes were watering from the cold when she paid her coal bill this week—I'm not sure—but she said she appreciates what everyone is doing to help out. I know she's really grateful."

"It's the least we can do." Mother placed a large bowl of tapioca pudding in the center of the table. "Plus, it's fun to have little ones around the house again."

"On most days!" M.J., they realized, was growing just a bit weary of her new responsibilities.

* * *

By March the Panczyks had weathered their crisis. Lorene had started taking the pains to fix herself up each day before she went to wait tables at the truck stop and was now contributing toward the weekly grocery bill. The lines of stress that had etched the faces of Tommy, Doris and their mother had eased at last. And Charley's hand had healed just in time for the tournament.

"Oh, my god, I'm so nervous!" Doris chewed on her nails as the girls waited on the bleachers for the opening game of the regional.

Kate glanced around. Although the pep band was whipping up school spirit and their boys in blue and white were swishing balls through the hoop, their gym lacked the magic sizzle of last year. This season the Boulders had lost seven games—two early in the season, four while Charley had been injured, and the humiliating whipping administered by tiny Bakers Corners that nobody could explain. No college scouts had visited Rockwell this winter, and no features about the Boulders had filled the sports pages of *The Chicago Tribune*.

"Wonder how far we'll be able to go." Rosie fidgeted in her seat.

Mike, who was sitting in front of them, turned around.

"Hey, we're goin' all the way to state. Geez, what're ya talkin' about?" He sneered at Rosie.

"Yeah, yeah, yeah." Bored with his very presence, Rosie glanced around to see if Jimmy McPherson might be sitting with Nancy Dawes. Her face brightened when she realized that he and the other eighth-grade team members had positioned themselves behind the varsity bench along with the Boulder freshman squad.

"Well, even Brian said we might," Mike shot back. "And he oughtta know."

Kate and Cheryl giggled. Sometimes, Kate thought, it was almost as much fun to watch Rosie and Mike bicker as it was to go a Sunday matinee at the Pinnacle.

"I just hope Charley does okay." Focusing on every move that her brother made, Doris nearly jumped off the bleachers when the starting horn sounded.

Kate didn't think anyone needed to worry. After all, they were playing Onarga Military, and everyone knew that Rockwell could always beat the socks off the boys from a private school. After a lopsided victory of 54-22, they began to hope that they actually might take the regional again.

"Charley's gettin' superstitious," Doris confided later in the week as they waited for the regional championship game to begin. "I fixed spaghetti before we played Onarga and we won. Then I just happened to fix it again before the second game and we won. Now, guess what Charley thinks he's gotta have before every game?"

"Spaghetti, of course." Rosie understood Charley's philosophy completely. "Last year, remember, I had my lucky mittens. But I dropped 'em on the bus—and we lost. This year I've got Brian's rabbit's foot. And I've got it fastened to the loop of my belt so I can't lose it."

They stood as the band began to play the national anthem. Cheryl had been invited to sing, a rare honor for an eighth-grader. Kate held her breath, first as the microphone's intermittent hum drowned a few of Cheryl's words and again as her husky voice cracked on "land of the free." When she finished and the crowd cheered, she felt a surge of pride for her friend.

"Geez, she's really getting good. Ya don't s'pose she'll get to Hollywood before I do?" Rosie seemed genuinely concerned.

"Shut up and watch the game." Mike's words came from the side of his mouth as his eyes were riveted on the players. Rosie answered by punching him in the back.

Once again their team again jumped out to an early lead and never looked back. During a time out, however, Doris elbowed Kate and nodded toward Charley.

"Every time he goes out, they put an ice bag on his hand." Her brow was furrowed. "I think he's hurtin' more'n he lets on."

At the end of the game Charley's hand seemed to give him no trouble as he accepted the regional trophy and held it high above his head for the crowd to see. As the Rockwell crowd cheered wildly Mike threw his popcorn in the air.

"See? I told ya! We've got just two games between us 'n state!"

"Oh, my god, here we go again." Doris' worry lines indicated she was already afraid of a repeat performance of last year's game with Champaign. "I don't know if my nerves can take it!"

Mixed emotions ran high the following week as the Boulders prepared for Danville. Although they yearned for victory, the Rockwell fans dreaded the bitter taste of disappointment. They were well aware of the facts: Danville had bigger players, a better record and the advantage of their home court. Kate secretly thought that the Boulders were just like the Cubs in some ways. You knew they were going to break your heart. You just didn't know how they were going to do it.

But she was never so glad to have been wrong in her life. Danville's boys, thinking they were in for a cakewalk, showed none of their well-publicized flashiness during the first quarter. By the time they realized that they were up against a quality team in the middle of the second quarter, the Boulders had steadily built up a lead that the city boys never could overcome. Charley scored twenty-two points as Rockwell won, 58-47, and the stage was set for a rematch with Champaign.

The following night the girls could hardly stay in their seats as the lead changed hands several times. Slowing the pace, the Boulders found themselves behind, 29-28, with a minute and a half to go. Each team traded baskets and Charley sank a foul shot so that the score was tied, 31-31, with just seconds to go.

"Charley's only got nine points," Doris fussed. "No matter what happens, if there's any college scouts here tonight, they're not goin' to be impressed. I can tell his hand is really hurtin'."

"Charley! Charley! Charley!" the crowd chanted as he dribbled the ball, searching for an open shot. Then, with only five seconds to go, the ball left his hands—but not for the basket. Doris gasped as it headed for Alan Atwater.

146

Confidently Alan grabbed it and whirled, hung suspended in midair for an eternity, then swished the ball through the net. The final buzzer sounded with the scoreboard reading, "Rockwell, 33; Champaign, 31." The Boulders were going to their first state tournament in history!

Disbelief silenced their fans. First, they could not comprehend that Charley had sacrificed his chance to take the winning shot and, second, they were stunned that Alan had been able to step up and play like a champion. Finally, a roar from the Rockwell residents filled the gym with such a force that no one could hear the words of the little bald man who presented the team with its first sectional trophy.

Mike turned around and gave Kate a damp hug.

"This is even better'n winnin' the World Series!" Kate was so excited that she didn't mind that his sweaty Cardinals T-shirt left her own blouse damp. "And man! When I'm a Boulder, we're goin' again! You wait 'n see!"

Doris' happiness was subdued. "I wish Charley'd just gone ahead and taken the shot," she confided.

"But *he* knew Alan could make it. We didn't. Wow! What a play!" Cheryl was jubilant.

"And you know what? This year I've still got my lucky rabbit's foot with me." Rosie's smile spread across her face. "We're goin' to state! Wahoo!"

It was almost midnight when the celebration finally ended back in the Rockwell gym, and the girls gathered at Doris' house to share a few more moments of glory with Charley. Rosie, however, was furious with Mike for tagging along.

"Go on home," she hissed as they tumbled through the front door and headed for the kitchen. The faint aroma of spaghetti sauce still lingered in the air.

But he just shook his head as he followed her inside. "I wanna be with Charley."

147

Violet was scooping out bottles of cream soda from the bottom of the refrigerator, and Doris was splitting open a large bag of potato chips when she noticed the note on the table.

"Hey, what's this?" Casually she opened the folded piece of lined paper and began to read. The color drained from her face as she handed it to her mother. "Sit down, Mom," she warned.

A hush fell over the kitchen as the paper was passed around the room and each one read the note. Lorene had met a driver from Pennsylvania—Steve something, Kate couldn't read his last name—and had gone with him on a run to Texas. He would drop her off the following Wednesday, but they were making plans for their future. Vickie and the twins were spending the night with Cletus' brother, Emery. "Steve's a *good* man, Mom." She had underlined "good" three times with her blunt pencil. "You'll just love him. I do."

Kate watched as Lorene's message sucked the joy from the room faster than a nail could deflate an inner tube.

Doris clenched her jaw and reeled off the worst string of obscenities Kate had ever heard. "Why does Lorene have to ruin the happiest—"

"Watch your mouth, Doris Bernadette." Her mother's reprimand was automatic before she allowed herself to crumple into a chair.

"God," she whispered. "What am I gonna do with those kids while she's gone?" A tremor swept through Mrs. Panczyk's body.

"I'll tell you what we're gonna do, Mama." Violet squared her shoulders. "I'll let Mrs. Dawes know that I have an emergency and can't work for a couple of days this week. She'll just have to get by." A look of grim determination passed over her face. "I'll watch the kids till Lorene gets back. That way, we can go along as usual here at home and not upset nothin'.

"Charley—me'n you'll tell Lorene when she gets back that if she ever pulls somethin' like this again, she's takin' them kids with her." The way Violet fixed her eyes on Charley made all of them hold their breath. Clenching his fists, he nodded resolutely.

"But in the meantime," Violet continued, "we're goin' to state—and we're gonna celebrate! And nothin's changin' that, you all hear? Nothin'!" She raised her bottle of cream soda and took a long, deliberate drink. "To Charley. And to the Boulders!" she toasted as they all recovered their senses at last and cheered.

* * *

"ON TO STATE!" screamed the *Rockwell Messenger's* headline in the same huge type it had used on V-J Day.

Everyone in town—from the blue-haired ladies at the Methodist Church to Sweet Briar's scrawny first-graders— was consumed with basketball fever. Only Mr. Hartley, who proclaimed that an all-school variety show would be held in three weeks, seemed oblivious of the carnival atmosphere. Although Cheryl instantly began debating which song she would sing in the show, the other girls ignored his news bulletin. They were so keyed up about going to state that Mr. Hartley could have dropped dead right in front of them and they might not have noticed.

Even Lorene's return with her new love seemed insignificant. As Kate bounced along in the fan bus on the way to Champaign for their game against Hillsboro, Doris told her that Lorene and Steve had announced they would be taking the children and heading back to his home in Pennsylvania. He had a job waiting for him so he would not be on the road anymore and had told Mrs. Panczyk that he truly loved Lorene.

"Geez!" Rosie was genuinely shocked. "What did your mom say?"

"Somethin' like 'whatever'." Doris etched the words, "Go, Boulders," onto the steamy window with her finger. "To tell you the truth, I think she's so fed up with takin' care of Lorene that she's glad to get her and the kids out of our hair. She's just plain wore out from tryin' to work this week with all the excitement about state goin' on."

"It's going to be so quiet at your house," Kate said.

"Yeah—Lila kinda looks forward to seeing Vickie every week." Cheryl's eyes were solemn. "It's sort of like she has this little blond doll she can play with for a couple of hours and then give back."

"She'll get over it." Doris gave them a knowing smile.

As they piled out of the bus Rosie felt for her rabbit's foot.

"Gotta make sure I've got my good-luck piece." She patted her pocket confidently.

Never at a loss for words, the four girls fell silent in awe as they entered the University of Illinois' Huff Gym. As Kate surveyed the crowd she realized that there was an aura of orderliness with none of the wacky signs and goofy behavior that usually marked an important game in their home gym. They truly had hit the big time!

The Boulders clicked like clockwork as they disposed of Hillsboro, 45-39. Unselfishly each member passed the ball, patiently waiting for the best shot. Just when Hillsboro had decided that Charley was going to fire the ball to Alan Atwater again, Charley would surprise them by swishing a long one. Alan seemed to have found new confidence, directing the ball mainly to Charley and Wayne Stevens while managing to score several points himself. It wasn't until they were homebound that they realized the Boulders would have to go up against Mt. Vernon, a big powerhouse from the southern part of the state.

The next day they repeated the trip to Champaign. Doris had insisted that Charley eat spaghetti for breakfast, and Rosie had her rabbit's foot. Their players were at the top of their game but still were no match for Max Hooper and his Mt. Vernon teammates. By the beginning of the fourth quarter, the Rockwell fans could see how the script would play out and began chanting cheers of support for their beloved Boulders. When the final buzzer rang and the scoreboard read, "Mt. Vernon, 62; Rockwell, 55," they knew they had witnessed a game that would become legendary in local history.

"Thank you, Boulders! Thank you, Boulders!" came the roar from the blue-and-white section. In spite of the loss, they knew their boys had given it their best shot and had displayed a great deal of class against the team that eventually would win the championship. Charley scored nineteen points and made the all-tournament team, with Alan and Wayne getting spots on the second and third teams.

"We're from Rockwell, couldn't be prouder. And if you can't hear us, we'll yell a little louder!" With the sharp March air streaming through the open windows of their bus, they filled the streets of Champaign with their pride as they left for home. Never once did they want fans from other towns to consider their Boulders losers!

* * *

Chapter Eleven

K ate had thought their euphoria would carry them all the way through to eighth-grade graduation at the end of May. Nothing that she could imagine could begin to fill the space that the state tournament had held in their lives. However, much to her surprise, she and her friends were distracted by two events that made the roar of the basketball crowd begin to fade out like the end of one of her favorite radio programs.

The first was Rosie's bug-eyed announcement on Wednesday that Colleen and Danny were getting married.

"Ma's about to pitch a fit!" Rosie tossed her jacket over a hook in the cloak closet while the rest of them stood rooted around her like baby birds waiting for crumbs of information. "She can't believe that Colleen and Danny've gone together half their lives and now all of a sudden they've set the date for a week from Saturday."

"Well, your folks've always pretty much known that they'd get married someday." Doris didn't see it as a crisis. After all, Lorene and her kids were moving all the way to Pennsylvania as soon as Steve could find housing for them.

"Yeah, but Ma's gotta make a dress in ten days. And me 'n Mike've gotta get somethin' to wear." She brightened. "At least I get a new dress outta this!"

"Where's the wedding?" Cheryl, Kate could tell, was already picturing a romantic event straight out of one of Lila's magazines.

"In the little chapel at St. Peter's. Ma wants *this* marriage blessed by a priest."

"But," Kate interrupted, "Brian and Sandra didn't—"

"Yeah, they just ran off. But Ma was so happy for Brian that she just didn't care. I guess Ma wants Colleen to have a ceremony." Rosie scowled. "Fried fritters! How do I know? Maybe she's afraid that Colleen will end up workin' down at Rigoni's someday and wants her to be on God's good side, just in case."

Kate noticed that Rosie seemed moody as they collected their books and headed for music class.

"Geez," she heard Rosie mutter as if the news had just dawned on her. "It'll just be me 'n Mike at home." Her eye began to quiver as she smiled sheepishly. "I never thought I'd be glad to have him around, but I'd sure hate to be the only one left for Ma and Pa to pick on."

Cheryl glanced away but not before Kate saw her flush self-consciously.

"Where are they going to live?" Cheryl asked, recovering nicely.

"In a little apartment up over Rigoni's." Rosie shook her head. "Ma's not thrilled about that either—says the stink from the beer comes right up the stairs."

Kate was so intent on trying to imagine the beautiful Colleen living in a dark, foul-smelling place that she almost missed Mr. Hartley's reminder of the second event that demanded their attention. There were only two days left to sign up for the talent show, he announced. Cheryl had mentioned that she was practicing a solo and Doris had said Tommy was working with Gertrude Smoot on his piano piece. The rest of the Sweet Briar students were left scrambling to come up with an act, unaware that Mr. Hartley had been privately coaching several Longworth students for weeks.

"Why don't you and your friends do a pantomime?" Kate's father suggested that evening as he put down his newspaper. "There's a fellow from Danville who's having some success doing just that. Name's Van Dyke. I've heard he and his partner are really funny."

Kate weighed the possibility. "We'd sure have to know every word of the song," she protested.

Her father snorted. "You girls know the words to more songs than I do. Tell you what. I have the record of 'Doin' What Comes Naturally.' And you've all sung it along with me lots of times when I've played it on the piano. Get Doris and Rosie to stop by and practice mouthing the words."

His idea proved to be a good one, although Kate was sure that Mr. Hartley had something a little more sophisticated in mind. Poor Rosie was run ragged as she practiced with them for a few minutes before supper each evening, then raced home to help her mother with wedding decorations for the small reception in the church parlor. Doris turned pale every time they rehearsed and complained that the thought of getting up in front of "all them people" was keeping her awake at night. Still, they knew she was relieved to be working on a project that was hers alone and not something involving Lorene, Vickie or the twins.

In fact, it was Doris who suggested that they ask Jimmy and Stan and some of the other boys to dress like hillbillies and stand behind them as they did their number.

"Great idea!" Kate's father was delighted. It was the Tuesday before the show. "The more kids we get into this piece, the better it will go over with the audience. Ask the fellows to come home with you after school tomorrow and we'll run through it once or twice."

"I'll be the audience," Gran offered with a mischievous smile. "And the judge!"

Between their practices Rosie gradually unloaded every tiny detail she could recall about Colleen's "most perfect" wedding the previous Saturday:

"Brian and Sandra stood up with 'em, and Sandra sang 'Always.' It made Ma cry."

"Danny wore a dark blue suit. He had this one little lock of hair that fell over his forehead. I swear he looked like Guy Madison."

"Colleen and Sandra had these beautiful big white flowers that smelled so sweet. Gardenias, I think they were. I didn't tell her, but I thought Colleen's turquoise suit made her look kinda fat."

After the wedding Rosie had slept on a piece of cake. "I dreamt I was in Hollywood, so now it's gonna come true for sure. I just hope Ma doesn't see the big greasy stain the icing made on my pillowcase!"

By Friday night their newly created ensemble was restless with excitement as they joined the other contestants on stage just before the curtain went up.

"This event will be a true showcase of the musical potential that we have here in Rockwell," Mr. Hartley droned. "I know each of you will go out and do your best."

Later Kate wondered why he had even allowed the students from Sweet Briar to participate. They just weren't the kind of talent he had in mind. Dressed in their patched jeans and baggy shirts, she, Rosie and Doris took turns miming Ethel Merman's words while Jimmy, Stan and the other guys hammed it up in the background. Appearing second on the program, Kate's group set such a loose, light-hearted tone that the audience craved more. Instead, Mr. Hartley pummeled them with an assortment of light classics. People actually tittered as Nancy Dawes stumbled through her Jeannette MacDonald medley. They grew even more restless as Adele Atwater warbled "Indian Love Call"

155

and poor Peggy Birdsong struggled to reach the high notes of an unfamiliar number called "Pale Moon."

Right after the solos, however, Cheryl recaptured the audience with her catchy rendition of "A Little Bird Told Me." And when Tommy Panczyk finished playing "Rhapsody in Blue," people actually stood up and cheered. It was no surprise to any of the Sweet Briar contingent that Tommy walked away with first place in the instrumental division and Cheryl won the vocal competition.

Kate's father was the first one to congratulate them. Her mother and M.J., helping Gran move along at top speed, were close behind.

"You two are the best. We're going to hear great things about you someday." Dad clapped Tommy on the back.

"Aw, shucks, didn't you like my act?" Pretending to feel hurt, Kate could not keep the laughter out of her voice.

"Well, *I* liked yours. A whole lot better'n some of those screechy solos." M.J. had barely spoken before Mother clamped a hand over her mouth.

"You'd have won best in class if they'd given a prize for funny stuff." Gran's eyes twinkled. "You tell those boys they can come back to my house any day. We'll have cookies and listen to the Cubs games together."

The following week during music class, however, Mr. Hartley was tense and snippy. A muscle throbbed near the pinched corners of his mouth.

"Oh, oh—old Fartley's got a burr up his butt," Stan muttered. "Wonder what's eatin' him."

It didn't take them long to find out.

"Class." Mr. Hartley tapped his director's wand against his metal stand. "I would be remiss if I did not comment on the talent show."

"Sweet Briar kinda cleaned up." Jimmy spoke out of turn but with obvious pride.

156

"Cheryl, I would like for you to come up here with me." For some reason, the mirthless smile that Mr. Hartley directed at her friend made Kate's blood run cold.

Shrugging her shoulders nonchalantly, Cheryl grinned and joined him in front of the room.

"Now, just ever so briefly, let's run through the scales for the class, starting on middle C."

Cheryl obliged, belting out the first set, then the second. As she began with E above middle C, Kate grew apprehensive. During that set, just after her voice had cracked on one of the notes, Mr. Hartley rapped his baton and stopped her.

"Now, class, what you need to realize is that although Cheryl won first prize, she will never have the pure tones of a true professional." His eyes blinked rapidly. "Hear how her voice catches on some of the notes? I want you to understand the difference."

Kate felt her hands turn to ice as Cheryl stood paralyzed in front of the class. She had not seen her friend as ashen since the hobo had grabbed her under the railroad trestle.

"Yeah, but it sure sounds better than some of those—" Stan was cut off by Mr. Hartley's pounding baton and withering look.

"The students from Longworth, although they did not happen to win, selected songs by the masters which show off a well-trained voice. Maybe, with a great deal of work, she might—"

As Cheryl chewed on her lip to keep from crying, her shoulders began to droop. Desperately Kate looked around for Rosie to put an end to this humiliation as Mr. Hartley droned on. Then she grimaced as she remembered: Rosie was home with the flu! But something had to be done. In an instant, she realized that she would have to be the one to support Cheryl, no matter how much embarrassment she might bring upon herself. Stunned at her rush of courage, she heard herself speak.

"No, Mr. Hartley." Her voice quaked as she interrupted him. "Cheryl did a great job with her song. After all, she won."

Her face grew warm as she felt her heart begin to flutter under her blouse.

"Katherine, this has nothing to do with you. I'm sure your father—"

"My father *loved* her song." She knew she was gaining strength. How dare Mr. Hartley bring her dad into this! "He told her so himself."

"I will have to ask you to be quiet, Katherine. No one requested your opinion."

Cheryl had straightened herself and stared at Kate in amazement as she continued to unleash her anger.

"You just gave the Longworth kids the music that you happen to like." There. She had just stated what everyone already knew.

"Yeah!" A chorus from her classmates rose behind her.

"Because they were songs of worth—not cheap popular junk, like the one that Cheryl sang." Mr. Hartley's long, thin face had whitened, and his bloodless lips were set in a fine line.

"My dad says different people like different music. It's what you grow up with—you know, like people in Tennessee like country songs." Now she was on her feet, propelled by the rumbles of encouragement from her classmates.

"One more word, I'm warning you!" Pointing at her with his baton, he gave Kate the most seething stare she had ever endured. "One more word—and you will take an 'F' in this class for the rest of the year."

"I don't care! If a certain kind of music makes people

happy, then it should be okay." As she took her seat, Kate had never felt stronger in her life. Only her shaking hands betrayed her emotions.

It was then that she heard the whoosh of his baton as it sailed out of his hand clear across the room. Smashing against the side blackboard, it splintered as it hit the floor.

"Get out!" he screamed. "Get out of my class right now and go to Miss Wentworth's office. We'll see how you like standing before the principal!"

Kate sat motionless as a hush fell over the room.

"You're kicking me out of class 'cause I don't believe the same way you do?" She knew she was pressing, but he was dead wrong. Wrong to humiliate Cheryl and wrong to force his beliefs on her,

"Not another word. Do you hear?" Suddenly his voice sounded shrill and feminine, like Gracie Allen's always did when she yelled at George Burns. "Now!" he squeaked.

Kate rose slowly, collected her books and took the time to turn and give Cheryl a reassuring smile. As she closed the door behind her, she heard her classmates clapping and Mr. Hartley shrieking, "Quiet! Quiet this moment!"

Oh boy, Kate thought, as she made her way to Miss Wentworth's office. She's really going to throw the book at me. I'll have an "F" on my report card—and my parents will ground me for my entire adult life.

When she reported to Miss Wentworth, however, she found the principal contemplative but not cruel. She merely said that she would schedule a meeting with Kate and her parents and, in the meantime, Kate should report to study hall instead of music class.

In the days that followed, she learned to live in the eye of the hurricane that she had created. Her classmates praised her:

"You sure told off old Fartley!" Stan chortled.

"I didn't know you had it in you," Russell grinned with admiration.

"You're the best friend anyone ever had." Cheryl hugged her. "I mean it!"

"I just wish I'd been there. He'd have been really sorry." Rosie narrowed her eyes as she lamented her lost opportunity.

Even the Longworth kids approved:

"Everyone at school thinks you're great." Peggy Birdsong phoned to tell her. "We can't stand him either. Adele, Ellen—even Nancy—said they'd have liked to have been there."

Kate's parents, however, were ominously silent on the subject.

"We'll hear everything at the meeting at school." Her mother's face was stern. "I want to keep an open mind."

"Oh, Katie Sweet, you've gone and done it now." Gran's papery skin wrinkled over her brow as she inched her way to her radio after supper. "We had a rule that if one of the boys got in trouble at school, he got in trouble at home. I was always making trips to school because of Earl, the little devil." She pulled her handkerchief from her sleeve and blotted her damp cheek.

When they gathered a few days later in the principal's office, Kate felt close to throwing up. Staring at Mr. Hartley until he finally glanced away, she drew strength in the fact that Miss Wentworth had asked Cheryl to join all of them.

The radiator pipes squeaked and groaned as they hissed more heat into the stuffy room. Kate wondered if Miss Wentworth always kept her office so warm. Sucking the heavy air into her lungs, she tried to relax as Mr. Hartley spoke. It seemed, according to him, that few of the children at Sweet Briar had any appreciation for fine music and he felt it was his mission to expose them to it.

"But you made fun of me. In front of my friends." The words tumbled from Cheryl's lips before she had a chance to weigh their impact. Her eyes filled with tears.

Calmly Miss Wentworth asked Mr. Hartley and Kate to recount their exchange. When they had finished, the principal bristled as she drew herself up straight and tall.

"You really thought that you could improve our students' love of music by berating Cheryl?" She strode to the window and opened it with such force that Kate was afraid the pane would crack. "I myself thought she deserved to win."

"Me too." As her father spoke Kate could tell that he was trying to be diplomatic. "You know, Mr. Hartley, some people love all kinds of music. I happen to be one of them. Others prefer only one kind—the classics, for example, or country or jazz. You might fall into the latter category."

Mr. Hartley looked as if he had been slapped across his narrow worm face. "But your daughter. She questioned my author—"

"In her life there will be times when our daughter will run across people like you." Kate listened as her mother measured each word carefully, tilting her chin to let Mr. Hartley know she did not want to be contradicted. Staring him straight in the eye, Mother continued. "Sooner or later, she will have to learn how to deal with them. Either she will take a stand or let them walk all over her." She stopped and blanketed her daughter with an expression of love mingled with admiration. "Kate will take the 'F' in your class. It may be one of the most important grades she ever earns."

Kate thought she was hallucinating! Maybe the stuffy air had caused her to misunderstand. Shaking her head, she concentrated on her mother's words. Once or twice before she had seen Mother level someone without ever raising her voice. This was one of those rare times, and she had served up her best on Kate's behalf! Kate was speechless as Miss Wentworth told them that she had heard enough and advised Mr. Hartley that she would like to meet with him alone the following day.

As soon as they arrived home, she hugged her mother. "I can't believe you did that," she said with tears of gratitude in her eyes.

"I was only following your example, Kate," her mother explained as she slid her apron over her head and tied it firmly. "I was taking a stand, just as you did. And I would gladly take an 'F' too if they'd give it to me!"

* * *

Chapter Twelve

K ate was relieved that she did not have to face Mr.
Hartley again. Instead, Miss Wentworth asked her
to spend her music period tutoring two first-graders who
were struggling with their reading.

She knew her parents were happy with that decision.
They also were pleased that Miss Wentworth had soundly
reprimanded Mr. Hartley.

"Maybe that'll teach that bast—"

"John!" Her mother warned one evening as they settled
themselves to listen to the radio.

"That buzzard," he corrected himself, "not to use his
students as verbal whipping posts."

"Sounds to me, Katie Sweet, as if you took care of
things just right." Gran never looked up from the jigsaw
puzzle she was working.

Kate smiled. Secretly she was proud that her parents
had backed her so solidly. Secretly she basked in the new
respect she had gained from her Sweet Briar peers. And secretly she no longer dreaded being with the Longworth kids
after they had congratulated her on her courage at Peggy
Birdsong's birthday party near the end of April.

But, as she began to grow weary of the heat of the spotlight, she found she was also dreading the departure of
Vickie and the twins. Doris had mentioned that Steve had
located a small house and would pick up Lorene and the
children the following week.

When her mother suggested that they have an after-school picnic for the children, Kate was once again amazed at her generosity.

"The more the merrier," her mother replied when Kate asked if they could include Tommy and Mike along with Rosie, Doris and Cheryl.

Three days later Kate felt a swell of pride as she viewed Mother's mountain of fried chicken and three kinds of cookies heaped on their picnic table. With the chips and pop donated by the others, they she knew they would have plenty to eat.

"It's gonna be like a tomb at our house," Doris lamented as they watched Tommy and Gran show Vickie how to make a necklace from dandelion stems. In the distance, a turtledove cooed contentedly.

"Kinda like our place ever since Colleen moved out." Rosie blew the gray fuzz from a dandelion that had gone to seed. "Except Mike makes enough noise for three people!"

"I'd think you'd welcome the change, hon," Cheryl said to Doris as she watched M.J. and Mike play tag with the boys. "But you know what? Lila told me herself that she'll miss painting Vickie's nails once a week."

"Yeah, I think Mike's gonna miss feelin' like a big brother." Rosie sampled the chips she had brought. "He's really taken a shine to those little guys."

They attacked the platter of fried chicken like a litter of hungry pups. However, before Mother had a chance to sit down, Donnie knocked over his bottle of Grapette, and she had to run into the house for some old towels.

"Dummy!" Vickie chastised her little brother.

"Dummy!" Ronnie echoed.

"Dummy, dummy, dummy!" they all squealed.

"Hey!" The voice that boomed from Mike was full of authority. "Nobody's a dummy, so just shut up 'n eat." He tore off a chunk of breast meat and, with cheeks bulging, mumbled, "Anybody hear about the circus that's comin' to town?"

"Somebody mentioned it at the elevator today." Kate's father paused as he mopped up the rivers of sticky purple juice that ran across the picnic table.

"Didja hear who's gonna perform?" Mike shoved a handful of chips into his mouth.

With a drumstick poised in the air, Rosie stared doubtfully at her brother.

"President Truman?" She chortled at her own joke.

"You wish." Mike gave her look of disgust. "I'll tell you—Burt Lancaster, that's who!"

"Naw!" The chicken dropped from Rosie's hand and fell with a thud onto her paper plate.

"The movie star?" Tommy's gray eyes looked skeptical.

"None other." Deftly Mike slid his fingers under two wings to retrieve a plump piece of white meat.

"Why in the world would he be coming here? With the circus?" Doris sponged off the front of Donnie's shirt.

"I dunno. Guess he used to be a acrobat." Mike's mouth was so full they could hardly understand him.

"But he's getting to be a big name actor." Mother had mopped up Donnie's mess and was finally filling her own plate. "I mean, he starred in *The Killers.*" She sounded as doubtful as Tommy.

"Yeah." Disbelief echoed in Rosie's voice. "He was really good too."

"Are you sure, Mike?" Kate stopped eating to look him in the eye. "You're not just spoofing us, are you?"

"The boy seems to know what he's talking about." Gran gave Mike a vote of confidence as she poked a fork at the chicken Dad had cut up for her.

"Yep, I'm sure. And, no, I'm not shi—I mean, spoofin'

165

you. Teddy Moody's dad heard about it down at the *Messenger* where he works."

The next day Kate and her friends were relieved to see visible proof of Mike's claim. Posters had sprung up overnight all over town proclaiming: "COLE BROTHERS CIRCUS, STARRING THE ACROBATIC FEATS OF BURT LANCASTER!"

"I don't care what anyone says, we're goin' to the circus if it kills us!" Rosie was staking a claim that none of them would dispute.

Everyone in town seemed to feel the same way, Kate thought. Everyone, that was, but Gran. She said she'd have trouble getting her cane through the thick grass and sawdust and would listen to the Cubs at home instead. Kate promised to stay with her grandmother during the evening performance if her parents allowed her to go with her friends to the after-school show.

She could feel the anticipation bubbling inside her as the Fourleon Four mounted their bikes to pedal out to the circus site just beyond the railroad trestle. Not only was it the first time that they had ventured out on the cemetery road since seventh grade, but she had news that would stand her friends on their ears, as Gran always said.

"Guess where Burt Lancaster's staying." Casually she toyed with her friends as they began to move out.

"You don't know." Calling Kate's bluff, Rosie braked so suddenly that she wobbled and almost fell off.

"Do too." Kate passed her as Rosie struggled to regain control of her bike. "My dad told me that he's up at the Rockwell Arms."

"How'd *your* dad find out somethin' like that?" Rosie puffed as she caught up alongside Kate.

She told Rosie that he called from work and said that Uncle Henry and Uncle Art had been up at the hotel for

Rotary Club. They had seen him and another guy flirting with the waitress while they had lunch. Kate grinned, anticipating the impact that her next piece of information would make.

"Dad says he's driving a baby blue convertible."

"Oh, my god," Doris swooned. "Just the color of his eyes!"

"Naw!" Swerving out in front of Kate, Rosie protested, "He'd be riding with the rest of the circus. On the train."

"Nope." Kate pulled up even with Rosie's bike. "Uncle Art asked the hotel manager, and he said that Burt himself had told him that his contract allows him to drive a car if he wants to."

Rosie whistled low, her respect for Kate's information obvious. "What're we waitin' for?"

The sweet May air was laden with the scent of lilacs as their bikes scrunched through the thick gravel beside the road. On either side, brilliant fields of dandelions looked like liquid sunshine under a cloudless sky.

"It doesn't seem one bit spooky on this road today," Cheryl observed as they rode over the rickety bridge that spanned the branch of the Iroquois River. To their left stood the railroad viaduct where they had fought off the hobos.

"Not like the last time we were out here," Kate agreed. Still, a small voice reminded her that if it had not been for the two tramps, they never would have become such close friends.

"At least it finally quit rainin'," Doris called from behind. "If it was rainin' the way it did all day Sunday, this place would still give me the creeps."

"Yeah—and Dad's Aunt Edna came for dinner and left her umbrella open in our house. You'd think she'd know that could bring us bad luck!" Rosie led them to a spot just beyond the entry gate of the circus grounds, where they dropped their bikes.

"Hey—I've got an idea!" She snapped her fingers. "As soon as the last act is over, let's grab our bikes and get downtown. Maybe we can catch a glimpse of Burt at the hotel."

"Let's do it!" Cheryl's brown eyes danced with excitement.

"Yeah!" Kate and Doris chimed in together. Wow, Kate thought. She just loved these girls. Everything they did together always seemed to turn into something special!

At first they were disappointed that they were not allowed inside the main tent before the performance. Mr. Lancaster was doing some last-minute practicing, they were advised. Instead, they amused themselves by spending an extra dime to enter a musty tent where they could observe the fat lady, a three-legged cat and a furry pig.

When they emerged into the bright sunlight they pooled the rest of their change for a bag of popcorn and a stick of cotton candy, but it was hard to enjoy the taste of the fluffy pink sugar with the odor of warm animals consuming the air.

"Yuck!" Rosie held her nose. "Sure stinks! Gimme a handful of popcorn, Kate."

"What in the world is that?" Cheryl paused in front of a poster at another tent.

They stopped and studied the ad for the "hermaphrodite," a human being that was "half man and half woman."

"How can that be?" Kate wondered aloud.

"It's a queer or somethin'." Doris shuddered. "I wouldn't want nothin' to do with it. C'mon. They're lettin' people into the big tent."

Kate was grateful that Doris had nudged them along so they were among the first through the door and were able to find four seats together in the third row right on the aisle. The canvas walls seemed to trap the air inside the tent so that the smells of sawdust and animals almost overpowered them. Cheryl began to sneeze so hard that Kate was afraid she would have to leave.

"Id's okay. Id's okay," she assured them, her nose so stuffy that she sounded as if she had a heavy cold. "I'll get used to id. Don't worry." She wiped her eyes on her sleeve.

They'd have to carry her out before she'd miss this, Kate thought, as they watched the a troupe of trained dogs jump through a series of hoops and a dozen clowns climb out of a tiny car. Finally, as the circus band tooted a tinny fanfare, the ringmaster stepped to the center ring.

"Ladies and gentlemen and children of all ages," he boomed. "Cole Brothers Circus is proud to present Mr. Burt Lancaster and his partner, Mr. Nick Cravat!"

At a side entrance, a blue convertible split the flaps and began to encircle the tent. As the driver slowed in front of them, the star and his partner hopped out and waved.

"Oh, my god, I think I'm gonna faint." Doris had turned as white as she had been the day she had told them about Cletus crawling into her bed.

"Breathe deep!" Rosie instructed, her eyes never leaving her hero.

Before he performed, Burt took the microphone from the ringmaster and explained that he had been a circus entertainer before he had been an actor.

"I guess my heart will always be with the circus." The crowd cheered at the sound of his voice. He responded with his famous smile, then paused as if considering a spontaneous possibility. "Would you like to see us do a little something?"

"Yes! Yes! Yes!" A unified chorus rose from every side of the tent. As Kate glanced at Doris she was reassured to see that the color was returning to her face.

In one swift motion, Burt and his partner peeled off their street clothes and tossed them into the convertible. For the next few minutes, the world seemed to stop as the crowd focused on the center ring. With amazing agility the two went through their routine on the bars. Then, as quickly as they had appeared, they jumped back into the car and sped through the opening at the end of the tent.

As the crowd cheered and begged for more, Rosie suddenly grew alert.

"We gotta go. Now!" Her tone was urgent.

"But it's not quite over—" Kate hated to miss the rest of the show.

Elbowing them sharply, she prodded them into the aisle and out the door.

"C'mon!" Running toward their bikes, she motioned for them to join her. Not since the frightening escape from the hobos had they ridden so fast! Breathless but triumphant, they pulled up in front of the Rockwell Arms. Sure enough, there was Burt Lancaster's convertible, its top still down, straddling the first two spots near the door of the old two-story hotel.

"Fried fritters! He's already gone in!" Rosie's disappointment bordered on despair.

"Aw, hon, maybe it's just for a few minutes." Cheryl tried to reassure her.

"Wow!" Doris touched the hood as if it were holy shrine. "This is *his* car!"

"Not his—really," Cheryl corrected her. "It's his manager's. I read in one of Lila's movie magazines that the circus actually gave him his own railroad car but he borrowed his manager's convertible so he could go off by himself and stay at hotels if he wanted to."

After they had circled the car several times Rosie grew

restless.

"How do we know he's not gonna stay in there until the show tonight?" She brushed her hair away from her face emphatically.

"I've got an idea," Kate said. "Just wait here and I'll see what I can find out."

Charged with energy and imagination, she entered the dark lobby of the hotel and approached the desk clerk. Her words seemed to compose themselves as she confidently informed him that she was doing an assignment for the school newspaper and wondered when Mr. Lancaster might be coming outside. The clerk explained in hushed tones that he had overheard him making plans to drive somewhere for an early supper, so they should be leaving soon.

"Thanks." Kate grinned. She couldn't believe her good luck. "Thanks a lot. I'll just wait outside."

"Want this?" He held up a piece of paper and a pencil.

"What for?" She was puzzled by his question.

"Well, for your story. Or maybe even an autograph," he answered with a wry smile.

"Oh, yeah—right. Thanks!" Blushing when she realized she had not fooled him, she accepted the paper and pencil and tried to make her exit casually.

Outside, before she could deliver her news, Rosie raced up to her.

"Look!" Breathlessly she held up a cigarette butt. "I opened the car door, just a little, and lifted it out of the ashtray."

"Rosie, that's disgusting!" Kate shrank from the crumpled white tube that she cradled in her hand. "Besides, how do you know that other guy didn't smoke it?"

"That's what Cheryl asked. But I know, that's all." She set her mouth defiantly. "And I will keep it. Always."

When Kate told them that Burt and his partner should

come out soon, they could barely stand still. But fifteen minutes later, their enthusiasm waned as they parked themselves on the curb to wait.

"I gotta get home sometime." Doris picked at her thumbnail. "I'm starved."

It didn't help that the aroma of ribs and sauerkraut from the Downtown Cafeteria wafted across the street. Kate began to fidget as she remembered her promise to stay with Gran that evening.

"It shouldn't be long." She tried to reassure them. "Let's count the number of cars on that freight."

They held their ears as the northbound train rattled the C&EI tracks next to the hotel.

"They oughtta slow down when they go through town!" Cheryl shouted over the noise.

As the caboose faded from view, they began to bicker on how many cars they had counted.

"Oh, my—" Doris stopped still in the midst of their argument and pointed. They followed her gaze to the front door of the hotel, where two men had stepped out into the late afternoon sunshine. One was short with black hair; the other was tall and muscular with brown curly hair. "It's him."

Hurriedly they arose, brushed off their clothes and surrounded the convertible.

"Hi, ladies!" The one named Nick greeted them. "Beautiful afternoon to run into four good-looking girls—right, Burt?"

"That it is." Burt flashed each of them his toothy white smile.

"We wondered—well, um—uh—could we please have your autograph?" The words stuck in Kate's throat. "And yours too, of course," she hastily added to the man she assumed was Nick Cravat.

172

"Sure!" Burt agreed amiably. "Got any paper?"

With trembling hands Kate tore the sheet of paper into four pieces and distributed them to her friends. Rosie, who had stuffed the cigarette into the pocket of her blouse, was catatonic as she presented Burt with her scrap of paper.

"We saw you both at the circus," Cheryl's brown eyes were wide. "You were great."

"Thanks!" Burt beamed as he scribbled his name on her paper, hopped over the door into the driver's seat and turned the ignition key. Waving, he paused long enough to shout, "See you at the movies!"

As the car sped off, they stood with mouths agape.

Rosie was the first to speak.

"He—he said he'd see us in the movies," she stammered. "What'd I tell ya? Someday he knows I'm goin' to be in the movies . . . in Hollywood!" Her left eye had begun to twitch.

"No, silly," Doris chuckled. "He said he'd see us *at* the movies!"

"Yeah," Cheryl agreed. "But look, hon, we all got his autograph!"

"Well, I know what he said." Rosie walked slowly toward her bike. "And he talked with us. Burt Lancaster talked with *us!*"

"He sure did." Kate was still quivering from the experience. "Wow!" she yelled right for all of downtown Rockwell to hear as she realized what they'd done. "We've just had our best day ever. Together!"

Rosie and Doris nodded numbly.

"You got that right, hon." Cheryl ran out ahead of the rest, jumped and clicked her heels together. "You sure got that right!"

* * *

Chapter Thirteen

For the next two days Kate felt like a celebrity herself. "So, you got the big man's autograph?" Her father was amazed. "How did you pull that off?" He ladled up a bowl of potato soup from the big tureen in front of him and handed it to her.

When Kate recounted the story of how the girls had waited at the hotel, her parents nodded in approval, obviously impressed with what her mother called her "ingenuity."

"Next thing you know, everyone will be saying you're the new Hedda Hopper," Gran joked. "Maybe someday you'll have your own newspaper column." Using her good hand, she crumbled crackers into her soup.

Only M.J. was miffed.

"He wasn't even the best act at the circus," she complained, extracting bits of celery from her bowl and placing them neatly on her plate. "Besides, I haven't seen him in a single movie. Maybe next time they'll bring somebody really famous . . . like Roy Rogers!"

"Only he'll have Dale Evans along," Kate shot back. "And you won't have a chance!" Taking a huge bite from her grilled cheese, she gave her a look of contempt.

The following day Doris, Cheryl and Rosie came to her house to sit on Kate's front steps and talk about their triumph. Mother served them lemonade and asked them to repeat the story again so Gran could hear it. In the May sunlight they clustered around Gran as they shared every detail.

"It was our best day . . . ever!" Cheryl smiled up at Gran.

"Yea, it was," Rosie and Doris murmured.

Gran smiled.

"In all the days of my long life, what do you suppose the best day was?" Her keen glance lighted on each girl, then darted to the next. They shook their heads, unable to make a guess.

"The day you got married?" Rosie finally ventured.

"Nope." Gran took a long, slow sip of her lemonade and put the glass on the little metal table. "Although that was a fine one." She paused. "I think it was the day I had my stroke."

Stunned, they studied her.

"Naw," Rosie protested.

"Yes, in many ways it was. Because if I hadn't had my stroke, John wouldn't have moved his family back to my house so they could look after me. And then I never would have been able to spend so much time with Katie Sweet and the rest of you."

"Boy, that's sure takin' a lemon and makin' lemonade out of it," Doris murmured.

"And that's what Mother just did!" Kate laughed, proud of her own humor.

Everyone giggled, even Gran. At last, Kate thought, she felt like a permanent fixture in her group. Everyone was here, at *her* house, and Mother and Gran were enjoying her Sweet Briar friends as much as she was.

The following day was a sunny, golden replica of the ones that had preceded it. As Kate, Doris and Cheryl waited outside the school for Rosie, they debated about how to spend the next hour and a half.

"Well, at least I don't have to snip greens." Doris was relieved. "Mom said she could do without 'em, now that

Lorene and the kids're gone."

Kate noticed that Mike seemed to be begging Rosie for something and that his sister was losing her patience. Finally, Rosie turned toward the girls and ordered, "Get your tennis racquets! We're goin' to the park!"

That Rosie, Kate smiled in satisfaction . . . she always manages to think up something fun.

"Ours is busted." Doris gave them a plaintive look. "I think Lorene hit Cletus over the head with it before—well, you know, before he left."

"I've still got my old one in the garage." Already Cheryl was on her way. "I'll go get it and my new one, and we can all meet at the Naughton corner in a few minutes."

It was strange, Kate thought as she pedaled past the mansion, how the spring sunshine stripped the old house of its eerie qualities. Instead of looming large and formidable, it merely appeared dark and shabby. She waved to her friends and, once again in the comfort of their familiar formation, they made their way south toward the park. Rosie and Cheryl led the way, with Doris and Kate following close behind, just as they had that first day when they had headed out on the cemetery road together.

First they bounced over the east-west Nickel Plate tracks into the Longworth side of town. They rode south a few blocks, then turned west for about a quarter of a mile and bumped across the north-south C&EI line. Serving as Rockwell's link to Chicago, the C&EI skirted the community park that had been developed years ago from a donated piece of property that no one seemed to want.

"Great!" Cheryl chirped as they rode between the iron entry gates that were always locked at sundown. "No one's using the good court."

Like everyone in town, they preferred the court with the concrete surface to the one with cracked asphalt and the droopy net. Gathering around Cheryl, they listened for the familiar hiss as she opened a new can of balls. After ping-ing around for awhile they lined up for a game—Doris and Cheryl on one side and Rosie and Kate on the other.

"These things really fly!" Doris watched in dismay as her return shot sailed over Kate's head and hit the back-stop. "I'm too used to those old dead balls. Sorry, Cheryl."

When it was Kate's turn to serve, she zinged one right past Cheryl.

"Geez, when did you learn to serve like that?" Rosie's grin spanned her face. "Keep that up 'n the boys'll be wantin' you on their team next year!"

Kate glowed in the confidence that Rosie's compliment gave her. Hearing the thwunk of the ball as it hit their rac-quets, she could not remember a more perfect day. Around them the feathered branches of aging elm trees filtered shafts of light onto the court.

"Whew! I'm pooped!" Doris mopped her brow with her shirt as Rosie and Kate finished the match in two straight sets. "Let's get a drink."

Kate loved the shock of the fountain's icy water as it filled her mouth and trickled over her face. As they plopped onto a picnic bench for a few moments, she asked, "Got your dresses for graduation yet?"

"What?" Doris cupped her hand behind her ear. "I can't hear a thing." Behind her a freight train rumbled into Rockwell, headed for Chicago.

Kate repeated her question, and strained as she tried to listen to their replies. Suddenly the train screeched to a halt, each car jerking from the abrupt stop.

"Geez." Rosie turned around to look. "Freights usually don't stop for nothin' in Rockwell."

As they strolled back to the court, Doris confessed, "I don't know about you guys, but I'm kinda scared about high school."

Together they shared their misgivings—about making
the change from Sweet Briar, about having to do everything
with Longworth kids, about not being top dogs anymore.

"I just couldn't have made it through seventh and
eighth grade without the three of you." Doris was so sweet,
so open.

"I sure couldn't have handled Old Fartley without you,
Kate." Cheryl's eyes were filled with appreciation.

"And I—" Kate's words were cut off by Rosie's admonition.

"You guys! We're only goin' to high school. And we'll
all still be there for each other." She headed for the court.
"C'mon—let's play!"

As they started their second match, they never noticed
that the train had not moved. This time Kate and Doris
lined up against Rosie and Cheryl. Focusing all their energies on their game, they also were unaware that Skip Stone
and Walt Hamilton had ridden up on their bikes.

"You 'bout done?" Skip called impatiently. The tallest
boy with the most perfect crew cut at Longworth, he was
used to getting everything he wanted right away.

"Oh, my god—you scared me!" Doris dropped her racquet.

"Yeah, hold your horses." Rosie gave him the kind of
look she reserved for all Longworth kids. Since Jimmy
McPherson had taken up with Nancy Dawes at the sock
hop, she had no use for anyone from that side of town.

"Gosh, we had to ride six blocks out of our way, just to
get here." Walt strolled over to the side of the court. The
sun shone off his freshly combed black hair. "There was a
wreck, and the train can't get through."

"We wondered why it was stopped so long," Doris returned a serve, never taking her eyes off the ball.

"What kinda wreck?" Rosie continued to keep the ball in play as she spoke.

"I dunno," Walt said. "When we went by the *Messenger* office, Mr. Moody was leaving in a hurry. Screeched his tires and everything. Somebody said something about his kid being out by the trestle north of town."

Rosie froze so fast that Kate's return shot hit her in the stomach. Turning slowly she faced Skip and Walt. "Not Teddy? Not Teddy Moody?"

"Yeah, I think that's what they said, wasn't it, Walt?" Skip seemed unfazed.

Walt nodded.

"Hey," Skip prodded them. "You girls gonna play or just stand around?"

"Mike." Flushed from exertion, Rosie's face suddenly went from a deep burgundy to colorless. She looked at each of her friends in desperation.

"What's the matter, hon?"

Cradling her racquet, Cheryl approached her. "Tell us."

"Mike. Oh, God. Mike!" Her left eye was jumping. "He was on his way to Teddy Moody's when we left school!"

She ran for her bike, leaving the others to stay or follow. Together they pedaled so fast that Kate feared the breeze might topple them.

"I gotta get home—gotta see Mike. And Ma." As they detoured around the end of the train and headed for her house, she repeated those words like a mantra over and over again. The rest huffed and puffed as they forced themselves to keep up with her.

When they reached Mulgrews' house, however, no one was home. Kate saw several half-cooked hamburger patties that lay forgotten in the big iron skillet on the stove. As Rosie's blue eyes desperately searched each of them for reassurance, she gasped.

"Aunt Edna's umbrella—she opened it in the house, remember? Oh, geez!"

Kate felt an icy fear clutch her stomach. "Let's go, Rosie," she said. "We're with you."

"The trestle. Gotta get there. Gotta see Mike."

Kate felt a sharp pain sear her side as they mounted their bikes once again and started north. Ahead a knot of traffic blocked the cemetery road. However, she noticed that one car seemed to be pulling loose from the tie-up and moving toward them. As it passed, Kate recognized Mr. Moody at the wheel. Next to him, like a small ghost, sat Teddy.

"Oh, my god," breathed Doris.

"Mike. Gotta see Mike. Gotta see Ma."

They were uncertain where to go next as they came upon Rockwell's two police cars, the hearse which doubled as an ambulance, Dr. Dawes' black Cadillac and a few other trucks and cars.

"Sorry, girls—no one's allowed up there." One of Rockwell's policemen tried to turn them away.

"Oh, Jesus, Mary and Joseph." Rosie's face began to crumple as she crossed herself. Kate turned to see Dr. Dawes, his arm around Rosie's mom, guiding her gently into his car. Rosie's dad stumbled along behind them.

"Ma!" shrieked Rosie and bolted past the fireman.

The rest of them could only stare helplessly.

Kate was so numb she could scarcely speak. "Wha— what happened?"

"A boy got hit by the train up on the trestle." Tears filled the officer's eyes.

"Killed?" She had to know.

He nodded his head.

"Not Mike. Not Mike Mulgrew." Denial was turning her insides to water.

"'Fraid so. Got his foot caught in the track and couldn't get off."

The impact of his words hit Kate across the face like a blow from a wide board. Take them back, she wanted to shout at him. If you don't say them, they'll never be true!

"Don't," Doris whispered to him. "God, please don't tell us anything else."

"No!" Cheryl screamed.

"No, no, no!" Kate heard the word spewing over and over from her own mouth. Instantly they fell into each other's arms and began to weep. From the west the sun provided no warmth as it mocked them with its perfect-day light. The three huddled together, shaking as if they had just waded coatless through a blizzard.

"Kate!" It was her father. "Oh, Kate. Doris. Cheryl." His eyes, too, were red. Kate knew that if she lived to be one hundred, she would never forget the strength of his arms as he wrapped them around the three of them. "Get in my car and I'll take you to our house." When Doris looked questioningly at him, he added, "I'll come back in a few minutes and pick up all of your bikes."

In the dappled light of that May afternoon, her father steered them up the front steps and into the house. Her mother, who always had the right words for every occasion, said nothing but merely shook her head silently and gave each of them a hug and a blanket. Then, motioning for them to follow, she carried a pot of hot chocolate and several mugs into the living room. The sound of those cups, clattering on the tray, made Kate aware of just how shaken her mother was. From the bathroom Kate heard the muffled sobs that she knew were Gran's. And when M.J. joined them, her round face paled by the tragic news, Kate did not protest. She would never think of her younger sister as a pest again, she vowed, as she began to cry.

Quietly her parents comforted them, then her father took Cheryl and Doris to their homes, where he spoke with their parents. Later, when her family picked at their supper plates, the food in front of Kate only triggered dry heaves and she spent most of the evening gagging in the bathroom.

That night her mother crawled into bed with her and held her close, something she had not done since Kate had suffered a string of nightmares when she was four years old. She could feel the moistness on her mother's cheek as they huddled together, each seeking comfort from the other, all night long.

* * *

Chapter Fourteen

E very person Kate knew was consumed with grief. Tears puddled in the eyes of the teachers at Sweet Briar and streamed down the cheeks of strong men and little children. Even the priest had to stop during the funeral mass when a sob escaped from his throat. The only person who was not crying was Rosie.

When the girls had visited the funeral home the day before, Rosie had taken them over to the closed casket and pointed toward a telegram that her parents had received from the St. Louis Cardinals. In a monotone, she told them that Peggy Birdsong's dad had called a friend of his who worked for the Cardinals and told him what a great fan Mike had been. But Kate thought Rosie acted the way she might if she had been showing them the canned goods in her mother's cupboard.

Everyone else in her family was a swollen, soggy mess. Rosie's dad and Brian tried to blink back tears as they greeted friends. With Danny at her side, Colleen wailed from a corner of the room. And Rosie's mother, too weak to stand, wept continually. Kate saw Gran whispering condolences as she wiped away her own tears. When Mrs. Mulgrew nodded, Kate was sure Gran was recounting her own nightmare when she lost Earl so suddenly.

But Rosie was as stoic as one of the heads on the Mt. Rushmore picture they had studied in geography class. Throughout the funeral and at the cemetery, she clenched her teeth and ignored her twitching eye while her family and hundreds of friends were dissolved in grief. Danny even had to lead Colleen through a side door in the middle of the mass. And in the days that followed, Rosie mechanically turned her attention toward their eighth-grade graduation.

Although the spring air was filled with the sweet fragrances of lilacs and mock orange blossoms and the sun beamed down from an untroubled sky, it seemed to Kate as if the gray gloom of deepest February had descended upon all of them. After the flurry of activities, after all of Rosie's out-of-town relatives had fled with relief to the normalcy of their own lives, after all of the baking dishes had been returned, there was the terrible quiet.

"Come home with me," Rosie pleaded after school the last week of classes. "I gotta talk to someone, and Ma and Pa—well, you know."

Reluctantly they went, each of them privately dreading the moment they would cross the threshold into her house for the first time since Mike's accident. Inside it was just as Kate had feared: Mike was everywhere but, of course, was nowhere. The rooms shrieked with his presence, yet there was that devastating stillness that filled every bit of space.

"Let's go upstairs," Rosie whispered. "Ma's busy."

Mrs. Mulgrew nodded in their direction and attempted a wan smile. Surrounded on the sofa by stacks of cards, she seemed to be reading every single word. The lack of cooking aromas and activity in the kitchen reminded Kate of Cheryl's house. At one time, she recalled, she had not been able to soak up enough of the raw energy in this home; now she squirmed uneasily, eager to embrace the security of her own family.

"Looks like I got a picture of John Garfield." Rosie ripped open a small white envelope, then laid the glossy photo aside. "You guys get any new ones lately?"

"Lana Turner," Cheryl plopped down on the bed. "You could have it if you want it."

"Naw." Rosie's lifeless blue eyes seemed to roam the room. "Did I tell you that's what Colleen and Danny're gonna name their baby if it's a girl—Lana?"

"Colleen's pregnant?" Doris' face lit up. She snuggled herself into a pillow, making herself comfortable for the rest of the story.

"Yeah. Didn't you see her trying to faint at the funeral?"

"I just thought Danny was helping—" Kate began.

"When's she due?" Doris' sat straight up, her expression revealing she was mentally counting the months since the wedding.

"I dunno. Sometime in the fall, I guess." Rosie's tone was flat, disinterested. "She's kinda vague about it."

"Well, that's great news. Oh, hon, you'll be an aunt. Aunt Rosie!" Cheryl gave her a hug.

"Yeah."

"Hey, Rosie," Kate suggested. "We've still got plenty of time before supper. Want to play some tennis?" Golly, she thought, we've just got to distract her, get her out of this depressing house and into the sunshine.

"Naw. I don't never want to use that thing again." Rosie motioned toward the family's racquet, which leaned against the wall in the corner beside her bureau. "Doris, just take it. You need one." She set her jaw resolutely.

"But—" Doris protested.

"Go ahead. Just get it outta here." Rosie slid off the bed and went to the window, where she stared at the budding maple so hard that Kate wondered if were imagining Mike on one of its branches.

"Well, okay." Doris was hesitant. "Gee, thanks."

"You don't want it 'cause we were playing tennis the

day that—" Cheryl began slowly.

"I don't want it 'cause, oh, geez—" Rosie's face was a roadmap of misery. "You gotta promise never to tell this. Just like the hobos and all our other stuff. Okay?"

"Okay," they responded in one voice.

"'Cause I can't never tell Ma or Pa or Brian or Colleen. Not even the priest at confession. But I gotta tell somebody." She twisted her loose shirttail around her thumb and drew it tight.

"You know you can trust us," Kate reminded her.

"I know." Rosie turned again and, weaving the cotton back and forth through her fingers, studied the tree again for several moments. Finally, when she spoke, her voice was so soft that they had to strain to hear her.

"After school last week, when you guys were waitin' for me and we hadn't decided what we were gonna do, Mike came up and said—" She stopped and continued to gaze into space. Finally she took a deep breath and tried to continue.

"Well, Mike said him and Teddy Moody thought they'd—they'd play tennis. He was gonna use—" She nodded toward the corner.

Pausing, she breathed deeply and began again. "You know how me 'n him—well, how we always fight over everything." Kate noticed that she was still referring to Mike in the present tense. "I told him—and I was kinda mean about it—that there was no way he was usin' it 'cause I had promised to play with you guys."

The three drew one sharp breath in unison but never uttered a word.

"He was mad—said him and Teddy would just go off and look for Indian beads. And if they found some good ones, he sure wouldn't give me any of 'em." She uttered a grim little mirthless snort. "As if I'd want 'em."

Again the girls waited in painful silence.

"And that's what he was doin' up there with Teddy. Looking for Indian beads instead of playing tennis. I—I wish to God he'd of been playing tennis!" Sighing deeply, she released her wrinkled shirttail. Her face seemed to be carved in stone with never a flutter in her eyelid. "Just get the damn thing outta here, Doris. Now." Her eyes held a tense, startled look as they swept the room. "Maybe all of ya better go so I can help Ma."

As they left, Doris said dejectedly, "I really don't want this racquet—not this way."

"Oh, hon, just put it somewhere—anyplace where you don't have to look at it for awhile," Cheryl advised.

"I—I just wish that Rosie would cry." Kate could not stem the flow of tears that spilled down her own cheeks. "All last week I couldn't stop bawling—and Mike wasn't even my brother."

"She's just gotta cry." Doris stopped and gazed at them. "We've been through this at our house, and I'll tell ya one thing—ya just gotta cry!"

"It's an awful thing," Cheryl's voice was choked. "She's blaming herself."

"And now it's our secret too," Kate added. "And we can't ever, not ever, tell another soul."

That evening at supper her mother asked about Rosie.

"She—she's so down," Kate spooned a small helping of beans and franks onto her plate. "I wish we could help her."

"I tried to talk to her at the funeral home," Gran looked so fragile as she spoke. "Told her she has to let herself go. I tried to bottle it all inside me when Robert died, and it just didn't work."

Dad reached out and covered Gran's frail hand with his own. "We know," he assured her.

"Then when Earl was killed, I was a blubbering fool."

Gran reached inside her sweater sleeve for her handkerchief and patted her eyes. "Either way, you just never get over it. None of them will either, no matter how they handle it."

Rosie's grief cast a long shadow over their eighth-grade graduation. Sitting stiffly in her itchy white dress with the sweet pea corsage threatening to make her sneeze, Kate gazed around the Sweet Briar auditorium. These moments would be her last as a student there. She was in such a deep nostalgic trance recalling her classes, the operetta and her tangle with Mr. Hartley that Russell Logan had to nudge her when her name was called. Diploma in hand, she flashed Rosie a triumphant grin as she returned to her seat. Dutifully, Rosie spread her lips in an empty smile.

After graduation Kate realized that the four of them had not given their summer a thought. It seemed that Mike's death had sapped each one of them of their joy and anticipation. Cheryl was the only one who knew how she would fill her days.

"You take care, hon," she told Rosie as they watched her pack for another long session at music camp. "When I get back, we'll be freshmen. Rockwell High had better be ready for us!" The theme music of Oxydol's own, *Ma Perkins* filtered up the stairs from Lila's radio.

Rosie nodded absently. "I guess me 'n Ma and Pa are goin' to Missouri for a couple of weeks. Pa's got relatives in the Ozarks who want us to come visit."

The others nodded dumbly at her news. Kate could not imagine Rosie spending hundreds of lonely miles in the car with her parents and no Mike to tease her along the way.

"My mom's lettin' me wash dishes part-time at the truck stop," Doris confided. "It'll give me a chance to earn some money so I can get me some new school clothes."

"At least you'll have a job." Kate shook her head in disgust. "My mom and dad have got me so busy that I won't even have time to read the newest Nancy Drew book when it comes out."

"Doin' what?" Doris wondered. Rosie didn't seem to care.

"We're taking a little trip to Florida at the end of June—probably about the time you get home, Rosie. Then they've signed me up for Methodist church camp—that's a whole week—and they promised my uncles that I'd cut their grass for them in between all that." Kate pretended to be annoyed, but she knew her parents wanted her to stop thinking about Mike so much. "Plus, I've got a bunch of extra appointments with the orthodontist."

"I'm gonna detassel corn in August," Rosie straightened her shoulders a bit. "Shirley Ann Melowicz told me you can make a dollar an hour."

"Really? Maybe I'll sign up too." Kate thought that detasseling for that kind of money sounded better than cutting grass for her uncles.

Doris snickered. "My mom won't let me go out in them fields—too many rough kids, she says. She let Vic and Charley but she says it's no place for a girl."

"Maybe I can talk them into it." Kate continued to watch Cheryl as she folded two new pairs of jeans and placed them in her suitcase. "I'd love, just once, to earn enough money so I can shop for the school clothes that *I* want for a change."

Once again, however, Kate felt as if her summer slipped away from her control. As soon as Rosie and her parents returned from Missouri, Uncle Art and Aunt Janet came to stay with Gran while Kate and her family left for a ten-day trip to Daytona Beach. There she and M.J. spent hours discovering shells and riding the waves of the Atlantic. In the soothing rhythm of the ocean and the comforting warmth of the sand, she began, very gradually, to let go of

Mike. They all talked about the tragedy on their way home.

"I don't get it," M.J. mused as Dad inched the car through a construction site filled with red dust in the middle of Georgia. "If God loves us, like everybody says, why did he let Mike get killed?"

"Good question, honey." Her father's knuckles whitened as he gripped the wheel a little harder and maneuvered the Pontiac through a series of barricades. "Mike made a mistake. A really bad mistake."

"But why didn't God stop him? Or why didn't He let Mike get his foot loose?" Kate was astounded as her little sister verbalized the agonizing questions that had haunted her every night since Mike's death.

"God gives us a lot of freedom." Dad chose his words carefully. "Damn!" he muttered as they lurched into a deep chuckhole.

"I heard Lila tell Rosie's mom that God wanted Mike to be one of his angels," Kate offered. "And that's why He took him. That's why He took him now." She recalled Lila's attempt to offer condolences at the funeral home. "I was scared Mrs. Mulgrew might hit her."

"I'm surprised she didn't." Mother shook her head. "I'm afraid I might have if someone had said that to me."

Kate was confused. "So what's the answer?" she asked as Dad steered the car into a Stuckey's parking lot.

"The answer is that your mother could use some pralines." The roadwork and the depth of their conversation had shaken him.

"No—really!" Kate insisted on an explanation, not a truth-dodging attempt at humor.

"The answer is that there just isn't one, Kate." Turning around from the front seat, Mother let her warm brown eyes rest lovingly on them. "But I'll tell you what I think. I think that God is just as heartbroken as Rosie's family. Especially right now, when he's—" She winced and corrected herself. "When he was so full of life. I think that God is grieving just as hard as Jack and Mary and Brian and Sandra and Colleen and Danny. And Rosie. Especially Rosie."

"Oh," M.J. tried to absorb Mother's words.

"Oh," Kate echoed, then added under her breath, "I just wish that she could cry." As they entered Stuckey's, an exact replica of the one they had visited in Florida, she wondered if Rosie had been able to give in to her pain.

When they returned to Rockwell, however, Kate knew the moment she saw Rosie that she still was walking around with that bag of unleashed tears stored up inside her.

"My mom and dad won't let me detassel," Kate complained one evening as they shared a bottle of blood-orange pop on Rose's front-porch steps.

"Yeah? Well, I'll tell ya all about it."

"Your mom and dad think it's okay?" Kate knew she was treading on thin ice, but she couldn't believe that the Mulgrews would allow Rosie to do something that could be bad for her in some way.

"My ma and pa are still thinkin' about Mike so much that they don't care what I do." She drained the bottle. "And that's the God's truth."

In mid-July, Rosie vanished from the horizon and did not re-surface until mid-August. Kate worried about the long hours, the sweltering cornfields, and the bawdy company Rosie was keeping. But she convinced herself that Rosie needed the distraction more than she needed the money and that the four girls would be together as soon as school started.

Finally, by late August, the four of them were able to reassemble for the first time since early June. Shunning their bikes because they didn't want to look like children, they decided to walk the seven blocks to Rockwell High for freshman registration.

"I wish I didn't have to bother with algebra and general science." Cheryl kicked a stone as they approached the Nickel Plate tracks. "At Interlochen I got so used to studying music that I don't want to have to bother with the other junk. I almost wish we had enough money so I could go there all year, but then I wouldn't see the rest of you."

"You could sign up for general studies like me and just forget the rest," Doris stepped carefully over the silver rails. "I'm taking business courses. Mom says maybe I can get a job as a secretary down at Midwest when I get out of school if I'm good enough at shorthand."

"That's what I'm gonna do." Rosie's jaw was set resolutely. "Shirley Ann Melowicz and Norma Jean Coleman told me them college courses are a pain in the ass."

"Where did you run into them?" Cheryl wondered.

"We detasseled together. And know what? Them and their friends're a helluva lot of fun!"

Rosie's words seem to sail over Doris' head, but Cheryl shot Kate a puzzled frown to acknowledge the change in Rosie's vocabulary.

They strolled in comfortable silence for a few moments before Kate decided to throw out the idea that had nibbled on her for the last few weeks.

"I may try something new, but I want to see what you all think of it." Sidestepping a red tricycle that blocked her path, she failed to mention that Peggy Birdsong had made the suggestion during one of their trips to the orthodontist.

Her friends looked at her expectantly.

"I might run for Student Council." Before they could voice their opinions, she hurried on, eager to explain. "Each class elects two boys and two girls, and you get to plan a lot of the dances and stuff that go on all year. There's a bunch

of kids running from Longworth, but we need some of us
from Sweet Briar too."

"Oh, hon—go for it," Cheryl slowed her pace and
grinned. "After what you said to Old Fartley, you could
stand up to anyone."

"Yeah." Doris' sweet smile was genuinely encouraging.
"We'd be so proud."

Rosie continued to stride along at full pace.

"What do you think, Rosie?" Kate held her breath,
waiting for the approval she wanted more than anything.

But Rosie merely hunched up her shoulder in the same
"don't-care" manner that Kate had seen Shirley Ann
Melowicz use when she'd been at Sweet Briar.

"Whatever." She shrugged. "If it gives ya a thrill, then
do it."

* * *

Two weeks later Kate could not believe her good fortune.

"Hey, it's me 'n you, kid!" Peggy rushed up to her
locker. "They just posted the Student Council results—and
we're in!"

Kate's mouth fell open. "But Nancy and Adele . . . they
were running—"

"No buts. It's the two of us plus Walt Hamilton and
Russell Logan. Wanta know something really jivey?" Her
eyes twinkled with the prospect of sharing big news.

"Sure."

"You got the most votes of anyone in our class. By a
lot."

"Me! No . . . no . . . no . . ." Someone must have made a
mistake, Kate thought.

"Nope. It's true. Know what happened?"

Kate could only shake her head.

"All of us from Longworth who ran—well, we split up the vote from our school. But you—" Peggy patted her on the back—"you must've gotten a bunch of votes from Longworth and every one of them from Sweet Briar too!"

Kate began to feel her disbelief give way to gratitude for her Sweet Briar friends and their vote of confidence. "Suppose I should call Mr. Hartley, wherever he is, and thank him?" she asked dryly.

Peggy thumped her again. "Oops—sorry! Hope that didn't hurt. See, I told you you'd win if you'd just run!"

A few days later, Kate realized that the Student Council results also seemed to impact their class election. Skip Stone was named president and Adele Atwater vice-president, but she was chosen secretary. Suddenly she had new responsibilities and a schedule bulging with commitments. With her demanding college-prep classes and her desire to help manage the props for the fall production of *My Sister Eileen*, she was busy every day after school and most evenings too.

She knew she was not the only one with a full plate. Doris had kept her job at the truck stop and was working several hours a week. Cheryl had landed a coveted spot in the school show choir and was one of just two freshmen cast in the play.

"The four of us need to get together." Cheryl rushed up to her breathlessly in the hall one day between classes. "We never see each other anymore."

"How about Friday night after the football game?" she suggested. "We could have everybody stay at my house. My parents wouldn't care, and Gran would love it."

Their plans fizzled, however, when they checked with Doris and Rosie.

"I've gotta work till eleven that night. Then I'm on

again Saturday morning," Doris apologized. "Maybe next weekend I can do a different shift."

"Sorry." Rosie stuffed books into her locker and slammed the door before they could spill out. "I'm goin' to Danville with Shirley Ann and some of the kids that night."

"After the game?" Kate could feel her eyebrows raising.

"No, Goofus, during the game." Rosie gave her a tolerant, "I-can't-believe-you're- so-naive" look.

"Your mom and dad don't care?"

"Ma and Pa don't *know*." In an instant Rosie was off, hurrying to catch up with Norma Jean Coleman. "Yeah, try me some other time."

Kate never realized it at the moment, but there would be no other time for the four of them. As quickly as Mike was gone, Cheryl left. The following Wednesday night, when Kate answered the phone, she hardly recognized her friend's voice.

"Kate—we're leaving. Moving." Cheryl choked out chunks of sentences in little staccato phrases. "Tonight."

"Huh? Leaving?" Pulling the phone away from her ear, Kate stared at the receiver, unable to comprehend the words that were pouring through it. "What're you talking about?"

"Bertie and Lila. They're loading the car right now. I've only got a few minutes." She wept as she tried to continue. "I just had to call—"

"But—" Kate couldn't even think of the right questions to ask.

"It's got something to do with Bertie's job, and he says he'll have to tell me later. He's going to work in Decatur." Cheryl sniffed and swallowed again. "We're—we're staying with some of Lila's friends there till we find a place."

"But—" Kate's mind raced to Cheryl's place in the choir, her role in the play, their furniture, their hi-fi, their record collection. Still, she was so stunned that she could only stammer once more, "But—"

"We're only taking our clothes this first trip. And—and Lila's throwing all of her nail polish and stuff into a box right now. Oh, Kate," she wailed, "tell me. What am I going to do without all of you?"

"Can I come over? Just for a few minutes?" Kate knew she couldn't let Cheryl slip away so fast.

"No—in fact, Bertie's telling me to hang up. Oh, hon, I'll write you as soon as I have an address. Give Rosie and Doris a hug for me. I love you—"

"Love you too. Good luck." She could not believe what she had just heard. "Write!" As she placed the receiver on the hook, her father was passing through to the kitchen.

"Good lord, Kate, you're white as a sheet." He pulled up a chair and took her hand. "What's the matter?"

When, trembling and haltingly, she managed to tell him, he shook his head.

"Oh, boy. Oh, boy," was all he could say.

"But why would they have to leave tonight? So fast? I mean, Cheryl's got a part in the play!" The questions that she'd been unable to ask Cheryl tumbled out. "Why?"

"I'm not sure, but I've heard rumors." Her father removed his glasses and cleaned them with his handkerchief. "I promise you—I'll find out something tomorrow. And I'll tell you then."

Sleep did not come easily for Kate that night. Tossing from one side of her bed to the other, she felt as lonely as she had when they had first arrived from Texas. But this time there was the added sense of abandonment. She plumped up her pillow and tried to get comfortable. Everyone seemed to have left her. Doris was at work, Rosie was never at home, and Cheryl was on her way to Decatur. Decatur? She sighed. That was almost one hundred miles

196

away. What could have caused the Allisons to want to move so abruptly? When she finally fell asleep, she dreamed of the hobos for the first time in months.

The next day at school people wondered where Cheryl was, but Kate didn't utter a word. She wanted to wait until she had talked with her father. When he came home from work, he took her up to her room and shut the door. It was then that she knew his news would not be good. Still her mind reeled as he told her gently but firmly that Herb Adler, the owner of the dealership himself, had said that Bertie had been skimming funds for more than two years.

"He'd wait on three or four customers in the service department every morning before he'd start the cash register," he explained. "Then he'd pocket that money for himself."

"But that's stealing!" Her mouth was hanging open. "Cheryl's dad wouldn't do that!"

"He not only would, but he did." Dad took off his glasses, wiped them and put them back on. "If he's as guilty as Herb says he is, he's lucky Herb's not pressing charges. He could go to jail."

"Jail?" Her knees wobbled beneath her as she tried to imagine sweet, lively Bertie confined to a jail cell.

"But it doesn't sound as if that will happen," he assured her. "Herb caught him red-handed yesterday morning and just told him to get out of town and leave his furniture and stuff. Herb's going to sell it and try to recover some of his money that way." He shook his head. "Herb Adler's a good man, but he's so disillusioned. He told me that the one thing Bertie is guilty of is worshiping his wife and daughter so much that he'd actually steal just so he could give them the best."

"Oh, that's so sad." Her own voice sounded small, far away. "Cheryl never asked for a thing."

"I know."

"Dad?" She made a decision. "I'm not going to tell anyone about this—not even Rosie or Doris."

He studied her lovingly. "That's all well and good. But you know in a town this size that everyone's going to hear about it And a lot of people will make up some pretty ugly stories along the way."

She shuddered.

"Just tell Rosie and Doris that when any of you hear from Cheryl, you'll let the others know. And then all of you should write to her. She'll need every bit of help she can get from her old friends back home." She felt the strength and warmth of his hug, then he went downstairs and left her sitting on her bed to try to digest all the information he had just shared.

The next day the school was rife with rumors:

Cheryl's dad was on the "most wanted" list of criminals and had to leave town in a hurry. Kate felt that speculation did not justify a response.

Cheryl's grandmother had died and the family had merely left town for the funeral; after all, their furniture was still in the house. Kate didn't tell a soul that Cheryl's grandmother had died several years ago.

Cheryl's mom had taken ill suddenly, and they all had gone with her to Chicago for the best medical help. Kate never told a soul that Lila had taken the time to pack up her nail polish and other cosmetics before they had fled.

Kate suffered through each endless minute of each endless class. After lunch she steeled herself for more questions when she saw Peggy approaching her.

"Hey, kid, a bunch of us from Student Council are going up to the malt shop after school to talk about decorations for the fall sock hop." Peggy's voice was full of cheer, like a rainbow splitting clouds after a storm. "Wanta go?"

"Maybe. I'll let you know." Kate scanned the halls for

any sign of Rosie or Doris. With their classes in different subjects, it was often hard to locate them. At the far corner of the hall she caught a glimpse of Doris' new electric blue corduroy skirt.

"Doris!" she shouted, leaving Peggy behind as she broke both rules about making noise and running in the halls.

Doris turned and waited.

"I just heard that Cheryl is gone. And other stuff." Doris looked grim. "Somebody must be fibbin' for sure."

"It's true, all right," Kate panted. "She called me before she left. You were at work and Rosie wasn't home." She gasped as she caught her breath. "Wanted me to tell you she loves you and she'll write as soon as she can. She—she said her dad got a different job and they had to go right away."

"But—" Doris' gray eyes were puzzled behind her glasses.

"We've just got to write to her when we hear from her, okay?"

"Sure. Okay."

"Come on," Kate urged, "walk with me. I've got English last hour. What do you have?"

"General math." She stopped. "But I'm not goin' today. I'm leavin' early so I can work an extra hour."

"Did you get an excuse?" As soon as Kate heard her own words, she scolded herself for being such a prude.

"I sorta forged Mom's name." Doris glanced away. "You won't tell on me, will you?"

"You think I'd do that? Get out of here!" Kate reassured her. "I haven't seen you all day—right?"

As soon as the final bell rang, she searched for Rosie and saw her slip out a side door and jump into an old car with some other girls.

"Rosie!" she called. "Rosie!" It never occurred to Kate not to chase her down. When she reached Rosie at last, she stuck her head in the car. Edna Brinkhoff, who had been two years ahead of them at Sweet Briar, was driving, and Rosie was sitting in the back seat beside Norma Jean Coleman. Thick clouds of cigarette smoke curled out the window and the front door as Shirley Ann Melowicz slid into the front seat.

"Wait a second." Rosie told them as she climbed out of the car, holding one hand behind her back. "Whad'ya want?"

"It's about Cheryl. You know she's gone?"

"Yeah. I've heard all sorts of shit."

"I just wanted to tell you she called me before she left. She had tried Doris, but she was at work and you weren't home."

"So?"

"She—she just wanted us to know she—well, that she loves us." Desperately Kate searched Rosie's eyes for warmth, for concern. "She wants us to write as soon as she gets an address."

"I can do that." Rosie sounded tolerant, the way she might if she'd been talking to little Vickie. "Just let me know if you hear from her."

"And you—you do the same. Okay?"

"Okay."

"Hey, Rosie—you comin' or are you gonna stand there and gab all day?" Shirley Ann demanded.

"I'll be there. Geez, just hold on."

As she and Rosie faced each other there seemed to be nothing more to say. Edna revved the engine, but Rosie took her time.

"Hey, Kate." She drew her arm around in front of her so her cigarette was in full view. "Gonna turn me in?" Taking a long, slow drag, she gave Kate the look of defiance she had once saved for their Sweet Briar teachers.

Willing away the tears, Kate stared at her steadily. In seventh grade she knew she would have protected this girl with her life, just to ensure her acceptance. Now, with a stronger sense of her own self, she searched Rosie's blue eyes before she answered.

"Not you, Rosie. Not this time."

As Rosie gave her a quick little unexpected hug, Kate could smell the odor of cigarettes, rather than hamburgers and onions, embedded in her clothes. Suddenly she wished with all her heart that they could turn back the clock to the day that they rode like the wind to escape the hobos.

"Love ya, Rosie," she said softly.

"Love ya too," Rosie whispered. Then she turned abruptly and climbed in the car. Over the screech of the tires, Kate could hear Shirley Ann's shrill laughter as they sped away.

"Hey, Kate!" Wiping her eyes with the sleeve of her sweater, she turned to see Peggy waving at her. "Hurry up if you're going to the malt shop with us!"

Kate paused long enough to stare at Edna's car as it careened around the corner and roared out of sight.

"Wait, Peggy. Wait for me!" she called. "I'm coming!"

* * *

Part Two: Doris

1951 – 1962

Chapter Fifteen

"**W**ouldja just wait a second?" Doris yelled over her shoulder. "I'm comin'. I'm comin'. Fast as I can get there!"

That swine, Tooley Blunk! She knew he'd like to trip her just to get her attention. But with two plates of the meat loaf special lined up on each arm as she hurried to the booth next to his, she'd make a terrible mess if she fell. The fat hog, she thought. He'd already had a double helping of cherry pie loaded with ice cream and had the nerve to dangle his mug out in the aisle so she could fill it for the fourth time.

"Wait? Me wait?" His piggish face turned the color of pickled beets. "You're the one who's waitin' on folks, girlie. That's why they call you a waitress!" Out of the corner of her eye she could see his huge body, dressed in the same old bib overalls and plaid shirt he always wore, shaking in the booth as he snorted at his own stupid joke.

"Hey, give her a break, Tooley." Bill Lochschmidt whirled around on his stool at the counter. "I'd like to see you move as fast as she does, you big lardo."

"Thanks." Doris grinned at Bill, allowing Tooley to see that she was giving Bill a refill before she even thought about bringing the coffee pot over to his booth.

"Kinda like sloppin' the pigs, when you've gotta wait on old Tooley." Holding his coffee cup in both hands, Bill gave her one of those crooked smiles that made him look like Farley Granger. "Hope he's a big tipper," he added loud enough for Tooley to hear.

Bill understands, she thought. He's one of the few customers here at Pete's Truck Stop who really understands. And although she'd never slopped pigs before, she'd cleaned up plenty of messes that customers left. Cold eggs and syrup were the worst, 'specially when people wadded up their paper napkins and smashed them into the sticky circles that they'd slobbered onto the table.

Pushing up her glasses with the back of her wrist, she squinted through the clouds of cigarette smoke at the clock over the counter. Two hours to go. And she still had four pages of shorthand to transcribe and a bunch of bookkeeping exercises to finish when she got home. She hoped she could stay awake that long.

"Working late?" Bill must have seen her checking the clock.

"I'm off at nine." Wiping off a ketchup bottle, she replaced the lid and set it on the counter.

"I'll still be in town. I can take you home." His voice was as smooth and sweet as a Milky Way.

She couldn't believe her ears. Bill Lochschmidt was one of the cutest guys around—probably about twenty or twenty-one and already farming his own acreage near Bakers Corners. A little voice inside her warned that she shouldn't seem too eager.

"I dunno. Someone's already plannin' to pick me up." Doris, she chided herself, that is an out-and-out lie! You know you're goin' to have to call your mom to come. She busied herself filling the napkin holders so he couldn't read the guilt on her face.

"Let 'em know you've already got a ride," he said playfully. "Besides, if you do, I'll tell you what the name 'Lochschmidt' means in German." His brown eyes twinkled with mischief as he edged up so close she could smell his Old Spice.

"And what if I don't care?" Two could play this game, she thought—and it was fun. "Refill?" Her coffee pot hovered between them until he set the mug down so she could fill it again.

"Oh, but I think you do. It's an old family secret." Cocking an eyebrow, he looked her over till she felt herself turn pink. "And I'm betting you'll let me buy you a hamburger when you get off." Sliding down from his stool, he swaggered over to the jukebox and dropped in two nickels. She watched while he punched the same buttons twice. "Two for the price of two," he grinned.

"Put another nickel in, In the nickelodeon . . ."

Doris felt new energy surging through her as Teresa Brewer's brassy voice filled the smoky room. She began to wipe the counter a little faster.

"You sure must like that song to play it twice." She tried to sound stern as she plucked up six glasses and laid them in the dirty dish bin. Bill just sipped his coffee and gave her a slow wink.

Later, when she looked back on that evening, she swore at herself for having been so blind. If only she'd been half-smart when Bill had charmed her when she'd been so tired. If only she'd remembered Lorene's complaints that Bill was one of the biggest flirts back when she was working at Pete's. If only she had been strong enough to resist the attention that this movie-star-handsome farmer was heaping on her.

But that was the spring of 1951, and she was ready to be swept away by the first sweet-talking guy who came her way. After scrubbing mountains of greasy dishes at fifty cents an hour during her first year and a half of high school, she finally had been able to move up to waiting tables as soon as she'd turned sixteen. It seemed pretty weird that she felt more at ease with the customers, even jerks like Tooley Blunk, than she did at Rockwell High—mainly, she guessed, 'cause it seemed she hardly knew any of the kids anymore. After Cheryl moved away, Rosie started running with people Doris would've been ashamed to be seen with. And Kate, God love her—well, Kate was always so busy with committees and homework that it seemed like they lived on different planets. She'd resigned herself to the fact that Kate probably would end up going away to college anyway and she'd never see her again.

She allowed her thoughts to drift to her friends as she filled salt and pepper shakers. The four of them had always had so much fun together, but nothing had been the same after Mike got killed. To tell the truth, Doris had always wondered why the other three had ever bothered to include her. Her family had been so poor compared to the Freemans, but Kate and her folks had always made her feel comfortable. At Cheryl's she'd gotten to see how the other half lived—that is, till they'd left in a hurry after Mr. Adler found that Bertie had stolen money so he could buy all that fancy stuff.

She rolled paper napkins around fresh table service and piled them onto a tray as she thought about Rosie. She'd always been grateful that Rosie had accepted her way back in second grade, the very minute her mom moved the family to Rockwell. Just took her on as one of her friends, no questions asked. But after Mike's funeral, Rosie had set her jaw and moved through each day like she was on her way to the dentist. Still, she'd never cried once—not so's any of them could tell. They'd tried and tried, but they just couldn't get her interested in nothin'. Later, when Rosie'd hooked up with Shirley Ann Melowicz and some of them other wild girls, she'd started going to road houses south of Danville where they served drinks to underage kids. Doris sighed. Somehow, she couldn't blame her. Rosie'd just been doin' anything she could to try to forget about Mike.

So when she allowed Bill Lochschmidt to buy her a hamburger and take her out to his pickup truck and tell her, "Lochschmidt in German means locksmith—and I've got the key to unlock your heart," Doris felt herself melting like butter on a griddle. He was romantic and he took charge—not like those skinny, pimply boys at Rockwell High!

Right off the bat, that very first night, he kissed her— real tender, like in the movies—and made her feel so special she knew right then she wanted to spend her whole life with him. All summer long he took her to movies and carnivals at the county fairs. Afterward, he'd park his truck on a gravel road. First, he'd have her listen to the sounds of the country with him—said the songs of crickets and toads were his favorite music. He'd ask her about her family, then he'd talk about his.

She couldn't believe how sympathetic he was about her losing her dad. But his own father had died when Bill was fifteen, and he'd had to quit school to run the farm. She thought it was so sad that his four older sisters had married and moved away, and Thelma, the one just three years older than Bill, had convinced their mom to join her and her family in Missouri. It was tough enough to run the farm alone, but the worst part was just being so lonely. When she heard all his stories, she felt so sorry for him she just about cried. But then he started in with those warm kisses—well, right there in his truck, she promptly forgot all the warnings her mother had given her over the years. Later, when she recalled those sultry nights with Bill, her face grew hot just thinking about them.

She knew she was distracted all summer long. In the back of her mind she heard people at the counter say they were still mad at President Truman for firing General MacArthur, but she really didn't care. Others talked about how many cases of polio were popping up in the county, but their concerns just went in one ear and out the other.

By August, she was trying to figure out how to break the news to her mom that she wouldn't be going back to school for her junior year. Doris knew she'd get yelled at and that her mom would cry like her heart was broken. After all, she was still mad at Vic for quitting college to go into the Navy and was worried half-sick that he might get sent to Korea. But that wasn't the part she dreaded most. The real thing Doris hated to tell her was that she was pregnant.

"It's not like Lorene and Cletus!" she protested when her mother dissolved in tears. "Me 'n Bill really love each other. He's a hard, hard worker, Mom. The two of us—we're gonna farm together and raise our kids together. And someday, I swear on the Bible, I'll finish school. Honest!"

Bill took her mom's hands in his and said he understood how disappointed she must be. Doris felt her heart swell with pride as he pledged to take real good care of her and patted her mom's cheeks with his handkerchief. Finally, her mother heaved a big sigh and hugged both of them.

That Saturday morning it was hot enough to fry an egg on the sidewalk as she and Bill climbed the worn steps at the home of the local justice of the peace. She was glad to have her mother, Tommy and Violet along for moral support. Charley was away on a work/study program in Minnesota, and none of Bill's sisters or his mom could make it on such short notice. When she started thinking back on the whole affair, Doris thought that his family's absence should have tipped her off right there, but she was too devoted to Bill to give it a second thought.

Try as she might, however, Doris could not make herself feel like the romantic bride of her dreams as she stood beside Bill in the stuffy little office that reeked of mothballs. She felt her knees wobbling as she promised to love and obey and feared she was going to pass right out when Bill slipped the band of gold on her finger. Thinking they had spent at least an hour with the justice of the peace, she was surprised when they emerged into the blazing sunshine to discover that they'd only been in there ten minutes.

When her mother offered to treat all of them at Pete's, Bill thanked her but said they'd better get on their way to make sure they'd be able to get a room at the lodge at Turkey Run State Park over in Indiana. It would be the first time, Doris realized with a pang, that she'd ever been away from her mom, except for the overnights she'd shared with her friends.

She could barely contain her pride when Bill gave her his sly grin as he signed them in at the lodge as Mr. and Mrs. William Denzil Lochschmidt. She glanced around to see if anyone noticed this handsome man who accompanied her, but the only soul around was a maid pushing a sweeper in the corner. When he opened the door of their room, she was stricken with the fact that it smelled just like the office of the justice of the peace. Suddenly missing her mother, she sat on the side of the bed for a few minutes and tried not to cry.

The odor in the room didn't seem to affect Bill, but then he wasn't the one who was pregnant. He was quick to distract her and, enjoying the luxury of a real bed rather than the truck cab, they left the room only once that night to get a quick hamburger. Exhausted from their lovemaking, they checked out at noon the next day, drove back to Rockwell and stopped at her mother's to pick up a few of Doris' things. She couldn't wait to get to the farmhouse that would now be her new home.

However, she sucked in her breath when they drove up the bumpy lane and she realized how much the old two-story house looked like her mom's. Only worse. Curls of white paint peeled away from the boards, and the porch definitely leaned to one side. Bill mumbled a brief apology, explaining that he'd been too busy in the fields to do any fixing up. But when all the crops were in, he promised her with his sweet smile, he'd put new screens on the windows and paint some of the rooms.

Inside, the place smelled like Vic and Charley's dirty socks, and the wild shades of hot pink and mint green on the walls made her stomach churn. Still, she convinced herself that she'd died and gone to heaven. Here she'd have no more homework and no more slobs like Tooley Blunk to wait on. She could hardly believe her good luck. She was set for life with her own home and a handsome husband— and she hadn't even celebrated her seventeenth birthday! How many other girls could lay claim to that?

She savored her new independence. No longer grabbing a bite of breakfast and hurrying off for a long day of boring classes, she was up before dawn and frying slabs of bacon and a bunch of eggs for her husband. The very first week he taught her useful stuff, not ridiculous subjects like short-hand and typing. She learned how to tend the laying hens he'd given her as a wedding present and how to manage the tractor so the two of them could get the crops in faster. Sometimes, after a long day, they hopped in the truck and drove the five miles into Rockwell for pie and coffee at Pete's. Those were times when she felt so proud to be sitting on the other side of the counter for a change. She wished that they had time to stop at her mother's, but Bill was always in a hurry get home so they could make passionate love. Finally, she got so big she was afraid they'd hurt the baby.

"You tell that kid to hurry up and get out of there," Bill teased. "That's my territory, not his!"

The one thing she missed the most after she moved to the farm was Tommy's piano playing. She never realized how much his jazz and show tunes had calmed her down when she'd cooked in the kitchen and looked after Lorene's kids. Now the music of Joplin and Gershwin had been replaced by static-filled farm reports on the radio, restless moans from the cows in the barn at milking time and Bill's tuneless whistling just before he opened the squeaky back door.

When her water broke on a cool April morning, she was trying to help Bill work on the plow so it would run better. He sat her down on a bale of hay and asked if she thought she could make it to the house.

"My baby's not gonna be born in no barn!" she retorted. Suddenly Doris yearned for her mom. "Oh, my god, Bill," she gasped. "Just get me outta here!"

She knew she'd never forget the reluctant look he gave the plow as he helped her into the house. "Come on." Shoving her along impatiently, he seemed cross, but she knew he must be scared too. "I'll help you, then I'll call Hilda. I might still be able to get some plowing done yet."

She was glad they had made arrangements with Hilda Gundlach, the midwife who delivered most of the babies around Bakers Corners. Bill said he didn't have the money for a hospital and, besides, Hilda'd probably brought more kids into the world than all the Rockwell doctors together.

Doris felt helpless as she lay in their big iron bed and let Hilda's Gundlach's calloused hands do their work. She tried her best to follow Hilda's directions, but as the pains came—longer, sharper, closer and closer—she heard herself screaming for her mother.

"Hey!" Bill spoke sharply. "Forget your mom. This is our kid, not hers!"

Pushing with such intensity that she thought she might pass out, she vowed she would never go through this again. Moments later, Hilda held up a squalling, black-haired boy who peed in a great arc all over their bed.

"Oh, God, thank you." Bill dropped to his knees and clasped her hand. "We've got us a farmer, Doris. A brand new little farmer."

After Hilda had wiped off the baby and wrapped him in a piece of flannel, she placed him in Doris' arms. Awed, she cradled him as a wave of emotion washed over her. In all her seventeen years, she had held plenty of kids before, but this one took her breath away. She studied his tiny, scrunched-up features.

"He looks just like you." Gently she ran her hand over his broad face and felt the dimple under his chin.

Bill just grinned as he inspected the perfect little fingers.

"Someday these hands'll be big enough to plant corn." Already he had dreams for their son.

"We should name him after you," she said. "He's the spittin' image of you."

"I'm not much on juniors." He shook his head.

"Then let's just turn your name around and make it Denzil William. How's that?"

"Denzil Lochschmidt." He repeated it two or three times. "Sounds good. Sounds strong. He'll be a good kid, our Denny will."

During the next months she could not believe how perfect her life was. She marveled that Bill was thoughtful enough to fix her up with a backpack so she could take Denny everywhere with her—up on the tractor, out in the hen house and in the rows of her vegetable garden. She felt so complete as she fed him from her breasts, sometimes under the big elm that stood outside their kitchen window. Nursing a baby, she thought, must be about the best thing a woman can do.

The only trouble was that no one ever warned her that women can get pregnant while they're breastfeeding. Since she wasn't having her monthly periods, she never gave it a thought as she and Bill picked up right where they'd left off. By the following February—not long after Ike had taken office—Hilda paid them another visit and delivered David Chester. The new baby didn't look a thing like Denny. With his high cheekbones and the crop of light fuzz on his head he favored Tommy, but Doris decided against mentioning that to Bill. He wanted his kids to be Lochschmidts, not Panczyks!

That spring it was harder for her to get out into the fields. Although she didn't like to do it, she often had to leave David asleep in his basket just inside the back door and take Denny with her while she gathered eggs and planted the vegetable garden. One evening, as she indulged in a rare break on the porch swing and looked at the *Rockwell Messenger,* she saw the pictures of the graduating class of 1953.

"Oh, my god!" she blurted. Not once had she stopped to think that her friends had been finishing school while she'd been farming and having babies!

A lump filled her throat when she spotted Kate's picture on the front page, looking so pretty in her slipover sweater and string of pearls. The paper said Kate finished second in the class and would give the welcoming speech at graduation. It also mentioned that she'd won a scholarship to study journalism at a place called Butler University in Indianapolis. Good for her, Doris thought. The Freemans must be plenty proud.

She flipped through the pages till she found the pictures of all the graduates. There in the fifth row of little squares was Rosie. Somehow, she looked a lot older than most of them. That cocky expression in her eyes just dared anyone to challenge her. Doris wondered about Cheryl and if she would be graduating in the town where her family had moved. Was it Decatur or Springfield? She couldn't quite remember.

Automatically her finger traced down the rows to the P's. Gene Palmer. Alma Peterson. She'd have been right between them if she just hadn't been in such a hurry.

"Hey, Doris!" Bill's disgusted voice from inside the screen door interrupted her thoughts. "Better get your butt in here. David just spit up all over himself and Denny's got poopy pants."

"Comin'," she sighed. Someday, she vowed, she would get her diploma, the way she had promised her mom. Someday . . . when she had the time.

* * *

Chapter Sixteen

Two years later Doris could not believe how fast the seasons flew by, yet the days were so unbearably long. She sighed as she shifted her newborn to her other breast and tried not to let herself get upset as her mother continued her lecture.

"You know you just can't go on like this. I mean, honey, you do understand what causes this, don't you?"

Doris studied the flat, gray landscape outside her kitchen window and wondered how she'd get through Thanksgiving the next week. In spite of her mom's preaching, however, she was grateful to have her help that Saturday. After giving birth to her fourth child just days before, she felt that exhaustion had taken up residence in every bone of her body. Even her cheeks seemed to ache from fatigue. Still, she felt blessed as she gazed on little Douglas Charles, born just seventeen months after his sister, Debbie. With their round faces and dark hair, anyone could tell they were Bill's kids.

"Mom—I'm not stupid. It's just that Bill—well, he—"

"He's a man!" Savagely her mom twisted the dishcloth till there wasn't another drop of moisture left in it and attacked the stains on the kitchen counters. "How do you think *I* ended up with seven kids?"

Silently her mother scrubbed with all her might before she gave up and scooped a bundle of diapers out of the old dryer. "But at least I had a couple of years between kids— well, except for Vic and Charley. Denny's three-and-a-half years old and here you are with four already!"

"We're gonna be more careful, Mom. Honest. Bill promised." Doris knew she had to offer her a crumb of hope. Carefully she took a step toward the sink. In the last couple of days Debbie had started standing on her feet, with her arms thrown around her legs and giggling as Doris tried to move around. The extra baggage sapped her even more, but Doris figured it was better than putting her toddler down and listening to her scream her head off.

"Well, I'm gonna have Violet come out here and help you a couple of days a week when she's not busy at Dr. Dawes' house." Her mom folded diapers like a machine on an assembly line, never even pausing as she spoke.

"No, Mom. I can handle it. Really." Rinsing off Debbie's pacifier, she returned it to her daughter, who stepped down and ran to join her brothers. Once again she opened her blouse so Dougie could resume nursing and called into the living room: "Denny—you and David be careful with Debbie while you're playin'."

Wearily she turned her back so her mother couldn't see her close her eyes, even for a moment. She just couldn't find it in her heart to explain that Bill thought they didn't need any help—that he wanted—no, expected Doris to care for their children, run the house and still put in plenty of hours on the tractor. She was thankful that at least Dougie had chosen to arrive in November, when there was a break in the fieldwork.

Trying to steer their conversation onto a safer ground, she asked about Lorene and was glad to hear that she and Steve seemed happy. They had even invited her mom and Tommy to take the bus out to Pennsylvania the next summer so they could see the kids.

"I'd love to go see Vic too, but San Diego's just too far. At least he seems to like the Navy okay. And at least," her mom added, "we're not at war."

"You've gotta feel so proud of Charley." She patted Dougie's back to encourage a burp and went to stir a kettle of potato soup on the stove.

"He likes his job. That kid is smart." Mom smoothed out the wrinkles on a gray diaper. "Maybe we oughtta soak these in bleach next time. You know," she said without missing a beat, "sometimes I just don't understand the difference in my own kids. Here's Charley who let basketball take him through all four years at Purdue and is makin' good money in that factory office near Chicago." She shook her head. "Then there's Vic, who was too stubborn to stick it out with basketball—thought he knew everything. It's funny, come to think of it. He never liked to have anyone tell him what to do, then he quits college and goes off and joins the Navy where someone orders him around all the time!"

Doris laughed at her mother's insight. As they spent the next few moments in companionable silence, she looked at Dougie and wondered what differences there would be in her own children.

"I still miss Tommy and his music," she confessed. "Every single day that I'm out here."

"I wish I knew what will happen to that kid." For the first time Mom stopped working and walked over to the window to stare at the bare fields. "Did I tell you that Gertrude Smoot said she'd taught him about everything she knows? So Kate's dad got him lined up with a teacher in Danville and drives him down every week for his lesson. Sometimes he even takes him to the Steak 'n Shake for supper."

"That Mr. Freeman. He's a really good man." Gently she rubbed Dougie's back. "But those lessons've gotta cost him an arm and a—"

"Nope" Her mother picked up a handful of crayons from the kitchen table and stuffed them back into their box. "The Rotary Club offered to pay—provided Tommy comes and plays for 'em twice a year. Mr. Freeman volunteered to drive him every week."

Doris listened in amazement as her mother continued to talk about Tommy. In spite of his rigorous music schedule, he had taken over all of the household chores, now that the rest of the kids were gone.

"It kinda scares me sometimes though," her mother confessed as she carried the stack of diapers to the living room and set them on the big old table that was used for changing the babies. "I mean, his music is just so beautiful—and I don't know what to tell him to do with it. But he's gotta learn a trade, somethin' he can support himself with. I sure don't want him to end up in a factory . . . like me!"

"Oh, sh—" Doris caught herself before she swore in front of Debbie, who had glued herself to the tops of her shoes once more. "The soup is startin' to scorch. I can smell it. Bill'll have a fit."

"He is treatin' you good, isn't he? Like he promised when you got married?" Her mother gave her a quick glance as she turned down the burner and stirred the soup.

"Sure, Mom, he wouldn't lift a finger to hurt me. And he always lets me have the truck to go to eight o'clock mass on Sundays. When I have the time to get there."

She knew her mother would feel better if she realized that Doris still cared enough to go back to St. Peter's in Rockwell for mass. As she placed Dougie in his bassinet in the draft-free corner of the kitchen, she wished she could tell her mom some of the stuff that her neighbor, Bessie Yoder, had confided to her just after David was born—that Bill had been spoiled as a child and talked mean to his mother and sisters the way his dad had done; that his mom had moved to Bill's sister's place, rather than listen to him yell at her every day of her life; and, worst of all, that sometimes when he made fun of her best meals, his smile would lose its charm and become scary and triumphant when he realized how much he had hurt her feelings. No, Bill never hit her, she could honestly say that. But Doris could never tell her mom that his words sometimes stung her worse than a whip across her back.

"How's Violet?" Abruptly changing the subject, she grabbed a rag to wash the smear of hardened jelly that had been on Debbie's cheek since lunch.

"She's got a beau." Her mom put the lid on the kettle and wiped her hands on her apron. "Spud Zylstra."

"The garbage man?" Doris wrinkled her nose. "Not the garbage man!"

"Yes, the garbage man—who is a good fellow, Doris Bernadette, so don't make a face. And he also happens to have a very good business," her mother emphasized.

Doris shook her head. A farmer with manure on his shoes was bad enough, but a garbage man—ugh! Scooping up Debbie, she smoothed her hair and gave her the set of measuring spoons to jingle while she changed her diaper right on the linoleum floor. From the living room she could hear Denny and David fighting over a toy truck that her mom had brought.

"Shut up!" she barked. "You'll wake the baby!"

At the sound of her voice, Dougie awoke and began screaming.

"Now look what the two of you have done!" she scolded as she picked up Dougie and tried to soothe him. There just was no letup. If only, she thought, I could just have a minute to myself.

*. *. *

A few weeks later she felt like she'd been run over by Santa and his reindeer. Between having a new baby and trying to shop for Bill's mom and his sisters and get their packages mailed, she hardly knew what hit her. So when she had a call from Kate between the holidays, she went into a real panic.

"We haven't seen each other in so long." Kate didn't sound any different on the phone. "Could I drive out tomorrow, just for a little visit?"

Doris always believed that most of the time she did a pretty good job of not letting things get to her—not the messes, not the work, not the noise. But the thought of Kate Freeman coming to the farmhouse and seeing that she was no better off than Lorene when she'd moved in with their mom kept her awake most of the night. Before the earliest streaks of light appeared in the sky, she tiptoed out of their bedroom so she could put a batch of oatmeal raisin cookies in the oven and straighten the living room. At least Kate would see them at their best!

When she heard Kate tap on the door, her heart fluttered so hard she was afraid she might pass out right there in her own kitchen! Hanging her apron on a hook by the door, she smoothed the faded house dress she'd carefully ironed. She felt lucky that Debbie was napping, Dougie had fallen asleep during his last feeding, and Bill had gone into Rockwell to pick up some parts for the tractor and wouldn't be home until supper time.

"You boys be good while my friend is here," she warned Denny and David as they pushed their trucks and bulldozers around the living room.

The moment she set eyes on Kate, she realized with a pang what different worlds they had moved into. Kate looked like she'd stepped right off a poster with her shiny shoulder-length hair that turned under like Cheryl's used to. Someone at the college must have shown her how to put on makeup too. Surveying Kate's tailored navy blue coat, Doris thought of her own shabby pink jacket with the torn lining.

"Doris!" She felt like a seventh-grader again as Kate threw her arms around her then quickly lowered her voice. "Oh, oh—I don't want to wake any of the children." Setting a shopping bag on the floor and tossing her coat over the back of a kitchen chair, Kate added, "Look at you! Married with four kids and your own house. Oh, we have so much to catch up on!"

Feeling like a cow in the thin dress that couldn't begin to hide her bulk, she tried not to stare at Kate's tweed skirt and matching sweater set. She was embarrassed that her white dime-store socks seemed so wrong with her black ox-fords, while Kate's, double-rolled into perfect cuffs, looked just right with her brown-and-white saddle shoes. Again Doris' heart began to dance across her chest.

But Kate, just as sweet as she'd ever been, never seemed to notice their differences. Pulling four little packages from her bag, she said, "I brought something for the children. I hope they don't already have these."

Doris was so overwhelmed by her friend's kindness that she was afraid she was going to have to sit down. Kate had actually gone to the trouble to pick out a book for each of the kids. A book, for God's sake! She turned her head so Kate wouldn't see the tears in her eyes. After all, Bill never allowed her to spend money on silly stuff like books.

Denny and David were thrilled with their presents and were so taken with Kate that they fought over who could sit on her lap. Doris feared that they were headed for an ugly scene, but Kate just smiled and promised to hold both of them after she had finished visiting with their mother.

God, Doris thought, it was like a breath of fresh air to see her! Before they began to catch up, she told Kate how sorry she was that Gran had died the year before.

"I felt just terrible that I didn't get into Rockwell to the funeral home," she apologized. "But two of the kids was down with colds and fever. She was always so nice to all of us."

"And full of good sense," Kate added. "I still miss her. The house just isn't the same."

She tried not to bombard Kate with questions but couldn't rein in her curiosity. Kate answered them all with humor, saying that, yes, she liked college but, no, hadn't found a boyfriend yet. Kate told her that she'd met lots of nice people but would never have friends as close as the Fearless Four had been.

As they comfortably spoke of old times together, Doris was glad to have news to offer. She'd seen Mrs. Mulgrew at mass a few months ago and learned that Rosie had gone to California. But Rosie's mom had seemed sad and told her that she really felt like she'd lost Rosie when she'd decided to move in with Danny and Colleen for her last two years of high school. After Rosie left, Mrs. Mulgrew said she and Rosie's dad had gotten themselves a different house . . . with indoor plumbing, she'd added with a little smile. The big old place was just too full of painful memories.

"I hate it that we let Rosie drift away from us." Kate bit into a cookie and stopped. "These are really good." She took another bite. "I mean *really* good. You could sell them, Doris!"

"Yeah, in all my spare time," she chuckled, but Kate's compliment felt like cool mist on a hot summer day. "Ever hear anything about Cheryl?"

"Just a couple of days ago, actually." Kate sipped her coffee. "I ran into Russell Logan while I was shopping on Christmas Eve. He sees her at the U. of I. In fact, they're in some musical revue together next semester. Oh—and he mentioned she's going with a guy from Chicago's north shore. Someone who's really rich, Russell said."

"S'pose we'll ever all be together again—the four of us?" she asked as Kate reached for another cookie.

"I don't know where or when. Sounds like the song, doesn't it?" When Kate smiled, Doris realized how much she'd missed her, but she didn't know the song she was talking about. Tommy probably would, but Bill only played farm markets and music from Nashville on their little radio. "But I'd really like that," Kate added.

Doris was grateful for the fifteen minutes they had together before Debbie climbed out of her crib and padded into the kitchen whimpering and carrying her crusty "blankie." She had wanted Kate to see her little daughter in her one good dress with her hair brushed, not in Denny's old stained T-shirt that she wore every day.

"She's beautiful." Kate whispered, smart enough to let Debbie warm up to her. As Doris tried to pull a comb through her daughter's stubborn curls she heard Dougie— hungry again—screaming from the upstairs bedroom. Usually Debbie cried when Dougie demanded her attention, but now she was distracted by the packages that Kate took from her sack.

"Want to unwrap one for you and one for your baby brother?" Kate handed her a small square.

Debbie smiled shyly and took the gift. When Doris returned with Dougie in her arms, Kate was seated in the overstuffed chair beside their spindly Christmas tree in the living room. She had taken Debbie onto her lap and was reading one of the books she had brought. Denny was perched on one arm of the chair and David on the other. They never looked up when Doris came into the room.

"She's nice," David volunteered when Kate had finished reading.

"Our mom put this chair here to cover a big spot on the rug." Denny shared one of their family secrets with Kate. "She didn't want you to see it."

Doris felt herself blushing.

"We always did that at my house too," Kate laughed. "Remember, Doris, how we always kept that ugly green chair in the same weird place? Now you know why."

By the time Kate left, Doris didn't care that her old friend had sat in the sagging chair and walked on the chipped linoleum in their kitchen. Kate hadn't even cringed when Dougie spit up a whole feeding all over Doris' clean dress.

"You are so lucky to have such beautiful children." As Kate buttoned her coat Doris could tell she meant every word. "I can't imagine ever being so blessed. Actually, I can't imagine ever meeting 'Mr. Right,' the way you did."

Doris felt a lump rise in her throat at that remark. She guessed she'd gotten into the habit of thinking about what they didn't have, instead of being thankful for what they did have.

"I mean—you're living the dream. The one we all had, remember?" As Kate fixed her hazel eyes on hers, Doris knew that both of them were thinking of the times when all they talked about was what they wanted to do when they grew up.

Doris swallowed hard and nodded.

"Can she come back sometime?" David wondered.

"I really hope so!" Kate told him. "Think your mom would bake those good cookies again if I do?"

"Yeah!" Denny screamed.

"Yeah!" David echoed as they punched each other and ran off to the living room.

Debbie, her nose running, gave Kate a gooey kiss that Kate never even tried to wipe off. She's a good person, Doris thought. Like her dad.

She was grateful for the fun and laughter her friend brought into their house that day. But as she watched Kate cautiously back her parents' car down the lane, Doris thought with a sigh of relief: At least Kate left before "Mr. Right" got home and gave her a verbal whipping for not having supper started yet. She closed the door and went straight to the refrigerator to take out a package of hamburger to brown.

* * *

Chapter Seventeen

K ate's visit had whetted her appetite. During the frozen days of January Doris realized she was hungry for more—more for her children and more for herself. As she reflected on some of Kate's comments, she wondered if education and a love of learning could be the key to a better life. Vowing her kids would enjoy school more than she had, she asked Violet to come out to the farm and take them all to the Rockwell library twice a month. There she would pick out books for her kids and Violet would check them out on her card, since Doris wasn't a Rockwell resident.

She had to make sure Bill didn't get mad and toss the books aside. He was afraid they'd make her and the kids lazy. So she'd wait to read their stories at bedtime, after all the work was finished. The older three would pile into bed with her while she stroked Dougie's cheek with one hand and turned pages with the other. She also made up her mind that once a week she would sit and read a book to an individual child. She struggled to find the time but sensed that she needed to get to know each one.

They were all so different. Denny was special because he was the first and because he was charming—exactly like Bill when he'd courted Doris at Pete's. David tugged at her heartstrings because he reminded her so much of Tommy. Although he didn't show any musical talent, he had Tommy's sweetness and the ability to tune out the chaos that swirled around him. She marveled at David's ability to sit in his own little world while all hell was breaking loose and quietly assemble a barn or a windmill with the Tinker Toys that Violet had bought for him.

She was so proud of her beautiful little Debbie and didn't mind a bit that her daddy called her "Princess." Debbie had Bill's looks and knew exactly how to get whatever she wanted. Dougie had learned in his cradle that the only way to grab Doris' attention was to pitch a fit. When he grew old enough to toddle and Bill spanked him, he glared at his dad and came right back for more. Doris feared they were going to have to address Dougie's temper, but she didn't know how. And it sure didn't help any that Bill had given him the nickname of "Grumpy."

Most of the time she was just worn out. Something was missing in her life but she didn't know what in the world it was. She'd tried to act excited when Kate had called the last time she was home to tell her she was going to work for a newspaper in Indianapolis after graduation. Kate also mentioned that Russell Logan had said that Cheryl and her rich boyfriend had eloped several months ago. She was happy for both of her friends, but she still wanted more out of life. For herself!

Well, she lamented as the months sped by, you gotta be careful what you wish for, 'cause she got more, all right . . . lots more. When Denny was almost six and Dougie just two-and-a-half, she gave birth to Darcy. For the first time in her life, she delivered a baby in a hospital. She gritted her teeth as Bill forced their old truck through a March blizzard to get to Danville. Uttering every oath he knew, he cursed her for having to go to the hospital. Now, he fumed, he wouldn't have the money to trade in their ancient tractor on a newer used one. Never once did he acknowledge that this child was his too!

If only she hadn't passed out one day at the library, she

thought as they made their way over the slippery back roads. After Violet had revived her, she had taken Doris and the kids straight to Dr. Dawes' office and marched them in ahead of everyone else. Dr. Dawes had been really nice—not at all like Nancy and her mom. When he'd told her she had high blood pressure, he'd given her some sample pills and said she should go to the hospital to have the baby so she'd get the right care and a little rest.

"Hell, it's no wonder they call women the weaker sex." Bill had shattered a coffee cup against the kitchen wall when she'd given him the news him at supper that evening.

The children had sat, welded to their seats, until David whispered, "I'll help you pick up the pieces, Mommy."

Doris had wanted her own mother so much that night that she felt an ache like a hot lump of coal in the middle of her chest. She longed for a dose of Mom's common sense and the warmth of her loving arms around her, but her mother and Tommy had moved near Chicago the previous summer right after Violet and Spud Zylstra had gotten married. Charley had found work for Mom in his plant—a job that had good benefits and gave her the chance to sit down. And best of all, Tommy was studying with one of the finest piano teachers in all of Chicago, someone who was even trying to get a college music scholarship for him.

When Mom had told them they could have most of her furniture, Bill had grudgingly gone with her and hauled it out to the farm in his pickup truck. Now Denny and David slept in Vic and Charley's beds instead of a double mattress on the floor. Debbie was in Doris' old bed, and Dougie was using Tommy's cot. Doris was glad that her mother and Tommy were better off than they'd been in Rockwell, but every time she remembered they were so far away, she'd start whistling or something just to make herself stop thinking about it.

As she examined her newest baby with her tangle of light hair, Doris knew right away that Darcy was their biggest one yet, although they'd never weighed the others. She decided Darcy must favor Bill's sisters because all of them were big-boned. Bill seemed to be proud as punch of her.

"This one may be able to outwork her brothers," he boasted to one of the nurses.

But Dr. Dawes was concerned about her size. "Nine pounds and ten ounces is a lot of baby." He shook his head thoughtfully. "She's a beautiful, perfect girl. But I'm a little worried about your health, Doris. I think we should have some tests run."

"Me? I'm as strong as they come!" she protested.

The following day Dr. Dawes told her that she was mildly diabetic.

"With your sugar up and your high blood pressure, I'd advise you not to have any more babies," he cautioned. "These children need a healthy, happy mom."

She wept as she tried to absorb the fact that this would be her last baby. Wiping her eyes, she assured Dr. Dawes that they'd try to be careful.

But her husband, she knew, never really understood the meaning of the word 'careful,' except when it came to tending his farm machinery. Just fifteen months later, on a June morning filled with the scent of wild roses, she returned to the hospital and delivered Dirk Thomas one month early.

Scrawny and spindly, Dirk had a crop of black hair that must have made up half of his five pounds.

"I shouldn't have tried to help Bill get that ornery calf back inside the fence," she confessed to Dr. Dawes. "Then I probably would have carried the baby full term."

"He'll be okay. It'll just take him awhile to catch up."

Dr. Dawes pulled up a chair beside her bed. "Go get Bill," he instructed the nurse. "I want him to hear what I'm telling Doris."

Sullen and anxious to get back to the farm, Bill shuffled his feet at the end of the bed while Dr. Dawes said that he wanted Doris to stay long enough to have her tubes tied.

"Hey, this is my family, Doc—and you've got no right messing with us." Bill gave him the same threatening, narrow-eyed look that he used on Doris when she questioned the lengthy hours he'd been spending in town lately.

"It's a decision that you and Doris have to make together," Dr. Dawes agreed. "But if you want a wife who's dead before her twenty-sixth birthday and feel like raising those kids all by yourself, you do whatever you damn well please."

"Shit!" Bill's heavy boot kicked the nightstand so hard that her box of tissues fell to the floor. "Go ahead and do it then," he snarled. "This last one's so little, he prob'ly won't be good for much anyway."

Although she closed her eyes, Doris couldn't stop the tears that streamed down her face. She hoped that Dr. Dawes had left, then she felt the soft tissues against her cheek.

"It's for the best, Doris," her doctor assured her. "Believe me." He was quiet for a few moments, then said, "I wish my Nancy had your capacity to work. She seems to think the world owes her everything on a silver platter." He took her hand in his. "Violet's told me about you and what a good job you're doing with all of your children. But she's worried too."

"About me?" she croaked.

"About you. Believe me," he repeated. "This will be for the best. Violet will think so too."

She blew her nose long and hard.

"Your sister's a real gem, you know. One of a kind. But," he squeezed her hand and chuckled, "I wouldn't want to get on the wrong side of her!"

"Me neither." Doris smiled in spite of herself. Violet, she knew, would lay down her life for any of her brothers or sisters—well, maybe all except Lorene. "Thanks, Doc."

* * *

After Dirk began walking when he was eleven months old, Bill never called him anything but "Runt."

"Stop that!" Doris warned, her mouth full of clothespins. The spring breeze billowed the legs of Bill's jeans as she clamped them to the sagging line in their side yard. "You'll have him thinkin' he's worthless."

The look Bill gave her indicated that was exactly how he felt about their youngest child. Full of disdain, the expression was one that he wore almost continually. She actually anticipated his wrath a few days later when she announced that she needed the truck to go to the one-room schoolhouse for her scheduled end-of-the-year meeting with Denny and David's teacher.

Doris always looked forward to visiting with Imogene Macy. A veteran instructor who had taught Bill and all four of his sisters, Miss Macy was starting to show some white in the fat braid that she wrapped around her head. At first glance, anyone would have mistaken her for just another heavy-walking farm wife with her gap-toothed smile and ruddy round face. But Doris knew better. She had learned that Miss Macy's head contained more knowledge about kids and education than a lot of so-called experts would ever hope to have.

"I wish I had more students like your boys." As Miss Macy opened her record book and smiled, Doris tried to get comfortable on the metal folding chair in front of her desk. "You've given them a head start by reading to them."

"But how did you know—" She felt invaded, as if the teacher had been peeking through the windows of her house each evening.

"I can always tell." Miss Macy rose slowly from her desk, picked up a piece of chalk and wrote her name on the blackboard. "Those children who have been read to watch what I'm putting up on the blackboard—the way you did right now. But those who've never been read to just stare at *me*. It's one of those things I've learned over the years."

"We have stories every night." Twisting her handkerchief, Doris tried to hide her embarrassment as they discussed her precious private moments with her children. "I try—but it's hard with six. I do my best to read one story to each one ev'ry week. It's our special time together."

"It shows," Miss Macy beamed. "That Denny's a worker. He keeps at something until he gets it."

She grinned. His teacher had him pegged all right, she thought.

"It's David I want to talk with you about." She opened her bottom drawer and pulled out a stack of papers.

"David?" Doris could feel the sweat popping out on her forehead. Was he having trouble she didn't know about?

"Don't worry." Miss Macy took the papers and lined them up neatly across her desk. "Denny is doing well—but your David is exceptional. Look at these."

Trembling, Doris picked up one sheet, then another. Each bore a picture of a different flag and the name of the state it represented. At the bottom of each, in precise letters, was printed "David L."

"They're the flags of each state," Miss Macy explained to her. "He's traced them from our set of encyclopedias after he's finished his class work so he won't get bored while

I'm busy listening to the older students read aloud." Her deep blue eyes were excited. "In all my years of teaching, I've never seen anything like this."

"Is it a bad thing? I can make him stop." Inside, Doris was scolding herself for encouraging David's thirst for knowledge.

"Oh, my dear, no! It's a gift." Miss Macy's radiant smile was proof that she believed every word she was saying. "David has the ability to educate himself almost. In fact, it's going to hustle me to keep ahead of him. He could probably skip second grade and go into third in the fall. But I wouldn't want to do that without getting your approval."

Doris stared hard at the red and yellow flowers on her handkerchief as she tried to sort out the load of information that Miss Macy had just dropped on her. In her heart she'd always known that David was smarter than Denny. Back when he'd first started to talk, David would ask questions about everything, like he could figure things out better than Denny. God, she thought, he'd be the first kid in the Panczyk family ever to get double-promoted—and wouldn't her mom be proud! Suddenly, though, she had a second thought.

"But that would put him up with his brother—" She began to allow her fears to spill out, like cereal from a box that had been turned over on the counter.

"And you're afraid that might not be good for either boy. I know." Miss Macy sighed as the lines in her forehead deepened. "Let's try this." Searching Doris' face for approval, she said, "I'll give Denny and David extra work to do any time they can handle it. You'll notice that David's getting different assignments than the ones Denny's had in the past, but don't worry. I'll just be pushing him along to make him stretch that mind of his."

"I—I don't know what to say." She rolled her damp

235

handkerchief into a tight wad. "Their dad—he's a farmer, you know—and he don't—"

"Oh, my dear, you forget. I had Bill Lochschmidt in my classes. And his sisters." Miss Macy allowed her words to hang in the air until Doris found the courage to look her straight in the eye. "I knew their home situation. They had never been read to because their father had not permitted it. But they had been yelled at. Every one of them. Made to feel like nothing."

Doris could almost feel the sparks flying from the angry teacher as Miss Macy remembered. "Your Bill was only in second grade when he started belittling those girls—his older sisters, mind you." She covered her mouth, afraid she had said too much. "I'm sorry. I didn't mean to—"

Now Doris felt it was her turn to console. "No. No, Miss Macy, it's okay. I know Bill gets his ways from his dad. One of the neighbors told me." She smoothed out her handkerchief across her lap. "Bill's a farmer and there's nothin' wrong with that. I just want my kids to know more about—well, about the world. I'm glad—really glad you're watchin' out for 'em."

"You're a remarkable woman—and probably not even thirty-five quite yet. Did you graduate from Rockwell High?"

Doris turned away from the penetrating blue eyes, mortified that the teacher had misjudged her age by almost a decade! Did she look that old, she wondered? Struggling to push aside her bruised feelings, she mumbled, "No. I didn't graduate myself."

She squirmed in the chair as she felt the teacher's steady gaze cover every inch of her. "I probably should get home now," she added.

"Just one more thing." Miss Macy patted her hand. "You are a wonderful mother. I hope you know that."

"I-I love my kids. They're my whole world." She could feel herself blushing at the praise. No one had ever said such a thing to her.

"I look forward to teaching the rest of them," Miss Macy replied happily. Then her voice took on a softer, more confidential tone. "But what I'm going to say now is for you." Doris wanted to shrink from the gaze that pierced her like a sharp knife slicing through noodle dough, yet she found the strength to stare right back

"Someday, as your children grow up, you're going to want to finish your own education. There's so much you could do," the teacher told her.

"Aw, Miss Macy, I never was much good in school. All my friends got better grades than I did." She hung her head as she recalled straining her eyes to copy the answers from Kate's test paper back in seventh grade.

"There's a difference between grades and knowledge. You, my dear, have knowledge, and someday you'll be able to gather all that knowledge together and put it to work for you."

Doris folded her handkerchief and stuffed it into her pocketbook.

"That'll be a long time off, Miss Macy," she sighed as she started toward the door.

"Let me help—just a little. I have some things that I think you might like to read." Miss Macy chuckled, a deep, warm laugh. "In your free time, of course. But, seriously all you need is just a few moments each day."

"Well, some days that's pretty much impossible," she protested. "'Specially with the summer work in the fields comin' up and the cannin' to be done and all."

"I know. But I'll drop off some papers that I'd like for you to look at whenever you can." Doris felt warmed by the expression of love and compassion that Miss Macy fixed

237

on her. "You have a special time with each of your six children. But there are seven days in the week. Save some time on that seventh day for yourself."

Miss Macy's advice landed on Doris' ears with the crisp tone of a command rather than a suggestion. But as the years began to unfold, she realized that the teacher's words were some of the most important ones she would ever hear in her entire life.

* * *

Chapter Eighteen

"**I**f you think you're going into town every damn week for a night class, you've got another think coming!" Bill pushed back his chair in disgust, leaving part of his sausage and sauerkraut on his plate.

"Why are you mad, Daddy?" Debbie's spoon, filled with fresh peaches, dribbled juice onto the table as it hung in the air.

"I'm not mad, Princess. Just thinking about the farm and all the work we've gotta do to keep it going." He ran his fingers through his hair, now peppered with gray. "'Specially since I bought those extra hundred acres from our neighbor."

"But *we* help. All the time." Dougie, in his usual persistent way, wanted to make sure his efforts did not go unnoticed.

"Don't argue with me, Grumpy," Bill cut him off. "I need your mom here every minute of every day." He walked out, letting the screen door slam behind him.

"Where are you goin'?" Trying to remain calm, Doris followed him out on the porch. The leaden August air took her breath for a moment. A storm was brewing for sure.

"Over to Gibson City. Need to talk with a guy about rotating next year's crops." He never looked up as he worked his toothpick up and down one side of his mouth. "Don't wait up."

She watched as he revved up the engine of his pickup and left a trail of dust as the truck roared down the lane.

Coming home late at night had become a habit. Crawling
into bed and not fooling around had become a habit. She
didn't much care about either. But making fun of her in
front of the kids had become a habit that he relished every
day, mostly because he knew how much it wounded her on
the inside. That was the habit that shamed her more than
anything.

"I'm damned if Bill Lochschmidt is gonna get the best
of me," she muttered. Ever since Miss Macy had come to
their house six weeks ago to drop off the materials showing
how Doris could get her high-school diploma, she had felt a
little rush of excitement whenever she thought about it.
She'd talk with Violet. Right away. Somehow, between the
two of them, she bet they could think of a way for her to
take at least one class when school started in two weeks

"C'mon, kids, let's get this kitchen cleaned up." She
opened the freezer door and counted the frozen little tubes
in their colorful wrappers. Good, she thought. There were
just enough. "Then we'll all take a popsicle outside and
watch the stars come out. I got a chart at the library so we
can find the Big Dipper and the Little Dipper."

"Anna Baby Dipper too?" Darcy asked. All the rest
laughed.

Doris smiled, savoring the lightness of the moment. In
fact, she realized, when she and the kids were home alone,
they didn't have many bad ones. It was just when Bill came
in and stirred the pot that everyone got all riled up. Sometimes, when she was mending or driving the tractor through
the rows of soybeans, she'd try to put her finger on the time
when things had started to go bad between the two of them.
She knew she wasn't foolish enough to think that they'd be
able to hang onto that red-hot level of romance they'd
shared that first summer. But never had she dreamed that
Bill could cut her into little pieces by the way he talked to

her. She'd have rather had a whipping!

When she'd think about how tender Bill had been when they started going together and how he'd changed, she'd have to stop and wipe her eyes with the sleeve of her shirt. Way back, when she was pregnant with Denny, Bill liked to tease her about her weight gain and how different her cooking was from his mom's. But after David had been born, he'd stopped smiling when he criticized her; and, lately, he'd been downright mean. Maybe he was smarting from losing last year's wheat crop to the string of freaky thunderstorms. Or maybe he was second-guessing his decision to buy that extra ground. Whatever was eating on him sure made life tense for all of them around the supper table.

She couldn't even remember when he'd last called her by her given name. He'd just yell out, "Hey, Woman!" or, worse yet, "Hey, Lardo!" and then glance around like an ornery schoolboy to see if the kids thought he was cute. Usually they all just stared down at their shoes when he did that. In fact, he had a nickname for everyone but Denny and David. She didn't mind that he used "Princess" for Debbie, but it really burned her up when he called the three younger children "Grumpy," "Blubber" and "Runt." And Bill knew it.

The other thing about Bill that had begun to bug her was the huge amount of time he was spending away from home. It had been years since the two of them had gone to Pete's for pie and coffee, but Bill hardly ever went into Rockwell anymore. Lately he'd started using a grain elevator and supplier over at Gibson City, eighteen miles west of their farm. He said that the old Freeman codgers in Rockwell weren't keeping up with the times and he got better service in Gibson City. She didn't learn until later that he liked to loiter at a little diner at the edge of town where he could flirt with a waitress named Flossieann who wasn't even a senior in high school and was looking for a ticket out of town.

With Violet's help, she took a stand against Bill for the first time in her life.

"I'll just come out and stay with the kids on the night when you have class, then you can drive my car into town," her sister volunteered. When she stuck out her lower lip determinedly, Doris knew Violet was digging in her heels. "And if Bill gets mad, he can just get mad. I don't think he wants to tangle with me!"

During the next weeks Denny, David and Debbie all thought it was funny that Mom had homework, but Bill didn't find it so humorous. He'd just warn her not to stay up so late that she couldn't do the milking the next morning. Then he'd take off for Gibson City.

Going against Bill's wishes seemed to give Doris a new burst of energy. Never before had she loved school, just for the sake of soaking up new information. When she'd been younger and had to go, being in class meant giggling and passing notes with Rosie, Kate and Cheryl. Now she studied hard and made a point of posting her "A" in general math and "B+" in basic English on the refrigerator door, along with the kids' papers. Bill sneered about her "worthless waste of time," but she was proud of her progress and was determined to show everyone that she was just as smart as her children.

She tried to hide her exhaustion, but the work was endless. She'd get up early to fix breakfast for the four older kids and see them onto the school bus, then she'd zip Darcy and Dirk into their jackets so they could trail after her in the barn while she milked and gathered eggs. Bill picked corn and took it to the elevator; she canned the fall tomatoes and made ketchup. But, somewhere along the line, they'd lost the joy of celebrating their efforts at the end of the day.

"Hell, Woman, is that the best you can put on a plate for supper?" he snarled one evening as they sat down to a big kettle of ham and soup beans.

"It's the best I can do with what I have to spend on groceries." She picked up Dirk's spoon from the floor and wiped it on her apron.

"Scotty Schroeder threw up today at recess and had to go home." Debbie poked a forkful of beans into her mouth.

"That's enough, Princess." Turning pale, Bill silenced her. Inside, however, Doris was smiling because she knew Debbie had upset his queasy stomach.

"Yeah. All over the swings." David spread a chunk of butter over the top of his bread.

"Goddammit! I said that's enough!" Bill stood up so fast his chair fell over. "How do you expect me to eat when you're talking about shit like that?"

"Language, Bill," she reminded him evenly. Early in their marriage they had pledged not to swear around their children. Challenged, Doris had been forced to clean up her vocabulary as she weeded out the expressions she had learned from her parents. She'd never given her profanity a single thought, but now that *she'd* made the effort, she sure as hell didn't want him saying bad stuff in front of their family.

He righted his chair and picked at his food while the rest of them finished their meal. Only the sound of little Dirk's chuckles as he blew bubbles in his cup of milk broke the fearful silence in their kitchen.

One night just after Halloween Violet arrived early.

"Whew!" She wiped her shoes before she stepped into the kitchen. "This wind's gonna shake all the leaves off the trees before the first snowfall!" She tossed her old jacket on the back of a chair. "I met Bill comin' down the lane.

Where's he headed?"

"Somewhere. Who knows? Gibson City probably." Doris hung her apron on a hook and began to gather her books together.

"Hey, kiddo. Come here and sit down a minute before you go." Violet's voice was unusually soft. She scooped Dirk onto her lap. "Denny, set up the Chinese checkers in the living room—and make sure Darcy's not puttin' the marbles in her mouth."

Realizing it was hard for her to defy her big sister, Doris did as she was told. "Spud—well, you know Spud's been over at Gibson City a lot lately too." Violet seemed a little flustered. "Been talkin' with that guy about a big contract for trash pickup. And it's lookin' pretty good." She grinned. "Even as hard as *you* work, you'd have a rough time keepin' up with Spud." Her pride showed as she spoke of her husband.

"I know—"

"But that's not what I wanted to say." When Violet trained a direct look at her, Doris knew that whatever was coming would be the truth. Her big sister had never been one to mince words. "I hate to be the one to tell you this, kiddo, but I'm goin' do it and I'm goin' do it real fast." Taking a deep breath, she made her announcement, short and simple. "Bill's foolin' around with some young girl over there at Gibson City."

Although she was sitting down, Doris grabbed the edge of the table to steady herself. In the swirl of mental pictures that rushed before her, she saw Bill's truck leaving the farm day after day and coming home late at night. Her deepest suspicions had just been confirmed.

"That sonofabitch," she murmured, forgetting that Dirk was within earshot.

In a brief account, Violet told her how Spud had seen

244

Bill in a corner booth at a diner one night when he'd stopped in for coffee. Bill hadn't spotted him, but Spud had been smart. He'd started asking around at different places about a girl named Flossieann and had learned from other guys in Gibson City that she'd had a string of hot romances with older boys when she was fourteen and fifteen. But now that she was sixteen, she was ready for the "big leagues," as one fellow put it, because she had a farmer from Bakers Corners wrapped around her little finger. In the several months that they'd been seeing each other, she had bragged about the locket and expensive perfume that he'd given her. No wonder he hadn't had the money to replace the kitchen linoleum at home. And no wonder, Doris thought ruefully, he'd been leaving her alone when he came to bed!

"And he's worried about me bein' gone one night a week. For *school*!" She pounded the table with her fist so hard that Dirk began to cry.

"Oh, honey, it's okay." She lifted her youngest from Violet's lap and cuddled him close. Sprinkling a few Cheerios into the palm of her hand, she let him pick them up and pop them into his mouth. Even at that moment, in the wake of Violet's revelation, she asked herself the question she often did when she had one of the children all to herself: Do I love this one best?

"God, I hate this. But I had to let you know." Violet's voice was rough with emotion. "I could just wring his neck. Nobody—I mean nobody—hurts my little sister!"

"Thanks—well, thanks for havin' the guts to tell me." She placed Dirk back in Violet's outstretched arms. "I've gotta get goin' to class. Somehow, I'm gonna be okay. I've just gotta make sure the kids will be."

On the way into town, Doris struggled to keep Violet's car on the road. The wind rocked the old Plymouth so hard that she gripped the steering wheel and peered through the sheets of rain that smacked against the windshield. "Now you know, now you know," the wipers seemed to chant as they scraped the glass clean.

She had guessed, but she had not known. Not for sure. She searched her memory for another time when she had heard that phrase used with great sadness. At last she had it—the first night when Rosie, Kate and she had stayed at Cheryl's and shared the best and worst days of their lives.

"My worst is just never knowing—well, when Bertie's coming home. It's the *not* knowing that's so hard," Cheryl had confessed. Eventually she had been forced to face the fact that her dad had been skimming funds from the car dealership. Their sudden move from Rockwell must have been a terrible blow to Cheryl. Especially when she knew he had used most of the money to buy nice things for her mom and her. Doris thought of the few letters she'd received from Cheryl, but they'd never mentioned the pain of discovering her dad was a common thief. After Doris had married Bill, she stopped writing to Cheryl, and the two gradually lost track of each other.

Pulling Violet's car into a space in front of Rockwell High, she wrapped a scarf around her head to try to keep dry. Cheryl had been right, she thought. It is the *not* knowing that's hard to handle. Somehow, now that she knew the truth about Bill, she'd find a way to cope. And, someday, he would be oh, so sorry! She welcomed the splatters of rain on her face as she ran into the building.

* * *

For weeks she never hinted to Bill that she knew about the girl in Gibson City. Instead, she concentrated on laying her groundwork. In the back of her underwear drawer, she kept all her extra grocery money and the cash she earned selling a few eggs. She might need it sometime; she just hadn't decided when.

Right after Halloween Bill dropped a bombshell at supper when he told the kids that they didn't need to ask Santa for anything that year. With taxes going up and the price of corn going down, he'd gotten caught in the middle, he explained.

"But Santa don't need money. He makes his own toys." Dougie's eyes narrowed as he questioned his dad.

"Santa's comin'," Darcy chirped while Bill lowered his head and scooped his stew against a piece of bread.

"God, Woman, this food's hardly fit to feed the pigs." He shoved his plate aside. "And you can forget about taking any more school this winter. Costs too damn much."

Quietly she placed her fork on her plate and stared at him. Avoiding her gaze, he left his meal unfinished, grabbed his jacket and slammed the door behind him.

"Finish your suppers." She passed the bread around for seconds.

"Tastes real good, Mom," David assured her as he reached over to finish his father's portion.

Two nights later, when Violet arrived, Doris told her about Bill's outburst.

"Don't you worry none, kiddo. I got somethin' else for you to think about." Plucking Dirk from his high chair, she waltzed him around the kitchen. "Dr. Dawes and some of his friends—well, they're havin' parties like crazy this year and want me to cater 'em. I'm goin' to need some help. And," she added breathlessly, "they're payin' real good."

"But how—"

"Oh, Spud'll come out and watch the kids while you help me. He's already said he would." She set Dirk on the floor and, with a love pat, sent him off to join the other children in the living room. "It's a shame that the mumps went down on Spud when he was fifteen and we can't have kids. But we love yours like they was our very own. You know that."

The timing was perfect. Since there were no crops to tend and no canning to do, Doris realized she could go to Violet's and help her make platters of cut-up vegetables and different kinds of dip while Spud watched the kids and Bill was off doing whatever. In fact, Bill hardly noticed she was gone; and when he did, he assumed she was doing chores or running errands. He never cared enough to ask.

At Violet's, she loved studying the pictures of food that her sister had cut out of magazines. She practiced so that she could curl carrot slices and carve little flowers out of radishes and rejoiced when they arranged the food into attractive arrangements on platters that Violet had picked up at a flea market. Sometimes, when they made big kettles of barbecued pork and tubfuls of potato salad, they laughed over nothing—just the way she had done with Rosie, Kate and Cheryl. God, she thought, that was centuries ago in another life. Violet liked to play records by a new singer named Elvis Presley. Together they swished around the kitchen like a couple of teenagers as they worked.

Doris couldn't believe that she was starting to feel almost young again. Better yet, she felt almost rich! With the money she made she was able to buy a decent toy for each of the kids and, thanks to Dr. Dawes' generous tip of fifty dollars, still had plenty left over to stash away in her "hope jar."

Christmas was good in the farmhouse that year. The only flaw was that Bill stayed home and everyone was walking on eggshells all day. But the smiles on her children's faces and the secret knowledge that she herself had made them possible gave her the feeling that she had accomplished something on her own for the very first time in her life.

***

Chapter Nineteen

After the glow of the Christmas of 1961 had worn off, Doris noticed that the smiles at their house were as scarce as hen's eggs during a cold snap. Bill paced like a caged animal while he was home, always searching for someone to pick on. When he continued to torment the younger children with his cruel nicknames, Dougie became even harder to handle. Dirk, as young as he was, soon learned that if he avoided his dad, he wouldn't have to answer to the name of "Runt." Even Darcy, who adored her father, shrank from Bill when he patted her on the fanny and called her "Blubber."

As tense as the atmosphere was when Bill was home, Doris felt it was thickening when he was away. Denny, who was a few weeks shy of his tenth birthday, seemed to think it was his responsibility to take over for his dad when Bill was gone.

"You stop callin' the little kids those awful nicknames," Doris chided him one evening in March when the two of them were in the barn alone.

"Dad does it." He shrugged.

"But it hurts their feelings. You can see that." She stopped squeezing the cow's udder long enough to look at him.

"They just gotta toughen up." Standing the pitchfork in the corner by the door, he flashed Bill's crooked grin at her and swaggered out. "Even you oughtta be able to see that," he smirked over his shoulder.

She felt as if he had just snapped a whip across her face. Stung and stung badly, she tried not to take out her anger on Clara, who shifted uneasily as Doris squirted the rest of the milk into the pail. Even their aging cow, it seemed, sensed that Denny was acting like a big shot and was pushing her to her limit.

Two days before Denny's birthday she hummed to herself as she parked Spud's truck by the farmhouse. Although she was late, she felt good about the twenty dollars she'd just earned helping Violet cater a spring luncheon for Mrs. Dawes. Spud had volunteered to come out and watch the kids—a setup that she knew Bill disliked but wasn't sure how to handle.

"Hell, Woman, where you been?" Bill's squinty little eyes reminded her of an old sow that's gone mean.

"Oh, just helping Violet. Hi, boys!" Denny and David shielded their eyes from the sun as they stood beside their father. She jumped down from the truck, brushed by a row of straggly tulips and headed for the house.

"Oh, yeah? What about us? Don't our farm count for nothin'?" Bill twisted her arm as he grabbed her. "We've sure got plenty of work around here that you could be doing!"

She stopped and stared in disbelief, first at him and then at the boys.

"You—you know how much this place means to me," she stammered angrily. "I'm goin' inside to start supper."

"Make sure it's worth eating!" he yelled.

When she heard Denny snickering at his father, she couldn't stem the flow of tears. She'd felt so proud of the beautiful lunch that she and Violet had presented that afternoon, but Bill could sap away a person's joy quicker than anyone she knew. Wiping her face on her shoulder, she tried not to let Spud see how upset she was when she entered the kitchen.

Although he was kind enough not to say anything, she could see his face had turned ruddy all the way back to the strip of hair that encircled his head. Instead, he made an announcement.

"I think me'n Violet are going to move pretty soon." His tone was as flat as if he was talking about the weather. He handed Darcy and Dirk a few saltine crackers.

"Move?" Her heart stopped. "Violet didn't say—"

"That's cause I asked her not to. Just yet." He popped a cracker into his mouth, chewed it thoughtfully and swallowed it. "We put a bid in on the old Raney home—and it looks like we're gonna get it." His brown eyes searched hers for approval.

"That huge house at the edge of town?" She could picture it—a two-story yellow place with five or six bedrooms at the east end of the Sweet Briar side of the tracks. "What do you want with all that room?"

"It's a good house. Well built. Got real nice woodwork—chestnut, actually. You know how I like to fix things up." He hummed to himself as he reached for a few more saltines. "I'll probably remodel it some, then sell it and make a profit."

"Wow!" She lowered herself onto a chair. Wait till Mom hears about this, she thought. She's gonna wonder if Spud and Violet have flipped!

"That's great, Spud." She forced enthusiasm into her voice as she dug out her iron skillet and began to stir up some hamburger for sloppy joes. The truth was that she was still smarting from Bill's way of welcoming her home and the humiliation he had heaped on her in front of the boys.

"Doris." The serious tone in Spud's voice caused her to turn around. "Someday you may not want to stay here anymore." Slowly he straightened the kitchen chairs around the table, then looked her straight in the eye. "If that time comes, you know me 'n Violet will have room for you and the kids."

Automatically turning off the burner, she wondered if she had heard him right. As she searched his face for an answer, she tried to find the right words for her question. "Are you sayin'—"

"You know what I'm saying." Carefully he brushed some cracker crumbs off the front of his blue denim work shirt into his palm and dropped them in the sink. "Every time I come out here I worry a little more about these kids. The younger ones—well, they're still just babies. But we all know Dougie can't control his temper and David seems kinda like he's just turning off from people and crawling inside himself. Denny idolizes his dad, and he's going to be just like him if we don't watch out."

Doris gripped the side of the stove. Spud was actually voicing every worry she'd had about the kids, like he'd been snooping inside her head. She was worried sick about each one of them, but no matter how hard she tried, nothing seemed to work. With just a few cutting words, Bill could erase her greatest efforts. She was losing control of her family. And she knew it.

"The kids, Doris." Spud spoke gently as he opened the door. "They're too good to waste."

Two weeks after Denny's birthday, Bill announced after supper that he was going to spend three days at a farm implement auction down at Springfield.

"I'm taking the truck over to Gibson City day after tomorrow and picking up a guy. So if you need something from town, you'd better stock up before I leave 'cause you won't be going anywhere."

"Won't you be here for our school program?" David

stopped sweeping the kitchen floor, his shoulders drooping as he leaned on the broom handle.

"Nope." Bill slid a toothpick between his teeth as he studied the big calendar that hung on the wall by the door.

"But I-I might get an award," David pleaded. "Miss Macy said we should have all our family—"

"Hell, David, the day I left that school Miss Macy probably went out dancin' and drinkin', she was so glad to get rid of me. She won't miss me, believe me."

"But *I* will—"

The sound of the slamming door muted David's protest. He stared after his father, then furiously attacked the dirt on the floor.

Doris was relieved that everything went so smoothly the first night Bill was away. After a relaxed supper together, she and the children walked the mile to the school for the program. She was proud when Denny received a certificate for "Most Improved in Spelling" but clapped loud enough for two parents when David was honored as "Best Student" in third-grade language and math. On the second night, however, the mood grew dark the moment she put supper on the table.

"Stew again?" Debbie questioned. "I wish just once that we'd have our food not all mooshed together. You know," she drew a line across her plate, "like the meat here and the potatoes over there like some people do."

"Stew? Is that what you call this garbage?" Using the same sarcastic tone as his dad, Denny winked at his brothers and sisters.

"Shut up!" Dougie snapped. "I think it's good."

"You're so grumpy and grouchy, you'd prob'ly eat anything," Denny goaded him.

"That is enough!" Pounding her fist on the table, Doris stood up and glared at each one of them. "The next one that

254

says a mean word goes to your room. With no more to eat tonight!"

"That'd sure be a big loss." Denny smirked as he smeared his stew around his plate.

The room grew quiet. Even Dirk stopped eating. Doris could feel herself slipping over the edge.

"That's it. You go to your room right now, Denzil William. Right now! Do you hear me?" She was shocked to her own voice screeching like chalk on a blackboard.

"I *don't* have to go anywhere. But I *am* goin' outside." He narrowed his eyes at her. "And when Dad gets back, I'm tellin' him you was a bitch and tried to make us eat your god-awful stew. You know what he'll say?" He grinned as he glanced around the table for support. "He'll just say, 'So what else is new with old Lardo?'"

Oh, my god, she realized, he sounds exactly like Bill. As Denny closed the door behind him, she could feel beads of sweat popping out on her forehead. Without taking another bite, she marched to the phone, as she'd known all along she would do one day, and called Violet. Spud answered.

"Spud?" She tried to keep her voice from quivering. "It's time. Bring your truck out right now and get us."

"I've been wondering what was taking you so long," was his response. "Be there in fifteen minutes.

In only three hours, they packed up ten years of living. Violet came in her station wagon and drove Darcy, Dirk and a load of clothes to her house, then asked her neighbor to stay with them while she returned to help. Denny's jaws were clenched as he helped Spud load the beds into the back of the truck. Doris wondered what Spud had said to her oldest son to make him shut up and mind. Whatever it was, it worked!

They labored in such a frenzy that she never once

thought of her normal chores. As they started to leave, she saw the barn.

"Oh, my god—the animals!" Jumping out of Violet's station wagon, she ran into the house to call Bessie Yoder to ask her if she and Leon could do the milking and feeding till Bill returned. "He'll be back by noon tomorrow." Doris' voice cracked. "Me'n the kids—well, we're goin' to have to leave."

"I know," Bessie answered calmly, like she'd been waiting for that call for a long time. God, Doris wondered, am I the dumbest one around?

Before she left, she made one last sweeping glance around the kitchen. The supper stew was now stuck fast to the plates that were scattered on the table. She smiled. Bill would either have to clean them up or he'd be so mad he'd just throw them at the wall. Then he'd really have a mess. She took time to scribble a note:

We'll be at Violet's from now on. All of us.
D.

When they arrived at Spud and Violet's, they didn't take time to unload everything. Spud threw the mattresses on the floor, and, exhausted, the children collapsed on them and fell asleep instantly. Only Doris remained awake, her heart in her throat. While she was reeling from the finality of her actions that night, she kept asking herself the same question: "What the hell am I going to do?" She had no money except the $781.38 in her "hope jar," no high-school diploma, and six kids to raise.

Maybe, she thought drowsily, she wouldn't have to worry. Maybe Bill would just come back and kill her and then he'd have to take over. She recalled that first summer when he'd take her out after work and they'd sit in his truck listening to country sounds. How could the same guy who'd been so sweet and tender back then turn into such a monster now? Just two weeks ago he'd come in late, had shaken her till she awakened, and had forced himself on her. Then he'd muttered some nasty words under his breath before he fell asleep. She'd laid awake a long time that night too, feeling used and pretty much good-for-nothing.

She tried to remember happier times, but Denny's sassiness seemed to override everything else. It was her *child's* words and tone, she realized, that had made the difference. Not the backbreaking work. Not ever having a little extra money to spend on the kids. Not even the way Bill treated her so she'd understand just how worthless she'd become. Nope, she thought, it wasn't none of those things. It was Denny, her firstborn who she loved more than she could ever tell him, talking to her like she was one of the hogs on the farm . . . or less. He'd sounded exactly like his dad.

Well, she'd gone and done it now. And she was good and scared. Punching her pillow so she could get more comfortable, she wondered what her mom would say. She tried to repeat the Twenty-Third Psalm but kept interrupting herself with one looming question: How will I get by? The only thing she knew for sure was that she'd take the older kids to Sweet Briar the very next morning so they could finish the school year there.

Somehow that plan comforted her as she pictured her kids sitting in the same rooms where she'd gone to school with Rosie, Kate and Cheryl. Oh, my god, she thought, those had been good times!

A sweet April breeze wafted through the window, soothing her at last. Bill could never hurt her again, she reassured herself. That pain was behind her now. She'd already taken one giant step into her new life by moving out that night. The next day she would take another one when she escorted her children into Sweet Briar. That felt like the right thing to do. Still, the last thought that flitted across her mind before a heavy sleep pulled her under was, "I hope it's not too late to save Denny."

* * *

Part Two: Cheryl

1963 - 1974

Chapter Twenty

"It's not too late. Honest, Sugar, I promise. Never again."

Her husband's voice was muffled as he pulled the lipstick-smeared shirt over his head and poked through the closet for a clean one.

Cheryl folded her arms in disgust as she watched him fumble with the buttons on his clean shirt. Already late for work in his father's office, Jamie once again had failed to come home the previous night.

"You say that every time." She spat out the words. "Every damn time!" The tone of her voice caused Jamie to pause, one leg in and one leg out of his dark gray trousers. As he looked at her, she searched his deep blue eyes until, finally, he squirmed and began to shove his other leg into his suit pants. Always before, when Jamie had begged for forgiveness, she had sighed and given in.

Even today, after all the rough times they had weathered, she knew she would have to be careful. His blond handsomeness and charming grin had hooked her the first night she'd met him at the Phi Delt house in Champaign eight years ago, and she'd been a sucker for them ever since.

Eight years! Had she known him only eight years, she wondered as she left him sorting through his vast collection of expensive ties to stroll over to the window of their brownstone apartment on Bellevue. Gazing down at the Gold Coast setting she had grown to love, she thought:

Lordy, here I am, about to make the gutsiest move of my entire life, and I'm not even scared! The only thing that gnawed at her confidence was the prospect of fighting the Loneliness again.

She doubted that any of her old friends in Rockwell had ever suspected that she might be lonely. After all, she'd never felt that way when she was with them. It was when she was at home that the tiny hollow inside her would swell until she was afraid it might engulf her and no one would ever see her again. All she'd ever wanted was for Bertie and Lila to spend time with her—but Bertie was usually down at Rigoni's, and Lila was totally absorbed with her radio programs and magazines. She had longed for Bertie to do something with her, the way Mr. Freeman played the piano with Kate, or for Lila to push up her sleeves so the two of them could roll out noodles like Mrs. Panczyk and Doris. Most of all, she'd yearned for a brother who'd tease her the way Mike Mulgrew tormented Rosie. But then, she'd realized at the end of eighth grade, there's the pain that goes with losing someone like Mike that can ruin you forever.

After failing to knot his navy tie with the red flecks, Jamie approached her for help. Mechanically, she firmed and tightened it, then smoothed it over the crisp white shirt that camouflaged his growing bulge around the middle. He gave her an appreciative wink, obviously assured that he would be forgiven for yet another frolic with a girl he'd met on Rush Street.

Barefoot, he sauntered over to the cookie jar and lifted out three Oreos. Cheryl rolled her eyes, disgusted to think he was stuffing cookies into his mouth before he went to work. Maybe his growing paunch wasn't strictly a beer gut, she thought. If he wasn't careful, nobody would give him a second look. She wished he would stop nibbling at the dark chocolate long enough to take her seriously.

Turning back to the window, she sighed as she watched four girls in school uniforms giggle as they approached the corner on the sidewalk below. She'd had friends like that once—and she'd never been lonely when she was with them. In fact, she'd known that deep down they actually envied her. Kate would have killed to have a collection of popular records like hers, Doris would have personally hauled away their living room sectional to replace her own sagging sofa, and Rosie would have grabbed Cheryl's clothes in a heartbeat if she could have fit into them. She smiled ruefully as she recalled that Bertie always bought the best for his family. Still, there had been those empty moments at home when the best didn't mean a thing and the little hollow of Loneliness would begin to grow.

That's when she would escape to the hi-fi and count on Judy Garland or Dinah Shore to fill the void. Later, after they'd moved to Decatur and the Loneliness threatened to swallow her whole, her closest companions had become Jo Stafford, Rosemary Clooney and Doris Day.

For weeks after they'd left Rockwell, she couldn't believe that their move might be permanent. Bertie had found them a furnished apartment with one bedroom in an old house and told her she could sleep on the couch for awhile. He'd confessed that he'd hit a bad patch down at Adler's Ford-Mercury because he'd borrowed a little money from the cash register now and then. When he'd hung his head forlornly, she'd put her arms around him and comforted him. But, inside, she had felt the Loneliness begin to pump up like a bicycle tire.

Now she battled that same feeling again. She'd forgiven her dad back then and she'd forgiven her husband plenty of times over the years. In fact, Jamie almost had grown to expect it.

"Come on," he coaxed, brushing the back of her neck

with his lips. "Give me a little kiss to get me through the day."

"What do you know about getting through the day?" Repulsed, she pulled away. No one—not even Jamie—had ever imagined how hard it had been for her to get through every day after Bertie had moved them to Decatur. Still, she'd been lucky that her choral teacher had encouraged her to sign up for the girls' choir right away. Before long, she'd won starring roles in the high-school musicals. No, she'd never found close friends like she'd had at Sweet Briar, but her singing had kept the Loneliness at bay most of the time. When she'd received a scholarship at the University of Illinois to study music education, she'd secretly hoped she could avoid teaching and become the next Kay Starr or Patti Page.

She'd discovered all kinds of opportunities to sing in college. During her sophomore year, when she'd had one of the four leads in the spring production of *Good News,* she'd been surprised to bump into Russell Logan from Rockwell. He'd chuckled when he said he was majoring in accounting but still had enough "ham" in him to want to be part of the show chorus. As they'd sipped Cokes after rehearsal, he'd mentioned that Kate was attending Butler and Doris was married to a farmer and already had several kids. The only thing he'd told her about Rosie was that she had gotten mixed up with a wild crowd in high school and had left for California soon after graduation. Russell's news of her old friends had made her wistful for their companionship and she'd wished, at that moment, that she had done a better job of keeping in touch with them.

During rehearsal a few days later, she and Russell had been amused by the antics of another cast member, Shep Bartlett. A wiry, nimble fellow who reminded her of a leprechaun, he'd invited her to his Phi Delt party the next week. It was there that Shep had introduced her to his high-school friend from Wilmette, Jamison Trent Foxwell IV.

When she'd first seen "Jamie" Foxwell, he'd been lean-ing against the grand piano in the Phi Delt living room. With his streaked blond hair, gray tweed sport coat and dress shirt open at the collar, he'd looked like Tab Hunter. And, when he'd grinned slowly at her, his blue eyes crin-kled at the corners.

"Jamie, this is my friend Cheryl. From the show." Shep had nudged her toward Jamie. "You two talk for a minute while I get us something to drink."

"Hi, Cheryl-from-the-show." Jamie had taken her hand in his and held it slightly longer than necessary. When Ja-mie had told Shep he was going to whirl her around the dance floor, her knees had trembled at the thought of shar-ing the same space with this Greek god.

"Just once," he'd promised.

And he had. Just once. But as The Four Freshmen crooned "It's a Blue World," it had taken just once for Cheryl to realize how perfectly she fit into his arms. She'd felt as if he'd placed her gently on a cloud when he'd deliv-ered her to Shep's side and strolled off to join a group of his fraternity brothers.

"He'll call you next week." Shep had licked the foam from his upper lip. "Happens every time."

"Oh, don't be silly." She'd punched him playfully. "Af-ter all, I came here with you."

"It's okay. Like I said, it happens all the time." Shep had drained his glass. "Want another one?"

She'd declined, amazed at Shep's capacity to hold his liquor and fascinated by his attitude toward his friend. The following week, when Jamie had indeed called, she also had been impressed with Shep's ability to predict the fu-ture.

Now she regretted that she hadn't asked Shep for some long-term advice. Once again, as she saw her husband swipe one more cookie from the jar, she decided that no one—not even a fortune-teller—could have foreseen the mountains that she and Jamie would climb together before they slipped into the deepest of valleys.

From her window, if she tilted her head just right, she could see a scrap of Lake Michigan beyond Bellvue. A sailboat skimmed across the blue ribbon, then slipped behind the buildings on Michigan Avenue. She recalled that first summer after they'd met. She'd clerked at the shoe store in Decatur where Bertie had become assistant manager, but every weekend Jamie had provided her with a train ticket to Chicago. He'd picked her up at Dearborn Station in his yellow Buick convertible and whisked her up the Outer Drive to his parents' home in Wilmette. For the first time in her life, Cheryl had realized there were people who had even more money than Nancy Dawes and her family.

She'd learned that the Foxwell fortune had come from the meat-packing business that Jamie's grandfather had started years ago. But, Jamie had explained in a bored tone, the family had "diversified its investments" and now owned a major share of one of Chicago's biggest banks as well as one of its newspapers. She'd hardly been able to comprehend that kind of wealth after she, Bertie and Lila had been forced to stretch a can of Campbell's soup into an entire meal for the three of them after they settled in Decatur.

She'd almost expected to see Elizabeth Taylor at the parties she'd attended with Jamie that summer. The splashy events at a friend's mansion or private club, had been straight out of *A Place in the Sun*. She'd tried not to stare as well-dressed ladies nursed something called a sloe gin fizz and silver-haired men ordered scotch on the rocks. She'd never been able to get used to the taste of the free-flowing liquor and often dumped her own cocktail into a potted plant when no one was looking.

"Remember all the fun we had out there on the 'Foxy Lady'?" Jamie now slid his arm around her, obviously aware that she was reminiscing about their evenings on his family's yacht. "We can do that again next summer. Just the two of us. I promise."

She grimaced as Jamie made yet another promise to her. She wished that they could recapture that first summer when Jamie had grown tired of the parties and had shown her Chicago from its waterfront. She'd loved sailing up and down the shoreline, admiring the sun as it dipped behind the Prudential building.

"You just about drove me crazy that summer," he murmured. "I'll never know why you felt we should wait to—well, you know—until we were married."

Sliding out from under his grasp, she poured herself a cup of coffee as she remembered the suffocating breakfasts at Jamie's home where his parents, Trent and Millicent, had exchanged polite conversation while their uniformed servant served them icy glasses of freshly squeezed orange juice. Shep had warned her that the Foxwells had a debutante all picked out for Jamie and that, deep down, they were afraid Cheryl was a fortune hunter. She would have married him if he didn't have a nickel to his name but had never found the nerve to tell them.

Now she watched sadly as he blew the dust off his wingtips and began to tie his shoes. How could the confident, attentive boy she'd loved eight years ago have allowed himself to fade into the irresponsible playboy who stood before her? It was Jamie who had insisted in the heat of passion that they needed to elope just before Thanksgiving during their junior year. And it was Jamie who had boldly driven them to Indiana so a justice of the peace could pronounce them man and wife. Cheryl had been ecstatic when he'd placed the plain gold band on her finger, knowing she'd spend the rest of her life with her one true love and would never have to confront the Loneliness again.

Now, as she stirred the cream into her coffee, she watched Jamie admire his reflection in the mirror as he ran a comb through his thick blond hair. He'd done the same thing at the Hoosier Hollow Motel that first night after they'd stopped off to get hamburgers and a six-pack of Miller's. Between combing his hair and fussing with the radio, he had chugged five bottles of beer while she toyed with one. When they'd finally made love, it was a short-lived moment that left her wide awake and confused while he collapsed and fell into a deep sleep.

The next day they'd gone straight to see Bertie and Lila, who promptly treated them to an all-you-can-eat buffet to celebrate. Jamie's parents, however, had greeted the news on the phone with stony silence before they recovered enough to ask if the union was legal and if Cheryl was pregnant. The following week, after one of the family lawyers had confirmed that she and Jamie were indeed married in the eyes of the law, the Foxwells had agreed to advance Jamie enough money to rent a small upstairs apartment in an old home near the campus in Urbana.

That following June there had been no north shore parties or romantic evenings on the "Foxy Lady." They'd stayed in Urbana so Jamie could pick up some credits during summer school when the professors were reported to be more lenient. Besides, by that time, Cheryl had been two-thirds of the way through a pregnancy that was making her deathly nauseated every day. Unable to work, she'd resigned herself to the fact that they would not have the money for her senior-year classes.

"How do I look, Sugar?" Jamie grinned playfully as he paraded in front of her. "And I'll be home on time tonight. You can count on it." When she shook her head in disgust, he shrugged and helped himself to one more cookie.

Those words had a familiar ring to them. He had hood-winked her with that line their entire married life. He'd always been so full of false assurance, swearing he'd spend less time at the fraternity house and promising to stand by her when Bertie had dropped dead just two weeks before her delivery date. She had learned soon in her marriage that the one thing she could not count on was Jamie's presence when she needed it.

Bertie's death of a heart attack one morning as he opened the shoe store had left her crumpled and over-whelmed with grief. More nauseated than ever at the fu-neral, she'd forced herself to endure the overpowering sweetness of the floral arrangements as Lila sobbed on one side of her and Jamie wiggled in his folding chair on the other.

Drained and devastated, she'd realized when they'd re-turned to their campus apartment that the Loneliness had moved in while they'd been away at the funeral. Each day, while Jamie was in class, she'd wept as she'd played old re-cords and pictured Bertie and Lila slow dancing in their liv-ing room to the Pied Pipers' honey-toned version of "Dream."

Since that time, she'd often wondered whether her grief over Bertie's sudden death had left her so depleted that she'd had no stamina to see her through her long labor. It had begun when her water had broken on a smoky Friday night as the sounds of a pep rally for the Fighting Illini filled the air. Jamie had rushed her to the hospital and actu-ally had stayed at her side the entire time. Thirty hours later, when she'd feared she might die from pain and weakness, her doctor finally had decided to take her into surgery in order to save the baby.

When she'd emerged from the anesthetic, she'd learned that their son had entered the world quietly and had whimpered only after he had received a sound thumping. But when she'd asked Jamie if they could name him Mark and use Wilbert as a middle name to honor her dad, Jamie had hooted at the thought.

"Not a chance! He's Jamison Trent Foxwell the Fifth," he'd proclaimed almost pompously from the foot of her hospital bed. "Gotta be. Can you imagine what my father would do if we called him something else? We'll name the next one for your dad," he'd added with his roguish grin.

The surge of nausea she'd felt at the thought of a next one passed the moment the nurse had placed little J.T. in her arms. As Cheryl examined their precious child, she'd vowed he would never have to fend off the Loneliness. She'd marveled at her little son's contentment in spite of his turbulent entry into the world and allowed the nurse to waken him for his feeding.

Now, as Jamie began to toss papers into his briefcase, she slipped around him to grab a tissue from the bathroom. The memory of her son's first days always brought tears to her eyes. Everything, as she recalled it, had seemed magnified at that time—her own desire to be the best mother a child could have, Lila's inability to function after Bertie's death, the wretched generosity that Jamie's parents showered on their grandson. When the Foxwells had hugged her and thanked her for giving them their "perfect little heir," she'd finally felt some degree of acceptance into their dynasty.

Wiping her eyes, she now refused Jamie's offer to dash with him to their favorite coffee shop before he left for work. She couldn't believe that he still thought he could charm her into forgiveness.

"I'll buy you a cream horn," he offered, as if a pastry would erase all his indiscretions.

"Lordy, Jamie, not now. Not ever." Picking up her favorite photo of J..T. when he was four months old, she wished with all her heart that they could return to that stage of their lives when all of them had been happy and innocent. Their son had appeared to be the picture of health, but by the time he'd turned eight months old he still showed none of the curiosity that Dr. Spock said he should have. Although he'd been a good eater and had slept well, he'd always toppled over when she'd tried to get him to sit up. When the pediatrician had reminded her that every child follows his own developmental timetable, she'd forced herself to remain optimistic by giving J.T. her undivided attention. Jamie had handled the situation by making more trips to the liquor store. Each had been too preoccupied with uncertainty to consider the romantic element of their marriage.

As she searched the photo of their four-month-old son for signs of abnormalities, she still could find none now. Sighing, she reminded Jamie to take his overcoat to work.

"It's supposed to rain and turn cold this afternoon," she said mechanically. Obediently, he went to the closet, glancing over his shoulder for a sign from her that she might stay.

Sliding her hand over the glass in the picture frame, she remembered how crazed the Foxwells had been to think that their "perfect little heir" might have a problem. They'd wanted nothing but the best for the baby and, right after Jamie's graduation, had arranged for them to move to Chicago so J.T. could see the finest doctors at Passavant and Northwestern. Jamie had gone to work immediately in a management position at the Foxwells' meat-packing plant, just a twenty-minute drive from the two-bedroom apartment on

Bellevue his parents had leased for them.

Around that time she'd begun to notice that, when J.T. was awake, his eyes remained unfocused and he drooled constantly. Unable to relax in the same room with his unresponsive son, Jamie had started living in the bars on Rush Street instead of coming home for dinner. Many nights she had felt like Lila waiting for Bertie to return from Rigoni's, except that Bertie had never arrived with traces of other women's cologne on him. When she'd shown Jamie the lipstick on one of his shirts, he'd merely laughed.

"Don't ashk. My mom never hash," he'd slurred as he'd tumbled onto their bed and fallen asleep immediately.

It was strange, she recalled, that her one true ally during those years when J.T. was still manageable had been Jamie's mother, Millicent. After Cheryl and Jamie had learned the heartbreaking news that their son was profoundly retarded, Millicent had emerged as both a friend and parent for Cheryl. She'd desperately needed someone to fill that role, since Lila had moved to Florida to help her sister, DeeDee, and her husband run their small motel.

While Jamie continued tossing papers in search of an important folder he swore he had brought home, Cheryl returned to the window and watched the people below bracing themselves against the wind as they headed east. How many spring mornings had she and Millcent put J.T. in his stroller and taken him for a walk along the Magnificent Mile? How many crisp autumn afternoons had she and Millicent ambled with him along the paths at the Lincoln Park Zoo? Although passers-by had gaped at them before their eyes darted in other directions, Millicent had simply stared them down and continued to push the oversized stroller. Cheryl had gained great strength from Millicent during those outings. She'd known that her mother-in-law, too, had begun to view her in a different light and enjoyed taking her into Peck & Peck to treat her to a classic addition to her meager wardrobe.

By the time J.T. had turned four, Millicent was making the trip in from Wilmette several times a week to help. She'd resigned her board positions with several charities and rarely entertained.

"Not important anymore." Millicent had raised her chin resolutely and stroked the smoothness of J.T.'s cheek.

Two years later, however, the two of them had admitted that he was getting too heavy for them to manage. They'd tried to protect him by having him wear a helmet as he lurched about the apartment in his unsteady gait; however, they'd been unable to protect themselves from his amazing strength when his temper flared. The day he'd broken two of Cheryl's fingers during one of his tantrums was the day that Millicent had insisted they place him in a special home. Ranting that she wanted to be a good mother, Cheryl had been almost delirious until Millicent had slipped a tranquilizer into her cup of tea.

Although her mind had turned to fuzz at the time, she could still remember Millicent's ramrod posture and expertly coiffed hair as she'd discussed Jamie's past and J.T.'s future.

Leaning across their dinette table, Millicent had spoken softly yet earnestly. She'd suggested that Cheryl and Jamie might be able to make a fresh start if J.T. were living where he would receive more consistent care.

"Marriage is hard enough without this kind of stress," Millicent had told her. She'd gone on to confess that she felt responsible for Jamie's behavior because she had always looked away when his father "had other interests." Thus, Jamie had always assumed that a roving eye was acceptable. "I hope," she'd said as a weary sadness settled over her features, "that you'll give your husband a second chance."

Cheryl had promised she'd try, but now, as she

watched Jamie fiddle with the snap on his briefcase, she wondered if she should have just walked away back then. However, with the Loneliness nibbling at her heels, she had aimed at perfection as she'd tried to be a better wife for Jamie while devoting endless hours to J.T. at the special home in Lake Forest where they had placed him. Relieved by their son's absence, Jamie had started spending more time in their Bellevue apartment.

"I'll promise to do better," he'd assured her. "You can count on me."

He'd lived up to his word for six whole weeks before he'd started missing meals and coming home drunk again. When Millicent had advised her that she needed to think long and hard about her own future, Cheryl had been afraid to ask what she meant.

On a bleak November evening as she'd sat alone and watched their dinner grow cold, she'd made up her mind to go out and look for her husband. After circling three bars and four restaurants near Rush and Division, she'd finally found him wrapped around a platinum blond in a corner booth of a famous steak house. As the strains of "Moon River" filtered from the piano at the bar, she'd waited beside a nearby table long enough for both of them to see her, then threaded her way back to the front door. She hadn't screamed. She hadn't even shed a tear. Instead, she'd felt a strong sense of calm settle over her.

That had been only a week ago, and Jamie had not come home. Now, several days later, there he stood, giving her that slow sheepish smile that he knew always turned her to butter. She shuddered to think where he might have slept last night.

"It's not too late. Honest, Sugar, I promise. Never again."

Cheryl felt her knees weaken, knowing this moment was

decision time. She could stay and reenact this scene repeatedly for the rest of her life, always certain that Jamie eventually would return. Or she could hoist the suitcase she'd packed, stride out the door and take the first step toward her new life. The Loneliness would be there. She knew it would. But this time Millicent was on her side, confiding to Cheryl recently that she'd already established a trust fund to cover J.T.'s needs as long as he lived. Cheryl had been humbled beyond words when Millicent had added that she would pay every cent of her senior-year expenses at Loyola and would help her with the rent on a small apartment in the Lincoln Park area.

"Still, you'll want more. You'll *need* more," Millicent had been firm as they'd lunched together at a small cafe on North Michigan. Cheryl had felt herself near tears to think that she and Jamie were parting just days before their eighth anniversary. For the rest of her life she'd wonder if it had been their marriage—or their separating—that always made her melancholy in the month of November.

"No, I won't." She'd held her head high. "I'll make it. Wait and see."

"But you deserve more." As Millicent poked at her Bibb lettuce, Cheryl had seen a tear trickling down her lightly rouged cheek. She was suddenly touched to think that this woman who had once considered her a gold-digger would now provide her with anything she needed.

"Who's to say?" She'd reached across the little table to touch her mother-in-law's hand. "Oh, Millicent, you may not realize it but you've given me so much already. So much that money can't buy."

Obviously shaken, Millicent had responded with a wan but appreciative smile. "I think you're the first person who has ever told me that." She'd taken one sip of her white wine, then set the glass down again.

"You know—you may not believe this—but J.T. has given *me* more joy than I could ever have imagined. My—my whole outlook on life has changed because of him." Lifting a linen handkerchief from her purse, she'd begun to dab her eyes.

"Me too," Cheryl had answered.

Now, as she faced her husband, she realized that she would always have feelings for Jamie. But they bordered more on pity than passion. J.T. would never grow up, but neither would Jamie. He would always be a fraternity boy, never a husband or a father.

Struggling with a loose cuff link, he extended his arm for help.

"Honest, Sugar, I'll give you anything you want if you'll just stay." Again he flashed the winsome smile that had always been her downfall. "Anything in the world."

Cheryl thought of her son in Lake Forest and of Millicent whose friendship and support were now the bedrock of her life. Surveying the room, she hesitated. She'd never live in a place like this again, with its high ceilings, rich woodwork and cozy fireplace. It was here that she and Jamie had nurtured J.T. And it was here that they had both loved deeply and drifted so far apart.

"Honest, I'll give you anything." For the first time, he looked genuinely concerned. "Anything you want."

She snapped his cuff link into place and lifted her jacket off the hall tree. Flashing him her own ironic smile, she replied, "You already have." Firmly she closed the door behind her as she left.

* * *

Chapter

Twenty - One

C heryl knew she would have drowned in the Loneliness during the next few weeks if Millicent had not been there every step of the way. Because Jamie was staying in their Bellevue place, she needed to assemble all the basics for her new apartment. Millicent seemed to thrive on the unusual challenge of seeking out treasures at consignment shops and painting them in bold fresh colors.

Together they converted a chipped kitchen table and two chairs into a bright yellow dinette set. In the far depths of Marshall Field's basement, they found a blue-and-yellow pullout couch and bright blue pillows. The result, in the midst of dreariest November, was springlike cheeriness that chased away the Loneliness. When Millicent left on November 20 with Jamie's father to spend a few weeks in Arizona, Cheryl felt serene and secure in her new little nest.

Two days later, as she pawed through the albums in a small record shop on Fullerton, she was stunned when a woman burst through the front door screaming that President Kennedy had been shot. Customers clustered around the fuzzy television screen at the back of the store to hear Dan Rather confirm the unbelievable. Shaken, Cheryl returned to her apartment, where the brightness of her new décor seemed to mock the chilling gray that seeped in around the corners of the windows.

She wrapped herself in an old afghan and numbly watched the chain of events unfold on the television that Millicent had given her as a housewarming present just before she left. After John-John had saluted his fallen father and Jackie had ignited the eternal flame, Cheryl herself felt depleted as she faced the stark reality of her personal tragedy. Her marriage was over, her son was in an institution, and she had no job and no prospects. She found herself wallowing in such a depression that she used most of her meager savings to buy an Eastern Airlines ticket so she could fly to Florida and visit her mother.

There she savored the warmth of the sun as she searched for shells along the beach but found the atmosphere at the modest motel musty and unbearable. Lila was still glued to her soap operas, Aunt DeeDee chain-smoked until the air was thick, and Uncle Vernon suffered from what Jamie had always called "diarrhea of the mouth" with his non-stop opinions on every subject imaginable. As she kissed all of them good-bye at the airport, she couldn't wait to return to her spot in the city and the classes she'd registered for before the holidays.

Once she started school, it didn't take her long to realize that she'd been living in a cocoon for the last few years. After she noticed the amused glances that other students gave her Peck & Peck skirts and sweaters, she took the bus to a cheap shop on State Street and bought two pairs of jeans, a couple of T-shirts and a baggy royal blue dress called a "shift." She stashed away the clothes that Millicent had assured her would always be in good taste in the back of her closet and decided that if she were going to start life over again, she was going to start in style.

After she'd updated her wardrobe, she noticed that her luck seemed to change as well. During the next year and a half, she delighted in the unexpected turns that her life began to take. Following the tip of one of her Loyola instructors, she applied for an opening as a music teacher at St. Agnes Elementary School near her apartment. She reveled in discussing her love for music with her interviewers but never expected to land the job. When the contract arrived in the mail, she exclaimed, "Lordy!" right out loud, amazed to learn that she had been hired for the fall term of 1965. For the first time in years, she found herself singing as she went about her daily routine in her apartment.

She also rediscovered the joy of camaraderie as she and some of her co-students who were approaching their thirtieth birthday fell into the habit of hitting Pizzeria Uno on Fridays. One evening, as they threaded their way through the crowd to leave, she bumped into a fellow as he turned from the bar with a full mug of beer. Apologizing profusely when she saw foam splash all over his expensive suit, she couldn't help but laugh when she realized that it was Shep. She told the other girls to go on without her, then she and Shep spent more than hour catching up on the last few years. He told her he was now an attorney with a large firm in the Loop and was still married to Helen, his Kappa girlfriend who'd agreed to wear his Phi Delt pin the year that Cheryl had dropped out of school. Jamie, he lamented, was already floundering in his second marriage and still hadn't given up any of his bad habits.

A couple of weeks later, she was surprised to get a call from Shep. He wanted to tell her that a little combo that played at one of the places in Old Town was losing its vocalist. Shep, who always seemed to know everyone, had talked with the leader and suggested that maybe Cheryl could fill in until they found someone else. Feeling brave, she strolled over to Wells Street, found the funky spot called Eliot's Nest and, in the dark room filled with the lingering odors of cigarette smoke and last night's beer, auditioned for Gus Chakir.

The band's leader and piano player, Gus nodded his dark curly head as she ran through her repertoire of old standards. Then, he smoothed his bushy eyebrows with a thick finger and said he'd have to help her get up to speed with newer numbers. He advised her to part her hair in the middle and brush it out straight. And if she really insisted on singing some slow stuff, he suggested that "Blowin' in the Wind" and "Puff the Magic Dragon" would be acceptable.

"You mean you really want me to sing with your band?" She tried to keep the elation out of her voice as she considered that she now would have two jobs.

"Just none of that 'Sound of Music' shit, ya hear?" Hitching up his black pants, he explained, "Our customers aren't into that. Oh—" His shaggy brows made a black arch across his forehead as he considered an afterthought. "You want us to use your real name when we introduce you?"

She glanced around the room, taking in the enlarged photos of Chicago crime that blanketed the walls of this bar/coffeehouse hangout. She'd always been one of the few people who actually liked her own name. But maybe, since she was teaching such young children, she ought to sing under a stage name on weekends.

"I know. Let's use my maiden name and reverse it. Real original, huh?" She chuckled. "Make it Allison. Allison Sherrill."

Three years later she found herself comfortable in her somewhat schizophrenic routine with both jobs. On weekdays, as "Mrs. Foxwell," she devised creative new methods to make her St. Agnes pupils appreciate all types of music. But on Friday and Saturday nights, as "Allison Sherrill," she untied her hair, donned her flashy clothes and jewelry and switched to the Bob Dylan/Joan Baez repertoire that the band had adopted.

"So you're the babe who told one of Chicago's richest playboys to take a hike?"

She'd stepped outside for a breath of fresh air and now stood face to face with the new drummer, Rip Frederick, who'd just joined the band a few days before. Immersed in rolling his own cigarette, he sealed it, lighted it and offered it to her. Inhaling deeply, she took one drag and returned it to him.

"Who told you a thing like that?" Disgustedly she headed for the back door, wondering what other bits of gossip the band members had shared with this lean, frizzy-haired drifter from out west.

"I read it in the society news." The orange tip of his cigarette glowed in the alley as she heard him exhale slowly. "I don't read the sports pages much," he added lazily.

"Don't believe everything you see in the papers." She let the door slam behind her and left him standing alone in the raw March air.

During the next few weeks, she labeled Rip Frederick a brat and tried her best to avoid him. She complained to Millicent that he was such a showoff, taking off with his drum solos and leaving the band and her wondering what he'd do next. He made so many snide remarks about "rich bitches" that she decided he must think that she'd collected a ton of money when she divorced Jamie and was working just for the fun of it. He cursed the Midwest, claiming that California was the only "happenin' place," but he always seemed to be first in line when Gus handed out paychecks.

Sometimes, when Millicent came to hear her sing, the two of them went to a Lincoln Park bar for a drink after the show. Other times, when the band finished its gig, a few of the members walked to Gus' pad over a liquor store on Division Street. There they liked to unwind and share the weird experiences they'd had that night. Those sessions helped Cheryl stave off the Loneliness that had reared its head after Millicent and Trent sold their home in Wilmette and moved to Arizona for most of the year.

It was during those hours just before dawn that she felt the tension starting to build between Rip and her. Whenever he taunted her about something from her past, she always took the bait. His soft chuckle let her know she'd been had. At other times, when she sang at "the Nest," as they called it, he started a slow, rustling on the drums that would build up to the sexiest backup she'd ever heard.

When he phoned her on one of their rare off nights in August, she accepted his invitation to go up to the observatory of "Big John." The view from the top of the new Hancock building—the tallest in the world—was spectacular. Below them, like a diamond necklace draped on a piece of black velvet, stretched the lights of Lake Shore Drive. Even the grimy west side was transformed into a magical playground. She dropped a coin into the viewer and strained to see as far north as she could.

"What's up there that's so fascinating?" Rip wondered.

"My little boy. Past the farthest light you can see. He lives there." Pushing her face against the metal telescope, she squinted. She could feel Rip's eyes boring through her.

"Let's get the hell out of here." His voice was husky as he took her arm and steered her toward the elevator.

He continued to guide her toward a bar over on Rush—right next to the steakhouse, in fact, where she had confronted Jamie with his blond girlfriend a few years before. There they split a pitcher of margaritas and, for the first time, spoke openly about their pasts.

Rip went first.

"Never knew my dad." He stared into his glass until she wondered if he'd gone into a trance. "But I never lacked for male companionship, if you know what I mean. My mom—well, she moved around a lot. And she always managed to find a guy to bring home."

Quickly he recalled his childhood, and the spots he'd lived up and down the California coast.

"Never hurt for friends either." He folded his cocktail napkin into a tiny hat. "My drumsticks got me into any group I wanted." Draining his glass, he refilled it from the pitcher and picked up a handful of pretzels from the basket in front of them. "Then a buddy of mine called and told me Gus was looking for a drummer. That's how I landed here."

"Think you'll stay?" She nibbled around a pretzel, not really interested in his answer.

"Not for long." He shook his head. "Ol' Rip doesn't hang around in one place for long. And," he shrugged as if winding up his story, "that's all I've got to say."

"Well, I have a lot more to tell than you." Flushed from the margaritas, she spoke as if her life had been full of mystery and romance. As she licked the salt from her lips, she added, "because I'm five years older than you are."

"Hey, Babe, you've got more to tell 'cause you've had a harder life." Above the shadows of his high cheekbones, his green eyes burned intensely. "Plus, you're eight—not five—years older than me! Let's make sure we get that right." She could feel his pulse hammering through his hand as he placed it on top of hers.

Lordy, she thought, I don't want this complication. Not now. I'm thirty-three years old, and I don't need to get involved with a younger guy. I've got a thirteen-year-old son who needs me, even though he's not capable of understanding who I am. I've gotta see J.T. through, whatever becomes of him. I've always gotta be there for him.

"Drink up." Rip's eyes softened as he listened to her story about Jamie and J.T. "I'll put you in a cab. We've got some big nights coming up over at the Nest, and I shouldn't keep you out too late."

Woozy from alcohol and emotion, she still marveled at Rip's thoughtfulness. She'd completely forgotten that Gus had announced that the band would be performing from eight to midnight for the next five nights. The Democrats were coming to town—and they wouldn't be spending every moment nominating Hubert Humphrey, he'd warned. Later she thought that they may have been ready for the crowds at the Nest, but never could the city of Chicago have prepared for the events that were about to unfold.

During the first few days of the convention, cabs were so scarce that she walked from Lincoln Park to the Nest. By the middle of the week, the atmosphere began to grow eerie—the way the sky turns green just before a bad storm rolls in, she thought. There were none of the usual nannies chatting on park benches or children squealing at the playground. Instead, the city was swarming with dirty, long-haired protesters wailing about "police pigs," and the war in Vietnam. The traffic that clogged the streets was dotted with little VW buses bearing hand-lettered messages about love and peace in psychedelic colors. In the twilight, as she cut across one of the grassy patches lining Lincoln Park West, she almost stumbled over a couple having sex. Right out there for all to see!

"God, this is better'n California!" Outside Eliot's Nest, Rip cheerfully rolled a cigarette and stuck it between his lips. He laughed when she shuddered and told him what she'd just witnessed. "Tomorrow, Babe, we're gonna meet right here—just you and me at, oh, about five o'clock. We'll take a trip down to Grant Park before the band has to start playing. I wanta see for myself what's happenin'."

However, the following day neither she nor Rip was quite ready for the scope of the "happenin's" that he had so eagerly anticipated. They were able to cram into a bus that crept to the south end of the Loop but were forced to walk the rest of the way to Grant Park in order to join the fringe of the crowd. Flinching, she grabbed Rip's arm as they dodged camera crews from all the major channels.

"Hang on, Babe." He gripped her tightly as the force of the crowd began to carry them along. Then, eyes fearful and glistening, he muttered, "Oh, oh—we're getting outta here. Right now."

Taking one more look ahead of her, she understood why. In the throng that surged from the park toward the convention site, she saw policemen wielding sticks against the heads of the nameless demonstrators known as "Yippies." She heard the ching of car windows as they shattered and watched, horrified, as two cops were trampled when they tried to keep order. As the acrid odor of smoke filled the air, she and Rip used all their strength to fight their way against the tide. They never looked back again until they were almost across the Michigan Avenue bridge.

"Scared the shit outta me!" Rip panted. "I only wanted to see what all the fuss was about. Hell, they're usin' tear gas down there!"

In the sultry August air, she felt her teeth chattering. Glancing back to the south, she could still smell sweat, filth and smoldering rubber and wondered if their city would ever be the same.

"I'm taking you over to my place on Franklin." Rip put his arm around her. "We can walk from here. It's not much, but you need to get yourself cleaned up and back together before you can sing."

Breathless from climbing three flights in the dingy building where he was staying, she was unprepared for the atmosphere of his room. She'd pictured a hovel. Instead, the bed was made, the dishes were washed and put away, and a tall drinking glass filled with zinnias and pink daisies stood on the end table beside his sofa.

"I'm a sucker for flowers," he explained sheepishly.

"Lordy, Rip, I've never been so scared in my life." Putting her head against his chest, she whispered, "Hold me just for a moment. So I know we're safe."

As he wrapped his arms around her and led her over to his bed, she gave in to him completely. Later that night at the Nest, he caressed her songs with the tender tension of his drums. When she glanced in his direction and caught the raw hunger in his eyes, she totally blanked her lyrics. She hadn't done that since high school! Somehow she was able to hum a few bars until she could get herself back on track. Neither of them, she knew, could deny the powerful chemistry that was pulling them under. As the chords from their last song faded, they linked arms and ran back to his room for more.

* * *

In her sex-sated state during that golden autumn, she began to appreciate the differences between Rip and Jamie. Where Jamie had been soft and almost pretty, Rip was "lean 'n mean," as he liked to say. Where Jamie sported an excellent haircut by an expensive stylist and wore Brooks Brothers suits, Rip let his wild-and-fuzzy hair take on the look of a tumbleweed as he sought out the most obnoxious shirts in tacky little shops on South Wabash. But where Jamie had been distracted by his own desires, Rip focused his lovemaking on Cheryl's fulfillment. She even overheard her students at St. Agnes talking about the fact that "Mrs. Foxwell seems a lot happier these days."

After the paths of Lincoln Park were strewn with dry leaves and a gray chill whipped across the east-and-west streets from the lake, however, she began to feel the Loneliness trying to creep into her days.

"Hey, Babe, what's the matter?" Rip looked like a physician as he scrutinized her from head to toe one night after they finished their gig. "You're working those sad songs back into your sets again. What's eating you?"

Sighing, she confessed, "It's November." They pulled up their collars as they left the warmth of the Nest. "I get the blues every year at this time. Guess I start missing my dad—and beating myself up for not trying to go see Lila more often. And J.T." She shivered. "It was just this kind of day when I had to leave him at the home."

As they strolled in companionable silence for a few moments, she was comforted by the knowledge that the Loneliness would not come knocking at her door as long as Rip was with her.

"I know!" Jumping ahead, he knelt in front of her on the grubby Wells Street sidewalk. "We could get married the day before Thanksgiving. We'd have two nights off to—well, you know, just do whatever. To be happy." He looked up at her, his green eyes glittering at this unexpected turn of events.

"But—"

"Thank you, ma'am, I assume that's a yes." Leaping to his feet, he curled his arms around her and kissed her. "And I can guarantee you one thing."

"What's that?" She was half-laughing, half-crying.

"After Thanksgiving you'll be singing only happy songs. That's a promise!"

* * *

287

Chapter Twenty-Two

Cheryl had never dreamed that marriage could be so much fun. Because they were accountable to no one else, they were free to let their whims dictate their actions as they established a crazy-quilt existence together. During Christmas break, there were days when they binged on doughnuts and nights when they dragged out their pots and pans to experiment with exotic Asian recipes. Once in awhile, they punished themselves with frigid marathon runs along the lakeshore, but on most afternoons they merely curled up under a blanket and stared at television reruns for hours.

After school started again in January, she rarely had time for her old friends from Loyola. On Monday evenings, she and Rip usually opened a couple of cans of something and spooned their suppers straight from the can while they giggled through *Rowan and Martin's Laugh-In.* On other week nights, she found herself in shabby hole-in-the-wall bars as she trailed after Rip and the guys he'd met at places all over the city. Sometimes, though, she'd have to beg off so she could stay awake to teach her classes the next day.

Later, when she thought of the rollicking times that she and Rip had shared, she couldn't recall a single fight during their first year and a half together. Those days they'd just been a couple of overgrown kids who couldn't think beyond the next few hours. In fact, when Rip greeted her after school one afternoon with the news that he'd located a bigger apartment for them, it never occurred to her to question his judgment.

"Your lease is up pretty soon, and now's a good time to find a place that'll hold all our stuff." He nibbled at her ear and mumbled, "You know it makes me nutsy when the clutter piles up."

She agreed, as she always did with his impulsive moves, that they should jump at the chance to swap their Lincoln Park nook for a two-bedroom apartment north of Diversey. The neighborhood wasn't as pretty, but she knew they could use the space. And, she rationalized, they could get all that for just fifty dollars more a month.

Soon after they moved, however, she was bewildered to find cartons of cleaning supplies stacked beside their front door one afternoon when she came home from school.

"You're looking at a soon-to-be successful salesman—something that I can make good money at during the days." Rip was scavenging through one of the boxes like a child at Christmas. "The thing of it is, Babe, if we can get our friends on board so they're selling Klean-Max stuff, we'll get a cut of their commissions." His face glowed with anticipation. "We can't miss!"

"But—"

"No buts. I signed us up for a new credit card and already charged these samples." He challenged her with his naughty-boy "what-are-you-going-to-do-about-it" look.

"But what about those daytime dance classes that you and Gus are playing for?" She shuddered. The pay wasn't much, but they needed a guaranteed paycheck to help cover their new rent.

"Long gone. I canceled out." Shaking a small supply of tobacco onto the thin white wrapper he held in his hand, he avoided looking at her as he began to roll his cigarette. When he finished he stuck it between his lips and, before he lighted it, added, "This stuff will sell so fast that we'll have it paid off in a couple of months. And even if we don't, the minimum payment is only thirty dollars a month."

"It'd better be good." She brushed by him and went straight to the bathroom, where she tried to compose herself.

The next day when she arrived home, he presented her with a check for eighteen dollars.

"There!" he pointed triumphantly to the amount. "The building super bought four bottles of Klean-Max. This is just the beginning, Babe!"

They celebrated by eating at a Chinese restaurant, seeing *Love Story* at the neighborhood theater and going home to make passionate love, grateful that—unlike the movie's heroes—they still had each other.

That spring, she regretfully said good-bye to her beloved parochial school and signed a contract with the public school system so she could take advantage of the benefits that the teachers' union offered, something that so far had been unavailable at St. Agnes. She knew the tough kids who lived in the marginal neighborhood north of Addison Street would challenge her on a daily basis but liked the financial package.

Saying he needed more time to concentrate on Klean-Max, Rip stopped going with her to see J.T. When Cheryl failed to notice any evidence of additional orders for cleaning supplies, she merely suspected that Rip just couldn't handle the scene at Lake Forest Manor any longer.

She, herself, was finding it harder to visit her son. Now almost fifteen, J.T. appeared to be a strange distorted combination of Jamie and her. Under the helmet that was almost welded to his head lay a golden mop of blond hair just like Jamie's, but his unfocused eyes, were brown like hers. And, the nurses told her, he hummed to himself most of the time.

Cheryl never tried to fool herself into thinking that he knew she was his mother. Each time when she arrived, he'd become extremely agitated when he realized someone different had entered his room. Then she would sit beside him and begin to sing softly the song she had always crooned to him when he was a baby:

"Hush little baby, don't you cry; Mama's gonna sing you a lullaby."

She'd rub his back gently and feel the rigidity evaporate while a peaceful expression came over his features. When she considered the hundreds of times she'd sung for audiences, she knew in her heart that this was her best performance—the one that counted above all the others.

She'd leave with a feeling of contentment, only to encounter resentment and sarcasm when she returned home.

"Hope you enjoyed your little outing." Rip was strung tighter than a banjo when she entered their apartment on a drizzly Sunday afternoon late in October.

"Yeah?" Cautiously tentative as she caught the sweet, expensive aroma of marijuana, she tossed her raincoat over the hall tree. Rip drew deeply on his joint as he stared at the piles of paper he'd stacked neatly on the coffee table.

"'Cause *I've* had a helluva afternoon with this paperwork shit. They've got me filling out so many forms, I don't have time to get out there and sell, much less try to sign up our friends!"

She shook her head in disgust as he offered her a puff.

"Well, you'd better find time to make some sales so we can pay for that stupid pot you're hooked on!" Striding past him, she slammed the bathroom door between them.

The next month was not a good one for Rip. First, Jimi Hendrix choked to death. Then, about three weeks later, Janis Joplin died of an overdose.

"The gods are trying to kill off all the great musicians." Rip's eyes were bleary as he sorted through a new order of cleaning supplies on the kitchen table. "You be careful not to use any bad stuff, Babe—you hear?"

His cure for melancholy was to register them for a short cruise while the Nest was closed for the few days around Christmas. Cheryl sighed. Once more, he had made another big mistake; he'd never consulted her first.

"We're going to shake the blues and celebrate life." He waved the tickets in front of her. "These are non-refundable, Babe, so don't give me shit that we can't afford them!"

"How much?" she asked wearily.

"Just twenty-five dollars a month for the next twenty-four months." Lordy, she thought, he looked like a ten-year-old who'd just blown his allowance for the next two years on a baseball glove. "And we don't even have to start paying on it till February!"

A few weeks later, she found herself on a boat for three days with a queasy husband who vowed that 1971 would be a better time for them. And, as she observed his behavior during the first months of the year, she did admit to herself that he tried . . . in that half-assed juvenile way of his. He meant well, she knew, but he was erratic. One day he was stashing all the Klean-Max boxes in their basement cubicle so he could "sell at a better time," and the next he was peddling Florida real estate over the phone out of a seedy office near the south end of the Loop. When no sales materialized, he became so discouraged that his music began to suffer. Fortunately, in June, Gus made an announcement that swept over them like a breath of spring air.

"We're going on the road. Taking a swing downstate

for a week—an insurance gathering in Bloomington for two nights, Champaign and Charleston one night each and a special celebration in Danville for two nights." He stared hard at Rip. "Hope you're all on board with me for the long haul, 'cause the pay is sweet." Cheryl knew he'd never quite forgiven Rip for walking out on that daytime job at the dance studio.

Right after the Fourth of July they loaded their equipment into the band's van and Gus' '62 Chevy Corvair and, with windows wide open, watched the Illinois farmers harvesting acres of golden wheat and cultivating rows of waist-high corn as they headed toward Bloomington. Cheryl was grateful that the change of scene seemed to revitalize Rip. As his drums came to life, she felt herself charging each song with the energy it deserved.

"They loved us in Bloomington!" Gus chomped on his unlighted cigar triumphantly as they cruised through the streets of Champaign. "Let's do it again here."

"Lordy, this is a real sentimental journey for me." She pressed her nose against the window to get a better look at her old campus. "I can't believe all the new buildings."

"Cool it, Babe." Rip had grown to love taunting her in front of the band. "You're showing your age."

She laughed as she punched him, but inside she was seething. In four years she'd be forty—and she did not like to be reminded by someone eight years younger.

By the time they arrived in Danville, she was consumed with such a severe case of homesickness that it almost rivaled the Loneliness in its strength. Suddenly she ached to see Kate, to sit around the table in Doris' kitchen, to roll with laughter up in Rosie's bedroom.

"Gus," she declared at last. "I've just gotta run up to Rockwell for a couple of hours before we perform. Can I borrow your car?"

His eyebrows merged in concern. "You drive?"

"Sure. Still got my license too."

"Okay." He muttered under his breath, "You takin' Shit-for-Brains too?"

"I guess. If he wants to go." She shot him a look of mock disapproval at his reference to her husband.

"Just don't let him drive. Promise?"

"Sure. Yeah, sure." As she studied Gus, he turned away. "What's the deal?" she asked.

"You haven't noticed how mean his sarcasm has been lately? You know he gets that way when he's restless." Gus sniffed and shook his head. "He's a good drummer, honey, but he's so goddamn moody."

"I know what you mean." Lately she and Rip had avoided conversation the same way they avoided health-food stores. Every time they opened their mouths, they found themselves ensnarled in non-stop bickering. "I won't let him drive."

Later she thought it would have been a pleasant afternoon if only Rip had stayed at the motel and napped. But he insisted on seeing the town where she had grown up and the house where she had lived with Bertie and Lila.

As they drove past the park where she had played tennis with Rosie, Kate and Doris, she could scarcely believe that more than twenty years had passed since she'd left Rockwell. But she wasn't going to make the mistake of verbalizing her thoughts so Rip could wound her with another nasty dig that made her feel as if she were practically on her way to the old folks' home!

She was amazed at what she saw, by what had changed and by what had not. The Pinnacle Theater, still needing a coat of paint, would be showing *Dirty Harry* that night. Adler's Ford-Mercury had been sold and now offered an array of rusting used cars. But the bank, the clothing shops

294

and the Grab-It-Here looked amazingly as they had in the fall of 1949.

She guided Gus' car carefully over the railroad tracks.

"You're in God's country now, Rip." Was she fooling herself, she wondered, or could she actually feel the difference? "This is the Sweet Briar side of town."

She had to drive down Doris' street twice before she realized that a duplex had replaced Panczyks' house and the one next door. The ragged lawn, however, still looked as if it might be dotted with dandelions in the spring.

Rip grew antsy when she insisted on parking across the street from her old house so she could just sit and reflect for a few minutes. She thought that it appeared to be in pretty good condition in spite of the fact that it had been painted gray with burgundy trim. Several toys were strewn across the front yard, and a small boy clad only in stained briefs dashed out of the front door in a futile attempt to escape his older brother. As the larger boy tackled him, they tumbled to the ground and a teen-age girl who reminded her of Lorene Panczyk stomped out on the porch and yelled at both of them.

"It's noisier than when we lived here." She started the engine. "Lila would have a fit."

There was no answer from Rip. Slouched in his seat, he was snoring softly under his wide-brimmed western hat. She breathed a sigh of relief, grateful because she wanted to dawdle past Rosie and Kate's houses and Sweet Briar School.

Rosie's old homestead hardly looked like the same place. Now covered with gold aluminum siding and trimmed in brown, it had been updated for the seventies. Even the outhouse was gone! As she stared at the old Mulgrew home, Cheryl could picture Rosie on the front porch, urging Doris, Kate and her to hurry so they wouldn't miss the previews down at the Pinnacle.

Ahead, she couldn't wait to see if the old Naughton mansion still dominated the block with its eerie presence; however, as she searched the treetops for its familiar turrets, she saw none. Slowing the car, she realized that the landmark was gone. In its place, on pie-shaped plots spilling over with feathering shrubs and flower beds, stood fashionable brick homes—French Provincial, she guessed. The massive iron gate that once had marked the entrance to the long drive to the mansion was the only reminder of the once-forbidding structure.

She edged the Corvair on up the block until Kate's house came into view. It was the only one of the four homes that looked exactly the same. A silver-haired woman on the porch was scolding a man perched high on a ladder.

"Lordy!" she said aloud as she stopped the car by the curb across the street. "It's Kate's mom and dad. Oh, Rip, wake up. You've gotta meet these people."

He shook himself, like a dog rousing out of a deep sleep and brushed his sleeve across his face.

"Let's make it quick." Slapping his hat on his head, he opened the door.

The Freemans frowned slightly as the two approached their porch. Cheryl wondered if they thought she and Rip were salesmen or Jehovah's Witnesses. But the moment she spoke, Mr. Freeman broke into a broad smile. "Cheryl. Cheryl Allison! I'd know that voice anywhere."

Although they greeted her with hugs and shook Rip's hand warmly, Cheryl noticed Mrs. Freeman's glance settle for an instant on Rip's hair. Kate's mother excused herself to get glasses of lemonade—"instant," she apologized. "I don't bother with fresh anymore."

During the next forty-five minutes, Cheryl soaked up every bit of information that the Freemans could share with her about Kate and their friends. She was not surprised to learn that Kate had graduated from college and had gone to work for a newspaper in Indianapolis but shook her head when she heard that Kate was now married to another reporter and had three children. She just couldn't imagine her friend playing the role of the harried housewife and mother.

"Marty—her husband—he covers sports." Mr. Freeman nodded at Rip as if he would appreciate that fact.

Rip replied that he wasn't much into sports and launched into a monologue about his love for music. Mr. Freeman was quick to pick up on their mutual interest; but when he mentioned that he'd played the organ at church for almost twenty-five years, Rip yawned and muttered under his breath that it must have been one helleva gig.

Throughout their visit Rip kept mumbling sarcastic comments, as if he thought the Freemans were deaf. Each time they offered a bit of news, he made a snide remark to himself. Cheryl could feel the perspiration begin to stand out on her forehead, knowing if she could hear his comments from across the porch, certainly Kate's parents could too! She wasn't close enough to elbow him or kick him— and he knew it. When he asked for a second glass of lemonade, she could see how much he was enjoying playing the naughty boy.

She was sad to hear that Doris had left her husband several years ago. Mr. Freeman said that Doris and her children now lived with Violet and Spud and that Doris and Violet had a thriving catering business together.

"All but the oldest boy." Mrs. Freeman corrected her husband as she returned to the porch with Rip's refill. "Doris' oldest boy moved back to the farm to help his father. I'm not sure he even finished high school. Doris couldn't talk about it for a long time, said she couldn't feel worse if Denny had died."

They all considered Doris' situation in a silence broken only by Rip's audible belches.

"I wish I could talk to Doris." Cheryl set her glass down on the little round table. "My son doesn't live with me either."

The Freemans had not heard about Jamie or J.T., so she tried to tell them as briefly as possible while Rip shuffled his feet impatiently.

"Doris isn't in town right now." Mrs. Freeman watched uneasily as Rip began to wander around the porch. "Melba Dawes had wanted Doris and her sister to cater her summer luncheon, but they've gone to New York."

Cheryl almost choked on the piece of ice she was nursing in the side of her cheek.

"Doris? In New York?" To her, Doris visiting New York seemed as likely as Rip doing a gig at The Drake or The Palmer House.

Mr. Freeman then told them that Doris' brother, Tommy, had gone to college at Julliard and had played with several classical groups before zeroing in on his real passion—the piano bar at one of the city's most fashionable hotels.

"They love him in New York." Mr. Freeman scratched his head. "But I never can remember the name of the place where he plays—The Algonquin, I think.

"No, John, it's The Carlyle. I've read little articles about him in *The New Yorker*. Mrs. Freeman corrected him kindly. "Everyone goes to hear him. One reviewer said the music of Tommy Panczyk has the effect of three martinis without the hangover."

"Wow!" Cheryl could hardly believe that "little Tommy Panczyk" had achieved such great success.

"Must've been in the right place at the right time." Rip chomped his ice between his teeth.

"I don't think so, young man." Mr. Freeman stepped over Rip's sprawled legs as he walked over to the side of the porch. "Tommy's always had talent. But he's worked hard to get where he is." He studied Rip intensely until Rip began to squirm. "Virginia and I are going out to New York in the fall. It'll be worth the trip just to hear him play."

When Cheryl announced that they needed to leave, she still was full of questions.

"What happened to the Naughton place?"

Mrs. Freeman explained that the property had been sold a few years ago, shortly after the second Mrs. Naughton died.

"Charley Panczyk lives in one of those new homes." Her eyes sparkled with pleasure. "He's general manager of Midwest Manufacturing now, but he wanted his children to grow up on the Sweet Briar side of town."

"Good for him!" Cheryl paused for a moment, remembering Charley and his brother, Vic, guzzling milk straight from the bottle in their kitchen.

When she asked about Rosie, however, she gained no more information than the news that Russell Logan had given her years ago in Champaign—that she'd gone to California. The Freemans nodded sadly as they agreed that neither Rosie nor her parents had ever been the same since Mike's death.

"And how about Russell Logan? And M.J.?" She wondered as they ambled down the front walk lined with pink roses.

"That's funny you should ask about the two of them in the same breath, because they're both in California." Mrs. Freeman stopped to flip a beetle from the leaf of one of her roses. "M.J. and her husband, Evan Gerard, live in San Diego. He has a design studio, and she's teaching and loves it there. Russell's with an investment firm in San Francisco,

I believe."

"Did he ever marry?" Cheryl knelt to bury her nose in the sweet ivory blossoms at the end of the sidewalk.

"Oh, no." It was Mrs. Freeman's tone of voice that made Rip wink confidentially. In an instant Cheryl realized that Russell must have joined the gay community. She also realized that she wasn't surprised.

"California. Now, that's God's country." Rip ran his hand across his frizzy hair as if he were checking to make sure it was still there. "You guys oughtta move out there."

"I don't think so, son." Mr. Freeman rubbed his chin. "This is the house I was born in."

Rip's mouth dropped open.

"Must've been a real blast to spend your whole life in the same place," he grunted under his breath as he opened the door of the Corvair.

"That it has!" Mr. Freeman not only heard but responded heartily to Rip's whispered sarcasm. "Cheryl— wait!" He snapped off the ivory rose and handed it to her as she started to climb into the stuffy car. "Do come back soon. Sometime when you can stay longer. I'll play the piano. And you can sing."

"And maybe I'll make cookies. Just like the old days." Mrs. Freeman had a way of sweeping all of them back to sweeter, simpler times.

"Wonder where that leaves me." Curtly Rip tipped his hat to the Freemans as Cheryl started the car. "Let's get the hell out of this god-forsaken town."

* * *

Chapter
Twenty-Three

She'd always poured herself into the lyrics of every song, but that fall Cheryl knew she was describing her own life when she sang Bob Dylan's words. She realized that "the times they were a'changin'" and with the stone of Loneliness anchored around her neck, she could feel herself sinking as the weight of it pulled her under.

She'd run out of things to say to Rip. Continually rolling his cigarettes as he paced around their apartment, he grew more caustic by the hour. Each day's mail brought a stack of new bills, unfamiliar credit-card charges that shocked Cheryl so badly that she merely tossed them aimlessly onto the mounting pile on the desk.

However, it was Gus who dropped the bombshell that knocked the breath out of her one evening late in October. As the band warmed up for its evening show at the Nest, Gus banged on Rip's drum and shouted that he had an announcement. His words came rapidly as he told them that Sonny Eliot had decided to sell the business and that the new owner would be changing the entire format. Different look. Different sound. In short, they would be out of their jobs.

"I know I can find us work, goddammit." Gus' brows danced up and down as he watched the band members absorb the impact of his news. "For awhile it may be just special occasion stuff—and the holidays are always good for that, with parties and weddings and shit." He mopped his face with his handkerchief. "You can bet your sweet bippies that I'll be calling you soon with our new permanent spot."

"And you can bet your sweet ass that I—that we—won't be waitin' around for that announcement. Right, Babe?" Viciously Rip kicked the end of the bar. "Besides, I hear they're looking for drummers in Vegas."

Limp from the news and embarrassed by his reaction, Cheryl shot him a dirty look and walked away. She knew they'd have a huge fight when they got home. There would be no avoiding it. Ever since their visit with the Freemans three months earlier, she had found it difficult to muster any respect for Rip because of the condescending way he had treated Kate's parents. Still, she had continued to make excuses to herself and everyone around her for his behavior; he was under pressure . . . and pressure made him restless . . . and restlessness made him mean and sarcastic. Worst of all, she kept recalling that same look of desperation on Bertie's face when the bills were piling up years ago.

Later that night, back in their apartment, Rip argued that it was time for them to move on. When she reminded him that she'd signed a contract for the entire school year, he snorted in contempt.

Trying to keep a cool head, she insisted that she could not leave. She had promised herself that she'd always be near J.T., in case he needed her. But Rip roared right back at her, sneering that J.T. hadn't the foggiest idea who she was.

"Shut up." She tried to keep her voice calm, mature.

It was then that Rip played the trump card he'd saved since the day he met her.

"Isn't it about time you dug into that pile of Foxwell money you've got socked away somewhere?" An unnatural brightness simmered in his green eyes. "*You* know where you've got it. So use it!"

His tirade washed over her like an eight-foot wave on Lake Michigan as he pounded her relentlessly with verbal blows. He claimed there had to be money the Foxwells had given her in a settlement that she'd never told him about. But he was no quitter, by God. He'd figured it all out shortly after they'd met. And he knew that, sooner or later, she'd have to dip into her wealth. Now, he figured, it was time for him to cash in on it too!

Never before had Cheryl felt such rage seething up from the depths of her soul. As she hurled every item that wasn't nailed down at him and called him names she didn't realize she knew, he backed toward the door until he finally opened it and ducked out. Then, just when she thought he was gone, he opened the door a crack and poked his head through it.

"Got a few bucks to get me down the road, Babe?"

She flung his precious vase of flowers at the door and heard it shatter.

A week later, when the end-of-the-month bills arrived, she was both staggered and scared by the size of the debt Rip had left. However, she felt a curious feeling of lightness settle over her as she began to comprehend that the times really were a-changin' and the stone around her neck had not been the Loneliness. Its name had been Rip.

* * *

That winter she developed the art of dodging creditors. Although she tried to pay each one the bare minimum every month, her teaching salary and the band's unpredictable work schedule wouldn't stretch far enough. When Millicent flew in for her annual holiday shopping binge on Michigan Avenue and she told her former mother-in-law that she had also added an evening job at Marshall Field's, Millicent offered her money but Cheryl refused. She couldn't bring herself to accept charity. For the first time in her life, she felt a hint of the desperation that Bertie must have experienced. Knowing she couldn't use his method to cover her bills, she set her jaw and decided she'd do it her own way—and that would have to be the hard way!

She'd always think that Millicent called Shep and told him about her problems. Otherwise, she couldn't imagine why he would have phoned her at home one evening after the holidays and suggested that they meet for a drink at The Berghoff around five the next day.

"What about Helen?" His wife, Cheryl knew, ran a tight ship and might take a dim view of an enlightened woman like her sharing the evening with Shep.

"She'll join us. It's her day to volunteer at The Art Institute, so she'll be in the neighborhood anyway." He paused for a moment. "Hey, we'll all be starved. Let's just have dinner while we're there."

Amazed that after all these years, his voice was still filled with its old contagious charm and vibrancy, she agreed to meet them.

The next evening, when Shep's wife emerged from her mink coat in the darkly paneled restaurant, Cheryl was relieved to see that that Helen had finally ditched her classic Michigan Avenue look and was wearing a mini skirt and fashion boots. She'd never had much patience for Helen's brittle efficiency and buttoned-up demeanor, so maybe there was hope for her yet!

As they sipped beer and exchanged superficialities, Cheryl learned that Shep and Helen had just returned from a skiing trip to Aspen with their three children. She, on the other hand, had spent the holidays alone—except for Christmas Day, when she'd visited J.T. Helen added that she was swamped with a heavy slate of volunteer obligations while their children attended classes in private schools. Cheryl refrained from tossing out a Rip-like bit of sarcasm that she herself had not only given her all to Marshall Field's but had promised to continue through the January sales.

Although their conversation was pleasant enough, she kept waiting for the other shoe to drop. As they savored their sauerbraten and creamed spinach, she began to probe for the real reason Shep had called. She asked about Jamie, but they had little to say.

"His present wife was a showgirl in Las Vegas." Helen raised her eyebrows as she carved her meat into dainty bites. "She and I don't have a whole lot in common."

"Sounds like Rip and me." Buttering a slice of rye bread, Cheryl saw Helen's face redden out of the corner of her eye.

"I didn't mean—" Helen stammered uncharacteristically.

"Hey, it's okay." She studied the texture of the chewy bread, bit into a thick slice and wiped her mouth. "We had our fun. And now he's gone. Easy come, easy go. And no hard feelings." After she took a long, slow drink from her mug she added, "Just a lot of credit card receipts to remember him by."

"That sonofabitch." Shep stabbed a piece of meat and stuffed it into his mouth. "He probably thought you had access to the Foxwell fortune from the first day he met you."

"It would seem so." Staring at her spinach dish, she fought off the urge to run her spoon around the inside to catch the last remnants. Instead, she requested coffee when the waiter asked if they'd like anything else to drink. Helen declined, but Shep took another beer.

"Do you need—" Shep seemed too absorbed in slicing his potato dumpling to look her in the eye.

When she reassured him she'd be fine, he nodded, took a notepad from inside his suit pocket and scribbled a name and phone number.

"You're proud, Cheryl. Too damn proud for your own good. But do me one favor. Call this guy at Boulevard Bank. It's the one in the Wrigley Building, you know." He handed her the scrap of paper. "He'll help you roll up all those nasty debts into one loan. That way, you'll have a lot lower interest rate. Otherwise, those credit card companies will eat you alive and you'll be working at Field's and God knows where else for the rest of your life."

Quickly she pretended to sneeze so she could bury her face in a tissue and neither of them could see the tears in her eyes. She doubted, however, that she fooled either one of them. Shep's animated features were frozen in concern, and even icy Helen reached for her hand with a look of resolve in her eyes.

A few days later, she decided to take Shep's advice and met with Peter Foley at Boulevard Bank. As the chubby little financial adviser began mapping out a new strategy for her, he told her that she was lucky to have Shep and Helen as her friends. In less than an hour, he set her up with one loan, suggested she find a cheaper apartment and steered her toward a divorce lawyer who could do the job quickly and inexpensively.

By spring, she had leased a modest studio unit just off Southport, northwest of Wrigley Field. Every time she moved, she lamented, she landed farther away from the lake. Still, she quickly realized that, by having one consolidated debt and paying half the rent, she could give up her job at Field's.

When she called Shep to thank him for his advice and to report on her progress, he asked how Gus' band was doing.

"That's my other bit of good news," she answered, cheered by his interest. "We've been getting more jobs than we know what to do with. Decent ones too. We're doing a wedding at a club in Kenilworth in May."

"I declare!" Shep's replied sprightly. It wasn't until after she had hung up that she had the oddest feeling that perhaps Helen had been promoting the band among her suburban peers. Well, Cheryl chuckled to herself, we could do worse! Humming "Nice Work If You Can Get It," she began rinsing off her dishes and stacking them in the drainer.

* * *

"Goddammit, we're gettin' so respectable we stink!" Gus plinked out a few notes of "Dueling Banjos" before the band started its practice session in the dance studio he'd been able to sublet for rehearsals. "I ain't been advertising, but I keep getting calls from people up and down the north shore. I've already signed a contract for our first Christmas party—a big hairy deal for Great Lakes Insurance down at the Hilton."

"All 'Star Dust' shit, I s'pose," shouted out Lionel James, the drummer who'd replaced Rip.

"Naw." Gus chomped on his unlighted cigar. "They want a lot of standards, but we're also supposed to do some of the stuff we did at the Nest. And for what they're payin', we'll play like Lawrence Welk standing on our heads if they ask us!"

Lionel howled at the thought. Secretly Cheryl was thrilled. At least this Christmas there'd be no evening shifts for her at Field's with all the gigs Gus was lining up!

She felt so giddy that she splurged on a shimmery royal blue dress to wear at the holiday parties. Bertie would have encouraged it, she rationalized as she recalled her father's weakness for keeping her in the latest attire.

Later she swore that her new blue dress had turned out to be her good luck outfit. She knew it was a crazy theory, but it seemed that whenever she wore it, she sang better! Sometimes guests at the parties asked if she'd dance with them, but she always smiled and told them that they weren't allowed to mix business with pleasure. She even used that line on Jamie at a charity ball at a private club in Winnetka in order to cover her shock at his appearance. His sun-bleached hair had darkened and thinned, and his entire physique had taken on a thick, puffy look. Pouting at her rejection, he winced as a piercing laugh rose above the crowd. Cheryl watched, saddened by his paunchiness, as he turned and lumbered toward the Barbie-doll owner of the shrill giggle, a well-endowed blond who seemed to be the current Mrs. Jamison Trent Foxwell IV.

But later, when Jarvis McTavish, president of Great Lakes Insurance, made his request for a dance near the end of the gala he'd thrown for his employees, Cheryl glanced in Gus' direction and saw him nod almost imperceptibly. She accepted Mr. McTavish's outstretched hand as she stepped off the bandstand and joined him.

Judging from his silver hair and the deep lines in his face, she guessed that he must be in his mid-fifties. Because he was only five inches taller than she and seemed to be all muscle, she thought he would be a natural on the dance floor. Instantly, however, she was surprised by his awkwardness as he tentatively led her around the ballroom floor to the strains of "Close to You." Damn that Gus, she thought. She should singing this one, not trying to follow some rich old fart around the floor!

"Do me a favor before you leave, will you?" Mr. McTavish's brown eyes were thoughtful as he helped her back up onto the bandstand. "Ask Gus to play 'People Will Say We're in Love' so you can sing it. It's always been a special song for me."

As she tried to give Oscar Hammerstein's lyrics her smoothest delivery, she was puzzled that he requested an old number from *Oklahoma* to be the closer for his 1972 holiday party. She searched the crowd of dancers for Mr. McTavish but finally found him seated at his table, his eyes so riveted on her that she almost spaced the line, "Give me my rose and my glove." Distracted by his intensity, she shrugged and decided she was not the one to question the man was paying for the party.

After the holidays, that same man began to call. At first, she felt a little spooked to be spending time with someone who was approaching sixty, but he seemed so lonesome. His voice broke when he spoke emotionally of his wife and the long battle with multiple sclerosis she'd finally lost two years before. He expressed surprise when Cheryl said she couldn't join him for lunch on a weekday because she was teaching.

One thing she learned about Jarvis McTavish was that he did not give up easily. He finally convinced her to meet him for lunch in the Lincoln Park area on a balmy Saturday in April. Afterward, as they strolled around the zoo and he asked about her family, she did her best to make light of her two marital attempts.

His own marriage had been a once-in-a-lifetime kind of love, he said as he guided her into the zoo's ape house. He and Mary Grace had been together since he'd sat behind her in first grade at their rural school in Indiana. Their families had been dirt-poor, he continued. But, as he and Cheryl watched two monkeys squabble over a piece of lettuce, they found it hard to talk of serious matters.

"I'll have to fill you in later." Leaning on the railing, he chuckled in appreciation. "These guys always crack me up."

Throughout the summer months, Cheryl grew impatient as she waited to hear the rest of his life story. Eventually she was able to piece together the facts: He had won a scholarship to college and married Mary Grace the day after he had graduated. Even during the Depression, he'd had a job teaching school. But after the bombing of Pearl Harbor, he'd enlisted in the Navy and had left Mary Grace at home with their two little daughters.

When the war ended, he'd returned home to Mary Grace, tucked away the medals he'd won and decided to take the risk of starting his own small insurance company in Fort Wayne. By 1960, his firm had done so well that Great Lakes had "come a'courting," as he put it. A few years later, the Great Lakes board members had asked him to take over as president. By that time, his daughters had moved to Boston and Oregon and "Mary Grace, God-love-her," as he usually referred to her, was confined to a wheelchair.

Cheryl enjoyed listening to his stories and, she admitted to herself, actually looked forward to spending time with him. When he took her sailing on Lake Michigan, she felt as if she were relaxing with an old friend, even though their trips lacked the tingle of those early sun-splashed days that she'd savored with Jamie on the "Foxy Lady." Later, when Jarvis introduced her to a new pizza place with a delightful table near the window, she experienced none of the electric sizzle that had charged the air when she'd first dated Rip. Each evening, after they had shared a few hours filled with excellent food, wine and conversation, he studied her with his soulful brown eyes and politely escorted her back to her apartment.

Because they never did anything wild and spontaneous, she was totally unprepared for the events that unfolded while they attended an open-air concert at Ravinia near the end of August. Mesmerized as the beauty of Debussy performed by a Japanese orchestra swept over her, she recalled her days at Interlochen, when classical music under the stars was a routine occurrence. The only flaw in the aura of serenity was Jarvis' unusual restlessness that seemed to increase as the last strains filtered through the summer air. She assumed that he was edgy because of the humidity. Thus, she nearly fell over when he blurted in one breath that he wanted to marry her and, in case she had been wondering, he was sixty-three years old!

She felt her heart begin to pound and her jaw drop. In the dark, Jarvis reached for her hand as the musicians switched to a number by Ravel.

"Don't give me an answer tonight," he whispered. "But, when you do, please don't let it be 'no.'"

She could recall very few times in her life when she had been rendered speechless—perhaps when Bertie had told her the family was moving immediately and when the doctor had pronounced J.T. profoundly retarded. She could not consider giving Jarvis an answer that night. After all, he was sixty-three and she just thirty-eight. As she quickly calculated the numbers in her head, she realized that he was twenty-five years older than she was.

Distracted by that fact, she drifted down another train of thought. If Bertie were alive, he'd be only fifty-nine. And Lila, happy as a clam with her second husband in central Florida, was a mere fifty-eight! The whole generation ahead of her was still younger than Jarvis McTavish. And *he* wanted her to marry him!

"I—I can't—" she began.

"I know you can't say anything now." He cupped his hand over hers. "We'll have plenty of time to talk about it later."

That was in August. Six weeks later, his question hung like an invisible barrier between them. Cheryl had to acknowledge that together they'd shared some of the best times of her life. On a warm Sunday in September, he'd driven the specially equipped van that he'd used for Mary Grace and suggested they treat J.T. to a trip to the beach. She'd been gratified that he'd known exactly how to maneuver a wheelchair. The sight of her son, with his pale face pointed toward the late afternoon sun, gave her indescribable joy. For J.T.'s eighteenth birthday, Jarvis had suggested that they take him to an outdoor concert that several high-school bands were presenting. Later she'd realized how insightful his idea had been when J.T. had hummed all the way back to Lake Forest Manor. Still, Jarvis still never pushed her for an answer.

When she began to wonder what life would be like without Jarvis McTavish, she was surprised to feel the familiar fingers of the Loneliness begin to wrap around her like a bristly blanket. Afraid that the Loneliness was preparing to pay her another long visit, she did not want Jarvis to suffer because of her insecurity.

The one thing she knew she must not do at that stage of her life was to make another disastrous commitment. Nor did she want to ruin the rest of Jarvis' days because of her inability to maintain a long-term relationship. She began to tick off her list of reasons why she believed his marrying her would be bad for *him*.

"For one thing, I'm a two-time loser, Jarvis," she protested one brilliant October day as they ambled along the shoreline near North Avenue "You don't want to get hooked up with someone like me."

"You were not the loser." He rested his hand gently on her shoulder, giving her a sense of peace and well-being. "They were!"

"And there's this ridiculous debt." Picking up a stone, she gave it an angry toss and watched it skip three times across the lake's surface before it dropped out of sight. "I've still got Rip's bills to pay off."

"I could—"

"But I won't let you." She stopped, hoping the sharp wind would clear her thoughts. "I have to keep teaching 'til I get the thing paid off."

He nodded as if he understood how vital her independence was to her. Like a child careening downhill on roller skates, she began to sputter out the elements of her life that were absolutely essential.

"And singing too. You couldn't stop me from that," she warned. Lordy, she thought, I hate this! Blinking back her tears, she forged ahead. "Besides, I make real good money with the band."

"I'd never want you to stop." It was then that he confessed that he had fallen in love with her while she sang at his company Christmas party and that he'd been unable to take his eyes off her all evening. When he'd requested the song from *Oklahoma*, he'd been trying to piece the two halves of his life together.

"Mary Grace and I had seen that show during its first run in Chicago." He paused to watch a speedboat bounce through the waves toward the Lincoln Park harbor. "We just loved the music. And I figured, if I could sit there and watch you sing it and not feel guilty, it was time for me to get on with my life."

"But I'm just not sure—" She couldn't begin to verbalize the worries that had stacked up inside her head. People would think he was robbing the cradle or that she was marrying the man for his money. Most of all, in her own heart, she questioned whether she was the right person for him.

"Who is?" He turned from the lake, engulfed her in his arms and kissed her. Cheryl felt the world around her slipping away as they embraced in broad daylight on the North Avenue beach. Succumbing to the security she felt when he held her, she was vaguely aware of a group of guys standing in their cut-off jeans in the sand cheering them on.

"Just one more thing." She pulled back. "We can't get married in November. It's gotta be after the first of the year."

"Why not November? The sooner, the better." The puzzled look on his face made her question again if she were the right person for him.

"Because." She knelt and plucked a penny, heads up, from the sand. "I've already done that twice. And let me tell you, if I've learned one thing in this world, it's that getting married in November is nothing but plain bad luck!"

Laughing, she tumbled into his arms and kissed him soundly, feeling at that moment like the luckiest woman alive.

* * *

Part Two: Kate

1975 – 1987

Chapter Twenty-Four

"**H**ow's *that* for luck?"

Startled by her husband's outburst, Kate turned down the burner under the spaghetti to see why Marty was so excited. She picked up the letter he had tossed on the kitchen table.

"It's the luck of the Irish—that's what it is!" The grin on Marty's freckled face could have lit up the entire circle of downtown Indianapolis. Scanning the page, she felt her stomach flip and delved deep into the refrigerator so he couldn't read the expression on her face.

"*The South Bend Tribune* offering me the Notre Dame football beat! And they want me right away so I can be a part of spring practice. God, Kate, it's my lifelong dream!" Enthusiastically he thumped the table with his fist, then reached around her to extract a can of Miller's Lite. Popping it open, he raised it in the air. "To our new life!"

Kate attempted to keep a smile pasted on her face as she hugged him and tried not to think how much she loved their old life. She'd fallen in love with Indy since her first day as a student at Butler and had carved her own comfortable niche here. After joining the staff of *The Indianapolis News* as a feature writer, she'd met Marty Kirkpatrick, who had been covering high-school sports. They'd married in Indy and were happily settled into their routine with their

317

three children. Now Marty wanted to uproot all of them so he could accept his dream job. She shared his joy but could feel the old "Sweet Briar insecurity," as she always called her feelings about change, creeping up on her. Still smiling brightly, she decided to test the waters by playing the devil's advocate.

"John Michael's doing so well in the gifted cluster for fifth-graders. Think he'll have any trouble with the move?"

"Naw—they'll have something similar in South Bend for him. He'll be on cloud nine when he gets to see the Notre Dame players up close." He took another swig of his beer.

"It shouldn't be hard on Shannon," she mused as she lifted a bag of raw veggies from the hydrator. "She's gotten along pretty well in third grade and always seems to bloom where she's planted. And Kevin?" She began to scrape carrot peelings into the sink. "I'm not sure."

"Kevin's barely four. Give him a little space where he can run, and he'll hardly notice the difference." Marty reached into the Ritz box for a handful of crackers. "In fact, with his natural athletic abilities, he could have some great opportunities growing up near the Golden Dome."

She knew it was silly and selfish to mention her own misgivings. But everything she loved was here: Her writing assignments with guaranteed paychecks, even though she'd switched to freelancing after Kevin was born, and her friends, especially dear, dependable Peggy Birdsong. The children's roots were here, their little footprints imbedded in the patio cement that she and Marty had poured two years ago. The thought of leaving so much security and starting over in uncharted territory made her head spin. Taking a deep breath, she steadied herself against the sink.

That night she tried to present an optimistic front to her children as she heaped piles of pasta onto their plates.

"Can we get a house with four bedrooms so I don't have to put up with Kevin anymore?" John Michael raked his fingers through his blond bangs as he always did when he was confronted with a new situation.

"That's what we'll look for." Expertly, Marty twirled several strands of spaghetti around his fork.

"Can I get a new bedspread and curtains? And have my friends come and visit? And have—" Shannon refused to let her mouthful of pasta keep her from placing her requests.

"One thing at a time, honey. And don't talk with your mouth full." Marty paused and looked at Kevin. "How about you, pal?"

In the waning rays of April sunshine, Kevin's blazing red hair glowed unusually bright. But his face seemed pale and drawn as he sighed.

"Can we get a puppy?" He nibbled around the crust of his garlic bread.

"We'll see." Marty's face clouded as he weighed the possibility. "We—we'll just have to s-see."

Kate glanced quickly at her husband's strong, earnest face. His tendency to stammer under stress indicated that, in spite of his elation, he too might be suffering from a few reservations. As she deftly changed the subject by asking Shannon about her field trip that day, she made a mental note to herself to meet with Peggy Birdsong. Someone had to provide ballast for her tipping boat.

* * *

"I'm afraid it's a done deal," she told Peggy after the two had ordered lunch the following day at a shabby little deli on Thirty-Eighth Street just off Meridian. "I'm thrilled for Marty . . . I really am. But we haven't even considered the option of staying here." She studied the reuben sandwich that the waitress set in front of her. "After all, my whole life is here and . . ." Her voice trailed off uncertainly.

"Then I'll tell you what I think. I hate it—absolutely loathe it— that you might leave." Peggy scowled as she attacked her grilled chicken salad.

There, Kate thought. The words that had been clawing at her heart were finally out in the open. That was one of the reasons she'd always loved Peggy. Her friend never was afraid to verbalize what everyone else was thinking.

"Thanks." She chewed off a chunk of her reuben, then decided she wasn't hungry. How, she wondered with a pang, could she ever function without her faithful confidante? Their affinity had budded when Peggy had rescued her during that terrible attack of stage fright in seventh grade and had spanned the years ever since. After Cheryl had moved to Decatur and Doris and Rosie had drifted in different directions, Peggy's friendship had filled a void in her life. Together, they had weathered their trips to the orthodontist in Danville, worked on Student Council for four years and served as the guiding force behind *The Stonecutter*, Rockwell High's monthly newspaper.

It was hard to imagine that the svelte advertising executive who sat across from her was the pudgy girl she'd met when they were pre-teens. Her longtime friend now wore her hair in a short fashionable razor cut rather than simply anchored with a headband and had managed to shed pounds in all the right places.

"I mean, it's been you and me, kid, since we started high school. Remember the first apartment we rented right out of college? Talk about spooky!" Peggy's brown eyes sparkled at the memory of the efficiency they'd shared just north of downtown Indianapolis.

Kate smiled as pulled the crust from her sandwich.

They'd felt so worldly at the time—she as a rookie feature writer at *The News* and Peggy as a general ad writer for L. S. Ayres.

"And remember how the floor slanted so much that we had to keep turning a cake when we baked so it wouldn't come out crooked?" she asked.

"Yeah, and the night the wallpaper started falling off the wall when we had a party?" Peggy guffawed. "That was the first time you ever brought Marty around. And," she added, "that was the first time you realized you were actually dating *the* Marty Kirkpatrick, Indiana's renowned basketball star."

Kate felt her face redden at the memory. She'd had no idea at the time that Marty had established himself as a legend among Indiana basketball fans when he'd tossed in his famous last-second jump shot to give tiny Tylerville the state basketball championship over Muncie Central during her junior year in high school. After all, she'd been entrenched in Rockwell High School activities and hardly knew the world stretched beyond the Illinois state line.

"It's a good thing someone mentioned it at that party," she admitted. "Otherwise, I'd have been embarrassed to find out in public." Just the next weekend, as she and Marty had listened to an improvisational jazz combo at a little pub, four different men had spotted his auburn hair and lanky frame and had come over to tell him they'd never forget listening to that Tylerville game on the radio. Always reluctant to be in the spotlight, Marty had sputtered a few words of thanks and had tried once again to explain the beauty of improv to her.

"Yeah," Peggy agreed as she munched on a hard roll. "But I'll never forget the Sunday night we were sitting around watching the Ed Sullivan show on that tiny little TV my dad had given us. The national college football champions were guests, and Marty told us his biggest sports passion was Notre Dame football."

"I remember that." Kate bit into the dill pickle beside her sandwich and felt her mouth pucker. "He said his school was too small to offer football, so he was content to play basketball and read everything he could find about the Irish. And I remember that he laughed right out loud when he realized that I could rattle off the names of most of the Cubs for the last fifteen seasons."

"You guys were more like friends than lovers." Thoughtfully Peggy stirred some skim milk into her decaf. "I had to tell you he was head over heels in love with you when he gave you those silver earrings for Christmas. I think I warned you not to let that one get away."

"And still we waited five whole years to get married," Kate reminded her. "I've never been one to make changes in a hurry. I guess," she added ruefully, "I'm still the same old girl."

"Well, you didn't have any trouble with change when the kids started coming along. For awhile that's about all you did was change . . . diapers, that is." Peggy chuckled at her own humor.

Kate sipped her coffee recalling the stacks of diapers that filled the apartment she and Marty had rented.

"Poor John Michael," she said. "We had to learn on him." Glancing at Peggy, she wondered if her friend still recalled that she had named her son for her father and for Mike Mulgrew and how much they had speculated about Rosie's whereabouts at the time.

When their daughter had arrived less than two years later, Peggy had been touched because Kate and Marty had chosen to name their daughter Shannon Margaret. Marty had explained that they had decided on Shannon "because she's an Irish lass" and Margaret in honor of "some obscure saint." Peggy had dissolved in tears when she'd peered through the nursery window at the squalling infant with the pink ribbon taped to her red hair and realized they had bestowed her own proper name of Margaret on their baby.

Four years later, when Kate had learned she was pregnant again, she had confided to Peggy that she really didn't think she could handle a third child. She'd never confessed her fears to Marty that she didn't see how she could manage three children through their morning routines and face the demands of her job at *The News* all day. Peggy had consoled her and suggested that she consider freelancing from home. After they'd assimilated bright-eyed Kevin with his wispy orange hair into their midst, Kate had realized that Peggy had offered the perfect solution.

Now, as the two lunched companionably together, Kate paused to appreciate the tenderhearted Peggy that she knew so well. Slim and confident from her weight-loss program, Peggy had founded her own agency during Kate's last pregnancy and was highly respected in the advertising community for her unusual combination of clear-headed logic and creative instincts. When Kate asked her how business was going, Peggy shrugged casually and mentioned that she just landed two plum accounts, including the 1976 re-election campaign for Congressman Keith McCord.

"I'm probably going to have to increase my staff and move to larger quarters." Cradling her coffee cup with both hands, she winked across the table. "Wanta come along? We were dynamite together when we ran *The Stonecutter*."

"Wouldn't I like to?" she asked dejectedly. "Then I could stay put." But that would never do—not now that Marty was so excited over his new job. Recently she had read in a trade journal article that, "Peggy Birdsong's no-nonsense demeanor screams Madison Avenue." She never ceased to be amazed at her friend's ability to cut through corporate red tape and assemble a sizzling ad campaign and still remain the compassionate girl who had bailed her out at Nancy Dawes' party long ago.

When Peggy spoke sharply to their server, however, Kate recalled a comment that Marty had made right after Kevin was born and she'd asked him to fix up Peggy on a date with one of his friends.

"She intimidates the hell out of most guys." He'd objected from behind the issue of *Sports Illustrated* that he was devouring.

"Not Peggy," she'd protested. "Both of us know she's a sweetheart."

"Maybe we do. But my buddies say she's a ball-buster. Spouts off more information than any of them care to hear." He'd buried his nose in his magazine, signaling that he didn't want to discuss the topic anymore.

Now, her appetite nonexistent, Kate pushed her sandwich aside. No matter how formidable Peggy had become in the advertising world, Kate knew she would miss the warmth and wisdom of their friendship more than anything. When she told her so, Peggy waved her words aside.

"As I said, I hate that you're leaving. But you've got to, kid. It's that old 'whither thou goest' crap. You know that."

Kate smiled. Peggy always could cut straight to the chase. Her friend was smart, she was decisive, and somehow she had just managed to clean up an entire grilled chicken salad without spilling a drop of Russian dressing on her cream-colored suit.

She felt a change in the atmosphere as Peggy began to switch gears and pelted her with logic. What would Kate gain, she wondered, if she stayed in Indianapolis? Write more freelance features? Save the kids from painful upheaval? Exist for the rest of her days with a husband who resented her for denying him the opportunity of a lifetime? Was that what Kate really wanted?

"Damn it, Peggy." She shoved her uneaten sandwich into a styrofoam box. "You should've been a lawyer."

"You think I can't drive the hundred plus miles to South Bend? You think you'll get rid of me that easily?" Hammering her with questions, Peggy finally sensed she had delivered her message and flashed the bright smile of a winner. "Not a chance."

Dropping her eyes to study their bill, Peggy quickly turned to pick up the caramel leather Coach purse that Kate coveted. Although Peggy moved swiftly, she wasn't fast enough to hide the one tear that cut a path through the well-applied Elizabeth Arden foundation on her cheek. Kate knew that Peggy Birdsong, the crisp, incisive advertising executive, would have to repair her makeup before her two o'clock presentation to her prospective client.

And Kate would trudge home with a heavy heart and start calling movers for estimates.

* * *

Chapter Twenty-Five

Later, when Kate looked back on the months just after they moved to South Bend, she wished she'd had sense enough to appreciate them. Instead, she found herself dwelling on what she had left behind instead of what they had together as a family. John Michael and Shannon were quick to find new friends to bring to the older two-story home that she and Marty had bought just north of the St. Joseph River. As Marty seamlessly transferred his skills from *The News* to *The Tribune*, he happily lapped up the Notre Dame mystique.

For Kevin and her, however, the adjustment was even worse than she had anticipated. She honestly felt she'd tried as she'd donned her best little career dress one sultry July morning and delivered her resume to an editor at *The Tribune*. Tapping his bald head, he'd glanced at her carefully typed credentials and told her he had no openings at the present. But, he assured her with a patronizing smile, she was welcome to submit freelance articles to their Sunday magazine section.

Feeling dispirited, she joined Kevin on the back step that afternoon. Together they stared glumly at the overgrown shrubs and patches of chickweed that threatened to take over the yard.

"Want me to push you on your swing?" she offered.

"Not now." His small shoulders slumped as he traced the letter "K" with a stick in the dirt beside the step. "I miss Jeffie from home. And I miss my old digging place. There's nothin' to do here, Mom."

She wanted desperately to tell him that she couldn't agree more. Marty, John Michael and Shannon were already comfortably entrenched. But she and Kevin had no friends, and he was dead right. There was "nothin' to do!" At that moment she resolved to try to find a pal for Kevin the next day.

"We could start a new one." She picked up a stick and began doodling in the dirt.

He gave her a suspicious look. "A new what?"

"Digging place."

"But there's no one to—" His face was sad, resigned.

"There's me. Come on. We'll find a good spot and make some mud." Heading for the garage, she unearthed the hose, dragged it to a bare place next to the garage and flooded the spot with water until the ground grew mushy. On their hands and knees they discussed the differences between their old house and the new one.

"This is okay." He sank his spade deep into the damp earth. "But I liked our old one better. I don't want to change."

There it was. In one simple sentence, Kevin had just stated the fear that had dogged her all her life.

"We'll work on it, sweetheart," she assured him, realizing that he felt the same way she had when she'd entered Sweet Briar School for the first time. "And it'll get better—you'll see. Let's get out your box of Tonka trucks."

The next day she drove Kevin to a nearby park, where they stood at the edge of a pond and watched a family of ducks. Kate had brought a bag of breadcrumbs; and, as they began to attract the ducks, she heard a raspy little voice ask,

"Can I feed 'em too?"

That was their introduction to the adventurous dark-haired Joel Newburg and his pregnant mother, Rachel. In half an hour, Kate learned that Rachel's husband, David, was teaching English literature at Notre Dame, that they had moved a year ago from New Jersey, and that Rachel felt she was hanging by her fingernails onto the fringe of civilization.

"Here's the thing. Sometimes ya'd think it was 1945, not 1975, from the look of this place. It takes forever for a new film to open—and ya can't even get a decent bagel here." Kate tried not to smile as Rachel emphatically shook her black curls to punctuate her sentence. "I mean, it's such a small town and all."

Kate nodded sympathetically. She could only imagine how difficult this woman's move had been, compared to her own. She suggested that maybe Rachel could show her the ropes, advise her about the best places to shop, tell her about any cultural treasures in the area.

Rachel did not have to be asked twice. In her broad accent she warned, "You're gonna have a hard time findin' veal around here too!"

That evening she and Marty relaxed on the front steps, watching their children chase fireflies. "Just look at that Kevin go." Marty sipped his beer. "He's keeping up with John Michael and Shannon."

When she mentioned that Rachel had said Kevin's feet seemed to skim over the grass, Marty predicted softly, "He'll be good at whatever sport he chooses—but I'm putting up the basketball hoop this weekend."

In the days that followed, Kevin's first question each morning was, "Can Joel come over?" Within an hour, Kate would see two heads, one mass of blue-black curls and the other a brilliant red-orange, bent over in their digging place. Later they would race their tricycles up and down the sidewalk and try to convince her to give them Kool-Aid and cookies. She began to relax, now that Kevin had found his friend.

Still, his earlier protest, "But I don't want to change!" had etched itself in her mind. She began to jot down notes about a child who is forced to cope with a move he doesn't want to make. The words seemed to spring from her Royal portable, molding themselves into a short story for children.

"Will it sell?" Marty rubbed his eyes with fatigue after he'd read it late one evening. "I think a lot of kids could identify with this."

"I didn't write it to sell. I wrote it for Kevin." Grimacing at his suggestion, she scooped up a scattering of school papers and grocery lists from the kitchen table. She wanted to put their best foot forward when Peggy arrived for a weekend visit the next day. "Besides," she added, "I don't know a thing about the children's market."

When Peggy arrived, she surveyed their new situation and quickly made her evaluations. Of all their new advantages, she loved most of all their proximity to Lake Michigan and that they could drive to the shore with a picnic lunch in less than an hour. As they dug their toes into the sand and watched the children flirt with foamy waves, Peggy mumbled casually that she and Keith McCord had shared a few drinks after some strategic planning sessions.

"He's close to fifty. You may remember that his wife died a few years ago and left him with a son and a daughter. They're both in college now." Drawing a circle in the sand, she added that she and Keith were "just friends." Kate thought it strange that her usually forthright friend never raised her head to look her in the eye.

The next day Peggy was awed by the beauty of the Notre Dame campus. She was less than impressed, however, with the retail sector.

"Looks as if downtown is giving in to the shopping malls," she observed as Kate and Marty completed their tour on Sunday. "And isn't there a decent deli anywhere around here?"

Marty assured her that the next time she came to visit, they'd take her out for real Polish sausage at one of the bars on the west side.

"You'll be okay here," Peggy pronounced as Kate helped her load her yellow MG convertible late Sunday afternoon. "But don't forget where I live. I miss you, Kate, more than you know. I mean it!" Gracefully she folded her frame into the tiny front seat. "Come see me—okay?"

When Kate leaned over to hug her friend once more, she saw Peggy's eyes were glistening with tears. Both swallowed hard and waved, then Peggy backed her car down the slope of the driveway and roared down the street. Feeling a combination of regret and relief, Kate knew she was ready for a quiet Sunday evening with her family.

"Let's walk the kids over to the ice-cream shop," she suggested to Marty.

* * *

By the time their maple trees were tinged with yellow and orange, Kate was almost too busy to notice the change in seasons. She missed Marty, who always seemed to be packing his suitcase for an out-of-town game but seemed to have acquired Joel as a fourth child after Rachel came home from the hospital with his baby sister, Ronni. The day that she packed her children and three of their new friends into the station wagon to go see *The Apple Dumpling Gang* was the moment that she realized that her entire family had settled in.

They began to look forward to Marty's mealtime stories about a quarterback named Joe Montana, a couple of Browner brothers and their coach, Dan Devine.

"Bad news tonight." Studying the mountain of mashed potatoes he had put on his plate, Marty decided to put one spoonful back into the serving dish in an attempt to curb his expanding waistline. "Montana broke his finger in the Navy game last Saturday and probably won't play this week."

Everyone around the table groaned.

"But there's some good news too." He gestured with his drumstick at Shannon. "Especially for you. They're starting a state girls' basketball championship tournament in February."

"Hey, maybe I'll be like you, Dad." Shannon's freckled face broke into a wide grin.

"Fat chance," muttered John Michael.

Kate sighed. Her son's comment triggered the usual barrage of insults. Once she had nurtured the dream that her family's dinnertime discussions might ascend to the same lofty levels that President Kennedy's parents had reached with their brood as they debated the importance of making contributions to society. Instead, her children had developed an uncanny ability to steer the mealtime topic toward flatulence and any other bodily function. She tried, without much success, to talk with them about their upcoming visit to see her parents for Thanksgiving.

The following Wednesday as she folded clothes for the Rockwell trip, Kevin gave her a handful of letters.

"Mailman came!" he announced cheerfully.

Bills mainly, she thought crossly. Then she spotted the unfamiliar return address from a New York publisher. Intrigued, she tore open the envelope, scanned its contents, and gently lowered herself to the bed so she could reread the message. An editor whose name she did not recognize wrote that she had very much enjoyed her children's book, *But I Don't Want to Change*, and was pleased to tell her that they would like to publish it the following spring. Hands shaking, she did something she never did: She called Marty at work.

She could hear the joy in his voice as he confessed that he had shown the book to Peggy during her visit. Peggy had loved it and asked if she could take it and "maybe submit it to an editor or two."

"We didn't want you to be disappointed, in case it didn't work out," he explained.

"Way to go, Mom!" John Michael and Shannon shouted in unison when they heard her news. Kevin just grinned when he realized that the story about his new friend, Joel, and their digging place, would be shared with other boys and girls.

"All right!" Peggy laughed triumphantly when Kate called to thank her. Although they chatted only briefly, Peggy added that Keith had asked her to join him at Williamsburg for Thanksgiving.

"All right, yourself!" Kate could barely contain her excitement.

"That's not exactly what my mother said," Peggy answered dryly.

Later that evening, after they had unpacked in Rockwell, her parents were ecstatic when they learned of her success.

"I'll have to get a copy for the Rockwell library." Her mother was so giddy that she let the giblets boil over on the stove.

"And don't forget the libraries at Sweet Briar and—" Her dad snapped his fingers as he searched his memory for the name of the other school across the tracks.

"Yeah, I guess we could get one for Longworth too." Kate said quickly, trying to cover the fogginess that her father had shown lately.

"And I'll deliver the copies in person." As he smiled and embraced her, Kate closed her eyes and allowed herself to nestle into the familiar roughness of his brown cardigan. In that moment, she felt herself swept back to the days when a hug from her dad could make everything right with the world.

* * *

By the time her book came out in print the following spring, however, her father was in no shape to live up to his promise. On Thanksgiving morning, the day after he had pledged to deliver her book to the local schools, Kate found him wandering in the upstairs hallway. Totally unresponsive to her questions, he allowed her to guide him back to bed. After an arthritic Dr. Dawes hobbled up their stairs fifteen minutes later, he announced that her dad had suffered a stroke. Then the good doctor called the ambulance.

In shifts, they forced down their makeshift holiday dinner—pale sliced turkey and instant potatoes with yellow gravy—in the hospital dining room in Danville. Marty took all the children to a movie so that John Michael and Shannon could see *Jaws* while he endured a cartoon marathon with Kevin. Kate and her mother never once thought about the twenty-pound turkey that sat spoiling on the kitchen table at home.

"I hate for you to have to see John like this." Bravely her mother smoothed his sheets as she prepared herself for the worst.

"But he's my *dad*. I need to." Kate felt her words stumble over the lump that had wedged itself in her throat. "I'll call M.J. and Evan just as soon as we know anything."

Because of the holiday, however, they had little concrete news from the doctors until late the following day. By that time, her father was sitting up and enjoying a full tray of hospital food. But the warm intelligence that Kate had always sought in his eyes had been replaced with curtained confusion. His smile seemed empty and childlike.

She knew they needed no sophisticated diagnosis from a specialist to tell them that her dad's health had been severely impaired. As soon as they arrived back at the house in Rockwell, she called M.J. and urged her to come home for a few days. Then she and Marty, with help from John Michael and Shannon, rearranged the furniture in order to create a downstairs bedroom for her parents.

Thanksgiving marked the beginning of a seven-month roller coaster ride for all of them. Her dad would come home for a few weeks, only to be rushed back to the hospital after another stroke. Kate brooded over the fact that every time her dad suffered an "incident," as her mother called it, both of her parents paid dearly with dwindling physical strength and waning optimism.

"Grandpa's kinda silly sometimes," John Michael whispered during Memorial Day weekend, as they gathered in her parents' living room. "When he talks, the wrong words come out."

"And he cries 'cause he can't play the piano anymore." Shannon's face was a mask of misery as she sorted the marbles from Gran's old Chinese checkers game. "I feel sorry for him."

"But sometimes he gets the giggles without anyone tickling him." Kevin idly picked out an unknown tune on the treble section of the piano. "I like it when he laughs like that."

Kate lifted his hand from the keyboard and motioned

for him to be quiet.

"Grandpa's trying to nap right now," she explained.

Two weeks later, just as M.J. and Evan were boarding their plane in California to fly in for a routine visit, their father died. It was almost as if he had timed it to coincide with their trip, Kate thought. He never had liked to inconvenience anyone.

Numbed by grief, Kate felt they were all such good soldiers during the next few days. For the children's sake, they rationalized that Grandpa's quality of life had been poor and that he didn't want to become a burden. The evening after the funeral they gathered, exhausted, in the living room. For the first time that Kate could remember, M.J. was quiet and subdued, while the usually reticent Evan repeatedly cleaned his wire-rimmed glasses and made a gallant attempt at small talk with Marty. As they sat, subdued in the deepening shadows, Kate wondered if she were the only one touched by the sweet scent of her dad's roses that drifted in through the open windows. At last, her mother spoke.

"I'd like for each of you children to choose something of your grandfather's." She bit her lip. "He would like for you to keep whatever you want."

Kate was proud of them as they gave thoughtful consideration to their selections.

"Could I have those books he always read to me? You know, *My Book House?*" Shannon's eyes were round with the wonder that her grandmother might give her such a treasure. "Unless, Grandma, you still want 'em."

Kate turned to her mother, who smiled and said that Shannon could read to *her* about "Little Orphant Annie" and "The Raggedy Man" next time she came to Rockwell.

John Michael pulled his fingers through his bangs as he deliberated.

"Would you care if I took his tackle box with those neat baits that he kept out in the garage?" He looked down, embarrassed at his choice. "Some of 'em really used to scare me when I was little."

Kate and Marty glanced at each other in surprise, but her mother agreed and reassured John Michael that she did not plan to go fishing in the near future.

"I want his piano." Kevin, who was just ready to celebrate his fifth birthday, staked the biggest claim of all, boldly and confidently. "Someday I'm gonna play as good as Grandpa."

"As well." Automatically, Kate corrected him. "But Kev—"

"It will be his," Mother declared firmly "Marty, you rent a truck and we'll get some of the neighbors to load it up. Besides," her voice cracked, "I—I can scarcely bear to look at—"

Abruptly she left the room, and M.J. dashed upstairs. It was, Kate realized later, the closest that any of them came to falling apart when her father died.

* * *

Chapter Twenty-Six

K ate knew that she would never forgive herself for being distracted on that muggy morning early the following August. Torn between the emptiness she felt following her father's death and the pride she experienced over the acceptance of her book, she allowed herself to dawdle at the kitchen table. Her day ahead would be a busy one because she had promised to take her children to see the Freedom Train that had stopped in South Bend as part of the bicentennial celebration.

Pouring a second cup of coffee, she reflected that even *The Tribune* was taking a fresh look at her abilities. Just the day before, one of the editors had called to ask her to write an article on children's books. She was savoring the glow of success when she heard the screech of tires that frequently would rip her from a sound sleep for the rest of her life.

First, there was a blunt thud, then total silence and, finally, a wail of panic that she identified as Joel's. Later she remembered running through the house and onto her front lawn, where she watched a weeping woman jump from a gray car. She recalled seeing and rejecting the twisted green bike and the small carrot-topped body that lay silently next to it. She knew nothing more until an ambulance attendant revived her on the way to the hospital. She had never fainted before.

Later Kate would discover that neighbors had dialed for help, called Marty at work and taken a distraught Joel home to Rachel. Later she would learn why Kevin had been in the street where he was forbidden to ride. But at the moment when she regained consciousness, she could hold only one thought: Kevin had to live! As she held smelling salts to her nose during the short ride to the hospital, a wiry young ambulance attendant tried to assure her that Kevin would be in good hands.

Marty met them at the emergency entrance as Kevin was being transferred onto a hospital cart.

"Wh—what ha-happened?" His face so drained of color that even his freckles were pale patches.

Shaking her head, she felt as if she were suspended, a feather floating in a cloud that insulated her from the raw pain she would face later. As Marty held her tight, however, she could feel the quivering fright that betrayed the calm exterior he was trying to present. Together, they clutched hands in the waiting room, oblivious to the din from the television shows that assaulted their senses throughout the long, long day.

Finally, that evening they met Dr. Fischoff, who later would seem like a member of the family. Sitting with them as an older brother might have done, he quietly reviewed Kevin's injuries—a severe concussion but no brain damage and a broken left arm and wrist. His badly crushed leg would require additional surgeries.

"Nothing life-threatening, thank God." Pushing up his rimless glasses, Dr. Fischoff bit his lower lip as he weighed the best way to present the rest of the news.

"We were able to save the leg—at least for now. At first we were afraid we would have to amputate." She felt Marty's hand tighten around hers as she fought off a wave of nausea. The doctor's voice seemed fuzzy, far away.

"He has a long road ahead of him—and it's just too early to predict how well the leg will recover." Dr. Fischoff's scalp, framed by a ring of steely gray fringe, reddened as he spoke, but his blue eyes gazed sympathetically at them. Even in her fragile state, Kate realized that it must never be easy for even an experienced doctor to deliver this kind of news.

That evening she and Marty were so grateful that Kevin was alive that they gave little thought to the long road ahead. Sitting stiffly on hard-backed chairs at the bedside of their chalky-faced son, they picked at rubbery beef and noodles and swallowed a few bites of red gelatin that a thoughtful nurse had delivered on a tray. Then they began to make their calls—Marty to his family and she to her mother and to Rachel. Bravely she assured Joel that his buddy would be out of commission for awhile but, eventually, would be okay. Kate's composure disintegrated, however, when she spoke with her mother.

"Can you come, Mom?" she asked tearfully. "We need you. I mean, we're *really* going to need you. For a long time, maybe."

* * *

In the weeks that followed, her mother ran the household while Kate and Marty devoted their attention to Kevin. From Joel they were able to piece together the scenario before the accident. He and Kevin, both proud that they had just discarded their training wheels, had decided to ride their bikes down the driveway and onto the sidewalk. Joel, the more experienced rider, knew enough to slow down before turning onto the sidewalk. But no one had ever taken Kevin aside and taught him how to use his brakes; he only knew how to pedal. Therefore, he had careened down the slope and into the path of the car while Joel stood by helplessly.

During the next months, she and Marty felt just as helpless as they watched Kevin endure two more surgeries and struggle through painful physical therapy sessions. "Crumpled" was the only word Kate could find to describe her son, for it was as if the car had flattened the very spirit out of him. When he was able to come home between operations, he perked up enough to build a few Lego projects with a patient and attentive Joel. But his friend's unabashed enthusiasm about kindergarten sometimes plunged Kevin into deeper depression as he realized that he was being left behind.

All of them felt the strain as their world revolved around Kevin and only Kevin. Kate heard herself bark at John Michael and Shannon over trivial misdemeanors. She often spoke so crossly to Marty that she suspected he welcomed the opportunity to cover out-of-town games so he could escape from home. Just before Thanksgiving, while Marty was away and the rest of them sat silently around the kitchen table poking at the pot roast her mother had prepared, Kate realized how strained the atmosphere in her home had become. Eating quickly and mechanically, John Michael had little to say. When she asked him about his next basketball game his reply was tinged with bitterness.

"What do you care? You won't be able to come anyway." He shrugged and stuffed a huge forkful of meat into his mouth.

"Nothing matters around here anymore. Grandma's the only one who cares about anything." Shooting Kate a mean look, Shannon curbed her comments when her grandmother reproved her. Since Kevin's accident, Shannon had sought and received all the approval and attention she wanted from her grandmother. Kate decided to deal with that problem later.

"Mom, do I have to finish my meat?" Kevin fidgeted listlessly in his wheel chair.

"Three more bites." She patted his hand encouragingly.

"They don't make me clean up my plate at the hospital." He pulled his hand away and made a face. Kate saw her mother lower her head and stare at her plate so no one could see the tears in her eyes.

* * *

"God knows you guys need help." Rachel's blunt perceptiveness set Kate on edge when she brought her children to visit on a Saturday morning early in December. Her timing could not have been worse, Kate thought. She had just broken the news to Kevin that he would need another surgery late in January. His head and his arm had healed completely, but Dr. Fischoff's final prognosis was bleak. Kevin would never be able to bear full weight on his injured leg again. Eventually he would graduate to crutches and, with hard work and a great deal of courage, might be able to manage with just a cane in a few years.

"My mom's doing her best to keep us going." Kate tried to keep her voice low and even so her mother, who was baking in the kitchen, could not hear.

"But Kevin was so ready for school—so eager to go with Joel. He's going to miss the whole year, and the boys will never be together." Bouncing Ronni on her knee, Rachel took a deep breath and launched her campaign.

"Here's the thing. David's got this teaching assistant with some extra time on his hands. Why don't you hire him to tutor Kevin so he can start first grade on schedule next year?"

341

"But he's got to get over this next surgery—" Kate put down her coffee cup. "I can't push him, Rachel."

"Oh, yeah? You think he's gonna like bein' a year behind his classmates his entire life?" Kate felt Rachel's piercing gaze. "Ya gotta get tough, Kate. It's time. And Christopher's just the guy to get him started, believe me."

She glanced at her son, who was ignoring Joel's requests to play a game of "Sorry." Instead, he stared blankly at a rerun of *The Andy Griffith Show* in the former dining room that now served as his bedroom. Life had indeed stopped for him, in more ways than one. Again, Kate forced herself to be grateful that Kevin was still alive. She did not want her own jealousy of Joel's mobility to sneak to the surface where Rachel would spot it in an instant.

"Besides," Rachel whispered. "Aren't you and Marty ready to have your mom go home so you two can—well, you know, get back to normal?"

Kate felt her lips stretch into a plastic smile so Rachel couldn't possibly see how intrusive her question was. "Probably not as ready as Mom is," she admitted.

That evening, however, Marty was less receptive when she told him about Rachel's comments.

"Hell, n-no!" Disgustedly he threw the supper silverware into the sink. It clattered so loudly that Shannon and Kevin glanced up from *The Brady Bunch* to see what had caused the commotion. "He's *our* son. I th-think we can h-handle this."

"It was just a suggestion." Kate could feel her defenses springing into place. She was glad that her mother had gone to pick up John Michael from basketball practice and wouldn't hear the two of them bickering. Never looking up, she began to fill the dishwasher.

"God, I don't know where you f-find your f-friends," Marty sputtered. "I used to think Peggy could be pushy, but this Rachel seems to think she's got a l-license to run everybody's l-lives!"

Kate knew she didn't have the strength to fight. Wearily she vowed that she would find the time and the stamina to tutor Kevin herself.

Rachel's proposal, however, became a non-issue as they plodded through the motions of celebrating the holidays. Stoically Kate and her mother switched off the radio because the carols made them ache for her dad. Not wanting to hurt the other, each silently nursed her grief and never referred to his absence. Kate could hardly face the ordeal of Christmas shopping and purposely avoided the sporting goods stores where she had always discovered surprises for all three children. Because she knew she couldn't bear to see Kevin stare longingly at his siblings' new athletic equipment, she brought home lackluster items that nobody really wanted.

She longed for her father that holiday season. She wished that, for just one evening, she could be a seventh-grader again riding in her dad's old Pontiac while he spoke of the decency of the hard-working people in the Sweet Briar neighborhood. And she yearned to hear him play carols on the piano that now occupied more than its share of space in their crowded living room.

On the twenty-ninth, as soon as she returned from delivering Marty to the airport for his trip to the Cotton Bowl, she and her mother began to dismantle the holiday decorations. She had always hated taking down the tree, but this year was even worse. On top of everything, this was the very day that Peggy had asked her to come to Indianapolis to serve as matron of honor in her wedding. With Marty's assignment being a command performance, she had told Peggy that she would have to stay at home.

Yanking strands of lights with a vengeance, she fought

back tears as she realized that even if Marty had been available, she would have felt too guilty to leave Kevin so she could go to Indianapolis. Sensing her frustration, her mother stated quietly that she would be returning to Rockwell when Marty came home from Texas.

"It's time. Time for all of us." Gently she wrapped three fragile ornaments in tissue and placed them in a box.

When Kate stopped in surprise to look at her mother, she realized how haggard she had become. As always, her mother was right.

"Thanks, Mom. For everything you've done." They embraced and sighed, wishing they could change the circumstances.

A few days later, when Marty got off the plane after Notre Dame's one-point victory over Houston, he had a spring in his step that Kate had not seen since Kevin's accident.

"Pretty potent chicken soup, wouldn't you say?" He grinned as he picked his bag off the luggage carousel. Confused, she shot him a quizzical look.

"Well, Montana didn't feel good, and they gave him chicken soup at half-time." He threw his bag over his shoulder as they headed out of the airport. "That's all it took for the 'Comeback Kid' to do it again."

She shook her head and grimaced, wondering how an adult man could drum up so much enthusiasm over such a trivial accomplishment.

"I m-mean, we won, Kate. We won the b-ball game." He looked at her as if she must have just landed from another planet.

Wearily she opened her door and slid in.

"I g-guess you had to b-be there," he mumbled. Deflated, he stared at the mounds of dirty snow.

"I guess so." They sat in wordless silence as she drove

344

him home.

Two days later as she watched her mother back her car out of the driveway, Kate felt a wave of panic wash over her. John Michael had slammed the door to his room, Shannon was weeping uncontrollably, and Kevin seemed more anxious than ever. How was she going to cope on her own? She had come to rely on her mother almost more than when she was growing up.

That evening, Marty apologized softly in the kitchen so the rest of the family couldn't hear.

"I'm sorry, Kate. I-I truly am." He brushed his sleeve across his eyes. "Every day I write about players who can run like champions. And every day it eats on me a l-little bit more, j-just knowing that Kev will never be one of th-them."

"What are we going to do?" Her words barely filled the emptiness that hung between them, in that intimate space where they once had shared knowing winks and suggestive glances. She felt as if all their lines of communication had been severed.

"I called that guy—Christopher—from my office today. He's g-going to come over tomorrow morning." Marty glanced at her for an instant, then pulled a Miller's Lite from the fridge. "I spoke with Rachel f-first and g-got his number," he added, answering my next question. "He s-sounds okay."

She touched his arm in appreciation, then went to the stove to stir the chili that simmered on the stove.

"At least we're doing something for Kev." She thought the tightness around his mouth had eased a bit. Neither of them had ever been able to verbalize the fact that cut them so deeply—that they would never see Kevin run again. There had been moments, just before she'd fallen asleep at night, when she'd known Marty was crying into his pillow.

Once, when she had reached over to comfort him, he had pulled away, sending her the obvious message that he would rather suffer privately.

"Why don't you tell Kevin?" She fumbled for the right words. "He'll be more receptive if he thinks the tutor is your idea."

When the doorbell rang just before ten the next morning, Kate expected to find a slim, scholarly English literature major on her front step. Instead, she discovered a tall, muscular young man with spaniel-type eyes. In fact, if he had not had his brown hair tied back in a neat pony tail, she might have mistaken him for one of the football players.

"Christopher Munn." His hand grasped hers firmly but lightly. "I'm here to work with Kevin."

* * *

At first they were all wary of the stranger who seemed to have joined their family circle for the sole purpose of watching television with Kevin. For three long weeks, from her vantage point in the kitchen, Kate stared holes into the back of Christopher Munn. The more time he spent chuckling at reruns, the more she scolded herself for having let Rachel talk her into hiring a tutor. Tutor! She laughed bitterly at the term. Couch potato was more like it.

Later she learned that Christopher's casual approach was part of his well-planned strategy to gain the confidence of her broken son. Only Joel had been able to communicate with Kevin on a regular basis since the accident. Sometimes, on rare occasions, he would whimper and cuddle into her arms, but he had shut out his brother, his sister, his grandmother and even his father most of the time. If he would not allow family members into his tortured little world, Kate wondered how he ever would accept an outside intruder.

After all traces of snow had disappeared just after Easter, however, she noticed that Kevin began casting curious sidelong glances in Christopher's direction. From the kitchen she could see her son observing Christopher warily as he strolled to the window and watched a spring rain hammer their brave little crocus blossoms into the ground.

"I sure know how much you hate to go back to the hospital." Turning from the window, Christopher rolled up the sleeve on his denim shirt to reveal a collection of angry red scars on his right arm. "See this? I've been in the same place, buddy."

Kevin studied the once mangled arm before he asked, "What happened?"

In his calm manner, Christopher explained that he had caught his arm in his father's corn picker on the family farm in Iowa, thus ending his promising career as a football quarterback.

"Thought I'd died and gone straight to hell." He smoothed the sleeve and rebuttoned the cuff.

"Did you cry?" Kevin wondered.

Christopher was silent for a moment. "Not at first. I was too mad and thought I was too tough." He picked up a Nerf ball and tossed it toward Kevin, who instinctively reached for it and caught it. "Then the weirdest thing happened."

"What?" Kevin was hooked.

"I began to see other kids in the hospital who were sick. You know, really sick—like with cancer and other bad stuff." He shook his head. "That's when I cried. I realized that I was going to get my life back and they wouldn't. I bawled like a baby. But for them."

He stuck out his hand, as if he expected Kevin to return the ball to him. Looking it over like a veteran infielder, Kevin gave it a perfect toss that landed in Christopher's palm.

Christopher stared him straight in the eye. "We got work to do, buddy. And let me tell you something. You'll get a few days off while you're in the hospital but that's it. We're going to have you so ready for first grade in the fall that everyone will think you're a genius." Kate saw him wink at Kevin confidentially. "Especially your pal, Joel."

Kevin grinned and held out his hands to make another catch. For the first time since the previous summer, Kate witnessed a flicker of the old competitiveness in her son's eyes.

* * *

A week later, she sat alone with Kevin as he fought off the effects of his anesthetic. During a few moments while he dozed, she turned over the list of post-op instructions she had received and began to jot on the back the fears and revelations that a few young patients in the ward had shared with her. As she wrote, she found herself forging their comments into something that could become the framework for another story. Scribbling faster, she already knew its title. She hoped that a book entitled *But I Don't Want To Go To The Hospital!* might ease the pain of other children facing traumatic situations.

This time she worked directly with Madeline Martindale, who had edited her first book. Embracing the concept, the editor felt Kate's second attempt could be marketed to children's hospitals as well as to the general public. When Kate received the call early in June that her book would be published the following spring, she felt none of her previous exuberance. Not wanting to pocket a penny earned from Kevin's accident, she immediately began to consider worthy causes that could benefit from the proceeds—a major donation in Kevin's name to the orthopedic department or perhaps special items to brighten long-term stays for pediatric patients.

Marty perked up when she told him her news during one of their rare moments alone in the house. Christopher had driven Kevin and Joel to a new McDonald's, and John Michael and Shannon were involved with after-school activities.

"We need so many things that I just haven't been able to get for us on my salary—especially since . . ." Marty's voice trailed off as he offered her his opened bag of pretzels.

"But that's just it. I don't *want* the money from this book." She shook her head, declining the pretzels.

He turned and studied her for a few moments as if he hadn't really seen her for a long time. Then using a ploy that he knew frequently intimidated others, he stood up to take advantage of his full height as he towered over her.

"D-don't want the money?" His tone was incredulous. "Good God, Kate, you're c-crazy!"

"And *you* want to profit from Kevin's tragedy?" She stared at him, wondering how she could have married such a monster. Then she leapt from her chair and heard herself hurling the strongest string of profanity that she'd heard since her days at *The News*. Telling him that she would use the money any way she damn well wanted to, she stomped out of the house, fired up the station wagon and roared down the driveway. Sobbing so hard that she could scarcely see the road, she drove into southern Michigan. Finally, she took solace in a greasy hamburger in the darkened corner of a bar and wished with all her heart that Peggy were not in Washington with her husband.

* * *

Chapter
Twenty-Seven

Two years later, as she reflected on the scarring effects that Kevin's accident had left on all of them, Kate was amazed that she and Marty had bothered to stay together. One thing she knew for sure: They never could have survived if it had not been for Christopher. As she lifted a basket of laundry fresh from the dryer, she wondered how a stranger could actually wiggle his way into the hearts of an entire family with the mere toss of a Nerf ball.

But that was exactly what Christopher had done. From the moment he had thrown the ball and had shown Kevin his injured arm, he had become a fixture at their house. He often stayed for supper and refused any pay for the extra time he spent helping John Michael with his freshman assignments. Shannon had developed such a crush on him that she frequently feigned confusion over her seventh-grade homework so she could bask in Christopher's undivided attention. Even Marty enjoyed his company, especially when they discussed jazz.

Because Kevin's mental and emotional progress continued to please them so much, they began to regard Christopher as some sort of security blanket. Kevin now concentrated on his own capabilities, not his limitations. He zipped through his advanced third-grade math and English assignments, but best of all, he had regained his confidence and sense of mischief. Kate had to keep herself from smiling as she scolded him for "unintentionally" tripping Shannon with one of his crutches and for whipping Joel at every board game they played.

"We're going to have to be careful that he doesn't turn into a brat." Marty stuffed a handful of peanuts into his mouth as he watched the local sports news at ten.

"I'm more worried about the other two." Kate frowned as she threaded a needle and began to stitch Shannon's junior-high basketball letter to her athletic sweater. "Sometimes I can't believe the sass that comes out of their mouths."

She sighed when Marty didn't answer, realizing once again that he had tuned her out. Reflecting on her humdrum existence as cook, maid, laundress, nanny, nurse and, on very rare occasions, an unresponsive sex partner, she continued to stitch until she pricked her finger.

"Ouch!" she exclaimed, throwing down the sweater and automatically sucking the end of her finger. Marty's gaze never left the television set. Blinking back tears, she tried to fend off her growing feeling of isolation that only seemed to increase when she spent time with her husband.

With Rachel now involved as a part-time day-care volunteer, Kate began to yearn for companionship. The only times she experienced any adult conversation came during Christopher's after-school visits three times a week. She began to look forward to the moments he spent with her, telling her about a new book he'd read or describing a show he'd seen in Chicago. One afternoon he shared his cast recording from *Annie* because he knew the lively upbeat score would energize the entire family—even John Michael, whose sullenness hovered over their household like a storm cloud.

It was through music that she saw Christopher begin to

reach Kevin on a deeper level. He had dusted off her father's piano and encouraged Kevin and Joel to follow along as he picked out some simple melodies on the keys. Silent and dusty since the accident, the piano now rocked with the easy duets that Christopher had taught Kevin and Joel to play.

"God, make 'em stop!" Shannon whined one evening in April as she passed through the living room. "The only way I can get any peace around here is to go out and shoot baskets. How can you stand it, Mom?"

Shannon slammed the back door on her way to the driveway before Kate had a chance to tell her that she was happy indeed to stand it. She was sick of the Bee Gees' "Stayin' Alive" that surged in a continuous stream from Shannon's room each day. Thrilled to hear Kevin channel his energy into something positive, she thought about how proud her dad would have been to hear his piano sing again. Kevin was no Tommy Panczyk—yet. But he was having a great time and was showing all of them through his music that it was possible to live with a disability.

By early May, Kate was just beginning to feel that her days were starting to return to normalcy when she received a call from her mother that threatened to flip her life upside down once more. In an uncharacteristic tizzy, her mother told her that a young man who was moving his family to Rockwell had driven by her house and had fallen in love with it. They had agreed on a price, and Aunt Janet had helped her find an apartment with a lovely view on the Longworth side of town. She had one month to make the move and asked Kate if she could spare a week—"just one"—to help her sift through the items in the house. Reeling from the sudden weight of it all, she told her mother that she would let her know the next day.

"A whole week! How can she expect that?" After hanging up the phone, she slammed Kevin's notebooks down onto the kitchen table in front of Christopher. "She knows how bogged down I am with Kevin's schedule, plus everything else I have to do for the rest of the family!"

"Maybe," Christopher replied as he bit into an oatmeal cookie, "she also knows that you could use a good excuse to get away from here for a few days." He said no more but went to join Kevin on the piano bench.

"Oh." Slowly she sank onto a kitchen chair. That thought had never occurred to her.

Later that evening, after Christopher had agreed to be at the house when the children arrived home from school each day, she called to tell her mother she would arrive the next day. As she listlessly packed her suitcase, she hoped that Kevin would be able to manage without her and that Marty, John Michael and Shannon would not live on junk food. But she had to sit down to catch her breath when she realized, with a sense of guilt and shock, that she would miss Christopher most of all.

The first night in her old bed in Rockwell she cried herself to sleep. If only, she thought, she had warned Kevin about riding down the driveway. If only she had held her ground so she and Marty could have stayed in Indy. If only she had never left home to go to Butler. If only she could be twelve years old again and make some different choices.

She awakened the next morning to the welcoming aroma of pancakes and strong coffee. As they sat at the Formica kitchen table, Kate began to understand her mother's decision to move.

"I never could have suggested going somewhere else while John was alive, you know. After all, he was born in this place." She surveyed the red-and-white paper that had covered the walls since Kate's sophomore year in high school. "But it's time to get on with my life—you know, to have a place that is just mine."

After breakfast, when they started on her bedroom, Kate wished that she had followed M.J.'s example and had cleared out her memorabilia. She found her dresser drawers stuffed with souvenirs . . . a program from the seventh-grade operetta when she had reluctantly portrayed Miss Liberty, her collection of autographed movie star pictures, a black-and-white photo of herself with Rosie, Cheryl and Doris. Her dad must have taken the photo, she thought, as she gazed at the four of them sitting on the front steps of her house. Doris was squinting uncertainly into the sun, she and Cheryl were grinning broadly and Rosie was mugging as she held up two fingers behind Cheryl's head.

"We'll never make any progress if you dawdle over every single item." Her mother chided her gently, then she stopped to look at the picture and shook her head. "You girls," she smiled as she remembered. "John never got tired of playing the piano for all of you. And I never got tired of baking for you either."

"We were tighter than M.J.'s braids back then." She blew the dust from a second photo of the four of them.

"How did you get so close?" Her mother took the picture and tilted it toward the light. "I mean, you all had so little in common."

"It was at the beginning of seventh grade—one day after school." She shivered as she thought of Cheryl fighting off the hobos under the railroad trestle. "There were—" She stopped short, remembering their solemn pledge in Rosie's bedroom. "There were—just lots of things that we liked to do together," she finished lamely, feeling her face redden. "Gosh, you're right, Mom. I'd better wade through this stuff if I'm going to be any help at all."

Still, the photo had sent her right back to seventh grade and the strong ties she had developed with her best friends.

When she asked her mother about them, she learned Cheryl was teaching and singing in a band in Chicago and had married a "most disagreeable young man." Rosie was drifting somewhere in California, the last her parents knew. But Doris—steady, dependable Doris—was right there in Rockwell living with Spud and Violet. Kate dropped her pictures and went straight to the phone. When Doris answered and Kate told her she would be in Rockwell all week, her old friend promised to come over late the next afternoon.

"And don't fix supper," Doris warned.

Full of anticipation, Kate answered the doorbell the following day and found Doris laden with two heavy baskets. As Doris set down her load so the two of them could hug, she explained, "One's full of hot stuff, the other's cold."

"Oh, Doris!" Mother's eyes filled with tears as she watched Doris unpack the scalloped chicken, fresh asparagus, hot rolls and Waldorf salad and place them on the kitchen table. "You realize, Kate, that we are going to dine with Rockwell's premier caterer."

"Well, yeah, what're you gonna say? Gotta make a livin' somehow!" Blushing from the compliment, Doris busied herself preparing her wares as if the kitchen were hers.

Kate found herself almost moved to tears. She thought Doris looked so—well, so together. This time *she* felt like the frumpy one. Doris had tied her hair in a neat chignon, and her fashionable pants suit showed that she had not fallen victim to her own excellent cooking. Kate had never seen her friend so trim.

As they dined together, however, Kate soon learned that this competent chef was still the same dear Doris. Poking fun at herself, Doris recalled the time she had cried when Nancy Dawes and her mother had brought food for the

Panczyks' Christmas.

"Now I deliver meals to people all the time and don't think a thing about it." Doris smiled as Kate heaped second portions onto her plate.

After supper, she surprised Doris with her collection of old movie star photos, and they snickered like junior-high girls at some of the old pictures she had unearthed from the bottom of her dresser drawer.

As they swapped stories of the last few years, Kate felt as if she had snuggled into a comfortable cocoon. She realized that Doris Panczyk never had and never would judge her. Even Peggy Birdsong might be quick to point out some of her obvious mistakes, but Doris would not. She would merely shrug and say, "Yeah, stuff like that happens. What're you goin' to do?"

Kate learned that Doris still lived with Spud and Violet. "Kinda like their pet dog or somethin'." Pausing to study another picture taken at Cheryl's fourteenth birthday party just before she moved, Doris went on to say that the catering business she and Violet had started had grown to such proportions that they had hired additional help. All of her children were on their own, some doing better than others, she added.

"Nothin' hurts quite as bad as knowin' one of your kids is hurtin'," she sympathized when she learned of Kevin's accident and the toll it had taken on Kate and her family.

"It about killed me when Denny went back to the farm." Sadly setting the pile of pictures back on the kitchen table, she grew pensive. "Didn't do him no good neither—he's been married three times and he's still chasin' skirts. That hurts me too." She glanced at Kate's mother for affirmation, as if she and Kate were seventh-graders again. "I guess you never get done bein' a mom, do you?"

Kate watched as her mother considered Doris' words

and abruptly strode to the counter to get the coffeepot. "How right you are, Doris," she murmured as she filled their cups with hot decaf, her voice laced with concern.

"Well the acorn—that's Denny—sure didn't fall far from the tree, like they say." Doris slammed a lid on one of her dishes and shoved it into her basket. "His dad, that son-of-a bit—billiard ball," she caught herself at the last moment, "died two years ago. And not a minute too soon neither."

They turned their attention to Cheryl and Rosie. No one had heard anything about Cheryl since she and Rip stopped to see Kate's parents several years before.

"Doris, if it's any consolation, we didn't like *her* husband either." Mother's rare critical comment caused Doris to laugh so hard she almost spilled her coffee.

"And Rosie?" Kate wondered, setting down her cup.

They fell silent for a few moments, as they always did when they thought of Rosie. After all those years, the unfinished business of Rosie's withdrawal after Mike's death still weighed heavily. Deep down they wondered if, somehow, they had failed their friend and leader when she had needed them most.

"Same old stuff—just what Colleen and Danny pass along. She got married some years back to a guy whose wife had died. They live out west somewhere—Arizona or New Mexico." Doris shook her head. "I'd give anything for the four of us to get together just once more," she whispered in her subdued seventh-grade-Doris voice. "You guys always made me feel like I belonged. Even if I didn't."

"Me too," Kate agreed as she carried their dishes to the sink. "I've never had such a special group of friends in my entire life."

"No kiddin'? And you goin' off to college and then writin' books for kids and all?" Doris stopped folding the checked cloth that covered the "hot basket" and gaped.

"Never." She started some hot sudsy water so their dishes could soak. "Oh, I've had a good friend here and a good friend there. Peggy Birdsong and I got to be pretty close after the four of us drifted apart. But somehow," she paused, recalling the times they had played with Vickie and the twins in Panczyks' shabby living room, "it was never the same."

Studying her perceptively, her mother announced that she'd leave them so they could visit alone for a few minutes. Inwardly Kate smiled, knowing it was time for *Jeopardy*. Her mom never missed a show because, she insisted, it was quite educational.

"Did you ever tell anyone about—you know?" Although there was no one else in the kitchen, Doris spoke in hushed tones as she gestured in the direction of the cemetery road.

"Never. Not a soul." Their eyes met in mutual understanding.

"God, that's amazing—after all those years." Considering that fact for a moment, Doris then flashed her a confidential grin. "Me neither."

* * *

By the end of the week, Kate felt emotionally and physically drained as she traced her way over the two-lane highways that led back to South Bend. The gigantic tasks of filling a dumpster with trash and deciding which items would go to the Salvation Army had left her depleted. While she found herself despondent about saying good-bye to each room in her beloved home, her resilient mother seemed energized by the entire process. Mother almost appeared to be shedding longtime burdens as she disposed of years of accumulation. She even seemed to look forward to moving day, when the Methodist men's group would transfer her things to her new apartment while the ladies from the church provided lunch.

Kate slowed as she drove through the crumbling business section of a small town just over the Indiana state line. Once again, she recognized the familiar anxiety that nearly suffocated her when she had to face a major change.

She smiled grimly, thinking the situation resembled the uncertainty she had fought in seventh grade when she had been wedged between Sweet Briar and Longworth camps and felt she belonged in neither. Now, as she grieved over the loss of the Rockwell house, she was reluctant to return to the demands in her own home. If only Marty could be more supportive, she mused. If only he could be more compassionate like—well, like Christopher. If only . . .

She hated change—no doubt about it. She'd fought it by packing her car with nostalgic treasures from her mother's house. The kids, she knew, would be intrigued with some of the items she'd salvaged. Dodging a cavernous pothole on the west side of South Bend, she vowed to try to make life more pleasant for all of her family. As she imagined her house and her loved ones in it, she floored the accelerator.

When she pulled into her driveway, she was grateful to discover that she truly had been missed. Her heart skipped a beat when Kevin's crutch caught in a patch of grass as he hurried to meet her. Shannon gave her a quick kiss and was gone; a tolerant John Michael endured her hug; and Marty's grin revealed that he was glad to see her. His smile faded, however, when he opened the trunk.

"What's all this crap?" He flipped through her collection of movie star pictures.

"It's not crap. And I'll put away every bit of it. Don't

worry about it," she bristled as she scooped up an armful of memorabilia.

"God, you're gonna have our h-house looking just like your m-mother's." Blowing the dust from a stack of boxes, Marty hauled them straight to the basement entrance.

* * *

A few months later, when she finally had the time to sort through her souvenirs, she found that Christopher was the only one who showed any interest. He was fascinated with the autographed pictures of Ronald Reagan, Peter Lawford and Esther Williams and carefully examined her old Disney toys.

"These are valuable, you know," he advised on a crisp evening in early September after he had returned from Iowa for the fall semester. He had just shared supper with them and rinsed his plate before placing it in the dishwasher.

"Better sell 'em then," Marty advised as he came through the kitchen to get a drink. He and Shannon were shooting baskets in the driveway. The thump from their dribbling had served as accompaniment to Christopher Cross' "Sailing," which bleated non-stop from Shannon's radio.

"Not on your life," Kate shot back.

Two years later, she realized that Marty was still smarting from her decision to donate two-thirds of the proceeds of her second book to the children's ward at the hospital. Recently she learned that Madeline Martindale had scheduled her third book for publication the following fall. Based on a poignant plea from Kevin, *But I Want to Be Like Other Kids*, it addressed the needs of children with disabilities as they searched for ways to turn negative situations into positive ones.

360

She had already decided that the money from the new book would go directly into their children's college fund, but she wasn't ready to tangle with Marty over finances again. Not just yet. Madeline had already told her that the publisher was lining up promotional spots for Kate to do on the *Today* show and *Good Morning, America* in November. She'd been so excited when she heard the news that she'd shared it with Christopher but couldn't face opening another Pandora's box with Marty. She knew he would only find reasons to shoot holes in the entire project.

When she finally did tell Marty, she felt ashamed that she had ever doubted him. Proud beyond her hopes, Marty seemed as overjoyed as he had been the day he had received his offer from *The Tribune*. When he checked his calendar and found that he would be covering a game out east right after her television appearances, he suggested that they hire Christopher to watch their children so the two of them could have a fling in New York together.

Ambivalent about the trip, Kate approached the tour with great trepidation. She was excited to think that she, Kate Kirkpatrick, would be appearing on network television and touring Manhattan. Still, she was hesitant to discuss the emotional roots of her book with an aloof Bryant Gumbel. Most of all, however, she tried not to dwell on the qualms she experienced when she considered spending long hours alone with Marty for the first time in years.

Later she scolded herself for all her petty little worries about situations that never materialized. Just two nights before she and Marty were scheduled to leave for New York, she received the phone call from a shaky Aunt Janet that would change all of their plans as well as their lives. Trying to maintain her composure, her aunt instructed her to sit down, then she began her narrative. As she listened, Kate wanted to scream impatiently for her to get to the point while another part of her never wanted to hear the finish.

Aunt Janet explained that a freak late autumn storm had caused puddles of rain to freeze in the driveway of her mother's apartment complex. Unsuspecting, Mother had slipped on her way to her car, hit her head on a large landscaping stone and had lain unconscious for an hour. When she failed to show up for her bridge game and did not answer her phone, a few members of her club had gone to her apartment and had found her.

"I am so sorry, honey." Aunt Janet's voice broke. "She died at the hospital a few minutes after she got there."

* * *

Chapter

Twenty-Eight

"Died?" Kate could only whisper one word as she fought to reject Aunt Janet's message. People didn't just die when they were starting a new phase of their lives; people didn't just die on their way to play bridge; people just didn't die. Not *her* mother.

"Died?" she repeated in disbelief.

Later, when she tried to recall the events of that evening, she conjured up blurred images of John Michael finishing the conversation with Aunt Janet and fixing her a cup of tea to sustain her until Marty arrived home from a jazz concert at the university. She remembered marveling, in her precarious state, that her son who rarely spoke a word to her had suddenly turned kind and attentive.

During the days that followed, she could not believe the support she received from family and friends. Marty canceled their trip to New York and, for the first time, asked *The Tribune* to send another reporter to cover the Notre Dame game. Back in Rockwell, Doris visited the funeral home with some of her children, but Kate had no idea which ones she was meeting. Colleen and Danny paid their respects and reminded her again of how much Rosie had loved spending time at Gran's house. A large floral arrangement from Peggy and her husband arrived the morning of the funeral; a card explained that they were on a political junket to several Asian countries but would get in touch as soon as they arrived back in Indianapolis.

Many people from all walks of life offered their comfort, each one bearing the same message: "Your mother was always so nice to me." While M.J. and Evan chatted pleasantly and coherently with visitors, Kate felt disoriented and detached. She seemed to have put her body on automatic drive.

In the weeks that followed, she trudged through the holiday season and tried not to let her gloom ruin Christmas for the family. She became a socially acceptable robot, clapping mechanically every time Shannon swished the ball through the basket for her high-school team. She even drove to Kokomo to meet Peggy for lunch and tried in vain to absorb her friend's words of wisdom about how to handle the loss of one's mother. She was so strong, in fact, that everyone around her, including Marty, agreed that she seemed to be doing real well. But she couldn't fool Christopher.

One early April afternoon, he stopped by unexpectedly. Kevin was at Joel's house, Marty was at work and John Michael and Shannon had gone to the mall with friends. She offered to make them some tea.

"It doesn't get any easier, does it?" His brown eyes studied her over the top of his cup. "Cut yourself some slack, Kate, and forget about being strong for awhile."

Something in his tone reached a spot deep inside, a hidden hollow for her grief that no one else knew existed. It was a secret sanctuary where she could recreate scenes from her lifetime as she recalled the love her mother had shown for her. Often she slipped into that private place to suffer silently because she knew there would be no more memories to add to that sacred collection.

"I still miss my mom. And she died nine years ago." He

refilled his own cup and motioned toward the teapot. She declined wordlessly.

"It's something you never get over." Stirring a spoonful of sugar into the liquid, he said thoughtfully, "Oh, you don't dwell on it. But still, you miss her so much. Every day."

No one had described ongoing grief to her in quite those words. Instead, everyone had been brutally chipper and cheerful.

"I-I never had a chance to thank her. For everything. To say good-bye—" Oh, God, she thought, as she felt the sobs emerging—great wracking heaves that were going to embarrass both of them. "And now there's no one left—"

"Except Marty and the kids—"

"I mean no one who really—well, really cares about me the way my mother did." There. She'd admitted her selfishness at losing her mother and Christopher could just think less or her. She put her head down on the table and wept.

He never tried to stop her as she poured out her emotions. Finally, when she looked up at him through bleary eyes and saw his own tears, he spoke.

"*I* care, Kate." He walked over and put his arm around her. "I have from the first moment I walked into this house. And I always will."

She threw herself against him, snuggling into the strength of his arms. "Oh, Christopher," she began to weep again. "What are we going to do?"

* * *

Once she had allowed Christopher to know her true feelings for him, she began to transfer each of her mother's finest qualities to him. Strong like her, he seemed to comprehend Kate's grief better than anyone in her immediate family. Warm and sensitive, he knew how to brighten her days. Hungry for cultural diversions like her mother, he suggested that she read the novels of Anne Tyler and listen to the cast recording of *Evita* that he left at her house.

She looked forward to the times, when Kevin and Joel were engrossed in a duet on the piano and she could permit him to cup her face in his hands and place a tender kiss on her lips. Warm from desire—and the fear that they would be caught—she would scurry back to the kitchen while Christopher checked on the boys and their music.

The ever-observant Rachel was the first to make the comment that brought her down to earth.

"Here's the thing. David thinks Christopher's fallen in love," she mused at Kate's kitchen table one morning as she and Ronni were on their way home from nursery school. "He says he's singin' to himself all the time. Like a subway musician, he is."

"He's always been pretty upbeat. Look how much he's done for Kevin. And Joel too, for that matter." Deftly Kate tried to turn the conversation toward Rachel's family as she placed a cup of milk in front of Ronni. "We can never thank you enough for suggesting that he come to tutor Kevin."

"David says it's more than that." Rachel trained her eyes on Kate. "Has he ever mentioned a girl to you?"

Feeling her face grow warm, she turned away to pluck a box of Ritz crackers from the cupboard. "Not to me. But, then, you know how we are around this house—pretty kid-centered."

"Yeah, well maybe he's just happy 'cause he's had a couple of teaching offers."

Rachel leaned over to wipe the white mustache from Ronni's upper lip.

"Here in South Bend?" Kate tried to keep her voice cool, disinterested.

"Naw. You know how they are here at the Dome. They want you to go away to cut your teeth, then someday, if you're lucky, they'll take you back. Come on, Ronni—we gotta stop at the store on our way home."

As Kate watched Rachel buckle her daughter into her car seat, she realized how often their chats together left her feeling prickly and uneasy. She couldn't ask for a friend who was more loyal, but Rachel definitely had the ability to unsettle her stomach.

That afternoon, when she asked Christopher about job offers, he brushed off her questions. He agreed that they needed to discuss his future but not at her house. They needed more privacy. The ideal spot would be at a small inn on Lake Michigan, he added casually—perhaps the first weekend in May. The intensity in his eyes conveyed the unspoken message.

"Are you suggesting—"

"Yes." He took her hands in his for a brief moment, then dropped them when he heard Shannon bang the back door behind her. "I'll make the plans. You figure out a way." He lowered his voice. "We're not kids, Kate. And I'm not sure how much longer—" He whirled to greet Shannon, whose smile revealed how much very she adored him.

For the next ten days, Kate could hardly sleep. After mentioning to Marty that she was going into Michigan for a couple of book signings and would be back late Sunday afternoon, she was stricken with guilt. He had believed her without question. Still, the urgency . . . the opportunity . . . the thrill of the offer to break free from the chains that had bound her since Kevin's accident outweighed any second thoughts that might have kept her at home.

Their plan was to meet at the inn early in the afternoon.

Certainly she didn't want anyone to see her picking up Christopher, so she would drive her own car. When she arrived at the inn shortly after two o'clock, he was already waiting for her, pony tail neatly fastened, long sleeves of his denim shirt covering his scarred arm and a tender smile signaling how glad he was to see her. She registered and took a key from the matronly lady, who scrutinized Kate for a moment.

Gallantly Christopher guided her to their room and closed the door. She admired the romantic backdrop of the dainty floral wallpaper and antique furniture, then felt his warm lips on hers. Initially he was hesitant, like a boy on his first date. Then, sensing her nervousness, he suggested that they stroll around the gardens and climb to the top of a sand dune where they could view the lake.

Outside, she tried to calm herself, taking deep breaths of the heavy air that was unusually oppressive for May. Branches of red buds brushed their cheeks as they ambled hand in hand along the stone path.

"Looks as if we could get rain." She glanced toward the west, then wondered why the most inane comments seemed to fly from her mouth at the most crucial times of her life. Christopher merely nodded, then beside a trellised arch bordered with lilacs, he stopped and kissed her again. His lips left her trembling and begging for more.

Abandoning thoughts of climbing a sand dune, they tried to make their way through the inn's cozy living room as casually as possible. But once in their room, they could wait no longer. As they peeled off their clothes and she saw his muscular body firm with desire, Kate dismissed every moral thought that could ruin their perfect moment together.

Wildly they made love with all the finesse of two teenagers in the back seat of an old Nash, then fell into an ex-

hausted sleep. Later she awoke to his touch, tenderly arous-
ing her. This time they savored their union, each gently and
slowly anticipating the needs of the other. Without shame,
Kate gave herself to him completely.

"This is the best book signing I ever had," she mumbled
happily as they lay together afterward.

Propping himself up on his elbow, he grinned at her.
"And if we're going to 'sign books' all night, we'd better
get something to eat. I hope they have a good steak!"

Showering together, they allowed themselves to get carried away again before they finally were able to dress and
make their way to the dining room.

Sated from their afternoon activities, Kate declined the
wine but echoed Christopher's order for a filet with mush-
rooms, special baked potato and large salad. She shoved all
thoughts of her family to the farthest corner of her mind
and asked him about his job possibilities.

He'd had three now, he explained, but he hadn't wanted
to talk about them in front of her family. Each was for a
beginning faculty position in English literature. And although he was flattered to have had offers from Carleton in
Minnesota and Xavier in Cincinnati, he was considering
accepting the one at Western Michigan because he would
be close to her.

They discussed how difficult it would be for Kevin to
adjust but agreed that he no longer needed Christopher to
lean on.

"I've become more of a crutch than the one he walks
with." Christopher speered his salad. "It's time for him to
go it alone."

Kate could feel her questions mounting but decided to
save them for later: What about the two of them? Where
did he see their relationship going? How could she live
without seeing him every day?

They enjoyed their main course in comfortable silence.
Then, as they waited for the creme broulet to arrive, he
tipped back in his chair and told her jauntily, "You should
realize that this is the longest courtship I've ever endured."
Flashing her a devilish smile, he let her know that he had
paid her the supreme compliment.

His words jarred her. What did he mean? "Longest . . .
endured?" Puzzled, almost disoriented by his remark, she
looked at him questioningly.

"I mean—those girls from St. Mary's, well, and Notre
Dame too, for that matter. They're easy and they're quick."
He rubbed his chin thoughtfully. "But you, Kate, were
worth every minute that I waited for you. You are absolutely unbelievable."

Her head buzzed as she wondered: Where was this going? What was he trying to tell her? What St. Mary's and
Notre Dame girls? She tried to calm herself as she replied.

"It was worth the wait for me too, Christopher. I guess I
never realized how much I needed—well, and wanted—
you too until after Mother died and you were so understanding." She cracked the thin caramel layer of her dessert
and let the silky-smooth custard melt in her mouth.

"*I* knew the moment I set eyes on you—that first day
when I came to tutor Kevin." Swiftly he ladled his dessert
into his mouth. "Man, when I think about all that I had to
go through—" He stopped, realizing he might have said too
much.

"Such as?" Feeling a sudden draft in the room, she set
her spoon on her plate. Reaching for her sweater on the
back of her chair, she snugged it around her shoulders.

"More coffee?" Their waitress hovered over them, then
filled their cups.

"Well, you know, pretending to enjoy Marty's company
and Shannon's silliness." Christopher blew on the steaming

liquid. "I mean, that Marty—he may be a basketball legend and all that, but he's really kind of an old fuddy-duddy. Of course, there were times when Kevin wasn't so much fun either—especially when his bratty friend, Joel, was there."

His words, tossed into the air like innocent drops of rain, descended on her and turned her to stone. Sitting still as a statue, she recalled the events of the afternoon. The two of them had not been able to get enough of each other. Now, she pondered in disbelief, was he confessing that he had endured—yes, actually endured—experiences with her precious family, just to get her into bed? Steadily, pleasantly, she posed the question straight out.

"Oh, yeah, and I wouldn't have had it any other way. Except it took you so damn long!" Again, he smiled smugly. "And we have a whole night ahead of us—plus lots of other weekends for who knows how long?"

"Excuse me. Just for a minute, Christopher. I need to go to the ladies room." Although she had tasted no wine, she had never felt as wobbly as she did as she blindly made her way through the dining room and the lobby. Once out of his view, she bolted for their room, grateful that she had taken the second key when they checked in. Hastily she threw her things into her suitcase and shut the door behind her as she left the room.

"Hey—what's going on?" Christopher was just leaving the dining room in time to see her stride through the lobby with her bag.

"You jerk!" She could not find words strong enough to express her anger. "You big miserable jerk. You *used* me! Used all of us, just to get what you wanted!" A chill wind whipped her sweater as she fled through the front door and felt the sting of a light rain peppering her face.

"Hey!" He shouted as he chased her through the parking lot. "You wanted it just as much as I did!"

"And I," her words sounded thick and hoarse as she started the engine, "am a damn fool!"

Hail the size of marbles pounded her windshield by the time she reached the highway. Inside the car, she made no effort to wipe away the bitter tears that streamed down her cheeks and etched warm paths on her neck. She realized that the beauty of the sultry afternoon had all been a cruel hoax as she pushed her Chevy through the storm.

As she turned the corner of her street, the rain slackened and she suddenly faced conflicting emotions. She couldn't wait to feel the security of Marty's arms; on the other hand, she knew that she had a terrible confession to make. Walking through the kitchen, she saw that her husband had nodded off in front of the television. As she stood and watched this decent man, deep in tranquil slumber, she never in her life had felt so worthless and undeserving.

She tiptoed over and kissed Marty on the forehead. Surprised, he roused and glanced at his watch.

"You're home early." He rubbed his eyes, confused by her untimely arrival. "Was your book-signing canceled?" Then, regaining his focus, he stared at her. "You okay?"

"No, Marty, I don't think so." She fell into his lap, weeping. "Just hold me, please. Hold me real tight."

* * *

Chapter Twenty-Nine

Damaged. It was the only way Kate could describe her family. They were bruised and dented like a set of pots and pans that had been dropped from a two-story window. Although they tried to make repairs, they found that all the tears, all the apologies and all the counseling could never transport them to that golden place where they had once lived.

When their counselor explained that a family tragedy has a ripple effect on every one of its members, Kate understood for the first time in her life, why Rosie's behavior had changed so abruptly after Mike had been killed. In their own case, she and Marty had adjusted their course by focusing so narrowly on Kevin that they had neglected John Michael and Shannon. And, most certainly, she and Marty had neglected each other.

They waded through ugly times after she confessed her infidelity to Marty. Harsh, judgmental, angrier than she had ever seen him, he had stormed out of the house. A few days later, when Shannon had called him at the motel and begged him to come home, Kate knew that he had done so only because she herself was so unstable. Once he returned, he began the sad, arduous task of putting their broken family back together again.

They never told the children what had transpired between Christopher and her. Maybe, Kate mused, when I'm approaching my one-hundredth birthday, I will share with them the worst chapter of my life. But, for the time being, neither she nor Marty wanted to destroy Kevin's image of the young man who had helped him in so many ways.

Christopher came to the house just once after their time together at the inn. He wanted to tell Kevin that he had accepted a teaching position at Stephens College in central Missouri and that he was expecting great things from him.

"Keep in touch, buddy." He gave Kevin a quick hug, then as he left by the back door, he flashed her a knowing smile. "Thanks, Kate . . . for all the good times."

If Kevin had not been there, she knew she would have chased Christopher down the driveway with a butcher knife. Instead, she glared at him, silently wondering how many conquests awaited him at the all-girls' school in Missouri.

During months of painful counseling sessions, Marty began to understand that he had been too preoccupied with his own bitterness over Kevin's injury to realize that Kate was suffering too. She discovered that she had buried her emotions—her guilt over Kevin's accident, her grief over the deaths of her parents, her confusion over John Michael and Shannon's surly moods. She even realized that she had resented Peggy's election to Congress after Keith had been killed in a helicopter crash. All that unresolved turmoil had opened the door for Christopher, and she had permitted herself to be seduced both mentally and physically.

As they struggled to rebuild their lives during the next few years, she and Marty were side by side as they shared moments of extreme pride and moments of darkest pain. They were elated when John Michael received a scholarship to Butler, then shattered when he dropped out of school to join the Navy.

"He has to feel that he is writing his own script," their counselor advised them.

They were immensely proud of Shannon when she led her basketball team to the state finals her senior year. She and her father were featured in a three-column picture on the front page of *The News*. However, after she went on to play for Purdue, Kate and Marty learned only by chance that their daughter had undergone an illegal abortion just before her junior season in high school.

"Hard, hard choices these kids have to make," their counselor sympathized. "Shannon will have to live with that one all her life. The bad news is that she felt she couldn't come to you at that particular time. The good news is now she realizes that you'll be there for her from now on, whatever happens. And that, folks, is progress."

When Kevin entered high school, he was mature beyond his years. He and Joel remained good friends, but Joel spent every waking hour in the chemistry lab, while Kevin had begun arranging special numbers for the swing choir. Still drawn to athletics, he secretly met with Dr. Fischoff to discuss the different scenarios that lay ahead for a leg that seemed to be withering rather than growing stronger. When he announced at supper near the end of his freshman year that he and Dr. Fischoff agreed that the best course of action was amputation just below the knee, Kate and Marty rebelled vehemently.

"Not after all you've been through!" She could not even think about it.

"Wh-what does he think you can do with a prosthesis and a lot of th-therapy?" Obviously shaken, Marty was open to the possibility.

Frightened as they were, she and Marty finally gave their consent. After all, it was Kevin's leg, Kevin's life and Kevin's choice. Less than two years later, he entered his first basketball game as a substitute with his pals chanting, "Kev-in! Kev-in!" Patting his prosthesis, he grinned and gave his buddies a thumbs-up sign. When he swished his third attempt at a field goal and moved steadily down the floor on his artificial leg, Kate felt Marty squeeze her hand so hard she feared he would crush her fingers. It was the first time either of them had ever cried at a basketball game.

Battered but surviving, she and Marty learned to give each other space and, as a result, seemed to want to be together more. On a May afternoon in 1987, six long years after her afternoon with Christopher, Marty waved two tickets to Wrigley Field in front of her as she worked at her computer.

"Hey, Kate. Look what I've got."

Shoving down her glasses, she read the fine print.

"June 3. That's next Wednesday. And my birthday." She stopped to check her calendar and sighed. "That's the day I promised to talk about my books at the downtown library. Plus, you know I'm working on a deadline—"

"That's okay. Ryno and Andre Dawson will understand." Sauntering away, he added, "I'll see if Jerry down at the paper wants to go with me."

She hesitated only a second. "Don't you dare give away my ticket. I can make it."

His smile reminded her of the one he'd shown when she had accepted his invitation for their first date.

The following week, as they took their seats in the terrace-reserved section behind third base, a strong breeze whipped the flags over the centerfield scoreboard straight out toward the lake.

"A hitter's wind." Setting down the cardboard holder with their drinks and hot dogs, Marty wadded up his jacket in the corner of his seat. "Glad I'm not Sutcliffe today."

"What a great birthday gift." Slipping her arm under his, she added, "Did I ever tell you how lucky I am?"

"Hey, I've learned. The way to *my* girl's heart starts at the corner of Clark and Addison. Right here in Chicago." He took a giant bite from his hot dog.

Gazing at the ivy-covered walls under the bleachers, Kate couldn't think of a place she would rather be on her birthday. As the players clustered around their dugouts, the announcer mentioned that the afternoon had been designated "Great Lakes Insurance Day." He asked that the two-hundred and fifty-eight employees stand to be recognized and was greeted with a boisterous cheer from a block of royal blue shirts on the first-base side.

"And now," he added almost as a footnote, "our national anthem will be sung by the wife of the Great Lakes president emeritus, Jarvis McTavish. Ladies and gentlemen, Miss Allison Sherrill."

Kate tingled as they stood and saluted the flag. No matter how many times she came to this ballpark, she always was covered with goosebumps during the national anthem. Listening carefully, however, she became distracted.

"And the rockets' red glare . . . the bombs bursting in air . . ." As the singer caressed each word, Kate realized she'd heard a vocalist with a catch in her voice like that before. But when, she wondered. And where? Turning her full attention from the flag to the singer, she murmured to herself, "Who *is* she?" Allison Sherrill? She'd never heard of her, and yet the woman had a voice that was as familiar as Kate's own mother's.

Squinting as hard as she could, she repeated her name aloud. "Allison Sherrill." A surge of disbelief washed over her. Sherrill . . . *Cheryl.* Could it possibly be?

"And the home of the brave." The premature cheering of the fans almost drowned out her two-syllable treatment

377

of the last word.

"Marty." Stepping over his feet, she was on her way. "I think that could be my friend, Cheryl, from Sweet Briar. I'm going to try to track her down."

"Huh?" Bewildered, he called after her. "Who?" he asked again. "Well, hurry—" His voice died in the wind.

Moving steadily through the aisles so as not to be chastised by the diligent crew of ushers, Kate kept her eyes trained on the vocalist as she was escorted back toward the sea of blue shirts. She caught up with her just as she was about to take her seat next to a silver-haired man.

"Cheryl!" she shouted. "Cheryl Allison."

Obviously puzzled that someone had reversed her professional name, the singer glanced in Kate's direction but failed to recognize her.

"Cheryl," she repeated. Dodging the beer vendor, she touched the singer's arm and removed her sunglasses. "It's Kate. Kate Freeman."

"Oh, lordy! Kate!"

Paralyzed by the shock of seeing each other again, they stared, mouths agape.

"Hey, ladies," yelled a rough voice from a few rows back. "Ya wanta chit-chat over da backyard fence or ya wanta watch da game?"

"I'll be under the stands by the entrance," Kate told her, motioning toward the exit and giving The Voice a dirty look all at the same time.

She nodded. "Jarvis, honey, an old friend just showed up. I'll be back in a little while." Kate watched as Cheryl tenderly touched the silver-haired man on the shoulder and hurried to join her.

As Cheryl trotted up the ramp to join her, Kate doubted that she would have recognized her old friend if she had met her on the street. Cheryl's cheeks were rounder, her hair was frosted fashionably and her muscled body looked as if she worked out on a regular basis.

After more hugs and a few tears, Cheryl stood back to survey her.

"I should have known you'd be here—you being such a Cubs fan and all. Where else would you want to be on your birthday?"

Kate's mouth fell open. "How did you remember?"

"Some things you never forget." Shrugging, she smiled as she reflected on past birthdays. "Your mother always made those beautiful three-layer pink-and-white birthday cakes with that fantastic frosting. I was lucky if Lila had popsicles in the house for us to eat on *my* birthday!"

Standing against a cool brick wall under the stands, Kate found herself oblivious to the crack of the bats and the roar of the crowd as she and Cheryl fired rapid questions at each other.

"Tell you what." Pursing her lips, Cheryl said, "Wait a minute while I let Jarvis know that you and Marty are here. We're having a supper down at our yacht club for everyone right after the game and I know he'll want you both to join us." Starting toward the entrance to the lower boxes, she whirled as an afterthought, "You can stay, can't you?"

Kate laughed. "I think I can talk Marty into that."

In a moment she was back, with the location of the yacht club scribbled on the back of Jarvis' business card. It would be their admittance into the supper, she explained. Hugging her once more, Cheryl assured her, "We'll be watching for you."

"You're missing a great game." Marty pulled back his feet impatiently when she returned to her seat.

Scanning the scoreboard, she saw that the Cubs already had a hefty lead. Being a long-suffering fan, however, she knew that no number of runs was ever large enough. Although she cheered heartily, she frequently let her eyes wander toward the section of blue shirts to make sure that Cheryl and her husband were still there. She was almost afraid to let her old friend out of her sight again.

By the time Reds were batting in the ninth inning, the Cubs had amassed twenty-two runs—a secure lead, even for them.

"I don't ever want this to end!" Kate shouted triumphantly.

Ebullient over the lop-sided victory, Marty agreed to go to the yacht club.

"Might as well let Great Lakes Insurance buy your birthday dinner," he said. Touching her elbow lightly, he steered her through the back gate on Waveland Avenue so they could get to their car on Irving Park and be ahead of the traffic.

At the yacht club, Cheryl introduced them to Jarvis and whispered an apology to Kate that she was obligated to mingle a bit. Between her duties, however, the two grabbed every opportunity to cover the major milestones of their lives. They smiled as they overheard Jarvis and Marty discussing Al Unser's recent victory at the Indy 500 and the Celtics' chances of beating the Lakers for the NBA title. Cheryl struggled for composure as she told Kate that J.T. had died the year before. Not once that evening, however, could Kate summon the courage to tell her about Christopher.

Agreeing to meet again soon, they exchanged phone numbers and addresses.

"We'll have lunch at The Art Institute," Cheryl said. "Then we can just find a spot on a bench somewhere and sit and talk. I'd ask you to come out and spend the day at Kenilworth, but it's such a haul."

When Kate suggested that Cheryl attend their thirty-fifth Rockwell High reunion in August, Cheryl replied that she never once had received an invitation. Blinking hard, she stared out at the lake. "After all, I didn't stay and graduate with all of you."

"But there are so many who would love to see you again. There's Doris—oh, Cheryl, Doris just looks so good." Kate found her words tripping over each other as she encouraged Cheryl to join them. "You'll come if they send you an invitation, won't you?"

"Well, maybe . . . on one condition." Cheryl's face expressed grave concern.

"What's that?" Kate braced herself, waiting for Cheryl's response.

"That Old Fartley won't be there to make fun of me!" Then she giggled with such contagious merriment that Kate, too, began to laugh—a hearty rumble that she had not heard out of herself since she and Marty had left Indianapolis. Convulsed, the two stumbled away from the group before they could embarrass themselves further.

"Oh, Kate." Cheryl's eyes misted as they watched three sailboats glide through the pink-gold rays of a brilliant sunset until they were safe in their harbor slips. "I can't tell you what this means to me. I think, for the first time since we had to leave Rockwell, I've got my life back together somehow."

Kate took Cheryl's hands and squeezed them. Looking into her expressive brown eyes that shared so many mutual memories, she finally was able to speak over the lump in her throat.

"Me too, Cheryl. Me too."

* * *

Part Two: Rosie

1988 - 2002

Chapter Thirty

"Geez! Our life's so together right now. Why in the hell would you want to change everything?"

Rosie winced at her choice of words as they bounced in their Jeep over the unpaved road. She never cussed at Bud, especially when they were on one of their camping trips in the Arizona mountains, but she could tell by the set of his mouth that he was digging in. And it scared her.

"It's time to move on, Ro." He ran his hand over his gray crew cut as if he were checking to make sure every hair was in place. "I've just had that feeling for awhile now."

Clamping her jaw, she looked out the window at the scrubby landscape she'd grown to love. She had never dreamed that their happy existence might be threatened when Bud's sister, Harriett, died and left him her Illinois farmhouse and eighty acres a few miles southwest of Kankakee. They'd been able to keep Harriett's hired man, Virgil Kletzig, to work the fields for them, so Rosie saw no need to trade the contentment they'd found in near Phoenix for the uncertainty they were sure to find an hour north of Rockwell. When she shuddered, Bud seemed to read her thoughts.

"Like I said, Ro," he emphasized as he pulled onto the main road. "It's time for a change."

* * *

"Rosalie Annette, I wish you wouldn't be so stubborn." Her mother's eyes filled with tears as they waited at the Danville bus station. Pacing on the worn linoleum, her dad tapped his watch to make sure it was running and muttered something about her going so "damn far."

"It's what I gotta do. It's what I've always wanted to do." She shook her head impatiently. "Geez, you guys, it's time for a change." Relieved, she saw the big Greyhound turn the corner and hiss to a stop in front of them.

"Change isn't always for the better, Rosalie Annette." When the tears began to etch paths down her mother's cheeks, Rosie knew her mom was thinking of Mike. "Call us and we'll send you money for a ticket to come home."

"You be good, you hear?" Her dad's words seemed to die in his throat as he helped her onto the bus. "I mean it, dammit!"

She shielded her eyes as she stared into the sun and watched her parents grow smaller as the bus pulled away. Triumphantly, she lifted her chin and glanced around at the other passengers, wondering if they were aware that she was on her way to Hollywood.

The monotonous landscape in Illinois and Missouri made her grateful she was leaving this god-forsaken part of the country for something better. She'd grown weary of well-meaning family and friends telling her to go ahead and cry for the last four years. Instead, she'd channeled her energy into her wild-and-crazy times with Shirley Ann Melowicz and her pals. Although she'd embraced the woozy effect from the booze she'd consumed, she could always feel the presence of Mike in the back of her foggy mind.

As the bus passed crumbling little storefronts in

dusty towns in Oklahoma and New Mexico, she thought of the tavern south of Danville where she and Shirley Ann had picked up lots of smooth guys. The Pacific Palms had been their official clubhouse where she'd cultivated close—really close—friendships with the sophisticated Danville crowd. Ma would have killed her if she'd known about the abortion she'd had in that creepy old doctor's upstairs office near the Palms. As moody as she had been for a few weeks afterward, she had never been able to bring herself to tell Colleen about it and she'd still been unable to cry.

Rosie didn't know what she would have done without her older siblings. When she'd had one too many nasty arguments with her parents, Danny and Colleen had found room for her in the tiny house where they lived with their two children. She wouldn't have been riding through New Mexico right now if Brian and Sandra hadn't loaned her the money for her bus ticket. They didn't have that much to spare either, now that Brian was teaching in southern Illinois and they had the expenses of the three little boys they had adopted. Sandra even had given Rosie her aunt's address in Glendale and told her she could stay there until she found a place to live.

She stared out the window as the endless desert finally began to give way to miles of fruit groves. Geez, she thought, just look at that—trees loaded with real oranges! Eventually the bus threaded its way past a few small clay houses and clusters of businesses. It turned, then chugged down a boulevard lined with palm trees and into a station that looked no better than the one in Danville . . . only bigger. She wondered if there was a drugstore waiting for her here, a place where she could be discovered just like Lana Turner.

"Los Angeles," called the driver. "End of the line."

She smiled as she picked up her suitcase. For her, it was just the beginning.

* * *

Rosie wasn't foolish enough to get into a screaming fight with her husband over the farm in Illinois. She knew it wouldn't do any good anyway—and it would only leave her more frustrated than ever. In the fifteen years she Bud had been married, they'd had only quarreled a handful of times, then she had been the one who had yelled, while Bud had silently managed to get his way. She set her jaw, determined that she wasn't about to let him win this one though. This was one big poker game, and she knew she'd have to play her cards just right.

For starters, she never brought up the subject of moving and avoided any topic that remotely touched on the farming or the Midwest. Instead, she went overboard to ensure that Bud continued to lead the life he loved in Glendale. After his retirement in the mid-eighties as a flight instructor at Luke Air Force Base, they had remained in the area and she had kept her part-time job in a small dry cleaning store. They savored the time they spent with friends and the trips they took into the White Tank Mountains.

Even when she saw Bud scanning back issues of *The Chicago Tribune* that he brought home from the library, she never uttered a word. She made sure that they continued to join their pals for the Friday-night fish fries at the Glendale Café and to stomp their feet to the western music at Mr. Lucky's on Saturday nights. When Bud suggested they join a couples' bowling league, she gave a secret sigh of relief and thought he must be settling in for the rest of their lives.

She made sure she was available on her days off to climb into their Jeep with Bud and cruise through the desert or bounce over a mountain trail. Regretting that she didn't have the stamina for long hikes, she admitted that her damn cigarettes were to blame but still couldn't give them up.

Like two savvy poker players, they held their cards close and didn't discuss their plans. She felt she'd won a hand the day they hauled Bud's fishing boat up the dirt road to Apache Junction and went on to make camp at Roosevelt Lake. With his Notre Dame cap plastered over his crew cut, Bud was ecstatic as he reeled in one bass after another. That evening, as the cobalt sky turned to flame behind the mountains, she knew the taste of the freshly caught fish grilled over an open fire would be enough to make him want to stay in Arizona forever.

She began to relax as their unspoken game continued for two years. Each time they revisited Roosevelt Lake, she felt both peaceful and exhilarated to know that Bud would never trade fishing in a mountain lake for farming in the flatlands.

Sometimes, after they had to hustle back to the Jeep to avoid getting drenched by a sudden downpour, she was amazed by the brilliant display of poppies that sprouted from the cracked desert floor. Living with Bud had produced that same effect on her, she thought one afternoon as she admired a parched gully that had sprung to life. Before she'd met him, she'd been like a piece of worn out, used up desert land, wasted by years of decadent living. Now she felt alive, eager for every day of adventure and contentment.

* * *

Maybe, she thought, just one margarita at her favorite little pub in Burbank would take the sting out of the nasty firing her boss at NBC had just dished out to her.

As she licked the salt from the rim of her glass, she couldn't believe that the warm April day that had started so nicely had taken such a rotten turn. Geez, she had only misplaced the guy's stack of phone messages. There'd been no reason for him to get so mean with her.

She strolled to the end of the bar and picked up the want ads from the stack of newspapers. Scanning the job categories, she wondered for the very first time if California really was the place for her. Her resume wasn't quite what she'd hoped it would be when she'd stepped off the bus almost twenty years ago—cleaning tables at the RKO cafeteria and answering fan mail at Republic and Paramount. She'd put herself right under the noses of the studio moguls, but no one had ever paid attention to her. The only people who noticed her were the bosses who canned her for coming to work drunk and the sleazy men she met at local bars who bought her a few drinks and took her to cheap motels for the night. No matter where she found herself when she woke up, she always had one thought foremost in her mind: Mike.

As she sipped her margarita, she recalled the time she'd gotten a stint as an extra in a cast-of-thousands MGM movie. She'd been sure that would be her big break, but her scene had been edited out of the final version. Although she'd been mad, she still hadn't cried. In all those good-for-nothing jobs, in all those lonely days and rotten nights, she'd never shed a tear for herself or for Mike.

She rested her head in her hands as she considered that maybe her whole life would end up on the cutting-room floor. That's when she noticed the Air Force guy with the sandy crew cut sitting three stools down from her. He glanced at her with the saddest blue eyes she'd ever seen, then stared into his beer. Later he told her that he'd been drawn to *her* sorrowful blue eyes.

"Hi." He moved one stool closer to her.

"Hi." She never looked up from her glass. Shocked by her own reaction, she could not imagine that she—Rosie Mulgrew who had kissed all the boys—was suddenly turning shy.

As he slid over next to her, he asked her if she cared if he talked. She shook her head, figuring she'd be out of there in ten minutes. But an hour and a half later—right after they discovered that they'd both grown up in east-central Illinois—he'd steered her toward a small grill where they wolfed down hamburgers together. By that time, he had her full attention.

He told her that his wife, Marie, had died a year earlier while he'd been home on leave. Then, just two months ago, his older son, Todd, had been killed in an accident near L.A. Rosie could see how proud he'd been that his kid had been one of the top students at UCLA. But now he was taking a break from his job as a flight instructor at Langley Air Force Base to tackle the sad job of tidying up his son's final business details. His other boy, Terry, had dropped out of school and was drifting around Wyoming. Sometime during their conversation he mentioned that his name was Lowell Laughlin, but everybody called him Bud.

She sucked in her breath two nights later when he asked her to tell him about Mike. They'd eaten Mexican food at a little hole in the wall, then driven out along the ocean. At first, her words emerged slowly as she dredged up her memories. Haltingly she described her rowdy, fun-loving family but admitted that Mike had been her favorite.

"That kid could make me so darn mad, push me right to the edge. But I couldn't help it—I loved him best. I loved the way his Cardinals cap always sat just a little cockeyed on his head. I loved how new freckles popped out all over his face after he'd been out mowing the grass. And I loved how he lapped up anything I cooked, like a stray puppy." She paused, listening to the waves washing gently onto the shore. "The trouble was, Bud, I never told him." She felt a peculiar sensation in her chest, like a huge turtle trying to swim to the top of a pool. "And I didn't let him borrow my tennis racquet. On—on the very worst day of my miserable life."

When Bud took her in his arms, she felt her cheeks grow wet. As twenty four years' worth of tears finally began to pour out of her, she clung to him and wondered if both of them might be washed away. Later, she realized, if she hadn't met Bud Laughlin, she might never have wept for her brother. But Bud taught her how to cry— and he taught her how to love, *really* love someone back.

* * *

Although Bud made one quick trip back to Illinois to discuss some of the farm's business with Virgil Kletzig, Rosie no longer felt threatened by the prospective move. She had played her cards like an expert and felt she could begin raking in all the chips. Relaxing her standards, she even agreed to take a few golf lessons with Bud, although she still believed in her heart that golf was a game only for the rich, like the people who lived on the Longworth side of Rockwell.

Sometimes though, she realized, a round of poker can turn on you just when you think you've won. One week in June, when they hadn't seen rain for weeks, she watched in dismay as her house of cards collapsed. On a Monday, she and Bud found themselves ambushed in the desert by a dust storm that left every corner of their Jeep filled with rusty grit. Back home, he swore under his breath as the two of them cleaned up the sandy grime.

A few days later, they drove their immaculate Jeep up to Roosevelt Lake to drop their lines into the water. Bud had grown vainly proud of the fact that he knew that lake like the back of his hand. But that afternoon, he grounded his boat on one of the lake's little desert islands that could pop up out of nowhere during a dry spell.

He fumed. He swore. He threw their life jackets against the sides of the boat. Not once in his whole life, Bud growled, had he ever had to wait for help on a lake. Finally, when they arrived home, Rose hid herself behind a magazine while he stomped around the house.

"That settles it, Ro. We're putting the house on the market so we can go back to Illinois." Angrily, he picked up the phone book and started thumbing through the yellow pages.

"Aw, Bud, we've only had a couple of bad days." She put down her issue of *People*. "Think of all the sunny—"

"Yeah, well I'm sick of them too. I'm just goddamn tired of sunshine every single day of my life." He dropped the phone book and walked over to the couch to take her hands in his.

"You know, it's not like we're actually going to be farmers ourselves. Virgil's told me he'll stay on to do the planting and harvesting. And we can always come back to Arizona in the winter, Ro. That's a promise. It's just that—" He ran his hand over his hair. "I need to get back to my roots."

"Not me, Buddy." She sighed. She wanted to stay as far away from her painful past as possible. "But I'd sure hate for you to leave without me."

The game was over.

* * *

Chapter
Thirty-One

J ust four months later, she found herself transplanted to the farm in Illinois. She had to admit that the two-bedroom stone house was neat as a pin, although Harriett had gone way overboard with her use of purple and lavender. Outside her kitchen window Rosie could see the picket fence that bordered the garden patch that Virgil had tended during the past summer. Beyond the stretch of harvested fields were clumps of neighboring farms and miles of trees ablaze with October color.

Privately she thought she could resign herself to their new country home, but she couldn't resist getting in a dig about Bud's old hometown.

"Geez, downtown Kankakee looks like everybody went home one night and forgot to come back."

Bud calmly assured her that there were a couple of newer shopping centers on the edge of town plus some good places to eat.

"Wait'll you see the lemon pie at Blues Cafe." His eyes sparkled, "You're going to need a stepladder to reach the top of the meringue, Ro."

She rolled her eyes. He'd never make a good liar.

* * *

She knew it was a sign of bad luck the minute she saw Bud's hat on the bed. Cringing each time he started a conversation, she waited for him to drop a bombshell. When he finally told her he'd been transferred from Langley to Luke Air Force Base in Arizona a year after they'd been married, she sighed and tried to hide her disappointment when she saw how excited he was.

"Man, Ro, this has always been my dream—to be an instructor at Luke. I mean it's like going to the major leagues. After all, they don't call it the 'Home of the Fighter Pilot' for nothing." When he planted a big kiss on her and grinned, she told him she guessed she'd go along for the ride.

She crossed her fingers for good luck when they started looking at houses that would be a short drive from the base. She'd grown so used to the hills and beaches in Virginia that Arizona seemed like the dustiest, most worthless stretch of land that anyone could imagine. But they managed to find a small ranch home in Glendale with a pink bush out front that was so bright that she practically had to shield her eyes. Later she learned its name was bougainvillea. She admitted that Arizona might have its good points and decided she might be able to tolerate it for awhile.

Once they started to settle in, she couldn't believe how fast they fell in love with their new spot. The pace was easy, every day was a sunny one, and they could scoot up to the White Tank Mountains in about half an hour. Bud liked it when she drove out to the base to watch the fighter planes go through their paces. She always had to cover her ears when the planes took off and swooped down for practice landings. The noise, she thought, was enough to rattle a person's rib cage. She never told Bud, but she was doubly glad that they'd decided to live off base.

..*

"They say the fishing's still real good on the Kankakee River." Running his hand over his hair, Bud continued to promote their new location. "I used to know it like my own back yard. But it's like Roosevelt Lake—you've gotta make sure you know where the shallow spots are. Some guy in the barber shop told me he and his buddy had to carry their canoe through a narrow spot during a dry spell last summer."

Rosie retorted that she'd fish with him but not to expect her to help him carry the boat if they got stuck. She was still smarting over sacrificing their perfect spot in Arizona.

When November rolled in and stripped the trees of their leaves, she realized she'd forgotten how depressing the Midwest can be before the snow comes. But they drove to Carbondale for a big turkey dinner with Brian and Sandra and their married sons and grandchildren. Best of all, she got to spend some time with her mother. All of them talked on the phone with Danny and Colleen, who bragged that they could see blue skies and water from the balcony of their condo in Naples that day.

"They always have to rub it in." Ma smoothed out her apron and returned to the kitchen. "Just wait until July. We won't be hearing how perfect Florida is then!" She lifted the lid on the potatoes, looked questioningly at Sandra and Rosie, and announced that she'd go ahead and mash them. They exchanged smiles, acknowledging to each other that they hadn't wanted the job anyway.

It made Rosie feel good to see her mother so happy again. After they'd buried Pa next to Mike in 1960, Ma had accepted Brian and Sandra's invitation to move to an apartment near them. She'd made new friends, started doing alterations for a department store and built a whole new

life for herself. That evening, after they'd stuffed themselves with too much good food and laughed together at
funny old shared memories, Rosie felt stabs of guilt for
having distanced herself for so many years. Bud never objected once when she suggested they return to Carbondale
for Christmas so she could do some more catching-up with
her family.

Being a realist, Rosie knew that they would have to stay
on the farm through that first winter. Bud and Virgil had
work to do, and she wanted to paint and paper over the lavender walls before spring arrived. Shivering every time she
stepped out of the house, she was thankful that the cold
snaps were relatively few. As soon as the threat of frost was
over, she planted her own flowers and spaded a small patch
for vegetables. During the summer months, as they ate her
green beans, sweet corn and juicy tomatoes, she was surprised at the sense of fulfillment she experienced from having cultivated her little crop.

Still, she was packed and ready to go when Bud fired
up the Jeep after the following Christmas and pointed it
back to Arizona. Rosie blissfully turned her face to the sun
as they neared the Phoenix area. She felt as if they'd never
left when they were able to lease a condo in Glendale for
three months. Their old friends welcomed them back into
the bowling league, and they all went to Mr. Lucky's afterward, as if nothing had changed.

By the winter of 1994, however, Arizona's appeal had
begun to fade. Several of their friends had left Glendale, so
she and Bud rented a place at Sun City. They tried to pick
up the pieces of their former lives, but the bowling league
had new people in it and nothing was the same. After
spending two full winters in Sun City, Rosie started to feel
antsy.

"I've had about as much this 'active senior community'

crap as I can stomach," she confessed to Bud. "I don't want to string beads and paint glass with a bunch of old people."

Bud agreed with her that three winters in "paradise" were enough for him too. Leaving before their lease was up, they loaded their Jeep and headed back to Illinois. Both were ready to settle into their real life in Illinois— unglamorous as it might be.

After they returned, Rose admitted that Kankakee didn't seem so bad. That spring they played a little golf and fished off the bank along the river. They even drove into town to go to mass at St. Patrick's occasionally. She knew they had carved out their own niche when the waitresses at Blues called them by name and brought them lemon meringue without even asking. A piece of pie and a movie at the Paramount made for a pretty good evening.

During the five years that they'd been in Kankakee, Rosie had made a few stabs at working part-time jobs. She delivered advertising papers for a few months, but Bud complained that all the stop-and-go driving was too hard on the Jeep. She signed up with a temp agency, but they always sent her to goofy companies that reminded her of some of the places she'd worked during her early days in California.

When her friend, Margie Snyder from church, asked her to join her dominoes club, she jumped at the chance. After all, Bud had his men's bowling team and ragtag poker group. With her skinny build and ability to crack her chewing gum, Margie reminded her of Cheryl's mom. She always seemed to be filing her nails and knew all the latest gossip, just like Lila. But Rosie felt she was a decent friend, even when Margie's non-stop chatter made her want to cover her ears.

She balked at first when Margie told her that Kennedy School needed tutors for kids who'd missed the basics of reading in first and second grade. However, Margie kept nagging at her until she surrendered and volunteered. Immediately she found herself face to face with a grubby third-grader named Colton Powers whose attention span wouldn't last through a thirty-second commercial. Although Colton had red hair, he had a winsome self-assurance that reminded her of Mike. Each week, as she experimented with new ways to maintain Colton's interest, she knew deep down that she was in the right place.

Thinking of Mike channeled her thoughts toward Rockwell but never enough to make the forty-mile trip. However, her curiosity about her former life finally won out during the summer of 1996, when she and Bud rented a cottage on a lake near Danville for two weeks.

On a perfect July morning when she casually mentioned that she just wasn't in the mood to fish, Bud shrugged and strolled down to the boat without her. As soon as he skimmed out toward the middle of the lake, she jumped in the Jeep and drove over to Highway 1 south of Danville. She wanted to see if any of the old roadhouses where she and Shirley Ann had spent some pretty wild nights still existed.

She felt foolish dawdling in front of liquor stores and tanning salons as she searched for a familiar landmark. Finally, to get her bearings, she pulled into the parking lot at a strip mall across from a Marathon station. She was certain that it was the site where the old Veterans Grill once stood, but there wasn't a trace of it left.

Sighing, she angled the Jeep back out onto the highway. She grumbled under her breath about the narrow and pitted road as she dodged potholes and several delivery trucks. Even the local radio station, with all its speculation about eastern Illinois crops, was making her edgy, so she turned it off and drove in silence for another couple of miles.

That's when she spotted it—the old Pacific Palms

Lounge. The square, two-story building on the corner was as familiar as her childhood home, but now it contained a shabby video store in the front section where the bar had stood and a couple of apartments in the back part where they used to dance and neck with the boys from Danville.

She parked and walked across the dusty lot. Over the door, she could still make out the faded plaster flamingos and swaying palm trees that had been the trademark of the Pacific Palms—every underage drinker's home away from home. Climbing up the three rotting wooden steps, she shielded her eyes and peeked through the front window. She couldn't see much—just enough to tell that the pink-and turquoise tropical motif had been covered with dark paneling.

As she placed her foot on the top step to leave, she was almost overcome with emotion. She recalled the night she'd drunk too many fancy tropical concoctions made with different kinds of rum and allowed a guy from Danville to talk her into getting into the back seat of his Packard. Later she'd wondered if that was when she'd gotten pregnant, but she couldn't be sure.

She opened the door to the Jeep, took out her cigarettes and inhaled long and slow as she thought about those days. Geez, she brooded regretfully, she'd been dumb! She, Shirley Ann and all their crowd had thought they were so grown up as they jitterbugged with each other and slow danced with guys from Danville who were barely conscious. She could almost hear the lively strains of Les Paul and Mary Ford's "How High The Moon" still hovering in the air as she smoked and remembered it all.

What was that guy's name, she wondered—the one in his early twenties who looked like Rory Calhoun? Cliff . . . Curt . . . Clay? Clay Breske, that was it. As she closed her eyes, she could picture handsome Clay bringing her yet another illegal sloe gin fizz. Each night, during the summer of '52, it was always the same. She'd felt so hip as her mind fuzzed out and she'd beg Clay to play Jo Stafford's "You Belong To Me" on the jukebox one more time. Then, when he knew she was past caring, he'd run his hand lightly up her leg under the table, and they'd go out to his car for an hour or so.

She cringed as she thought of all the nights of her youth that she had spent in this very parking lot and all the lies she'd had to manufacture, first for Ma and then for Colleen. Giving her half-smoked cigarette a toss into the gravel, she ground her wheels and, in a blur of dust, turned the Jeep back toward the lake. And her husband.

* * *

She was scared most of the time when she first met Bud—scared that he'd disappear into the mist and scared that he'd turn out to be another Clay Breske. When neither happened, she began to let down her guard.

After he left LA and returned to Langley, he sent her airline tickets twice so she could visit him in Virginia, and he managed to spend another weekend with her in California. She knew Shirley Ann Melowicz would howl in disbelief, but she and Bud never slept together until they were married—exactly three months to the day after they met. By that time, she teased him that he was getting a virgin bride.

"For me, Ro, you are." He held her face in his hands before he kissed her at the little inn where they spent their first night together. Those, she thought, were the sweetest words she had ever heard.

She worshiped the ground that Bud Laughlin

walked on.

Once, on the phone, she told Colleen, "He just treats me so good."

She felt like a queen when they drove through the mountains, relaxed on the beach and went into D.C. so he could show her the sights. When he told her that he'd been transferred to Arizona, she felt as if they were closing out a five-year honeymoon.

* * *

Bud was just climbing out of the boat with a stringer full of bluegills when she pulled up at the lake cottage. Still feeling in a sentimental mood from her visit to the Pacific Palms, she suggested after supper that they drive up to Rockwell the next day.

"I haven't been back since Pa's funeral," she told him, never including the fact that on that day thirty-four years ago she'd been so zoned she could barely function. Bud replied that he could sacrifice half a day of fishing to visit her old hometown.

The following afternoon when they headed north on Highway 1, she knew she was ready. As they passed the familiar sign at the edge of town stating, "Welcome to Rockwell—Home of the Boulders," she asked him to make a loop through the old park.

"Slow down," she instructed, sticking her head out of the window to get a better view of the six new tennis courts. "This is where the four of us used to spend so much time . . . where we were when we heard that a kid had been killed by a train." She could feel the massive lump growing in her throat.

"You sure you want to do this?" His knuckles were white as he gripped the steering wheel.

"Yeah." She took a deep breath. "With you along, I can do it. Yeah, I do."

As they crept through downtown, they spotted a restaurant called The Boulder. Might be a good place to have supper later, they thought. Then Bud drove her up and down every single street in the Longworth section. Rockwell's new high school dwarfed the old Longworth grade school next to it. Rosie wondered if the kids who went there were still so uppity. At last, after Bud steered the Jeep over the tracks to the Sweet Briar area, she commanded, "Stop. Stop right here, Bud." He braked by the curb in front of her family home.

"This is it." She heard the quake in her voice. "The old homestead."

"Wanta get out?" He started to turn off the engine.

"Naw, naw, I just wanta look for a minute." Sighing, she felt the same as she had the day before when she had found the Pacific Palms. The structure was still there, but the familiarity had vanished. "Aw, Bud, I can't believe somebody put that butt-ugly gold and brown siding on our house!"

The porch was gone, and the outhouse had been replaced with a garage. Gold and brown—what else, she thought. Blinking hard, she rubbed her eye with her fist to keep it from twitching. "Drive on up to the next block. I'm gonna show you the spookiest house you ever saw."

As they approached the plot of land once filled by the old Naughton place, however, she was amazed to see three beautiful homes.

"I can't believe it," she muttered. "It's gone! Honest to God, Bud, the old mansion that used to be here looked like something out of *The Addams Family*. It scared me so bad once, I damn near wet my pants."

He grinned. "Where to now?"

She asked him to drive on up the street past Kate's old house and wondered what had ever happened to her and her family. The place looked so different, like her old home. Covered with blue aluminum siding, it now appeared awkward and uncomfortable with its new deck clinging to the back porch like a tumor.

"This is where Kate lived—and where I used to eat the best cookies in the world." She could still smell the warm aroma that always greeted her when she walked through the Freemans' front door.

Next they snaked their way through the streets of the Sweet Briar section. Cheryl's house, now painted hot pink, was in pretty bad shape. Rosie smiled and thought that Lila might have liked that shade though. Geez, she recalled, they'd had fun there, drinking Grapette and listening to records on the hi-fi, but then Cheryl and her folks had left town in a hurry. She felt guilty when she remembered the letters she'd had from Cheryl. She'd been too busy keeping up with Shirley Ann to write back.

A duplex had replaced Panczyks' house, but the front yard looked like it might still be loaded with dandelions every spring. Colleen had told her a long time ago that Doris had divorced her husband after they'd had a bunch of kids. Her sister had also mentioned what Doris was doing, but the information had slid through Rosie's foggy mind like water through a sieve.

"Wanta go to the cemetery, Ro?" Bud asked.

She shook her head. It wasn't the cemetery so much that bothered her as it was passing the trestle where Mike had died. She just didn't feel she could handle it.

"Naw—let's just take this street up here and go by the old Sweet Briar School." She was beginning to tire of this sentimental journey. "Then we can grab a hamburger at that place uptown."

As they approached the playground, however, she sat up straight. Their old two-story school had been replaced by a building that took up half a block and put Longworth to shame. Good for them, she thought. The Sweet Briar kids finally got a decent school on their side of town.

It was 5:30 when they parked in front of The Boulder, so they went inside, slid into a royal blue vinyl booth, and scanned the menus. A high-school girl with a brown pony tail and a pretty smile took their orders.

"Make sure you give them folks decaf outta the fresh pot!" a woman called from the cash register.

"Okay, Grandma." Winking at them, their server assured them that all the calories had been taken out of the onion rings they'd just ordered.

As they waited for their food, Rosie glanced around the room and realized that the walls were covered with newspaper photos of Rockwell High events over the years. She told Bud to wait while she went to the back and studied the pictures of their 1948 and 1949 basketball teams. She couldn't believe how young they looked—Colleen's Danny, Vic and Charley Panczyk, Alan Atwater, all the rest. As she allowed her memory to wander, she heard a guy call from the kitchen: "Hey, Doris, you want me to stack up this order of paper goods that came in today?"

"Yeah—in the far corner." It was the woman at the cash register again.

Turning to look at her, Rosie caught sight of her profile. "Doris?" she echoed the name.

"Yeah," she answered, never looking up.

"Doris *Panczyk*?" Using the old name, Rosie caught her attention. The woman shot her a puzzled look.

"Yeah?" she repeated slowly.

For what seemed like an eternity, they stared at each other, trying to pick out any features they might recognize.

It was the kindness in her gray eyes that convinced Rosie.

"Geez, Doris, it's me. Rosie."

"Oh! Oh, my god!" She saw a little tremble run through the woman at the cash register as she steadied herself against the counter. Her mouth fell open in wonderment.

"What are you doing here?" Rosie was the first to speak.

"God, I should be askin' you that! I own the place." As Doris came around the corner and realized she was not dreaming, she gasped. Suddenly Rosie felt swallowed up by the biggest hug she'd had in a long time.

Doris' eyes filled with tears. "I—I just thought we'd never see you again."

"Fooled ya, didn't I?" Taking Doris' arm, she escorted her over to the booth. Bud, she noticed, had already eaten half the onion rings. "This is my husband, Bud. Sit with us, Doris."

"It's the only thing I *can* do. I'm so god-awful shaky." When Doris gave her the sweet smile she had always remembered, Rosie could have cried. Why, she wondered, had she made herself stay away so long?

Later, when she could not remember eating her hamburger, she surmised that Bud must have finished most of it while she and Doris traded stories. As they talked, Rosie tried not to stare. Doris looked good, really good. Her ash blonde hair had frosty streaks of gray, and the cut made her seem fifteen years younger. She told them all about her six kids and that she'd bought the restaurant a few years ago. But she and Violet still ran a catering business that they'd started about the time Doris left her husband.

As their conversation drifted toward their old gang, Doris told her that Kate had run into Cheryl in Chicago. When she added that Kate lived in South Bend and her husband wrote stories about Notre Dame football for the newspaper, Rosie thought Bud was going to fall out of the booth.

"Man, that's a guy I've gotta meet." His military reserve melted away so fast that Rosie couldn't help but laugh. "I've been an Irish fan since I was a little kid," he explained to Doris, trying to cover his embarrassment. As he picked up their bill, he commented, "Hey, Ro, your old friends are okay."

"Oh, no you don't." Doris grabbed the slip from his hand. "You're not payin' at my place. Just leave a little somethin' for Tiffany, my granddaughter." She nodded toward the kitchen. "She's one of Darcy's daughters. Nope," she gave Bud a look that showed she meant business, "This meal's on me."

While Bud went to the men's room, Rosie couldn't resist asking Doris if she were happy. She seemed so steady for someone who'd been through such tough times.

"Life's real good." She folded the paper from her straw over and over, just the way she used to when they'd share a chocolate Coke at the bowling alley in eighth grade. "But I never could have made it without Alan."

"Alan?"

"Yeah. You'd remember him—Alan Atwater. He played ball with Vic and Charley." A shy smile flitted across her face. "A Longworth kid . . . I know."

"You? And Alan? Adele Atwater's big brother?" Rosie was confused. She wondered if she'd mixed up names after all these years.

"Yeah." Briefly Rosie told her that she and Violet had taken food to his house during the years when his first wife had been ill with kidney failure. "We fell in love almost twenty years ago. But we never got married."

Rosie could tell that Doris seemed quite comfortable with her "arrangement," as she called it. "We thought about it and decided if ain't broke—"

"Don't fix it." Rosie grinned.

"That's what Charley says." Doris reached for her hands. "Oh, my god, Rosie. Did you know he just retired after bein' head of Midwest Manufacturing for years? He lives in one of them beautiful houses on the old Naughton ground . . . said he wanted his kids to go to Sweet Briar. As successful as he's been, he's always stayed on *our* side of town."

Rosie chucked appreciatively. She was glad to know that the Sweet Briar pride still existed. Then, as she and Bud finally left The Boulder, she and Doris hugged once more, exchanged scribbled phone numbers and promised they'd get together again soon. They had so much catching up to do—plus Rosie couldn't wait to hear more about Doris and Alan Atwater.

"Wouldn't hurt me to have another batch of your onion rings either." Bud lifted a toothpick from a box by the cash register and guided Rosie toward the door. "Plus you guys need to get this Kate and her husband down here. Maybe he could help me get some Notre Dame tickets."

She and Bud didn't say much as they sped down Highway 1 back to their cottage. As he hummed to himself, she knew he was picturing the bluegills he hoped to reel in the next day. Rosie silently reviewed the steady life that Doris had so stubbornly worked out for herself. Geez, she thought, a divorce, six kids and two businesses!

"And Alan Atwater," she murmured. "I just don't believe it!"

* * *

Chapter
Thirty-Two

S he'd always heard the road to hell is paved with good intentions. If that was right, Rosie knew exactly where she and Doris were headed the minute they died. They'd meant to get together soon after that night at The Boulder, but it didn't happen again for three more years. Every time they made plans to see each other, some unexpected bit of craziness would invade their lives. Instead, they just talked on the phone as often as they could, each assuring the other that she would survive her current crisis.

Soon after she had visited with Doris, Rosie was repulsed to discover Bud's son, Terry, on their doorstep. Brushing past her, he went straight for the refrigerator and pulled out a beer. Between swigs and belches, he told her that he'd come home to roost for a little while while he was between jobs.

"Just till I get back on my feet," he assured her. "What've ya got to eat?"

As his "little while" stretched into weeks and, eventually, months, Rosie began to wonder what it would take for him to re-enter the real world. He found a few odd jobs but usually was fired within days. She didn't feel she could criticize him because she knew she hadn't done much better herself when she'd been that age. But at least she'd always paid her rent—something he had yet to do.

Terry seemed much more adept at playing cards than at working. He slept past noon, then scavenged through the refrigerator and devoured anything he could find. Many afternoons and evenings he seemed to enjoy playing host to guys so scuzzy they made her skin crawl. Rosie felt she couldn't leave him alone in her house, so she just continued to stock up on groceries each morning while Terry was zonked out in their extra bedroom.

She complained bitterly to Doris on the phone but rarely said a word to Bud. Where Terry was concerned, her husband just seemed to look the other way. She guessed that he felt so bad about losing Todd that he couldn't bring himself to get tough with Terry. So the deadbeat hung around through Christmas, through the following farming season without ever tending a crop, and clear through another holiday season.

Rosie knew she would have lost her sanity during Terry's stay if it had not been for Margie's domino group and, of course, Colton. At the end of her first year of tutoring, she felt like a failure when he flunked third grade. But his teacher had explained that he'd be lost for the rest of his life if he didn't repeat the year now and whispered that he couldn't expect any help from home. His mom, Angel, Colton's teacher added, had had him when she was fifteen and on hard drugs. Now she spent her time doing part-time duty as a waitress and jumping from one boyfriend to another. Rosie set her jaw and decided that Bud could babysit Terry two or three times a week so she could work with Colton to make sure he wasn't backsliding.

After tolerating Terry, she found herself sympathizing with Angel. After all, she admitted, her own life at fifteen hadn't been much better than Angel's. And if she hadn't made that trip up the dark stairway to see the doctor in Danville, Rosie herself would have had a kid to raise!

Wanting to help, she pretended to have extra assignments for Colton so she could stop and see him in the apartment where he and his mother lived over a neighborhood tavern. She and Angel clicked so quickly that Rosie wondered if Colton's mother had sensed she'd found a kindred spirit.

Once she started visiting Colton at home, she was amazed by his artwork that Angel had taped to the apartment walls. Wow, she thought; if reading was a struggle for him, drawing must be as easy for him as breathing! Keeping him supplied with paper and plenty of crayons and pencils, Rosie often felt that Colton did more for her than she did for him.

He made her laugh, and he made her forget that Terry was still sponging off them and stealing some of their stuff. She never mentioned that to Bud. But when Terry finally told them that he was sick of "freezin' my ass off" and borrowed some money for a bus ticket to Florida in February of '98, she was never so thankful for a hard winter in all her life!

When she finally called Doris after Christmas, she was stunned to learn that her friend was coping with a challenge far worse than a lazy stepson. Her little brother, Tommy, had come home to die.

"Me 'n Violet—we flew out to New York to get him." Rosie could hear the tears in Doris' voice over the phone. "God, last time we went out, he took us all over Manhattan and we sat and listened to him play every night at the hotel where's he been for years."

It was AIDS, Rosie knew without asking, that was slowly taking sweet Tommy Panczyk. When Doris described the sores on his body and his blindness, she just couldn't hold back any longer. "He don't even want to go near the piano no more," she sobbed.

Again, they kept in touch by phone. This time, however, Rosie was doing the encouraging with Doris hanging on every word. Through Tommy's lingering illness and through his private memorial service, Rosie made sure she called Doris at least four times a week.

Finally, on a warm spring morning in 1999, after most of the planting was done, Bud agreed to return with her for lunch at The Boulder with Doris. Rosie admitted to herself that they all were a little bit older and a whole lot tireder than they'd been the first time they'd stopped there almost three years earlier. Doris looked worn as she recalled the amazing loyalty of many of Tommy's friends who'd come to see him all the way from New York during his last weeks.

"But people here in Rockwell didn't give a shit," Doris brushed her sleeve across her eyes. "Me 'n Violet didn't do much caterin' while Tommy was with us. I guess they was all afraid they'd catch somethin' from our kitchen." She shuddered as they sipped coffee in a booth. "God, Rosie, people can just be so damn cruel."

Rosie thought the wrinkles in her friend's pale cheeks seemed deeper than they had the last time they'd seen her. Doris brightened briefly when Bud told her how good the liver and onions were.

"That's one of his favorite meals, but it's something I've never fixed and don't intend to." Rosie rolled her eyes.

"He was cremated, you know." Rosie then realized that Doris hadn't quite finished with the subject of Tommy, so she and Bud let her ramble. "That seems to be the thing to do." Doris explained that they'd moved her father's remains to the Rockwell cemetery so he and her mom could be near Chet Jr.

Amid the chatter of other customers and the clatter of plates going into the tub of dirty dishes, the three of them sat quietly for a few moments. At last Rosie spoke.

412

"Guess we've both got our little brothers out there now." She and Doris exchanged glances of sad understanding, then she spiked her lettuce so hard she knocked some of it onto the table. A thought had begun to form in her mind.

"You wanta—well, you wanta go out there and visit both of 'em? Together?"

Rosie heard Bud's fork clatter against his plate as it fell from his hand. Doris studied her for a long moment before she replied, then checked her watch.

"Sure. Darcy's comin' in at 1:30 to run the afternoon shift. I can leave then."

When Doris saw her push the rest of her hot roast beef sandwich in Bud's direction, she stiffened. "Don't you like that? You want somethin' else?"

"Naw." Rosie rubbed her eye. "I just got kinda full. All of a sudden."

As they slid into Doris' Lincoln, Rosie hoped her friend didn't notice how tenderly Bud ran his fingers over the leather back seat. Sitting beside Doris in front, she couldn't help but remember the old beater Mrs. Panczyk used to drive when she took them to the local basketball games. Distracted by the luxury of the car, Rosie was pleased with herself for remaining calm—that is, until they turned onto the cemetery road. Then she felt her stomach start to reel the way it used to when she and Bud bounced along the steepest of mountain trails.

"The old trestle is gone, you know." Doris knew exactly why Rosie had stopped talking and was staring straight ahead. "Amtrack wasn't usin' that line anymore, so the railroad company tore up the tracks."

Rosie glanced quickly to the left and saw that Doris was right. Down the weed-covered path to the trestle there were only the two pyramid-shaped supports of cement blocks on each side of the stream. She found it hard to believe her

413

eyes. The bridge and its tracks *were* gone. A gaping hole about the size of the one in her heart was all that remained of the spot where Mike had been killed.

"Geez!" Her eyes smarted from tears. "If only—"

Reaching for the handkerchief that Bud handed her from the back seat, she blotted her cheeks.

* * *

"Hey, Rosie!"

What now, she wondered. She and the girls were just debating about what to do after school, then her pesty little brother decided to interrupt.

She watched him as he ran toward her, his baseball cap crooked as always over his blond crew cut. The burn he'd received when he ran into Ma's cookie sheet at Christmas was finally beginning to fade from his chin.

"Me 'n Teddy Moody're gonna play tennis. Where'd you put the racquet?" He trained his blue eyes expectantly on her.

"Someplace where *you'll* never find it." She smirked. She'd fixed him good when she'd hidden it behind some of Colleen's stuff in their closet.

"Aw, c'mon." He stood defiantly in front of her, his fists planted on his hips. She wondered if he'd ripped his jeans on the playground at school that day. Ma would kill him for sure!

"Me 'n the girls are goin' to the park to play anyway," she lied comfortably. "I've already promised."

"But you used it all last week," he protested.

"Tough." She lifted her chin in his direction. "Like I said, I already promised."

"But Mom said—"

"No buts, you little creep. Find something else to do."

Mike stuck his tongue out at her before he turned and headed toward home. She hesitated. She could change her mind, just this once. But then he might expect her always to give in.

Naw, she decided, she was going to use the racquet. He could wait until next time. Mike's shoulders slumped in disappointment for a moment, then she saw him pick up his gait and run after Teddy Moody.

"Get your tennis racquets," she ordered the girls. "We're goin' to the park!"

* * *

Doris and Bud stayed behind as Rosie approached her family plot. She had always expected this visit to blow her away. Instead, all she felt was a big ball of emptiness inside her. She stared at the three small stones imbedded beneath the Mulgrew family monument—the two weathered ones engraved "Michael Francis" and "John Patrick" and the one awaiting "Mary Rose" as soon as the staff at the Carbondale nursing home let her mother slip away. The scent of lilacs from a nearby bush sweetened the moment. In a budding maple overhead a cardinal whistled jauntily. The irony of its message was not lost on her.

"Wouldn't you know?" She turned to Doris and Bud.

Their puzzled looks told her how much they were worried about her.

"That Mike would have a cardinal singing over his grave." Blinking hard, she rejoined them. "Let's get the hell outta here."

As they threaded their way through a maze of markers bearing many familiar names, they walked to the plot where the Panczyk family members were buried.

"Remember the day we came out here on our bikes to

try to see the ghost at that little girl's grave and we stopped at Chet Jr.'s first?" Rosie reached down and straightened the artificial flowers in the urn beside Tommy's stone. "I could hardly stand to think that you'd lost your dad and big brother already."

"Yeah, it was hard. But we got through it somehow." Doris smiled. "Someday me 'n you'll have to talk about our bike ride back to town that day. You know— when Cheryl—when we all got scared."

"Scared of what?" Ahead of them, Bud had started toward the car but stopped and turned back in their direction.

As their eyes met, Rosie shook her head slightly at Doris.

"Oh, nothin." Doris winked at her. "We just thought we seen a ghost that day. Or somethin'."

"Yeah. Or somethin'," Rosie echoed. "We saw *somethin'*, all right! And so did Cheryl!"

When they snickered, Bud looked at both of them as if he thought they were a bit strange. But when they burst into laughter, right there among the graves of their own family members, he just charged ahead, opened the door and climbed into the back seat.

"You ever tell anyone about them hobos?" Doris' whisper sounded like the hushed secretive tone she had used back in seventh grade.

"Not a soul. Never." At that moment, she felt as if the years had slipped away and she was once again the old Rosie Mulgrew—the one who called all the shots. "We made a promise. Remember?"

"I sure do." Doris continued to giggle. "And I always keep my promises!"

They were totally out of control by the time they reached the car. Laughing hysterically as Doris drove the circular loop around the cemetery, Rosie could hear Bud muttering under his breath from the back seat. He must be ashamed to be associated with us, she thought. Then she laughed harder than ever.

* * *

All through that evening at home, Rosie felt as if she had been in prison for years and suddenly had been granted an unexpected parole. She couldn't believe that she'd actually forced herself to look at the trestle and to comprehend that it was gone. Gone forever.

"Thank God." She spoke out right in the middle of *ER*. When Bud didn't answer, she added, "I guess I've finally put that garbage behind me." Bud still was quiet.

"We got any Tums?" He finally responded at the commercial. Rubbing his stomach, he got out of his recliner and headed for the medicine cabinet. "I don't think that liver and onions set too well with me."

During the night Rosie heard him stirring around several times, rattling antacid pills from the plastic bottle and cussing under his breath.

"You all right? Want me to take you into the 24-hour clinic?" By 3:30 a.m., she was wide awake herself.

"Nope." He grimaced as he climbed back in bed beside her. "I just gotta stop eating so many goddamn onions. And you gotta stop thinking everything's a case for the ER!"

After that night, it seemed to Rosie that the chewable pills in their giant-sized bottle of Tums just evaporated and she began to catch Bud rubbing his gut when he thought she wasn't looking. By July, she noticed that all his T-shirts seemed to hang on him and vowed to be careful not to stretch them any more when she did the laundry.

When Bud casually mentioned that he thought they'd skip renting the cabin near Danville, her alarm system went off. Something, she knew, was very, very wrong. At first, she tried nagging him about getting a checkup, reminding him that they hadn't gone in for a physical since before Terry had arrived. But Bud just ignored her, keeping his eyes trained on the television. Finally, when a summer flu bug bit him hard, he agreed to see Ken Cole.

Sometimes, Rosie thought as she fidgeted in the office waiting room, it's harder to go to a doctor when you know him personally. Secretly she viewed Ken as a big, good-looking dark-haired hunk about twenty years younger than her husband. Bud had met Ken at a poker club, and the two had become fishing buddies after Ken's wife had left town with a golf pro. Ken liked to fish, but he'd been really grateful to have Bud around to help take his mind off his troubles.

Rosie could tell when Bud put on his macho act in Ken's office that he didn't want Ken to know how bad he felt.

"I just need something for cramps and diarrhea," he said.

Ken chuckled, patted him on the back as he handed him some samples and warned him that he wasn't going out in a boat with him until he could stay out of the bathroom for four hours straight.

She relaxed during the next few weeks when Bud responded to the medicine. She even took time to write a letter to Colton, who was spending the summer in Wisconsin with Angel's brother and his family. She couldn't believe how much she missed that kid!

On a steamy morning in August, when she came in from picking green beans, she saw Bud pushing on his stomach and realized how pale he looked. She went straight to the phone and called Ken to tell him she was worried about Bud.

The next day, on his afternoon off, Ken took Bud fishing. She hoped that Ken would talk some sense into Bud
but decided they must have danced all around the subject
of his health without ever mentioning it. Guys always
seemed to do that when they're afraid to admit that they're
scared, she thought. Ken did promise Bud that they'd
spend a few days in Wisconsin later that month if he'd
come into the clinic again. For that, Rosie was grateful.
She couldn't think of many doctors who would bribe their
patients, but that was exactly what Ken had done.

Rosie's hands turned icy when she and Bud stepped
from the sultry air into Ken's air-conditioned waiting
room. She continued to shiver while Bud went back to
have Ken examine him. Her blood ran cold, however,
when Ken called her into to his office and in a steady professional tone, told her that he wanted Bud to get a few
tests.

"I'm feeling something in his abdomen that I don't
like." Although she summoned the courage to meet Ken's
calm gaze, she could tell from the vein that throbbed in his
forehead that he was upset.

After that, everything went downhill so fast that it
made her head swim. The very next morning, Bud couldn't
eat because of the tests he was having at St. Mary's in
Kankakee. By that afternoon, Ken stopped at the house to
deliver the news that Bud had an obstruction that needed to
be removed as soon as possible. When Bud joked that he
didn't want anything to interfere with his enjoying the
sweet corn they'd raised, Ken just smiled tightly and told
them that he'd assist with the surgery. He'd already scheduled it for two days later.

During the next two nights, Rosie felt that she was
about to jump out of her skin when she tried to sleep. She
kept fighting the same feeling she'd had the day when

she'd pedaled from the tennis court to find out about the boy who'd been killed. Her heart wanted to believe that everything would be just fine, but her gut kept telling her something else. On the day before Bud's surgery, she even stopped at St. Pat's, found a side door open and allowed herself to be comforted by the beauty of the small sanctuary.

Her anxiety demanded action. She'd already picked her green beans, and the corn wasn't quite ready, so she stewed herself into a state of despair. Finally, she called Brian and Sandra in Carbondale to tell them about Bud's surgery.

"But don't say a word to Ma," she cautioned, forgetting that her mother had reached that blissful stage when her mind didn't permit her to worry anymore.

She then called Colleen in Naples.

"I'm kinda scared, Colleen," she confessed. Her sister tried to comfort her with the assurance that she and Danny would be praying for Bud. Rosie promised to keep her sister informed.

She even tried to call Terry at his latest location in Florida but learned his number was no longer in service.

She thought about calling Margie but didn't think she could tolerate her chatter. Instead, she called Doris.

"I'll be there," her old friend told her. "Darcy wanted to work that day anyway." Rosie could tell by Doris's tone of voice that she was lying but didn't care.

The day of Bud's surgery Doris brought her a sweater "'cause waiting rooms are too damn hot in the winter and too damn cold in the summer." She tried to read the new issue of *People* but it couldn't hold her interest. Finally, she went outside to pace on the curb until Doris yelled that Ken wanted to talk to her.

"Bud came through everything in good shape." She

thought that Ken looked as old as she felt. When he sank down in the chair next to her, she knew he wasn't finished.

"He had a pretty good-sized obstruction in there." He tugged at the surgical mask that dangled from his neck. "At least we were able to remove it without having to give him a colostomy."

"Thank God!" She began to breathe more easily, but when Ken didn't get up to leave, she felt her eye start to twitch. Finally she forced herself to ask: "Was it . . . is it cancer?"

Ken nodded and assured her they had removed the tumor. Rubbing his chin, he added, "There *is* some involvement with the liver."

"Shit." Doris' shoulders sagged. Rosie felt so dumbstruck that she couldn't utter a word.

Ken explained that they'd start treatment as soon as possible . . . if that's what Bud wanted to do. "We'll talk about it in the next day or two."

As he took Rosie's trembling hands in his, she could see the fatigue in his eyes. "We'll fight it together," he vowed. "After all, I promised him that fishing trip."

* * *

She'd never really climbed a mountain, only taken short hikes along the rocky ridges bordering the Phoenix area. But she'd held her breath during plenty of TV programs as a climber pulled himself up with a rope, then struggled as his foot slipped and he slid farther back than he'd been in the first place. She thought that's just how Bud must have felt during the next few months. When he finished his chemo treatments, he was as bald as Michael Jordan. Still, he slapped on his Notre Dame cap and escaped to Wisconsin with Ken during a fall weekend when his Irish team wasn't playing.

When they returned, freezing from the October chill, they were like two kids who had just won their first Little League game. Their coolers were so packed that Rosie told them the fish must have taken pity on them and allowed themselves to be caught. Groaning at her lack of appreciation, they retorted that she had no clue regarding their talents. Although she snapped back at them, she was grinning on the inside. She knew that the fishing trip was the best prescription Ken could have written for Bud.

She couldn't believe the change in her husband. For a few weeks Bud was like his old self, teasing her, taking her to movies at the Paramount, and calling to reserve the cabin near Danville for two weeks the next summer. He even traded their beloved Jeep on a used Ford Escort wagon saying he was ready for a smoother ride. Rosie thought a few times that she should call Doris to get Kate's phone number. If her husband could find a couple of extra Notre Dame tickets, Bud would be the happiest fellow in the Midwest. She became so involved with Colton again, however, that she completely forgot.

During the bleak days of mid-November, when naked branches stretched black across the bullet-gray sky, she noticed that Bud's energy seemed to fade. He grew as restless as Colton on a bad day, prowling around the house at night and dozing off for most of the afternoon. Even the floundering Notre Dame team couldn't hold his interest. She ignored most of his grumbling until he mentioned the work of Dr. Jack Kevorkian. When Bud launched onto that topic, she had to change the subject.

The two of them shared a quiet Thanksgiving. Brian and Sandra had invited them to Carbondale, but Bud didn't feel like traveling that far. When Rosie suggested they buy a Christmas tree the first weekend in December, he told her she could pick one up in town while he stayed home and played a few hands of solitaire. She didn't have the heart to remind him that they had always cut down their own tree. Instead, she drove like a robot to the Jewel, stuffed the first tree she found into the trunk of their wagon and hauled it back to the farm.

Knowing Bud's heart wasn't into Christmas, she asked Colton and Angel to help them decorate their tree. At first, Bud hated the idea, but Colton's enthusiasm was so contagious that Bud began hanging the paper ornaments that Colton and his mother had made. He even nibbled on a handful of popcorn when they were finished, something he hadn't done for months.

"What a great kid!" After Colton and Angel had left, Bud thrashed around in his recliner. He just couldn't seem to get comfortable. "His mom's a real piece of work though. Maybe she'd be okay if someone would teach her how . . ." He fell asleep before he could finish his sentence.

During the holiday season, Rosie learned that she and Bud were on several prayer chains—Margie's doing, no doubt. She'd never been one to talk to God much, but she discovered one thing: She found she'd much rather do the praying than be the one who's being prayed for! Friends from St. Pat's and the dominoes group brought them Christmas cookies, pumpkin pie and vegetable soup, and a group of carolers from the high school drove all the way out to their farm to sing to them on their front porch. Bud's military discipline helped him hold up during "Silent Night," but Rosie went straight to their bedroom and shut the door. As she rubbed her jerking eyelid, she muttered that she would be so glad when the holidays were over and they could get back to normal. Whatever that was.

Doris couldn't drive up from Rockwell until after the first of the year. She and Violet had been overloaded with private parties to cater, and Darcy couldn't handle the big office dinners in The Boulder's banquet room by herself. But once Rosie and Bud disposed of their Christmas tree and put the ornaments put away, Doris came at least twice a week. Bud perked up when she shoved a game of "Risk" in front of him. Rosie found she hated the game and knew that Doris did too, but they continued to play so Bud could show off his understanding of military strategies.

Often the three of them would eat lunch and get half-way through a game, then Bud would nod off and she and Doris would revert to their girl talk. One day she asked Doris to bring her up to date on the rest of her family.

"How much time have you got?" Doris went to the fridge, snapped open a can of diet pop and sat down at the kitchen table. When Rosie grinned, Doris launched into her account.

"Well, you know that Charley came back to the office at Midwest Manufacturing and got to be general manager." Thoughtfully she nursed her cola. "Mom—she lived long enough to have Charley take her on a tour of the lines in the plant after he was put in charge. Can't you just picture it— her an old hourly worker and him the head honcho? Oh my god, was she proud as a peacock that day!"

She went on to say that Lorene and Steve had stayed in Pennsylvania with her three kids. When Rosie asked about Vickie and the twins, Doris put down her drink.

"Remember how that little squirt used to twirl around our house? You wouldn't believe it, but Steve paid for some dance lessons after they moved. Vickie got to be real good. Danced in some shows professionally. She's had her own studio out there for years."

Then Doris frowned. "The twins? When Donnie tried to enlist, he found out he had a heart murmur. So he went into trucking with Steve. Too bad Ronnie didn't have one

too. He ended up in Vietnam and came home a quad—
quad—oh, shit, what d'ya call it?"

"Quadriplegic?" Rosie felt as if she'd been punched in
the stomach as she pictured little Ronnie as a toddler with
one blue eye, one brown eye and always, it seemed, dirty
diapers. "Aw, geez—how terrible!"

"Yeah, Ronnie finally got pneumonia and died. It just
about killed his mom too. I've never seen Lorene so low."
They sat silently together for a few moments, then Doris
mentioned that her brother, Vic and his wife, lived in California. "And of course, there's Violet. She's startin' to
slow down, but she's been my anchor most of my life. Her
and her husband, Spud. He died in '91, you know. They
never had any kids, but they always treated mine like their
own."

Rosie went to check Bud and found him still sleeping.
She began to grow drowsy herself as Doris spoke of her
kids. She knew if she lived to be a hundred, she'd never
quite be able to keep Doris' children straight. She fought
off sleep as Doris talked about Darcy and two of her
daughters who helped at the restaurant and Denny who still
lived on the farm and refused to see her much.

She began to wash their lunch dishes to keep herself
awake and listened while Doris bragged—and with reason—about David, who was now an engineer for a company in Atlanta. Her other daughter, Debbie, was running a
hair salon, and the two younger boys, Doug and Dirk, had
gone into construction with Alan Atwater. When Rosie
asked about Alan, Doris just said the usual—that he treated
her really good. His sister, Adele, had gone off to college
and lived out in New York state and didn't come back to
Rockwell much, she added.

Rosie ran a dish towel around the inside of their soup
pan as she tried to pay attention.

"Oh—remember Nancy Dawes?" Doris squished her soda can and dropped it into the recycling basket.

Rosie stopped, her towel in midair. She hadn't heard that name since she'd left for Rockwell to go to California. "Yeah. Little Miss Perfect, right?"

"Maybe back then she was. You know, Violet always worked for her family, so we did some of the catering for Nancy's first wedding." She rolled her eyes. "But not all of it. Mrs. Dawes had an uppity bunch bring in some fancy stuff from Chicago. They put up a tent in their yard and rigged up a champagne fountain somehow. That wasn't too long after I'd moved back to town with the kids."

"Nancy's *first* wedding?" She opened a bag of chips and put it between them thinking this was like old times after school.

"Yeah, she's had about five of 'em, I guess." Doris counted on her fingers. "In between, she'd come home and live with her folks for awhile, mess around with guys in Rockwell, then all of a sudden we'd hear she'd met someone and was off to marry him." She reached for a handful of chips. "It just about drove Dr. Dawes crazy."

"Any kids?" she wondered.

"Naw. She's back again, livin' in the old family home. Her mom and dad's both gone. She's skinny as a rail, wearin' tons of makeup and still prowlin' around lookin' for Mr. Right." Doris paused to inspect the cuticle of her thumbnail. "She'll come in to The Boulder and sit up at the counter drinkin' coffee till she's got the shakes. Then she'll hurry off, pretendin' she's got someplace important to go. You and Bud'll see her sometime when you come down."

"I'd just as soon not run into her, " Rosie chuckled. "We'd probably get into another fight." Reaching into the bag of chips, she thought better of it. "Remember all the trouble I got into at that dance in eighth grade when she wanted to be with Jimmy McPherson?"

"I sure do!" Doris started to giggle. "Oh, he's fat and bald now. Wonder if Nancy still thinks he's so cute."

They laughed so hard that they woke up Bud. He just shook his head and declared that she and Doris could make more noise than a whole squadron of fighter planes. They couldn't tell him what was so funny, Rosie thought. You kinda had to be there!

In mid-February, Ken came out to show Bud the new tackle box he'd bought for himself for Valentine's Day. Bud grinned and told Ken if he wasn't so ugly, he wouldn't have to get his own present. He puffed up his skinny chest and said he'd taken his wife into town for a good steak and a movie.

They traded friendly insults while she tried to watch *Jeopardy*. Then she realized Bud had grown quiet. Finally, he spoke to Ken.

"This is about as good as I'm gonna get, isn't it?" He shuffled a deck of cards while he waited for Ken's answer that was long coming. When Rosie took her eyes off Alex Trebek and turned toward Ken, she saw a huge sigh go through him.

She watched as her husband and his fishing pal looked long and hard at each other. While the *Jeopardy* song ticked away in the background, she and Bud waited, hoping Ken might give them the game-winning answer they were hoping for. When he spoke at last, his words were soft and not the ones they wanted to hear.

"'Fraid it is, Buddy. 'Fraid it is."

She and Bud sat still as statues, then he ran his hand over the top of his head, where his new hair was starting to grow in white and curly. She felt her entire cheek start to twitch.

"I'll get us some coffee." Rubbing her eye, she started toward the kitchen.

"None for me." Bud riffled through the cards again. "Just some ice chips in a glass."

"Same for me." Ken's voice broke. "Only pour a little whiskey over it, will you?"

* * *

Chapter
Thirty-Three

Some days Rosie felt that March 2001 was the longest month of her life. Other days, it seemed the shortest. Each morning she'd search for changes in Bud. Was he thinner? Was his skin taking on more of that awful yellowish cast? Was he sleeping a lot more? She worried herself sick as she tried to convince herself that he'd feel stronger as soon as warm weather arrived. She told Colton that, until Bud felt better, she'd only be able to help him at school once a week.

Still, in some wild-and-crazy way, she believed that those roller coaster days in March were the best that she and Bud ever had together. She always knew that he felt good when he declared that he wasn't going to "sit around the goddamn house." Those were the times that they climbed into their wagon and took off for the movie, the mall, or even down to Rockwell so Bud could go to The Boulder for liver, no onions. But on days when his strength failed him, he quietly pulled out his deck of cards and started dealing out hands of solitaire on the coffee table. While she pretended to dust or straighten up the room, they talked.

Sometimes Bud encouraged her to prattle on about her past. Little by little, she was shedding those bags of guilt she'd carried all those years about failing Mike, disappointing her parents and wasting her life. Bud made her realize that, ever since her early childhood, she'd been terrified of being alone.

"Look," he paused over a newly dealt hand of solitaire, "you surrounded yourself with grade-school friends that you could boss around. Then, when you were in high school you chased after guys that you thought would keep you company."

"Yeah." She sighed. "The only time I ever broke that pattern was when I got brave enough to go to California. Even then, I got off the bus and went straight to the bars to find myself a new group of chums."

"See? I finally swooped down and saved you from all that nonsense." He grinned wickedly. "Once you met me, you weren't alone anymore."

Throwing a pillow at him, she told him he was too smart for his own good. Then, as if guessing her thoughts, he assured her, "You'll never be alone again, Ro. I'll always be part of you, even if you can't see me. Got that?"

She shuddered and went to the kitchen to make them a cup of tea.

A few days later, as he unburdened himself during a game of solitaire, she finally learned his true feelings about Marie. Rosie had always thought he'd kept his high-school sweetheart on a pedestal and was stunned to discover that nothing was further from the truth.

"I tried to be a good husband, Ro, but she whined at me all the time for being so strict with Todd. And I got after her for spoiling Terry to pieces." He stopped to move a black queen onto a red king. "I really think we'd have split up if she had lived. We'd just grown too far apart, gone in separate directions."

"Aw, Bud." She went over to the sofa and took him in her arms.

"You know you've been the love of my life since we

met in that bar in Burbank. I took one look at you and almost slipped right off my bar stool." Without another word, he pulled her down on the sofa and kissed her. It had been so long since they'd let their passion loose that Rosie felt like a teen-ager again in the Pacific Palms parking lot . . . only this time it was right in the middle of the day!

She knew she'd keep that sofa forever. Every time she looked at it during the months that followed, she smiled and then tried not to remember that it was the spot where she and Bud had been able to make love for the last time.

* * *

April arrived and brought with it a full week of constant rain. She and Bud never left the house during that time and were grateful for their friends. Margie hauled in groceries twice a week, and Ken picked up carryout orders and ate his supper with them. Even Angel and Colton surprised them one night with lukewarm sandwiches and soggy fries from the Burger King. Later that evening Rosie felt guilty for snapping at Angel when she left her umbrella open in their house. After she'd yelled at Angel, no one was hungry except Colton. Bud was barely able to pick at his food by that time and hardly had the energy to deal out a game of solitaire. By the end of the dismal week, he said he didn't feel like coming out to the living room anymore.

"If the pain gets too bad, we'll put him in the hospital," Ken warned. "But I'll stop by every morning before I go to the office and give him a shot. That should help." He took a deep breath. "You should know I've called the hospice group. This is too tough for you to try to do alone."

Ken moved their little TV from the kitchen into their bedroom so Bud could watch the Bulls at night. He slept most of the day while Rosie fussed around the room, straightening pictures on their dresser and tidying up stacks of cards. Sometimes, when she stopped to look at him, she thought she could actually see him shrinking while his skin grew a darker yellow. She hoped, when it was all over, that she'd remember what the healthy Bud looked like.

On a Friday afternoon the sun came out, and Bud felt strong enough to sit up. He commented that there were daffodils blooming on the far side of the yard and allowed her to spoon some chicken broth into him. As she plumped up his pillow, he reminded her that the Bulls would be on at eight o'clock.

By the time Ken arrived, Bud had fallen asleep. She and Ken turned on the game but hardly said a word to each other. During the third quarter, Rosie stretched out on the little cot at the end of the bed. She didn't realize until early the next morning that Ken had dozed on the couch. All through the night, she wakened, heard Bud's rattled uneven breaths and drifted off again.

It was barely light when Ken shook her arm gently. Startled, she sat straight up. The first thing she noticed was the quiet. The terrible quiet.

"He's gone, Rosie."

"Jesus, Mary and Joseph." She crossed herself as she went to her husband's side. Geez, she thought, he looked so damn peaceful. "Aw, Buddy," she murmured as she laid her head across his chest.

Ken stood over them like a forlorn little boy.

"He was my best—" Tears streamed down his cheeks. "God, I wish I could've done something for him. Here I am a doctor and . . ."

"But you did, Ken. You gave him everything." She stood and put her arms around him to comfort him. And, unlike the day that Mike died, she gave in to her own grief as she and Ken wept for the one they loved.

432

* * *

She really thought she might be okay until events during the next two weeks knocked the props out from under her. Reeling from fatigue and emotion, she felt herself unraveling like a ball of yarn that had fallen from a table.

First, she couldn't believe that Terry appeared on her doorstep just minutes after Bud died. Ken had tried to locate him for several days so he could get home to see his dad but had trouble tracking him down because Terry frequently used an alias to avoid bill collectors. Ken finally caught up with him in Key West

She thought she was opening the door for the undertaker. Instead, there stood Terry. Her first thought was that she was grateful that Bud didn't have to see what a mess his son had become. His hair was long and oily, he was missing a couple of teeth since they'd seen him last, and one strap of his tank top had slid down over his shoulder, exposing a new tattoo of a snake. She couldn't bring herself to hug him and motioned weakly for Ken to take care of Terry.

Feeling anger beginning to seethe inside her, she sat on the sofa and looked the other way when Terry began to tell Ken how much he really loved his dad.

"Mom never would've let him get this sick." Terry turned his mean and vengeful face toward her. When Ken saw her struggling for composure, he suggested that Terry spend a few minutes with his dad before the undertaker came, then said he'd take him back to his place in town. She felt she'd always be indebted to Ken for handling that situation

When Margie called and offered to stay with her, Rosie was relieved that she could tell her Doris had already volunteered. She loved Margie but knew her endless chattering would give her the jitters. Doris always sensed when she needed to make conversation and when she wanted to be quiet.

With support from Doris, Ken, Margie, Angel and Colton, she was able to make it through the memorial service without falling apart. She kept reminding herself that Bud had told her she'd never be alone again. The following day, there were no surprises as they sat through the reading of Bud's will. He had left the house and acreage to her, a generous thousand dollars to Terry, and all his fishing equipment to Ken.

"Bitch!" Terry snarled. "A measly thousand dollars!" He scratched out an address so the attorney could send him his check and left without saying good-bye. His attitude gave Rosie the urge for a good stiff drink.

Instead, she and Doris split a beer at the kitchen table, then she assured her friend she'd be okay by herself. Ten days later Ken helped her scatter Bud's ashes over the Kankakee River. She was shocked by the weight of the bag and was glad that Ken had thought to bring surgical gloves for them to wear. When she saw that the gray powder clung to them and left a trail wherever they tossed it, she feared someone might arrest them for not having a permit. But as Ken said a few neat words about Bud on the bank of the river, she felt a calmness settle over her. After she and Ken left Bud's remains in the peaceful surroundings where he loved to spend his time, she felt she'd seen enough of death to last her the rest of her life.

Reassuring herself that she would be just fine, she returned to the farmhouse. The next morning, however, Brian called from Carbondale to tell her that their mother had slipped away. Two days later, Rosie found herself standing in the Rockwell cemetery at the plot that had been waiting for her mother for so long. Wedging herself between Brian, Sandra, Colleen and Danny, she heard a turtledove cooing

contentedly. Everywhere around her there was new life—
fat buds popping open on the peony bushes, a nestful of
baby robins cheeping hungrily from a branch on the maple
tree, and the sweet smell of freshly cut grass clinging to the
warm air. It had been a day just like this when they'd had
brought Mike there to be buried. Why, she wondered, did
everyone have to die in the spring?

* * *

"Rosalie Annette! Don't forget to start the pork
steak!"

"Geez," she muttered. "I have to do everything
around here." Tossing down Mike's copy of *The Green
Hornet*, she headed toward the kitchen.

"And don't be grumbling under your breath," her
mother scolded from the kitchen. "A bad attitude does
not make for a pretty face."

"Yeah," Mike added. "And be careful how you treat
my comic books too!"

She turned and stuck out her tongue at him as two
questions gnawed at her: How did Mike get away with
everything and where did Ma get her superhuman power
of hearing?

* * *

As the priest extolled her mother's virtues, Rosie
wished she could have apologized to her mother for all the
times she'd pushed her to the brink.

* * *

"Rosalie Annette, you've already been to the show

twice this week. You're not going again."

Ma untied her apron and hung it firmly on a nail on the back porch.

"Oh, yeah?" Rosie put her fists on her hips. "Well, Mr. Michael Mulgrew went twice, and he's planning to go."

"That's because Teddy Moody's father invited him." Ma lowered herself squarely onto the sagging couch and lifted the lid of her mending box.

"And Colleen—"

"Don't 'and Colleen' me. You know she earns her own money." Her mother spoke thickly around the thread in her mouth. "Besides, Danny pays most of the time."

"Geez, can I help it if I don't have a boyfriend?" Rosie wished immediately that she could erase her words that hung in midair.

"Well, now, that just settles it." Her mother poked her darning needle up through one of Pa's rough socks. "You won't be going next week either."

"But, Ma—"

"Careful . . . or you won't go to the show for a month. Take your sassy mouth and go upstairs."

As she left the living room, Rosie saw her mother wince, then suck a drop of blood from the thumb she'd just pricked.

* * *

She squirmed. The cemetery air seemed to be closing in on her. She longed to be back in her own kitchen and wondered if that bottle of schnapps that Bud had brought home from a poker game was still under the sink.

As the priest launched into the Twenty-Third Psalm, she sniffed and rubbed her cheek with her sleeve. Colleen handed her a tissue to blot her tears.

* * *

"Rosalie Annette, you watch what you do with that Melowicz girl. Your pa and me don't think she's the best company for you." Ma sighed as she placed the box of sympathy cards back on the shelf. Rosie wondered how many times a person could read the same cards over and over.

"Well, she's sure a lot more fun than anyone around here!" She wanted to pull out a cigarette and take a nice long drag on it. Since she didn't feel that brave, she caressed the cellophane-wrapped packet of Chesterfields buried deep in the pocket of her jeans.

Ma studied her for a long time before she spoke. Sometimes, Rosie thought, she could see the grief hanging off Ma's face.

"You're the only one we have left. You know that. If anything ever happened—"

"Well, I'm damn sick and tired of being the only one too. Did you ever stop to think about that? Huh?"

"Rosalie Annette—

"I'm not a baby anymore, Ma! I know what I'm doing. I can take care of myself!" As she let the door slam behind her, she yelled over her shoulder, "And don't try to tell me what to do!"

* * *

"Surely goodness and mercy shall follow us . . ." As the priest's words grew dim and fuzzy, Rosie crossed herself.

"Jesus, Mary and Joseph," she mumbled as she felt herself slip to the ground.

Each day, after her mother's funeral, she awakened feeling as if she'd been hit over the head with an iron skillet. Finding excuses not to go outside, she wandered around the house picking through Bud's clothes and shuffling through the sympathy cards. She felt like her mother after Mike had been killed. She knew Margie would have come to see her, but her friend had gone to Michigan to help her daughter, who was having her fourth baby in five years. After Colton left to spend the summer with his uncle, she didn't hear a word from Angel.

But Doris drove up from Rockwell two or three times each week. She brought tomato and green pepper seedlings to plant behind the house and petunias and marigolds to brighten up the front. During a June drought, however, Rosie forgot to water them. One morning in July, she gazed at them sorrowfully and realized that most of her seedlings had died too, just like Bud and Ma.

Each time Doris arrived, she unloaded enough food for several days. Rosie knew that Doris and Violet had fixed the special dishes just for her. She'd nibble at them a bit while Doris was there, then put the rest in the fridge for later. However, as she spent her days thumbing through old pictures and staring out the window, she would forget to eat. She always felt bad when Doris came to visit the next week and found all her salads and casseroles covered with mold.

When Ken drove out in mid-July and offered to take her fishing, she replied that she had too much to do. Maybe they could go later in the summer, she added. He left a big bottle of vitamins on the kitchen counter. By the end of August, they still hadn't gone fishing. And the bottle of vitamins sat unopened, gathering dust.

She turned down invitations from Brian and Sandra to visit one of their sons in Arkansas and from Danny and Colleen to spend some time with them in Naples. Although Colleen insisted that they would pay for her ticket, she couldn't bear the thought of getting on a plane. The idea of doing something Bud loved every day of his life nauseated her. So she made up an excuse and stayed home.

For Colton's sake, she did manage to drag herself to Kennedy School in early September but found she was exhausted for days afterward. One morning, as she recovered from her tutoring session, she grumbled at the television.

"Damn thing is showing the same movie on every channel," she muttered as she flipped through the channels and watched an airplane smashing into a skyscraper. In disgust, she hit the off button and strolled outside to stare at the limp remains of her marigolds.

She was confused when Doris called her, sobbing over the terrorist attack in New York. "Me 'n Mom 'n Tommy had our picture taken on a boat right outside the World Trade Center," she cried. "I just can't believe it. I just can't believe it," she repeated over and over.

After she had hung up the phone, Rosie returned to her set and turned it on. She huddled under a quilt as she tried to absorb the impact of the tragedy. She never thought about eating for the rest of the day.

Colton was so shaken by the events of September 11 that she felt she had to keep him on track with his reading lessons. But Christmas came along to distract him, and he asked if he and Angel could help decorate her tree again.

"I'm not doing a tree this year," she told him.

He studied her curiously.

"You're getting' awful skinny, you know," was his only response.

She spent Christmas Day watching television and piecing on food from Margie and Doris. Each had invited her to join them for dinner, but she couldn't bring herself to climb that mountain. Margie seemed a little upset, but Doris hugged her and told her she understood.

For the next few months, she found herself drifting through fuzzy-edged days. Each morning she pulled on one of Bud's old sweatshirts and her crummy navy slacks with the waistband that she had to fold over twice so they stayed up. Most of the time she watched old reruns. She couldn't get interested in a jigsaw puzzle but did make herself drive to Kennedy school for her weekly session with Colton. Once in awhile, she let Ken or Doris take her out for a sandwich.

She never noticed when the snow thawed. But one day she looked out the window and wondered why Virgil Kletzig was on his tractor in one of the fields. Then she realized: It's been almost a year since Bud left! Fighting off nausea, she reached into the back of the cupboard for a half-finished bottle of Jack Daniel's. She poured the amber liquid over a couple of ice cubes and went outside to sip her drink on the front step. As she sat on the stoop, she noticed the chipped paint on the house, the dead marigolds from last summer trailing over the front walk and the grass that had sprouted tall and uneven from the spring rains. Bud had promised she'd never be alone again. But there she was, feeling more alone than she'd ever been in her entire miserable life!

Suddenly she became so angry that she hurled her glass on the sidewalk and watched it shatter, the whiskey splashing into the thick grass.

"Goddammit, Bud Laughlin—you promised. But you lied! How could you just die and leave me like this?" Burying her head in her lap, she waited for the tears to pour forth, but there were none left. She heaved great dry sobs into her folded arms, angry at her husband, angry at the whiskey for spilling all over the grass, angry that someone was calling her on the phone. That meant she would have to get up and go answer the damn thing.

"You *know* I hate being alone!" she screamed at the cloudless sky as she mechanically headed for the door. "What in the hell am I supposed to do?"

When she finally picked up the phone, Doris was cross.

"Hey, it's me. Are you all right? I had to let the thing ring twelve times." Her voice was nervous and quivery.

"So?" she retorted. What did it matter anyway? "I wasn't sure I wanted to answer it."

"Don't give me that!" Doris snapped.

Stunned, Rosie stopped and stared at the phone in her hand. Could this really be Doris, she wondered. She seemed so upset—not nice and gentle like usual.

"What's wrong?" she asked her friend. "You sound . . . different."

"Now listen to me, Rosie, and listen to me good. I need you." She could hear Doris take a deep jagged breath.

"I've lost track of the number of times I've been up to your place in the last couple of years," Doris continued. "But this time *I* need *you*. Plan to be at The Boulder at 11:30 next Tuesday, you hear?" Pausing, Doris anticipated the next question. "And, no, I can't tell you why. Not on the phone. Just be there."

Rosie's hand shook as she hung up the phone. Jesus, Mary and Joseph, she prayed, please let Doris be okay. The tone of her friend's voice terrified her. What in God's name, she wondered, could be so bad that she needs help from *me*?

* * *

Part Three: Kate

May 2002

Chapter
Thirty - Four

F illed with anticipation over her trip to Rockwell, Kate rolled back her sun roof and inhaled the scent of freshly turned earth as she drove past the newly plowed fields west of South Bend. Admiring the yellow strands of willows and patches of wild violets and daffodils by the side of the road, she reminded herself that this was one of those days when midwesterners understand why they choose to live in that part of the country.

In spite of the glorious spring morning and Vaughn Monroe's crooning of his old hit, "Ballerina," she felt a shadow of misgiving creep over her.

"Are we presumptuous or what?" she muttered to herself as she headed south toward Rockwell. Who are we, she wondered, to think we can help Rosie? She winced when she thought of the number of years that had passed since they had been the Fearless Four. Acknowledging the mistakes she had made in her own life, she didn't see how she could ease the pain for anyone else.

Still, she thought as she slowed for the string of tiny towns along her route, she could not wait to see Rosie once more . . . to watch that smile spread across her broad face . . . to hear that tone of authority that had steered them through the tribulations of seventh and eighth grade! It was an opportunity that she'd feared might never present itself again.

Doris, of course, had renewed her friendship with Rosie, but she and Cheryl would be rewinding their lives to a time that she wondered if any of them truly recalled with accuracy.

She checked her watch as she pulled into the parking lot of The Boulder and was pleased to see she was a few minutes early. Gathering her purse and a light sweater from the front seat, she went inside to look for Doris. When she failed to spot her friend, she strolled over to the cash register to ask one of the employees about her.

An elderly lady stood nearby, a gaunt person with a familiar quality. Perhaps, Kate thought, the woman had been a friend of her mother's. In vain she tried to place her. Pansy Cunningham? No, too thin. Myrtle Belknap? No, too round-shouldered. Although she tried not to stare, she decided that the woman never should have allowed her straggly gray hair to grow to her shoulders—an unattractive length for anyone her age.

Clutching her purse nervously, the woman glanced at her. It was then that Kate saw the signature twitching left eyelid. She felt her stomach lurch and, biting her lip, turned away so the woman could not see the shock she knew was written all over her face. This frail wisp standing just a few feet from her, Kate realized, was Rosie. *Their* Rosie! She took a few deep breaths before she could bring herself to speak.

"Rosie?" she questioned softly. The woman's head jerked, then turned her blue eyes on Kate. "Rosie. It's Kate. Kate Freeman. From Sweet Briar."

Swaying slightly, Rosie reached behind her for the counter and sank onto one of the round stools.

"Geez." Squinting a bit as she gazed directly at her, Rosie showed a glimmer of recognition. As they hugged, Kate felt nothing but brittle bones encased by a bulky sweater. Overwhelmed with emotion, she wondered how long she could keep her composure. She was grateful to see Doris appear in the kitchen doorway.

"Oh, my god. Look at the two of you! And here comes Cheryl right now." Doris brushed tears from her cheeks with the back of her hand as she hurried to meet Cheryl.

Wearing a well-cut denim skirt and quilted vest, Cheryl might have stepped out of an ad for "country chic." Her frosted hair, a shorter version of her old page boy, still was thick enough to swing jauntily as she trailed after Doris to their booth at the back of the restaurant. Kate saw Cheryl's joy change to disbelief when she hugged Rosie and realized how fragile their leader had become.

After all of them ordered light items, Doris beamed with the pride of seeing the four in her own restaurant.

"Well!" Sighing, she took a moment to savor the success of their little reunion. "Here we are—together at last."

"You didn't tell me this was to be a party." Rosie's voice was flat. Sitting next to Cheryl, she looked worn and shabby. "I don't do parties anymore." Her eyes flicked furtively at Kate, then at Cheryl and back to the tabletop again.

An awkward stillness permeated the air around them, broken only by Doris' futile attempts at bright conversation. Uncertain if she could force down a single bite of her grilled cheese, Kate regretted their attempt to help Rosie. As she nibbled around the edges of her sandwich, she wondered if she and Cheryl should just finish their lunch and leave as gracefully as possible.

"Get this. I was a few minutes late because I drove by my old house. Would you believe it's *pink*?" Cheryl, cutting into the bits of grilled chicken on her salad, seemed to be making a brilliant effort to pretend that all was well.

"The last time I saw ours, it had blue siding on it. And a deck out back." When Kate offered Cheryl her pickle—an old habit from years ago—her friend took it without thinking.

"Mine's gold and brown." There, Kate thought as she took an easier breath. Rosie had entered the conversation with one tentative step, and the rest of them must be careful not to pounce on every word she uttered. "Butt-ugly is what it is," she added dully. "At least they had indoor plumbing put in."

"And at least your homes're still standing—no matter what color they are. Course, ours was half fallin' down when we was kids." Doris looked at each of them expectantly, but once again the cloud of uncomfortable quiet had descended over their table. She bit into her hamburger and tried again.

"My brother Charley?" Her mouth was full as she desperately tried to breathe life into their dialogue. "He lives in one of them big houses where the old Naughton place used to be. I'll show you after lunch."

The name of the creepy mansion seemed to crack the ice. Rosie relaxed her hunched shoulders slightly as Cheryl confessed that she had never wanted the rest of them to know how terrified she had been of the huge house. Kate recalled the time when she was sure she had seen a ghostly light shining from the top floor.

Doris hooted and chided them for having been "gutless kids." Then she, too, grew serious and admitted that when Charley was building his new home, she had been afraid that eerie spirits might still linger over the property. They smiled in companionable silence as they reflected on their childhood fears. Finally Rosie cleared her throat.

"Re—remember, Kate, how I'd always—I'd always make a phone call when I'd get ready—ready to leave your house?"

Kate felt her heart break at the hesitancy Rosie displayed. She yearned to take her old friend in her arms and assure her that everything would be all right. Instead, she asked, "You mean on those winter afternoons after school?"

Rosie nodded.

"I was—well, I was calling Ma to tell her to go out on our porch." She sighed. "She died, you know . . . Ma. Anyway, I wanted her to watch for me. Just—well, just in case something—something tried to get me."

"No! Not *you!*" Cheryl pushed away the remains of her salad. "You were always the bravest of all of us, Rosie."

"Not when it came to spooky stuff." Shuddering, Rosie studied the ice in her glass. Then she fixed her gaze on each of them. "I really had you guys fooled though, didn't I?" For the first time that day, a faint smile cracked through the wrinkles on her face.

"Oh, my god, we got so much to catch up on." Automatically Doris began to stack their dishes for the waitress. "Let's go to my house so we can just kick back 'n talk."

"Where do you live?" Cheryl opened a gold compact and repaired her lipstick.

"It's the old Raney place, on the Sweet Briar side of town," she explained. "Me 'n Violet—well, 'n Spud too till he died a few years ago—we've been there together since I left Bill. It's not fancy, but we've got all kinds of room."

As they lined up their cars behind Doris, Kate couldn't help but remember that first day after school when the four of them had hopped on their bikes and followed a confident Rosie to the cemetery. Now here they were again— more than fifty years later—winding their way through the streets of Rockwell together. This time, however, Doris was leading the way, and Rosie's car was tucked in securely between Kate and Cheryl.

Grateful for the few minutes alone, Kate checked her

own reflection in the mirror. Had *she* aged as much as Rosie? She didn't think so. And yet the realization that the most vibrant friend of her youth had lost every ounce of her zest had a devastating effect. Under the weight of her weariness, Kate had new respect for Doris' effort to bring them all together. But, deep down, she still almost wished that she had not made the trip.

The aroma of freshly baked cookies that greeted them inside Doris' home made Kate ache for her mother. As Doris escorted them into her sunny blue-and-yellow kitchen, Kate thought she must have read her mind.

"I always wanted a kitchen like yours, Kate. Someplace where we could enjoy good food and good friends." She straightened a pile of *Martha Stewart* magazines on her baker's rack. "Of course, it took us awhile to get it like this. When the kids was all home, this was a real mess!"

They waited while Doris made a pot of coffee, then joined her for a tour of her tastefully decorated downstairs. One wall in her living room was covered with framed photographs. "It's the Panczyk Wall of Fame," she chuckled.

Pausing, they studied the familiar black-and-white pictures of her dad and Chet Jr. that had stood on top of the piano in her old house. There were Vic and Charley in their basketball uniforms and all the rest of her siblings, nieces and nephews, children and grandchildren. Kate marveled at how many of them were blessed with the sweet gray eyes that had always been Doris' best feature. Doris motioned for them to sit down, then quickly brought in a tray of cookies and fresh hot coffee.

"You sure had me snookered, Rosie!" Cheryl was the first to launch the conversation. "To think that you were scared of that old mansion and we never knew it." She reached over to cover Rosie's hand with her own. Oblivious to the fact that Rosie seemed to have detached herself once again from their group, Cheryl sipped her coffee as she stared thoughtfully into space. "I guess in some way, we all lived a charade of one kind or another. With me, it was my dad, of course."

"You know," Kate told her, "to this day I can never hear the Pied Pipers singing 'Dream' without thinking of Bertie and Lila gliding around your living room."

"He worshiped Lila. And me too, I guess." She set down her cup. "That's why he did what he did—you know, stole from the dealership. Lordy, I thought the Loneliness would kill me when we had to move." They waited quietly as she struggled for composure. "When I'd think of the three of you having fun without me, I could hardly stand—"

"It wasn't like that. Not at all." Interrupting, Doris let Cheryl know that their high-school years hadn't been quite what they'd planned. "For one reason or another, we all went our different ways." Doris shrugged. "I know *I* sure as hell made one big mistake. But I'm not cryin' over spilt milk. I'm proud of every one of them kids and grandkids up there on the wall."

Cheryl's well-groomed exterior began to crumple as she allowed her vulnerability to show.

"Let me tell you, if—if I had a wall like yours, Doris, it—it would be pretty small." She walked over to Doris' photos, surveyed them again and sighed with longing. "I've—I've had three husbands, two of them real losers. And then there was my little boy—my little boy who never grew up."

As Cheryl shared with them the tale of her tumultuous years with Jamie and Rip and the tragic existence of J.T., her eyes filled with tears. This time it was Rosie's turn to cover Cheryl's hand in a gesture of comfort and understanding.

When she was able to continue, Cheryl smiled wanly

and admitted that Jarvis had been the surprise and joy of her life—an older man whom she had married for companionship and had grown to love with her entire heart.

"He took me into his world without batting an eye. But, better yet, he loved *my* world as much as his. He never allowed me to give up my singing." She paused and swallowed several times before she could continue. "But I lost him, you know."

"He died?" Rosie's reaction was blunt.

"He had Alzheimer's," Cheryl nodded. She went on to say that when he had begun to need round-the-clock care five years ago, she had sold their big house in Kenilworth and hired a team of nurses so she could keep him at home in their Lake Shore Drive apartment.

"It—it wasn't easy." She gripped Rosie's hand. "He was such a wonderful man. Kate, you and Marty met him. You tell them about Jarvis. I'm—I'm about talked out."

Enveloped in the coziness of Doris' overstuffed chair, Kate recounted the day when she and Cheryl had met by chance at Wrigley Field a few years earlier. As she described the evening that she and Marty had spent with Jarvis, Cheryl encouraged her with nods as Kate described Jarvis' energy, graciousness and magnetism.

"Lordy, Kate, no wonder you're a writer. Jarvis truly was every word you said about him," Cheryl agreed softly. "But don't just talk about *him*. Tell us about your family and your career. After all, you've had such a successful life!"

"It's not quite the one you may have read about on the jackets of my books." Kate squirmed in her chair as she began to speak. Staring at the carpet, she thought of telling them about Marty's accomplishments and that her children, though settled in their jobs and marriages, had yet to provide her with grandchildren. Instead, she mumbled halting phrases about the load of guilt she had carried—first, about Kevin's accident and, later, over her affair with Christopher.

"I had the perfect life," she confessed. "And I blew it."

The grandfather clock in the corner ticked off the seconds as her friends weighed the magnitude of her mistakes. Finally, it was Rosie's voice that broke the stillness.

"Hey, Girl—you're no different 'n the rest of us." A radiant smile began to spread across her thin face. "You think we could stand you if you was perfect?"

Instantly Kate felt herself engulfed by love as they wrapped her in warm, lingering hugs. Tears of relief streamed down her cheeks as she realized that the acceptance of three dear friends had accomplished more in a single moment than countless sessions of counseling had been able to do in years. She was so bathed in their compassion that she never heard Violet's heavy footsteps as she came through the front door.

"What in God's name is this? A love-in or somethin'?" Still stocky, Violet set her feet down carefully, as if arthritis must be waging a war in her joints. Her short-cropped hair was now snowy white.

Violet chortled as she surveyed the four of them, then proceeded to blurt out an embarrassing memory that she had of each one. For Kate, it was the day of Nancy Dawes' party.

"Remember that time?" Violet asked, scrutinizing Kate's puffy tear-stained face.

"As if it were yesterday." She studied the gruff countenance that masked Violet's great sensitivity. "I never would have made it through that stupid party if it hadn't been for you."

"And I never saw a more miserable kid in my life." Violet shook her head. "Boy, did I ever feel sorry for you."

"Served her right for going to a Longworth party." Rosie grinned slightly as she tried to recapture her old authority.

"Yeah?" Kate mimicked her own seventh-grade voice. "And if you're not nice, Rosie Mulgrew, I won't swap you my Gene Kelly picture for your Esther Williams!"

Violet stared at both of them as if they were daft and trudged toward the kitchen.

For the next hour, the four of them shared their innermost secrets as if they had never been separated. Doris glowed as she told them about her relationship with Alan Atwater, then grew serious.

"His family hasn't been the same since 9/11 though." Twisting the handkerchief she held in her hands, she explained. "His nephew, Ryan—Adele's son—was killed at the World Trade Center. He was one of the first firemen in. Just a great kid."

Kate reeled as she tried to absorb the terrible news. Adele Atwater . . . with the beautiful house . . . with all the right things. She could not imagine Adele's grief.

"I'd met Ryan once when me 'n Alan went to visit Adele," Doris continued.

Kate tried to imagine Doris being a guest in Adele's home in upstate New York and recalled the stiff atmosphere at the tea she herself had attended at Adele's house in eighth grade.

"He was funny, kept everyone laughing the whole time we were there. Even then, when he was fifteen, he wanted to be a fireman." Her gray eyes grew solemn. "Sure puts a face on the whole tragedy for me 'n Alan."

As a tremor rippled through Rosie, Kate feared that the conversation had grown too heavy for Rosie to handle. She was surprised, however, when Rosie spoke.

"Sometimes something good does come out of something bad," she mumbled almost to herself. "If Bud's son hadn't been killed in a car wreck, Bud wouldn't have been sitting on that bar stool in California the night I met him."

"Tell us about it, hon," Cheryl urged softly.

Kate and her friends had to strain to hear Rosie's words as she recounted her serene and spirited days with Bud and the deep sadness she'd felt since his death.

"Geez, you guys, I-I don't know what I'm gonna do." Folding her arms tightly across her chest, she tried to still her shakiness. "Now that he's gone, I'm too old to work and too young to die"

"Too old to work?" Doris showed no pity. "Shit, Rosie, I'm older 'n you—and I'm holdin' down *two* jobs."

When Cheryl added that she still sang in a band made up of "a bunch of old farts," Kate added that she was in the middle of writing her seventh book.

"Lordy, I never could have coped with some of the stuff that came my way if it hadn't been for my music." Cheryl held out her cup for a refill from Doris. "It helped me communicate with J.T., and it sure kept me halfway sane during two bad marriages. It—it helped me through—" Her voice broke as she thought of Jarvis.

"To tell the truth though," she rallied, "I'm not sure how I made it all these years without the three of you. Somehow, I've managed to struggle through on the strength of a good memory."

Kate agreed. "We just have to make a point of spending more time together, that's all."

"Yeah," Doris answered, "I know that right this minute I feel like a dyin' plant that's just had a good drink. God, there's just no friends like old friends."

Cheryl nodded. Then, thinking aloud, she began to devise a plan for all of them to spend a night in her apartment that summer. "We could go out for a nice dinner—maybe at the Cape Cod room at The Drake . . . or we could order Chinese carryout. Whatever." She glanced at them for approval. "At least we'd be together."

Abruptly, she turned to Rosie and asked if she planned to stay on the farm. Doris spoke up before Rosie had a chance to answer.

"I'm tryin' to talk her into gettin' an apartment in Rockwell." Doris passed the plate of cookies one more time. "Back here at home is where she oughtta be right now."

They all turned toward Rosie as the clock chimed four times. Its musical echoes faded before she breathed out little puffs of phrases, like feathers in the air.

"I—I don't know—" Her left eyelid had begun to jump. "I've been in—well, like in a deep dark hell hole. Ever since Bud left and Ma died." Her features contorted as she fought back tears. "I *hate* being alone."

"Oh, let me tell you, Rosie, I know all about the Loneliness." Cheryl's face reflected raw suffering as she spoke. "You guys never knew, I guess, how lonely I always was."

"But you had everything!" Doris' mouth fell open. "I mean—" She tried to recover gracefully. "You had such nice clothes. And everything!"

"Everything but Bertie and Lila's time. Oh, lordy—" She dabbed her eyes with a tissue. "I just wanted them to spend time with me, like all of your families did with you. Sure, I knew they both adored me. But they only had time for each other."

"Aw, we never had a clue. I—I'm so sorry." Rosie's genuine empathy was written all over her own grieving face.

"How did you fix it? I mean what'd you do?" Doris was ever practical.

"Married two jerks, for starters." Cheryl laughed bitterly through her tears. "Actually," she said after a few moments of reflection, "Jarvis taught me how to deal with it."

They all remained silent so Cheryl could finish.

"He said he'd fought the Loneliness too at different times in his life. Then one day, almost by accident, he realized that when he helped someone else who really needed it, the Loneliness was gone. Let me tell you," she lowered her voice confidentially, "it works. When I feel that bad old Loneliness starting to hang around, I know I've been thinking about myself too much. So I haul myself over to Children's Memorial Hospital or out to J.T.'s old school and I do something for somebody else. Funniest thing though," she flashed her beautiful smile, "*I'm* the one who always benefits."

"I—I think I kinda get what you're saying." Again, Rosie's quivering made Kate want to hold her until she could stop trembling. "You—you guys did just that today, didn't you?" Her face furrowed deeply as she studied each of us. "I mean, you came—came all the way home. To help *me*. Doris, you set this whole thing up." Her tone was half accusatory, half appreciative."

They sat motionless as they waited for Rosie to continue. At last she took a deep breath.

"Know what? You guys have made me realize it's time for me to get my butt in gear." Rubbing her eye, she continued. "I've had an offer from a neighbor who wants to buy our farm—a pretty good one, actually. And I may take the money and get myself a condo in Bourbonnais, right next to Kankakee. Might even get a job at Wal-Mart."

"Aw, Rosie, you don't wanta do that." Doris was testing her. "Come back to Rockwell. Come back home."

"I've gotta make my own home, Doris." Rosie's eye, Kate noticed, was now perfectly still. "You see, there's this kid I've been tutoring. His name's Colton. He needs me, kinda like what you were just saying, Cheryl. He needs me more than you do, Doris."

"When you've got a kid who needs you . . ." Cheryl's voice trailed off as her eyes misted over.

"And you know what?" Rosie sat up straight. For the first time, Kate saw a soft glow in her eyes. "Colton's mom does too. In our own weird way, we've kinda—oh, well, what d'ya call it? Bonded?" She reached for the last cookie on the plate. "Yeah, that's it. Bonded."

"I guess that's what happened to us that day when we got so scared on the cemetery road," Kate said. "We bonded."

"Hey!" Suddenly Rosie's voice displayed some of its former strength. "Did any of you guys ever tell anyone? You know . . . about the hobos?"

"Not me." Kate recalled the time when she and her mother had been sorting things at the house after her father had died. "I almost told my mom once. She wondered how the four of us got to be so close. But then I waffled and made up something. I couldn't bring myself to break our promise."

"Me either." Cheryl's brown eyes were earnest. "I thought about sharing it with Millicent, Jamie's mother. She'd have been shocked to hear the scariest moment of my life. We were so close back then, but I remembered our promise."

"I used to tell Bill everything after we was first married. Oh, my god, I loved him so much." Doris grew serious. "But I never said a word to him about it. And I've never told Alan neither!"

Rosie's face was transformed by her smile.

"Me neither—not even Bud." Quickly she turned to Doris and whispered something in her ear. Doris went straight to a bookshelf, pulled off a large Bible and laid it on the coffee table. Opening it, Rosie placed her palm on the Twenty-Third Psalm and signaled for each of them to do likewise.

"Now," she ordered, "I want you all to repeat after me. 'We promise not to say anything *ever* about what happened on the cemetery road'."

Like lemmings, they followed her every move.

"And," she continued, "we promise to be there for each other. For ever and ever."

Grinning self-consciously, they let the words tumble over the lumps that had formed in their throats. In the glances Kate traded with Doris and Cheryl she read the same thought: We must allow Rosie to lead the way for us on this. That's how it used to be, and that's how it will be from now on.

As they closed the Bible, the clock chimed five times. Cheryl looked at her watch in disbelief.

"I've gotta get going," she said. "I'm volunteering at the hospital first thing tomorrow morning."

"I need to go too," Kate echoed. "I can't take the late hours the way I used to. Plus," she paused as a thought struck her, "I want to get home to Marty."

"Take good care of him, Kate." Rosie was solemn again. "Give him all the love you've got."

Kate could feel her eyes filling as she nodded in agreement.

"You don't have to leave, Rosie." Doris urged. "Stay for supper with me 'n Violet."

"Naw, that's okay." As some of the color returned to Rosie's cheeks, Kate could not believe this was the same wilted woman she had met at The Boulder earlier that day.

"But you don't have to drive as far as Kate and—"

"Not on your life, Doris. You know me better'n that."

Rosie winked at Kate and Cheryl. "If you think I'm going by that old Naughton place by myself after dark—"

"But, Rosie, it's long gone—"

"No buts. And I don't care if Charley *does* live there. If you think I'm passing there by myself after the sun's gone down, you guys are crazy. I'm outta here!"

"Not quite so fast, Rosie." Cheryl put down her purse. "Lordy, when I think I came down here to help you this morning . . . that seems like another lifetime now. I-I'm the one who feels better now."

Reluctantly they inched their way into Doris' kitchen, where the cheery walls glowed in the rays from the late afternoon sun. Cheryl was the first to engulf Rosie with a hug, then Kate and Doris joined in as they had done so often many years before.

"Next time at my place," Cheryl reminded them. "Sometime this summer."

"Maybe you could get me a Notre Dame shirt for Colton." Rosie's face wore an expression of expectant hope as she spoke to Kate.

"It's a deal," she promised, knowing that Marty would get a kick out of selecting a shirt for Rosie's young friend.

As they approached their cars, Doris asked them about their routes home. Cheryl would go west to pick up I-57, Rosie would head straight north, and Kate would drive east into Indiana.

"Not like our old bike rides," Doris laughed. "We always had to go in a line together."

Not quite, Kate thought. We'll go our different ways today, but we'll always carry each other in our hearts. For the first time in years, she felt at peace.

* * *

Printed in the United States
210330BV00002B/52-66/P

9 781432 725136